I0699620

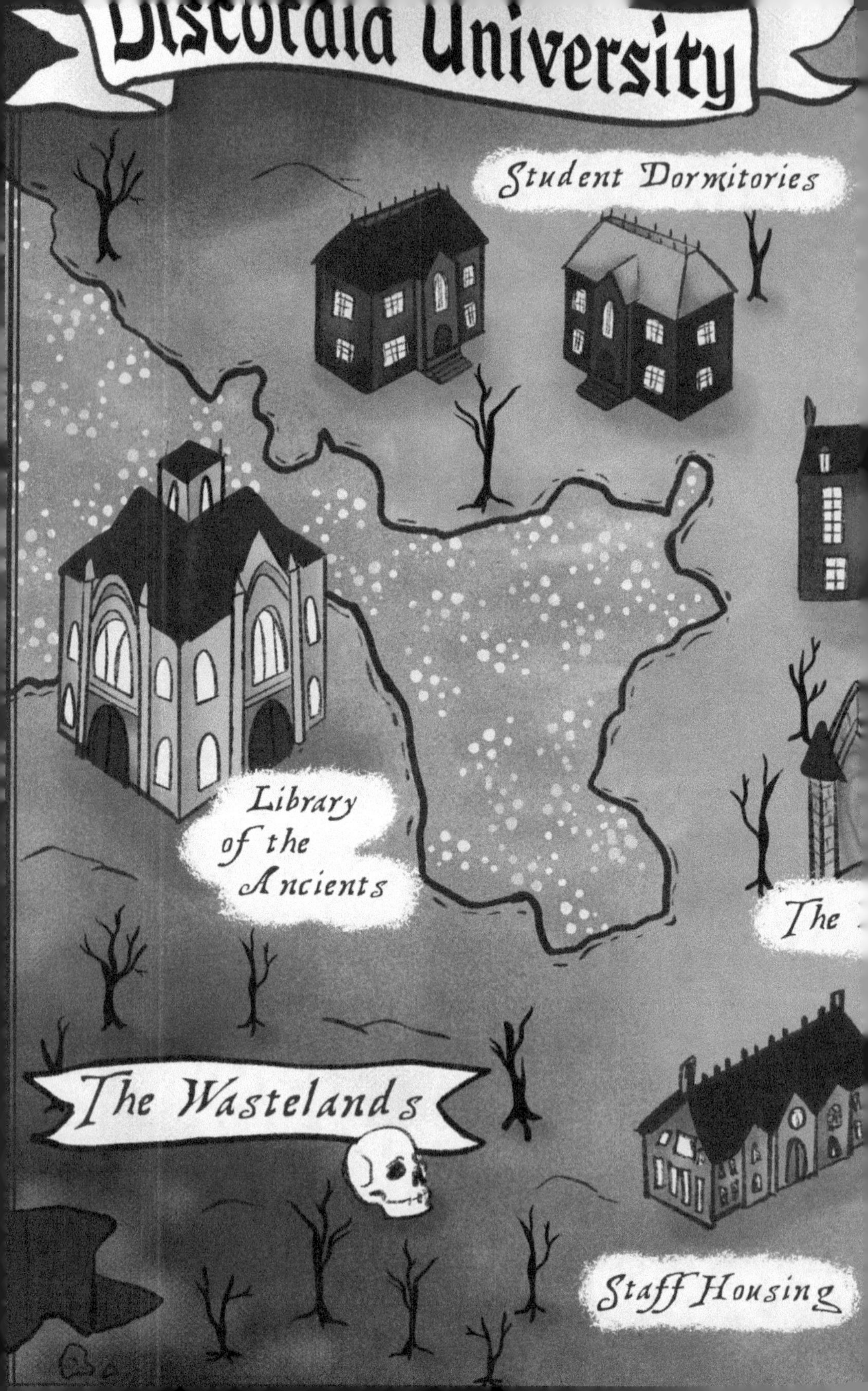

Discordia University
Student Dormitories
Library of the Ancients
The Wastelands
Staff Housing
The

Canto V
Region: Hell
Arena of Lost Souls
agic Enclave
Knowledge Enclave
Administration
& Health Annex

Special Edition VERSION ONLY

Original Ebook/Print Cover: Carol Marques Design
Alternative Cover: Sandra Faldo Designs
Map: Honeyy.Fae
Editing, Proofing, backgrounds, & Formatting: Dirty Sexy Words/ Storm shield
Editing/Little Tailfeather Publishing
Cassandra's logos: Pretty in Ink Creations/Artlogo
Goosebusters Alpha team: Kat Silver, Becky Ross, Erica Taryn
Sensitivity Readers: Brit Mason, Gail Jericho
Translation Consultant: Mo Jacobs
Legal Services: Joshua Farley, esq.
Images/Fonts: Depositphotos, Shutterstock, Canva, & Photoshop

No GenAI was used within this book. All errors and greatness are by an ADHD muppet.

DISCORDIA UNIVERSITY
COGERE EVOLUTIONE PER MUTATIONUM

Veiled FLAME

INTERNATIONAL BESTSELLING AUTHOR
CASSANDRA FEATHERSTONE

Content Information

This is a *paranormal whychoose romance with poly elements*—our FMC, Kat, will not have to choose between love interests.

I *purposefully* include **all** pertinent information in this section from tropes to triggers to included content to silly things. It's an attempt to cover my bases which is probably futile since some will be upset with *and* without it.

However, it's my book, and I'll do what I want, so here we go.

There are many situations included that are intended for _mature audiences (18+)_.

In these books, there may be instances/references (be they small or lengthy) that could trigger some individuals such as:

- discussion of mental illness
- demons
- attack on the FMC (physical)
- discussion about past non-consensual sexual event in FMC's past (description not on page, not MMC)
- non-consensual magical event by professor to FMC (not by MMC)
- within series: MM, MF, MMMMMMFM, and more
- bullying (light from MMC)
- foster kid
- alphahole/possessive MCs
- cinnamon roll MC

- girl disguised as a boy
- slightly unhinged chaotic MC
- big tough guy MC
- unhealthy coping mechanisms
- spoiled, selfish rich demons
- extremely aggressive boundaries
- age gap (unknown)
- cute familiar
- pre-existing pairings
- BDSM discussed (D/s relationship)
- horns, tails, and forked tongues
- traumatic childhood
- alcohol use and abuse
- threats of bodily harm
- death
- body modifications
- physical assault by non-MCs
- treacherous authority figures
- bullying (in person)
- PTSD
- blood
- emotional abuse
- body dysmorphia
- adult language
- pop culture references
- literary references
- emotional manipulation
- power play
- adorable nicknames
- physical intimidation
- emotionally abusive/manipulative parents (MCs)
- markings/tattoos
- Easter egg character cameos from other series in the universe
- family dysfunction
- absolute disrespect for shitty parents
- brief mentions of non-body positive dieting culture
- very liberal re-imagining of history
- ancient secret society who only cares about bigger picture
- official corruption
- discussion of arranged marriages
- rituals
- inappropriate professors

- name calling
- occasional misogyny
- shitty mothers and fathers
- discussion of parental physical abuse
- elitism
- bribery
- corpses
- drama
- physical threats to FMC and others
- species-ism

No practices in this book should be taken as safe or appropriate for real life application.

Content information is important and I don't ever want to harm a reader with inaccurate information.

Stalk Cassandra Featherstone in the Dark Corners of the Web

Join my Facebook group and follow me everywhere!

Want More?

Sign up for my bi-weekly manifesto for a free series sampler:

Join my Ream as a FREE follower or exclusive subscriber to get access to cover reveals, WIPs, Serial Stories, and personal chats from me!

CASSANDRA FEATHERSTONE
QUEEN OF SMART, SASSY SPICE

READER'S NOTE

A FEW THINGS YOU SHOULD KNOW...

I am so excited to bring this series from Vella to book format.

Veiled Flame is book **one** of the *Discordia University* series. There are five books planned and they will start on Vella/Ream, then come to print/KU after they are re-edited and formatted. This is a multi-book series, so *everything will not be revealed at once.* Some plot lines will continue through series in a larger arc and not get resolved in the first or even the third book.

I write lengthy books with intricate world building, strong character development, and *lots* of tiny threads that stretch throughout a series that may not always seem important at first glance. However, I promise nothing I put to paper and leave in the book is unimportant; it may simply become *more* important later on. There is no 'throwaway' detail in my worlds, so every scene will mean something eventually.

I promise it will all get tied up and have a HEA; don't worry!

Veiled Flame is a why choose/poly romance, which means our FMC will not have to choose.

I would consider it a **SLOW** burn—the slowest I've ever written. It will get spicier in the following books as Kat's situation changes. If you're looking for porn with little to no plot, no judgment, but this isn't the series for you. It won't be closed door or FTB, so I believe the spice will be worth the wait. I realize spice scales are subjective and everyone has different opinions on it, so forgive me if mine and yours aren't totally aligned.

Note: In the South (where I'm from), it is fairly common to call people by their full names when you're being condescending to dressing someone down. It's not just family, and if they don't know your middle name, sometimes they even make one up! It's an authority flex to do so. This happens in my books a lot—even if they are not set in the South—so I'm just giving you a heads up that it's stylistic and purposeful.

There are some characters and creatures that speak in other languages. I made the *translations clickable end of chapter notes* to help.

There are some words that are slang, jargon, or foreign that may seem to be spelled wrong—*please email the author or find her on social media rather than report to Amazon* if you think something is wrong. This has been proofed and edited *several* times since release; if you believe you found errors, you may not be correct. It could be a stylistic choice or a dialect choice. Please do not assume the two ARC teams, betas, alphas, and several proofers missed everything you believe is incorrect. Contact me if you find things; I want to make sure it doesn't get taken down so everyone can read!

If you see this book *anywhere besides Kindle Unlimited ebook format*, please reach out to me via social media or email. Pirating kills my ability to write full time and I am so grateful for your help.

Contact Cass for issues or to report piracy: teamcassandrafeatherstone@cassandrafeatherstone.com

Author Ramblings

Readers, you are going to adore my girl Kat.

She's very different than my other FMCs, and it's a good thing.

Her past is fraught with trauma and she's strong, but has a fragile psyche. She's doing the work, but as you know, it's a slow process when you're crawling out of the pits. Kat is doing it the right way, but doesn't have much support—then her world turns upside down.

There are Easter eggs for those of you who are inclined to read the faster burn series *Faetal Attraction* and some for *Secrets of State U*, but if you don't, those references won't leave you behind the curve.

As usual, I've done a lot of research and added quite bit of mythology, depth, and information to my rich world. But if I get something wrong, know I did the best I could to make certain I had the right information.

Plus, you know… magic. Magic explains everything. *wink*

Thank you to everyone who has read and recommended on Facebook, Instagram, TikTok, on Goodreads, and on Amazon. Your recs in groups and continued support help me get closer to my indie muppet dream of going full time.

In a world where there are hidden pitfalls and people that smile to your face and slide the knife in your back when you aren't looking, I want to thank my author besties who support me every day, my alpha/ARC team, and all the others who chat and help me every day.

Finding true support that doesn't require me to give up part of myself has been a goddess blessed event. I feel more and more like the confidence I had when I first entered this genre has returned and the abuse that caused me to falter is fading.

For that, I can never repay you.

However, I never give up and I never back down, so I'm going to be here with silly puns and smart FMCs who aren't afraid to show how big their hearts, libidos, *and* brains are.

Enjoy the newest series in the *Legends of the Ouroboros* universe, and fall for the bad boy demons like our girl will… eventually.

Blood and guts,

Cassandra Featherstone

QUEEN OF SMART, SASSY SPICE

A Note To My Loving Family Members and Their Friends...

THANK YOU FOR SUPPORTING ME BY BUYING THIS BOOK!

SO, YOU COULD PROBABLY READ THIS BOOK.

SHOCKER, I KNOW.

BUT TO BE HONEST, I DOUBT YOU'LL BE ABLE TO READ THE REST OF THE SERIES.

ONCE KAT'S SECRET COMES OUT, THOSE DEMONS WILL BE READY AND RARING TO GO... HOPEFULLY, SHE'S READY.

BUT YOU WILL NOT BE, TRUST ME.

WAY TOO MANY WEIRD ATTACHMENTS ON THE HORIZON.

SO... MAKE GOOD CHOICES, Y'ALL.

CAVEAT: IF YOU CHOOSE TO KEEP READING, KNOW THAT AT NO TIME WILL I EXPLAIN TERMS, POSITIONS, THEMES, TROPES, OR ANY OTHER PART OF THIS NOVEL AT FAMILY EVENTS, IN GROUP CHATS, OR ON SOCIAL MEDIA.

DON'T ASK.

Veiled Flame Playlist

CHAPTER TITLE SONGS

Veiled Flame Chapter Playlist

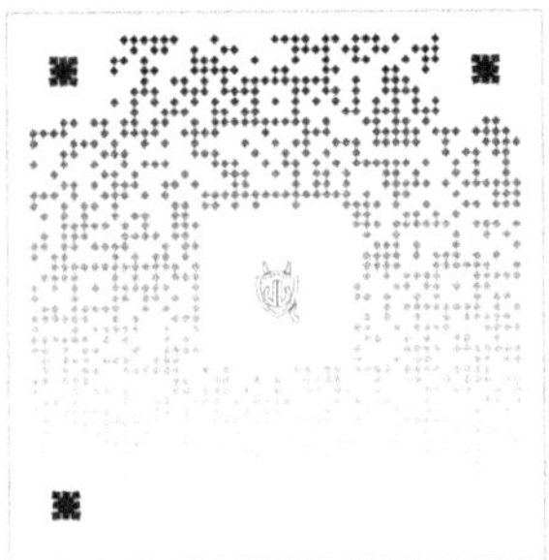

BONUS PLAYLIST

Kat's Emotional Rollercoaster Playlist

You are not crazy.
The things that happened to you hurt.
The things they said broke your heart.
The abuse you endured by their hands and mouth, you endured.
You are not crazy.
No, you lived through the trauma, the pain, and unbelievable hurt
that changed you forever.
That makes you a fighter, with a memoir written in scars.
You're a warrior birthed in the mess of life.
What a brave soul you are.
Never let them take that from you.

~Anonymous

CLASS SCHEDULE

All class schedules subject to administrative and professorial approval.

time	monday	tuesday	wednesday	thursday	friday
8:00 AM	Intro to Demons & Supes	Curses & Hexes 101	Intro to Demons & Supes	Curses & Hexes 101	Arms & Battle 101
9:00 AM	Lillibet	Wormwood	Lillibet	Wormwood	Eversore
10:00 AM	Deconstructing Human History	Mythology 101	Deconstructing Human History	Mythology 101	Free Period
11:00 AM	Alabaster		Alabaster		
12:00 PM	Free Period	Lunch	Free Period	Lunch	Dueling
1:00 PM	Lunch		Lunch		Lunch
2:00 PM	Ancient Demon Lineage	Free Period	Ancient Demon Lineage	Free Period	Dark Magic
3:00 PM	Kindervelt		Kindervelt		Salazar
4:00 PM	Literature of Dark Ages	Weapons & Tactics	Literature of Dark Ages	Weapons & Tactics	Intro to Fae
5:00 PM	Romero	Eversore	Romero	Eversore	Cedar
6:00 PM	Drama	Supe Law	Drama	Supe Law	Hackers Guild
7:00 PM	Dinner	Dinner	Dinner	Dinner	
8:00 PM	Thieves' Guild	Caliphate Mtg	Government	Caliphate Mtg	Dinner

COGERE EVOLUTIONE PER MUTATIONEM

Some pronunciations are very basic, but my editors believe they should all* have it to be uniform in style. *Obviously, I know you know how to read 'Bob', but it's just weird for things not to match, 'kay?*

Katarina Camponella (kat uh REE nuh CAM POH NELL uh) foster kid living with the Jamesons

Nicknames: Kat, Kit, Kit Kat, little demon,

Blake Jameson (blay-k Jay-meh-son) twin foster brother of Kat; plays football, popular kid; absolute ass; accepted to Alabama to play ball

Bryce Jameson (bry-ss Jay-meh-son) twin foster brother of Kat; plays football, popular kid; absolute ass; accepted to Alabama to play ball

Brett Jameson (Breh-TT Jay-meh-son) foster father of Kat; clueless; does whatever their mother says

Allison Jameson (al-uh-SON Jay-meh-son) foster mother of Kat; snobby; only likes the prestige of having the two foster boys who play ball; disdainful of Kat

Professor Horatio Alecto (hor-ay-she-o uh-leck-to) professor at Discordia; Dean of Admissions; sends a letter to 'Kit' Camponella

Mr. Jenkins (Jeh-kinz) school guidance counselor; overwhelmed and near retirement

Dottie (dah-tee) random kinkajou that shows up and is trying to break into the Jameson's bedroom floor safe; Kat finds her, and she refuses to leave; later, she's told it's a familiar

Sheriff Bob (Bahb) Useless, prejudiced town sheriff

Wilbur (will-BURR) deputy sheriff; four years older than twins; bully with a badge

Becky Sanderson (beck-ee San-der-son) town busy body

Lucian Darkstar (loo-see-en dark-stah-r) Headmaster of Discordia; sketchy AF; pit demon

Dank (DahNK) demon sent to fetch Kat; wears plague mask; aka Dr. Danckwardt

Silvera (sil VAIR UH) demon who does Lucian's bidding; fear demon

Beccarus (Beck-A-roos) toadie to Lucian; demon in Headmaster's office; chaos demon

Jasper Eversore (jas-PURR EVER-sore) Prince of Hell; leader of caliphate; dragon/demon hybrid; four years older than the others; working as teaching assistant while taking graduate classes to be with caliphate as they go to school; controlling asshole; fear demon

Nicknames: Asshole Demon, Prince Dickface, Prince Prick, Prince Prickface, Prince Cocknozzle

Salem Stryker (Say-lem Str-eye-cur) Panda/demon hybrid; likes to cook; Kat's roommate; dream demon

Nicknames: Lazy Demon

Anton Aldaric (an-TOHN all-dur-ick) peacock/demon hybrid; designer; lover of X; incubus

Nicknames: Flirty Demon, Annie

Xerxes (zerk-zees) cobra/demon hybrid; lover of Anton; enby; dream demon

Nicknames: Pretty Demon, X,

Oriel Bloodstone (or-ee-elle blud-stohn) crow shifter/demon hybrid; likes to steal shit; emo looking; quiet; shadow demon

Nicknames: Goth Demon, O,

Zavida Draven (zah-VEE-duh reh-ven) kitsune/demon hybrid; hacker; gamer; sleeps with Jasper; very smart; chaos demon

Nicknames: Gamer Demon, Zav, Zavvie,

Slash Scrum (slah-shuh skrum) Jasper's second in command; Fireball champ; shark; demon hybrid; vengeance demon

Nicknames: Big Demon, Big Guy,

Professor Alabaster (al-UH-bas-ter) Deconstructing Human History professor

Professor Kindervalt (kin-der-Walt) Demonic Languages professor;

Professor Wormwood (werm-wood) Curses & Hexes professor

Professor Basquez (bas-Kez) Culinary Art professor; ancient; stodgy; hates cell phones; bores Salem to tears

Professor Romero (rom-may-ro) Dark Lit professor

Professor Lillabet (lil-ih-bet) Intro to Supes professor; Cubi who feeds on boys in class; jerk to girls

Bastion Queznar (bast-ee-on qwehz-nahr) greed demon in Thieves Guild; species racist; drude

Cornelius Rhodes (cor-nee-lee-us row-dz), leader of the Southern demon contingent; crossroads demon

Phelps Brewster (fell-ps brew-stir) Leader of the Midwest demon contingent; dream demon

Allegra Masterson (UH-leg-ruh Mass-tur-sun) leader of the Eastern demon contingent; pit demon; ugly as hell

Professor Salazar (SALL-uh-ZAR) Dark Magic professor; chaos demon with a bent for making people nutty for his amusement

Professor Cedar (CEE-dur) Intro to Fae professor; hybrid Reaping Fae and incubus; actually a cool dude

Ivan Roquefort (ee-vahn ROH-kh-fort) demon in Kit's Waeapons class; super jackass;

King Tarron Eversore (tay-ron ev-er-soar) full nightmare demon; upset last royal rule in Hell; asshole; Jasper's father

Queen Daramah Eversore (dare-ay-mah ev-er-soar) Queen of Hell; arranged marriage; succubus; Jasper's mom; pays no attention to him or the kingdom

Locations

Woodlawn High School- school where Kat goes to school

Common Grounds- coffeehouse and diner where Woodlawn moms hang out

Woodlawn Mall- where Kat goes to create her Kit persona

Short Cuts- where Kat gets her haircut for Kit persona

Raging Trends- scene kid store in the mall

Wally World- mega store in town

Discordia University- premier demon college that invites Kat to attend

Canto IV- Section of Hell Discordia is located in; also the dorm the caliphate is in

State U- Supe college

Blackmoor Academy- reform school

Citadel- dorm Kat should have been in

Library Enclave- Building where many lectures take place

Magic Enclave- building where magic classes occur

Triclinium- cafeteria building

Infirmary- a dangerous place to go for treatment

Dr. Danckwardt's Office- the elite royal doctor's clinic

Arena- where the weapons and physical classes occur; also a large meeting space

Temple/Altar- ancient space where rituals are performed

The little blue icon on my app has been glaring at me all day, but I'm too damn nervous to open it. Everyone at Woodlawn High has been buzzing all day with their notifications, and the squeals of joy and moans of despair were too much for me to take. My anxiety is through the roof—this is the moment I've been waiting for since middle school, but I can't seem to force myself to bite the bullet and check.

Maybe it's because I don't have the support system most of my classmates have?

That's probably true, given I've always been a loner and I don't fit into any specific 'caste' here. It's hard to make friends when you get shuffled from foster home to foster home over the years. I've rarely stayed anywhere long enough to make a friend, much less a group of them.

I'm not a delinquent or anything—the families I got placed with just return me like a pair of pants that doesn't fit after a year. The caseworkers click their tongues sympathetically and hunt down a new placement, but I haven't been given a reason why people don't want me around. One lady said I must be born under a bad sign and hell if I knew what that meant, other than I'm not good enough to keep around.

It would be different, almost understandable, if I misbehaved or got poor grades. But I don't—I'm always in the top five percent of my class and I do everything I'm asked. I don't even lord my smarts over the other kids or adults. Being presentable and unassuming was something I adapted long ago to improve my probability of staying in a home long term.

Unfortunately, it never worked and though I should be a shoo-in for scholarships and acceptances galore, I can't bring myself to be rejected yet again.

So I wait for the last bell of the day, slinging my bag over my shoulder and trudging home to the latest in my temporary housing. I can't even contemplate looking at the heartache waiting for me in the college application system WHS insisted we use. The fear is too great and despite knowing I'll be on my own for good at the end of this year, I'm unable to risk the pain.

I hate being this way.

My court mandated therapist says it's some sort of attachment disorder that's common in foster kids, but I think that's bullshit. The problem isn't *me* not forming attachments; it's asshole adults not forming one for me. Being left at a safe haven in a fucking basket as a baby wasn't because *I* did anything wrong—again, fucking adults couldn't handle their commitments.

As usual, I arrive home to an empty house. There are two other kids who live here—Bryce and Blake—but they're at football practice. Of course, the Jamesons *love* them; they get to strut around at games because their strays are the stars of the team. I'm not mistreated, but I'm an afterthought. Both of my 'parents' are still at work, so I drop my bag on the couch and head for the kitchen to get a snack.

Don't get me wrong. I *could* have gone to far worse homes than any of the seven I've been in since elementary school. None of the ex-fosters starved, beat, molested, or abused me. They were all decent folks with jobs and houses that weren't hellholes, but they never liked me.

I have no idea why. I tried to be everything they wanted.

But when the end of each school year came, I got handed in like a textbook and off I went to some group home until the next contestant stepped up. It baffled everyone, not just me, but that's what happened every single time.

Sighing, I pull some fruit out of the fridge and grab a soda. I have homework to do and if I want to have time to work on my stories, I'll need to get it done before the house is full of people at dinner time. Bryce and Blake will have gotten messages about their applications too, and I'd bet my pinkie toe those idiots got into some serious sports school. Brett and Allison will ooze happiness for them, and I don't know if I'll be able to keep food down if I have to admit my failure when they ask.

Being eighteen sucks ass.

After I grab my books and tablet, I head down to the den. I have to give my current parents credit; they set up a very nice workspace for us to study in the converted basement. By the time they took me in, the Jamesons created a cozy room down here where the three of us could relax and do our work for school without being interrupted. It might have been more for the boys than me, but I appreciated it all the same. Desks, a couch, cushy chairs, and bookshelves fill the space, making it almost seem like our mini-library. They even put a small fridge for drinks and snacks in case we had to be up late to cram.

It's my favorite place in the entire house and I spend most of my time here.

I sink into the huge armchair, putting my drink and snack on the side table. It only takes a few minutes to arrange myself in the soft cushions, and I tug my headphones out of my pocket. Music always soothes my jagged edges, and I need it to stay focused on the bullshit AP Calculus I need to keep my average up in. My course load is heavy, but I applied to tough colleges. I wouldn't get in, especially on a scholarship, if I wasn't taking equally challenging classes compared to all the prep school kids.

As always, the sounds of Vivaldi carry me away as I scrawl equations on my screen and before long, thoughts of the blue notification completely fade away.

"KAT!"

The shouts barely register as I continue working on the problem set, gnawing on my lower lip in concentration.

"Jesus fuck, where is she? I could eat a hippo!"

"Kat!"

Thumping followed by what could pass for a stampede of elephants jerks me out of my math filled trance when Bryce and Blake come down the stairs. They smell as bad as the aforementioned pachyderm's cage, so they must have rushed home right after practice. The blond twins glare at me as if I'm the offending element, despite being sweaty and covered in dirt and grass stains.

This doesn't bode well.

Usually, they're tired and hungry after practices, so I'm used to cranky ass boys, but tonight, there's a light to their faces. That had to mean they've gotten their letters and dinner will be a gush fest in honor of their perfection. I'm going to need all of my strength to fake smile and nod as Brett and Allison fawn over them.

I don't begrudge them their success—not really. They work hard and play even harder on the field. It's not their fault they're the American dream teens and I'm the nerdy basement troll no one wants. But it's awfully hard living in the shadow of their bright light when I'm no less intelligent or talented.

"I'm finishing the AP Calc, guys. What do you want?"

They roll their eyes at me before Blake scoffs. "It's not due until Monday. You're so hyper."

Duh. I take anxiety meds, douchebag; of course I'm 'hyper.'

"I can only be who I am, Blake." That earns me a snort from Bryce, and I know it's because he thinks that's the problem. "Is dinner ready?"

"Almost. Get upstairs and set the table so we can shower—Brett's orders." Blake grins smugly.

The two of them seem to always arrange their lives so chores get passed to me for some half-assed reason and this is no exception. Sighing, I put my stuff aside, fully intending to hide down here after we cleaned the dinner mess up. Likely by me, but like I said, I could live in worse foster homes, so I let it go. Doing some chores isn't worth risking the group home for the last few months of my high school career.

They take off running up the stairs and I wait for them to disappear before I follow suit. I tuck my phone in my pocket and I feel like it's a stone of shame I have to bear. I know once the adults make over the twins' success, they will remember me, and I'll be forced to find out what disappointment lies in wait for me. The dread weighs on me, but I head into the sunny kitchen and pick up the pre-prepared pile of plates, silverware, and napkins on the counter.

Allison looks up from the stove and gives me a half-smile, nodding as I take the dishes into the dining room. Like I said, no one is mean or horrid. They just seem…obligated. After a while, it makes it hard to waste time trying to be bright and sunny. Being reserved makes it a hell of a lot easier not to feel rebuffed when they don't pay attention to you, regardless.

"Make sure you include champagne glasses for your dad and me!" she calls from the other room.

The twins got accepted somewhere big. Brett must have gotten the bubbly on the way home.

Once I set the table, I return to help Allison bring out the roast and sides. I'm a little amazed at her efficiency at getting housework done while working full time, but I suppose it's something people with proper parents get taught as they grow up. My home life has been so fractured that I haven't learned how to cook more than very basic shit from YouTube videos. That may be a problem after graduation, but I've never felt comfortable enough to ask Allison if she'd teach me. I'm sure she would try, but it doesn't feel right.

"How was school, Kat?"

I look over my shoulder, seeing Brett in the entry to the dining room. He's already changed from work and smiling, but I see the distraction in his eyes. He's waiting for the boys to come down. "It was fine. I've got a Calc test at the end of the week. I'll be studying a lot to get ready."

"Good, good. No matter what happens with applications, keeping your grades up will ensure no one pulls any offers," he says.

Those words aren't for me. They are for the two wet haired boys who just appeared behind him.

"Kat's too much of a geek to ever let her grades slip, Dad," Blake says as he pushes past his brother and drops into his usual chair at the table. "Grab me a Powerade since you're in the kitchen, mouse!"

Both Brett and Bryce stare at me and I turn around, heading to the fridge, although I was *no* closer than the other twin. Out of habit, I take two of the drinks and a soda for myself. I've been here long enough to know Bryce will send me back to get him one as well. It would feel like typical sibling stuff, but I *know* they do it to fuck with me. I have no idea why I feel that way, but trusting my gut has been the one thing that helped me get through all the upheaval in my life over the years. It's a good gauge for knowing when I'll get booted or if people are being earnest in their reactions.

The therapist says that's some sort of trauma induced early trigger warning shit, by the way.

After I hand out the drinks, I sit down on my side of the table and we wait for Allison to come out. Brett is at his seat at the far end of the table and the twins are punching each other as they look at something on their phones. I know where this is all going, but I drop my gaze to the table, swallowing the coppery taste of fear as it courses through my body.

I'm going to be exposed and there's nothing I can do to stop it.

Everyone piles food on their plates, including my parents, and I sigh with relief when full mouths put off the inevitable. My stomach is rebelling because of my anxiety, but I push the bits around so it looks like I'm eating more than I am. Silverware clinks against the dishes and awkward silence sinks over us until Allison can't wait any longer.

"So, kids. How was school? Anyone get any exciting news today?" She sips her wine casually, looking between both sides of the table as if this just occurred to her.

The boys drop their forks, pulling their phones out in sync. I stare at the food on my plate, waiting for the celebration as they pull their apps and wave the phones wildly. Their unison answers make my gut clench. "We got into 'Bama."

That's so much worse than what I expected.

I paste a cheerful smile on as Allison and Brett jump from their seats to rush to hug the boys. My hands clap, and the pleased looks my foster parents give me are telling. They knew this was coming, hence the champagne, and this little scene is solely so everyone can fawn over their achievement. Something inside of me curls up when Bryce eyes me and I know what's coming… He's going to ask where I got accepted because he's worked out that I'm uncomfortable. His elbow catches his brother in the ribs and they turn their smug smiles on me.

"Celebrate with us, Kat. Tell Mom and Dad your good news," Bryce says in a faux sweet tone.

Blake pretends to gasp and nods. "We would *never* want to leave you out, Kat!"

My hand shakes as I reach for my phone, dread coursing through me as Brett and Allison whirl on me as well. Their faces look eager and I wonder for a moment if they're hoping they'll have a third checkmark in their win column to hold up at parent meetings. They've never looked quite this excited to hear something I have to say before. "I… I haven't checked yet. Let me open up the app…"

"Oh, sweetie, were you nervous? I'm sure you're going to represent the family just as well as the boys," Allison coos.

I am so fucking screwed.

Everyone stares at me as I fumble with unlocking my screen under their intense gazes. I get the damn thing open and click the button for the app that's been taunting me all day. It takes forever to open, and I feel the fear sliding up my spine.

Then the doorbell rings.

"Honey, the cake is here!" Allison abandons her spot next to the boys to rush out of the room and my breath comes out in a slow sigh of relief. Brett claps Blake on the shoulder and follows her to help, leaving me alone with the twins.

"Afraid to see how badly you've failed, Kitty Kat?" Bryce taunts with a knowing grin. He's the ringleader and though they aren't truly mean, the boys know our parents favor them, so he starts shit all the time.

"No," I mutter as I give my phone another frustrated look. *Why isn't the damn app loading?* I know whatever ridiculous dessert Allison Door Dashed won't distract them forever, and I need an answer.

"She's definitely scared, bro. Her hands are shaking. Poor little Kitty Kat is going to be flipping burgers forever." Blake crosses his arms over his chest as he smirks.

Pushing out of my chair, I sit my phone down and glare at them. "First, even if I end up flipping burgers forever, that's not an insult. You couldn't eat fifty fucking burgers a week if no one was there to flip them, you dick. Second, there are plenty of options for people who don't get into their first choice schools. God, you two are so damned coddled!"

"Holy shit, she finally showed some claws!" Bryce hoots as he and Blake dissolve into laughter. "Maybe she can do stand-up when the colleges reject her for being a weirdo loser."

For the love of everything holy, how am I supposed to live four more months with these clowns?

I let out a growl of irritation, picking up my phone and deciding I don't give a shit who's pissed; I'm noping out of this little twin asshole love fest. "The two of you can get fucked. Tell Allison I don't feel well and I'm going downstairs to finish my homework."

"Trust me, once the ladies hear we're going D1, we will," Bryce says with an exaggerated roll of his hips.

Blake high-fives him and snorts. "For real, yo!"

Turning on my heel, I move to leave the room, but Brett and Allison are standing there with pale faces. Their expressions make me stop and even the boys quit howling like monkeys. Allison clears her throat and looks me directly in the eyes as she says softly, "Kat, you have a visitor."

"I do?" Confusion floods me and I look at my foster parents doubtfully.

"Kat *never* has visitors. Who is it?" Bryce starts towards the living room, only to run into Brett's hand.

"No, son. Only Kat. He was very specific."

I frown, looking at them both as if they're completely insane. They *never* tell the boys 'no,' and whoever this is was important enough to override that instinct. I can't think of anyone, outside of law enforcement, who might get that kind of response from my parents. "Okay…"

Brett and Allison move to the side, allowing me to pass before heading over to the boys to whisper to them.

Great. Not only am I going to find out they have rejected me for college, but now I have to worry about some mysterious stranger dropping by to ruin my night.

When I walk into the living room, anger washes over me. There's no one here and no sign of anyone ever being here. I'm about to stomp back into the dining room and give all of them a piece of my mind for tricking me when I see it: a large, cream-colored envelope made of thick, fancy paper. It's incongruent with the decor in the room, reeking of old world style and money. Stepping closer, I look at the beautiful black calligraphy on the envelope curiously. It simply says 'Mssr. Kit Camponella' on it.

What the hell?

My name isn't Kit.

I tried to explain to Brett and Allison that whoever they met at the door was gone, but they refused to believe me. The boys threw in their opinions, of course, and made a huge stink about the letter. They were convinced it was some kind of inheritance and my reluctance to open it was because I didn't want to 'repay' our parents for taking me in. That's not why I didn't want to open it in front of an audience, but they were right about the last part. I know for a fact that the Jamesons get checks to cover expenses for all three of us every month and they might not be rich, but they're financially stable. They aren't owed anything besides gratitude and I've always given back to the household without complaint.

Unlike those two morons who evade every task possible and do whatever they please.

The real reason I don't want to open the damn thing is because I sneaked a look at my status in the app while they were all freaking out and I don't have a single message in it. I'm not sure why it was blinking a blue 'three' in the notifications all day but now there's nary a damn thing waiting for me to check, but it's like the letter's arrival wiped it clean. Every fiber of my being is hoping this is some sort of fancy acceptance from some weird off-the-wall college the counselor made me apply to as a safety school. Otherwise, I'm going to need it to be an inheritance or I really will be stuck working in a fast food joint next year.

Lots of people have to take gap years to save, right? It'll be fine, Kat.

Of course, there's the matter of the letter being addressed wrong to deal with, too. What if the damn thing is meant for someone else? Camponella isn't a commonplace last name, but it's not super rare, either. I got abandoned within state lines, but I've moved all over Kansas since as they placed me with various families. Maybe there's an actual *Kit* located somewhere I've lived in the past eight years? That could be it and if so, that's almost worse than discovering a blank slate in the college app. Then I'd have *nothing*.

I look at the envelope again, willing myself to magically read it without having to open it. My hands are shaking again, anxiety damn near strangling me as I curl up in my favorite armchair. Being like this is a giant hurdle to overcome and although my therapist has given me a million exercises to help, it's something I'll have to live with for the rest of my life. High school kids aren't very kind with my episodes, but they wouldn't be any kinder to an epileptic or someone with asthma. Teenagers are awful, and no matter how hard parents might try to teach them good habits, that fades away in the presence of their peers. Humans are pack animals and adolescents are the neediest of the bunch—approval and acceptance trump their higher brain function every time.

Okay, Kat. You've wasted enough time dissecting the American teenager. Bite the bullet.

Flexing my hands to control the trembling, I slide my fingers under the flap of the envelope and detach the wax seal carefully. I don't want to rip it in case this really is a huge mistake. The possible 'other Kit' won't want to receive damaged goods; I wouldn't either if it came in this kind of fancy package. The smell of sulfur and cedar fill the air with an oddly familiar scent and I try to figure out where I've smelled it before. It's not good or bad; it's… known.

Warmest Regards, Mssr. Kit Camponella.

Your application to Discordia University has been received and we are pleased to offer you a place at the most elite school in Canto IV.

Despite the unusual method with which we received your information, our admissions department is eager to grant you a full scholarship based on your prior achievements. Your grant will include full tuition, uniforms, lodging, materials, and a monthly allotment you may use how you wish. This is one of our most generous offerings and we only give it to truly outstanding candidates.

Once you provide your signature on this document, we will fully admit you as one of our students. We will handle all necessary documentation to secure your release from any responsibilities you have currently, including but not limited to: transcripts, court documents, financial obligations, and guardian concerns. Our staff will obtain the records to provide you with any medical, financial, and personal needs upon your arrival.

You will be housed in the Citadel, a dorm for first-year students, with a roommate named Ari Zeno. I have likewise informed them of your eminent arrival and we will ensure your belongings are waiting for you. There will be an orientation on the first day where you will mingle with other new and upper-level students in order to learn about our institution from those who attend.

We wish you buona fortuna in your studies here as you navigate the challenging progression of your education and look forward to meeting you in two weeks' time.

Cogere evlotione per mutationem,

Professor Horatio Alecto
Dean of Admissions, Discordia University

I blink at the letter in shock, turning it over and over as if suddenly an invisible ink is going to appear and declare this a cruel prank. Nothing appears and the words don't change no matter how many times I re-read the damn thing and I suck in a sharp breath. Not only do I not remember even applying to this college, I've never even *heard* of it. But they're offering one of the best scholarships I've ever seen and with no prospects appearing in the school's program, I don't know if I can turn it down. I'd be crazy to even consider it, truthfully. How they work out all of that administrative stuff they mentioned, I can't fathom, but this place is offering to handle everything *and* get me out of this house before the end of the year.

It's almost too good to be true; that's why I feel so suspicious.

Brett and Allison wouldn't pull something like this, but I wouldn't put it past the boys to pay someone to create a cruel prank in this vein. They're not awful, but they're not nice dudes, either. If they even had an inkling they'd be accepted ahead of time, I could see them setting me up to look like an even bigger fool just to amuse themselves. Our parents might scold them, but they wouldn't attempt to punish them during the season. Their performance on the field could hamper their prospects, and I know for certain no one would risk that.

Tomorrow, I need to do some heavy duty research on this place and figure out if I can accept their offer. At the moment, I'd do damn near anything to get out of Kansas and start fresh somewhere new. I'll have to correct their typo in my name, but that shouldn't be a big deal. It's not as if my offer is predicated on a misspelling, anyway. They said my accomplishments were what they based the admission on and I should be proud—so I will.

At least, I will once I make sure this is all real.

"You don't recognize this college?"

Mr. Jenkins sighs as if I've asked him to cross the Mississippi on a paddle board, then puts his hands on his desk. "I don't know how I could be any clearer, Katarina. This letter you're describing must be some sort of childish prank. There's no record of it in the app system and it's not in the database. It does not exist."

"I heard you say that the first time, but someone hand delivered it to my house and the way the Jamesons acted, it didn't seem like it was some random kid." I cross my arms over my chest, giving him a suspicious look. "Maybe it's so exclusive that it's not *in* your system."

The guidance counselors at our school, much like the teachers, all wear the same tired look. Public schools post-pandemic are filled with adults who seem like they wish they could be anywhere but here. Most of the good ones left after the online year and now all we have left are unhappy people with few options. It makes finding hope for the future tough sometimes. Jenkins stands and walks around the desk, leaning against it as he looks at me seriously.

"Have you been seeing your therapist regularly? Your file says it's a requirement and if you've neglected it, that could be why you're refusing to accept the truth. Your sights were set awfully high and there are no responses in your app data, so this could be—"

I hold my hand up. "Stop. They document my visits in the file; obviously, you didn't read it before I came in. This letter is not some figment of my imagination, nor is it part of… the trauma."

"The incident that held you back a year when you were a freshman wasn't your fault, Katarina. And no one would blame you if you were still—"

My hands grip the arms of the chair I'm sitting in and I glare at him. Only a *man* could say something this ridiculous and assume he understands what happened and how I feel. "My name isn't Katarina. I go by Kat, though whomever entered it in your system put *Kit*, which is another problem I have to deal with."

"Listen, *Kat*." His body language and tone change immediately and I see a barely controlled rage behind his eyes. Mr. Jenkins hates his job, but he hates being corrected more. No wonder he's stuck in a failing school that depends on its sports programs to bring in the money. "Students enter their own information into the college admissions application. You cannot continue blaming everyone for your problems."

Ah, so he read my file. That's a gem my therapist loves to throw at me.

"My information was *pre-filled* when I got into the damn thing. The instructions said 'you may apply now' and so I did. I assumed that was standard and did as instructed. How is that blaming someone for *my* error?"

That earns me a baffled expression, and his posture eases slightly. I can tell something I've said concerns him, but he shakes his head. "The school you asked about doesn't exist. I suggest you Google it when you're at lunch. Now, if that's all, you need to get back to class, Kat."

Great. Yet another 'not my problem' adult leaving me to my own devices.

"Fine. But I'll be back."

"I highly doubt that. Have a nice day, Kat."

I know a brush off when I hear one.

With that, I gather my things and march out of his office, determined to come back with proof and shove it in his stupid face.

I WAS WRONG.

All day I've been surreptitiously searching for this blasted university, and I can't seem to find a single whisper of it anywhere. It's times like these where I wish I had actual friends because I might be lucky enough to have one who knew how to do computer hacker-type shit that would help me. But I don't; I'm not the heroine in some dystopian romance, so random NPGs aren't popping up to make my quest easier. In truth, various idiots and my teachers made it harder, if that was possible.

My mood is even more sour than when I left Jenkins' office this morning, so I grab everything I'll need for homework and slam my locker shut with a low growl. I shouldn't have expected anything to go right, but for once, I was hoping someone's ineptitude was greater than mine. Turning on my heel, I stalk out of the hallway and through the front doors of Woodlawn High. I'm sure my frustration and anger are written all over my face, but I can't be bothered to seem uncaring today. The universe and its bullshit won again.

"Hey, Kat! Find anything out yet?" The voice comes from across the front lawn of the school and I know exactly who it is. That spot is reserved for the jocks and cheerleaders, so my 'brothers' are there anytime they don't have class or practice. I keep walking and ignore Blake, but that only eggs him on. "Looks like the answer is no, guys. My brainy sis still hasn't gotten word about getting out of this place. Boo hoo."

Rage courses through me and I ball my fists at my side. I'd love to knock his teeth through the back of his head, but I have neither the skills nor the support to do it and survive. Even if I got my shot in, his crowd would eat me alive and when I got home, our parents would let me have it. I don't need the stress of their disappointment weighing on me while I'm trying to get through the rest of this year. College might be out of the picture, but I can work in the summer and then split as soon as I have enough saved. Maybe I can even get a job now since my grades don't fucking matter.

"Aw, did Blake hurt your feelings? What a shame!" Bryce adds.

God, I hope someone knocks them into next week at one of the playoff games this month; they deserve to know how it feels to lose.

The gaggle of admirers laugh like hyenas when I hoist my bag up on my shoulder and walk faster towards the street. I don't have a car and I hate the bus—the boys have one because they need it for practice and games. Allison and Brett sat me down when they bought it, straining like hell to explain why they did it, but I just nodded and let it go. It wasn't worth the fight and truthfully, besides the library, I didn't have anywhere to go. They could have said they couldn't justify the cost, but they pretended I'd be able to borrow the damn convertible when the boys weren't using it. Of course, that's *never* because they have it out constantly. Their parking spot in the driveway is pristine because it's almost never used.

Walking keeps me in shape, anyway. It's good for my heart and overall health, plus the quiet is soothing. No one bothers me once I'm away from the school grounds, so I actually enjoy it more than I'd let on. I don't want those idiots to suggest it's unsafe and get our parents to force me to ride the bus to fuck with me. They take a perverse pleasure in making sure that everything I love gets tarnished. I've never figured out why, but I'm sure it's damage from wherever they were before their placement with the Jamesons. Blake and Bryce aren't complete psychopaths, but they're narcissists, and my suffering makes them happy.

Yet another reason I don't bother with dating—who knows what lurks under pretty bows people put on themselves?

Sighing, I trudge down the main drag, considering a stop at the library. Our local branch is small, but cozy, and I can hide out there until right before dinnertime. They might even have more resources where I can try to locate this goddamn Discordia place. That would make me feel better and I'd be able to get my revenge on the asshole counselor. That thought swings my favor towards going, so I hang a right at the corner and make for the one place I used to escape outside of the basement at our house.

I walk past all the small businesses quickly, not bothering to glance at what's in the windows as I hurry to the almost storybook looking building at the end of the road. The library is in an old converted bank building, but the town toned down the harsh stone and granite by having local artists turn it into a wonderland of color. Murals, storybook characters, and friendly plants turned a cold, impersonal structure into a magical place that delights me every time I see it. I take the steps two at a time and pull open the wooden doors with a sigh of happiness.

Nothing beats that smell, even if it is decay and most people don't know it.

The desk has a scan station on it, so I wave my key fob to check in. A young librarian with colorful hair and funky glasses gives me a quiet wave, which I return as I head for the back of the building. I want to curl up in the reference section with my tablet and their laptops to do my research and I don't need any help with working on the equipment. I've been here so many times that I'm surprised the fat cushioned armchair in the corner by the window doesn't have my name sewn onto it.

When I get there, I'm annoyed to find a few other people on the desktops doing whatever old people do on computers. If I had to guess, it's genealogy shit—that's the number one thing I hear the librarians help people over sixty with. Being an orphan, I get wanting to find your roots, but I've never understood why they want to spend hours poring over shit just to brag about their people who lived in Ireland or Italy. What does that change for them? Absolutely nothing, that's what. Knowing who my actual parents are wouldn't change the fact that they abandoned me rather than live up to their responsibilities.

That's why I've never bothered with looking—I know what I'll find and I have no use for excuses.

Luckily, my chair is open, so I grab the laptop and a mouse from a table, then make a beeline for it. I drop my bag at my feet and pull out everything I need to take notes, intent on ruling out every place this fucking school could be hiding. If I don't find it then, I'll know Jenkins was right and I've been trolled. But until I rule it all out, I just can't accept that someone who scared the shit out of my parents and disappeared without a trace was a prankster. None of it makes any sense and I'll be damned if I give up because it's hard.

I may not know where my blood comes from, but they aren't fucking quitters.

y phone's been buzzing off the hook, and the only people who would call are Brett and Allison. I didn't think they'd notice me being at the library well past the normal dinner time because the twins have practice on Wednesday nights, but apparently, I was wrong. I haven't been able to stop working on finding Discordia to answer; it's like everything else has faded into the background. I've accessed the web, periodicals, newspaper microfiche… Still, I'm left with bupkis. It's like this place is *purposefully* keeping its existence hidden, and that makes little sense.

What college isn't looking for PR to get donors?

Stretching my arms over my head and cracking my neck, I pick up the phone to call Allison back. When she answers, her voice is strained. I don't know what's going on, but she seems very concerned. Instead of scolding me for not coming home on time, she tells me they are taking the boys out for a dinner with team members to celebrate their acceptance and there are leftovers in the fridge. My lip hitches in a sneer when I don't get invited to this wonderful night out, but I say nothing. I'd rather be eating leftovers in the basement while I continue my research than watching the twins hold court for their friends, anyway.

She hangs up and I sigh, shutting down the library laptop before I gather my stuff. It's time to walk the rest of the way home and do this in the comfort of my PJ pants and a tank top. The boys won't be home and no one will accuse me of dressing inappropriately for a unisex family space if I don't throw on a huge hoodie. That alone is hella appealing because I don't even have large boobs, but my foster mom likes me to keep them bundled up like Jesus is coming down to inspect my hemlines personally.

"You'd think boys being pervs was *my* fault, not theirs for lacking self-control," I grumble under my breath as I stand. A librarian cleaning up some of the used stations gives me a dark look for making noise, but I just wink and return my laptop. I don't leave messes and most of the staff here know me by sight, but this chick must be new. When I get out of range, I mutter curses under my breath about her judgmental stare.

The walk home isn't long and when I get there, the lights are off. That tells me no one came home before their little party and I'll have to make sure I put on the nighttime lamps Allison prefers. I'm not sure why she believes that having lights on in strategic places will deter break-ins; the idea is ridiculous. People are just as likely to watch the house for people coming and going as they are to randomly break-in; routines are absolutely fodder for baddies to learn where and when to do their thing with as little resistance as possible. We don't live in a high crime town, but I sure as hell don't stick to the same route or times when I walk home. You never know what lurks under people's skins and the worst serial killers were pillars of their communities. It's very possible we have a Ted Bundy hiding somewhere in one of the delightful houses—in fact, statistically, it's probable.

Enough of that, Kat. You're going into a dark house and you're going to scare the hell out of yourself.

My mental voice isn't wrong, so I let my mind wander from scary killers in my search for this college. I'm going to look at the letter I hid in my secret spot when I get everything settled inside. Maybe it had some secret barcode or QR on it I missed? That would explain not being able to pull up anything about it when I looked. They could be *so elite* that they aren't even publicly searchable. A little far-fetched but secret societies exist and so do elite rich people clubs regular people never see. Secret colleges can't be that off the mark.

When I unlock the front door, I step inside and turn on the lamp on the end table nearby. This is the first light Allison likes to have on and before I can relax, I need to make sure I get them all on. As my eyes adjust to the change, a skittering sound upstairs makes me frown. We don't have any pets; Brett's supposedly allergic to damn near everything. Did the boys leave so much shit in their rooms that it drew rats? I shiver, stalking towards the kitchen in irritation. There might be traps under the sink, but hell if I know if they're big enough for whatever made that sound.

Maybe a raccoon or bird got in through the flue?

I flip on the under-cabinet lights in the kitchen and bend to look for mouse traps. When I don't find any, I grab a can of bug spray that won't do a damn thing and head up the back stairs quietly. Halfway up, it occurs to me that there's a small possibility that what I heard wasn't an animal and I freeze. I mean, it *sounded* like a rat or something. What if it's some shadowy weirdo who could star in an FBI procedural about killers?

All I brought is fucking bug spray!

I press my lips together so I don't make a sound, as every plausible scenario runs through my head and my anxiety ratchets to a million. My blood pressure thrums and I can feel my body flushing as I continue moving up the stairs with the caution of someone who knows where every single creak and squeak is located. If I can get to the first bedroom, Blake keeps a baseball bat next to his nightstand. It's not because he'd ever be a hero; he just read a fucking comic where the guy carried a spiked bat, but Allison wouldn't let him wrap it with barbed wire. It's been sitting there ever since.

That's my savior—the not-quite Walking Dead baseball bat in my asshole brother's room.

I CREEP TO THE TOP STEP, HOLDING THE RIDICULOUS CAN OF CHEMICALS UP to defend myself if I'm approached. When I don't see anyone, I step to the right to miss the squeaky spot on the step and slide my back along the wall until I get to the door to Blake's room. I'm pushing myself as flat as I can, but I stick my arm out and slowly turn the knob, only to find it locked.

That motherfucker!

Brett and Allison insist we have to keep our rooms unlocked and though I never questioned it, clearly the boys ignored that edict. It makes me wonder what the hell he has in there that he's trying to keep secret, but now isn't the time. I can spy on my idiot foster brother later; right this second, I might come face to face with a crazed psycho and like a dumbshit movie heroine, I'm not running away. Instead, I'm silently tip-toeing even closer to the next door as I watch and listen for movement.

When I hear nothing, I try the knob on Bryce's door and have to bite back a curse when it, too, is locked. Those mouth breathers are going to get me killed and I'm going to haunt this place forever. Hell, I might even follow them to college and purposefully fuck up their sex lives until they die. I cannot *believe* this shit. I mean, the odds of their insolence and everyone's absence when I come home late almost feels *too* coincidental, right?

"I hope they catch a virulent strain of the clap and piss snot for months," I whisper to myself. My hand flies to my mouth when I realize what I did and I have to clench my entire body so I do nothing else stupid. Once my fury passes, I close my eyes and breathe in several slow, calming breaths so I don't start shaking.

Anger and anxiety are not good bedfellows.

The confluence of my issues fades as I look at the shadows in the rest of the hallway. The next room is mine, but it's on the opposite side of the corridor. I know I don't have any weapons in there, but I could probably find something to improvise? I've got books heavier than this bug spray can, so that might help. Although, I'm not sure anyone in history has defeated a Dahmer with a Dickens anthology, but there's a first time for everything, right?

Dropping to the floor, I watch for a few more moments, then slink across the carpet to the other side. I don't know why I feel like doing an army crawl like I'm trying to get under lasers in a heist job movie will help, but since a bleary-eyed sociopath hasn't appeared, I must be good. Standing slowly, I slide down the wall until I hit my door and turn the knob. It rattles a little and I flinch, swallowing hard as my blood pressure kicks up to the torrent in my veins. If I don't get inside without incident, I'm gonna start hyperventilating for sure.

I push the door open enough to slip inside and quickly close it when I'm in. My room is dark except for the glow of my lava lamp, and it doesn't look like anything is out of place. Breathing a sigh of relief, I pad over to my closet, holding up the can just in case there's a fucking axe-wielding murderer that pops out, and when it's not occupied, my shoulders slump. For a moment, I stand still, trying to let my nerves settle again, and when they do, I sink to my knees and crawl into the messy space.

It's dark, so I have to fumble around, but I work the vent open and grab the Discordia letter to stuff in my pockets. I don't know why I felt like it was important to get this before I grab the big ass Dickens compendium and finish searching the upstairs, but something told me I needed to keep it close. Once I tuck it away, I rise and head over to my bookshelf, looking for the biggest hardback I can find. Turns out it's not the Dickens, but a collected Shakespeare and I chuckle to myself. Willy would be cool with his books being used as weapons in a street fight, so I suppose this is kismet.

Don't judge me—my mind wanders off when I'm scared and it's even worse when I'm scared and anxious.

Now that I'm armed in a very Scooby fucking Doo way, I open the door to my room and sneak into the hall again. The only thing left to explore before I hit the stairs was Brett and Allison's room. I assume they must keep some important documents or jewelry there, so it would make sense if the intruder was in there. But I've seldom been in that room and I'm not sure I'd know if anything was taken unless it's ransacked. The door is always closed and we've been instructed *not* to go in without permission. Blake and Bryce may do it when our parents aren't home, but again, I'm the good one. I've stayed out of their space as requested.

Unfortunately, that streak is going to end because if there really is a person here, it has to be in their room. Biting my lip as I walk carefully to the door, I keep listening for the noises I heard earlier, but I don't hear them. There's a weird buzzing on my skin, but I chalk it up to the thumping of my heart in my chest. My hand reaches out and turns the handle slowly, watching as the room is revealed. All I see is the perfectly made bed and other furniture, but I know the person has to be in here.

Ugh. I'll have to go all the way in and look around.

I feel gross invading someone's private space and I should have called the police before I even came up here. But I didn't want the rest of them to come home to flashing lights and a donut eating dickhead lecturing me on wasting police resources if it turned out to be nothing. So I'm left with nosing around until I locate the animal or the killer clown—neither of which is appealing. My eyes scan the outer room and there doesn't seem to be anything out of place, so I walk towards the small hallway leading to what I assume is the bathroom and closet. When I look at the gorgeously designed bathroom with fancy fixtures, it's empty, so I know my last stop is the closed closet door.

Now or never, Kat, I tell myself as I fling the door open.

My eyes open wide as I look at the sight before me—*what in the fresh fucking hell is this?*

In the middle of the neatly organized closet is an open trap door that has a safe under it. It's hanging open and there's some sort of… *thing* digging in it. It's making weird little noises as it does so and all I can do is gape like a wide mouthed trout as I watch.

That's it… I've finally had an aneurysm from my damn disorder making my body act like a pressure cooker.

The creature senses me and looks up, tilting its head at me curiously. I stare back as my brain races to catalog the damn thing. It lets out an unearthly scream, and I yelp in response. That gets its attention and the weird, furry rodent thing drops to all fours, walking over to me. It has small ears and enormous eyes with a long tail like a cat, but this is *not* a cat *or* a weasel. I swear I've seen pictures of this before, but I'm so shocked that I can't seem to grasp thoughts as they fly through my mind.

When it stops in front of me and sniffs, I stand as still as possible. I don't know if this thing will get aggressive or not, but I'm not chancing it. It's small, but I saw those sharp ass teeth it bared when it yelled at me. I drop to a squat, looking back at it as it studies me. We're at an impasse and I have no idea if that's good or bad. I mean, what the fuck is some escaped zoo animal doing in Allison's closet and why did it seem to be rifling through her safe? None of this makes a damn bit of sense.

Did I knock my head somewhere, and this is all a fever dream?

Carefully, I reach for the papers strewn on the floor and look at what I find. This looks like birth documents and paperwork from when they adopted the twins. This stuff was flung aside, so it's doubtful the animal was looking for those. I pause for a moment as reality hits me.

Am I actually saying this thing was looking through papers and knew what to cast aside? I have to be dreaming or in a coma.

The animal gets impatient, making a high-pitched squeaking sound as it looks at me. I wrinkle my nose and shrug. "Dude, I don't even know what you are, much less what you're looking for." Its head jerks back to the safe and I frown. "Yeah, I get you were looking for something in there. I still don't know what."

Rising on its back legs, it sort of leaps over to the hole and stares at me, so I waddle my way over to the hole in the floor to look. It seems like there's a lot of papers in folders and it's all neatly stacked, along with small wooden boxes, cash, maybe some financial folders, and jewelry boxes. I point at the folders and the animal wraps its tail around my wrist, so I take that as a 'yes.' My eyes dart around the room quickly, then I lift the stack of folders out and place them on the ground.

As if it just *knows*, the damn thing picks one of the sealed folders and does a weird little dance.

I'm about to question it when I hear the garage door and my eyes widen in fear as I stand and race to the window in the main room. "Holy shit, they're home!"

Allison and Brett's car pulls into the driveway, followed by the twins, and I run back to the closet.

Everything is back where it belongs.

Most importantly, my furry little visitor is *gone*.

Covering my mouth with my hand to keep from yelling, I back out of the closet and shut the door. The sound of people entering the house adds to the urgency, so I high-tail it out of our parents' room and back to mine. My heart is racing as I turn on the reading light and pull a book out of the bag I ditched earlier, propping myself on my bed as if I've been there the whole time. Hopefully, if they peek in before they go to their bedroom, I won't look suspicious.

I'm not lying there for more than a minute when something falls from the ceiling, landing on me and making me curse in surprise.

The goddamned furry animal is sitting on my stomach, watching me with big eyes.

"What are you doing here?" I hiss in a low tone. "Brett is allergic and I know they won't let me keep a… a…"

I still don't know what it is, so I wiggle my phone out of my pocket and take a picture. Within seconds, I've done a reverse image search, and the internet does its thing. Apparently, I'm being haunted by a mother fucking *kinkajou*. They're not from around here, so either I was right about it escaping a zoo or someone wealthy is missing an exotic pet. It must be young, though, because the website seems to show a much bigger animal than the one perched on me. I have no idea what to do about it and I definitely know the fosters won't let me keep it.

Again, my life is absolute clown shoes through no doing of my own.

"Look, dude. I don't know where you came from, but you gotta go. They'll lose their shit and that's before they figure out you were rifling through their personal crap." I frown, tilting my head. Exactly where did the folder go, anyway? "And you stole something, for fuck's sake. The twins will make steaks out of you if they find out."

Its eyes get even bigger and it skitters under the bed. Blinking, I lift my hand to my head and rub my temple. Today is a complete wash: no Discordia info, haven't eaten, excluded from a party, homework untouched, and now I have a wild animal in my room. I don't know how it could get any worse, honestly.

That's when my door opens.

Allison pokes her head in with her typical fake bright smile. "Kat, you didn't turn on all the lights. What happened?"

Of course, her first thought is to criticize me.

Neither of my foster parents are horrible people; they just didn't get what they bargained for when they took me in. Allison would have preferred a sunny, cheerleading compliment to the boys she could hold up to the rest of her friends as a trophy and though I do well academically, that's not important to their circle. Brett likely has to listen to her bitch about my antisocial tendencies and snarky wit, so he's not pleased, either. It means they find fault when there really isn't any and can't wait for me to graduate, so I'm out of their lives. At least, that's the feeling I get and even my therapist doesn't convince me they're totally innocent. She emphasizes my responsibility to validate myself rather than seek it from others and skips to the things I need to do to let this shit go.

But right now, I have a secret and I need Allison to believe I'm contrite, so she'll leave rather than stay to argue. So I paste on a rueful expression and dip my head. "I'm sorry. I stayed late at the library and when I got home, I was eager to finish my work. I haven't eaten yet, either, but I'll go grab a snack and make sure the kitchen is spotless when I'm done."

That pacifies her and she nods. "Thank you. Aren't you going to ask how your brothers' celebration went?"

And the Universe tests my patience once more at the worst possible time.

Gritting my teeth to keep from shooting back a retort about how it would have been nice to witness this party, I give her a wide-eyed look of surprise. "Oh! I'm so sorry! How did it go? Did they have fun?"

Her smile gets bigger as she nods. "The *Coach* came! It was so exciting to see all the support the boys have from people in the community. Brett was so proud he almost burst and all my friends have been posting about it on social media. Your brothers are *stars*."

The silence hangs as an implied 'unlike you' floats between us. But I don't react; I nod with another grin. "They are. I'm *so* proud of them."

"You should be, Kat. They've worked so hard to get to the top. Perhaps telling them at breakfast would be appropriate, don't you think?"

I'd rather vomit acid into my hands, but I don't have a choice now that she's voiced it. "I will. What a brilliant suggestion."

A small squeak makes my eyes widen and Allison frowns. "Was that a mouse? Oh, I'll have to have Brett call an exterminator. Kat, you know food isn't allowed upstairs."

"No, no. My phone chirped; I know the sound. It was probably a study alarm. Don't bother Dad; it's nothing." I reach for the phone and open it, pretending to click something off. "There we go. Sorry it startled you."

"Okay. Make sure those aren't set at night where they could wake people up. Your brothers need their rest for the big game this weekend."

When I nod, Allison finally turns to go, shutting the door behind her. I let out a long breath and flop back against my pillows as I wait for enough time to pass. Feeling like she's been gone for enough time, I whistle softly, then say, "You almost got me caught, you know."

The kinkajou scampers out from under the dust ruffle and onto my lap, looking at me with a fierce expression. I suppose it didn't like Allison picking at me, but I'm not sure if I'm still giving this thing more credit than I should. Since I'm assuming it broke into our house to steal shit that has disappeared, that's not an unfair assumption. It keeps staring at me and I give in, reaching out to pat its head.

"You didn't mean to, right? It doesn't seem like you're trying to get me in trouble. And I don't know where you're from, so it's not safe to send you back to the streets. Wikipedia said you eat like bugs and fruit—it's too cold for you to find that anywhere. I'd be sending you to freeze and starve. I don't like that idea."

It chitters and leaps forward, sitting as close to my face as possible and wrapping its tail around my neck.

Now I've done it.

"Fine. You can stay, but you *have* to keep away from everyone, especially the twins. And this is only until I figure out where you came from so I can return you safely. No shenanigans. Got it?" I look at the animal sternly and it bobs its head quickly. "But I need to call you something because 'hey, you' will not work for me. I wish I knew if you were a boy or a girl."

It looks at me for a moment, then jumps again, moving quickly on all fours to my dresser. Hanging on with its toes, it opens a drawer and starts rifling just as it did in the safe until a pair of socks with little piggies in tutus comes flying at me. Wrinkling my nose, I ponder whether I should make a biased gender assumption, then I slap myself in the face. 'Gender is a construct' is *not* in the brain wavelength of a monkey. "You're a girl. Okay. Do you have a name?"

She just stares at me.

I might have strained the level of consciousness this weird fucking animal is capable of.

"No? Then uh… let me think about it." I frown to myself, rolling the balled-up socks in my palm for a moment. The damn thing has a good arm, that's for sure. *That's it!* I grin and look over at the creature. "I'm calling you Dottie 'cuz you have a hell of an arm like in *A League of Their Own*."

Dottie stands on her back legs and does a hopping dance, so she must approve.

"The next question is, what the *hell* I'm going to do with you while I'm in school?"

"This is the worst plan ever," I mumble to myself as I walk to school. The answering thump in my messenger bag makes me wince and I chastise myself again for thinking I'm ever getting through the day without being caught. "That's not helping, Dottie. It's Friday, so I only have to make it through one day, but we're not even there yet."

A much smaller wiggle against my side is the answer, and I rub my hand over my face. If we make it through the whole day, I'm buying a fucking lottery ticket.

The noise gets louder as I walk up to the front lawn. It's cold, but it's still dotted with groups of students hanging out before they go inside. There's a suspicious amount of smoke coming from behind the bank of parked buses and I know that's the smokers doing their thing. The administration tries to stop it, but there are too many places to hide and they're good at migrating from place to place like geese. On the opposite side of the grass is the area where the twins and their friends perch—I avoid even looking at it. I didn't have to talk to them at all this morning because they left early for a run and I don't want to ruin my almost two day twin-less streak.

Hustling up the walkway, I ignore the shouts that come from that area. It might be the twins' friends saying something nasty, but I don't have the will to engage today. I've got to figure out what's going on with this damned college that is hiding from me, and now I have Dottie along for the ride. Bullshit like the popular kids' taunts pale compared to the problems I'm trying to solve.

"Here we go," I murmur as I open the heavy doors and walk inside the busy atrium of my school. "Let's see if we can get through this with as little trouble as possible."

My locker is at the very end of the main hallway—something I've both appreciated and cursed many times. It's convenient, but it's also far too close to where all the idiocy happens. I try to schedule my trips here so I can stay out of the inevitable fights and groups hanging out near the cafeteria. This morning I arrived early enough to scoot in and grab extra textbooks so I won't have to come back here for the rest of the day. I figured the less I was around people, the more likely it'd be that my passenger will stay quiet so she isn't discovered.

I don't know why I'm risking this except I've always wanted a pet, but none of my fosters would let us have one.

Once I have the books, I head back to the center and down the hallway to the humanities section. I have AP English first and we're working on term papers, so we'll be in the library. I'm grateful for that; it will make it *much* easier to break off in a corner of the massive room and hide from the rest of the class. Woodlawn has an extremely nice library in the school because of wealthy donors and the space isn't as welcoming as the town library, but it's got plenty of nooks and crannies.

The only drawback to this class are Bryce and a few of his cronies. Eligibility for scholar athletes is no joke and though I'd bet a shiny nickel that he and Blake have more than a little help with their grades, they're both in more of my classes than I'd prefer. At least this is one where it's not both terrors at once, but I know I'll be ducking him and the other sporty jerks. Some of their queen bee counterparts are in this section of AP, too, and I can typically stay off their radar. I hate to say it, but I'm not different enough to evoke their ire.

They save that for people who do not need their brand of attention, as most mean girls do.

When I walk in, I make a beeline for the back corner where a single desktop with internet access is tucked behind reference shelves. That spot is mostly ignored, and it's where I want to be during this two-hour block. If I can work with my bag under the desk, Dottie can get some air and she won't be seen. All I have to do is get there before a randy couple or a cheerleader with a cell phone plops down and we're golden.

I slip between the shelves and walk down the deserted sections of the library with a cheerful smile until I reach my destination. Sitting in my favorite seat is my jackass foster brother, Bryce, and he's smirking as if he's been waiting for me. Adjusting the strap of the bag on my shoulder, I glare at him, waiting for his inevitable bullshit to spew.

"Hey, Kat. Whatcha doing back here?" Bryce leans back in the chair, his long legs splayed out in front of him.

Rolling my eyes, I kick at his fat sneakers. "I wanted to work in peace and quiet. Unlike some people, I have to earn all of my good grades. Now fuck off to your friends and leave me alone."

His smile only grows. "But this is such a *perfect* spot. I'm sure I could get lots of work done if I stayed back here and didn't go hang with my friends. Maybe *you* could help me study."

My face has to reflect the confusion I feel at his words. Bryce doesn't give two shits about studying unless he has to, and he does *not* care about using library time wisely. *What is his game and why is he bugging me?* I shake my head at him, gripping the strap of my bag. "I don't believe that's why you're here for a second. Tell me what you want, Bryce, and then get lost."

THE NASTIER TWIN FOLDS HIS HANDS OVER HIS LAP AND GIVES ME THE MOST fake smile I've seen in a long time. "Why do you assume I want something, Kat? Maybe I missed seeing you the past two days."

What the fuck is going on here? The twins are dicks, but they rarely corner me like this.

"I'm not assuming, Bryce. You and Blake spend any spare time you have putting me in my place. Outside of football and banging cheerleaders, I'm sure it's your only hobby." I cross my arms over my chest and suck in a calming breath, hoping he doesn't trigger my anxiety. He can't know… right?

"Oh, fine. But you're no fun at all. I want you to remember that," he says as he shrugs. His expression grows serious as he gives up the ghost. "I know you've been holding back your college shit on purpose. If you show up Blake and I with some fancy Ivy League announcement, I'll make sure you suffer. Brett and Allison need to focus on us and what we need for 'Bama, not run around waving a flag for you. Keep your shit buttoned up, pip squeak, or we'll make sure you regret it."

Like, what? Are they really that insecure and selfish?

One look at the hulking lineman says he is, and I'd bet Blake feels the same. Shaking my head at the gall of these two boys, I try to find the words to answer him. I don't know what he means by making me regret it, but I don't doubt their ability to make me even more miserable without laying a finger on me. They hold a great deal of sway over our parents and much of the student body. It wouldn't take much for my life to go from lonely and annoying to completely awful if they set their minds to it. That's just how it works around here and with four months left, he knows I won't make a stink to my caseworker—it'd be madness.

"Bryce, I'm not hiding some big acceptance to spite you guys. All their attention is already on you and I'm still waiting to hear from my applications. You don't have to worry." I feel movement in the bag and everything in my body tightens, making my heart rate kick up as I worry about the kinkajou popping out.

Rolling to his feet, he walks closer, looking down at me with a hard glint in his eyes. "That better be true. We won't stand for you trying to take our spotlight or our financial support. Just keep your head down and pray for scholarships, runt."

I'm not small; he's just huge. What a douchebag.

"I'm not lying."

"Who was that dude Brett and Allison seemed scared of, then? The one who came the other night?" Bryce cracks his knuckles and studies me carefully, like a predator waiting for its prey to come out of hiding. "That seemed important."

I shrug. "I have no idea. There was *no one there* when I went into the living room. The whole thing made me think it was some kind of prank that went too far."

Humming, he bends and picks up his nearly empty backpack. "Fine. As long as it isn't something that affects us, I don't care if people are pulling stupid jokes on you. But if I hear even a *whisper* about this shit, we're both coming."

"Got it." I stand as still as possible as he brushes past me imperiously, heading to the main part of the library where his cohorts are waiting. I wait to hear his heavy footsteps move as far away from my location as I can, then scamper over to the desk.

The bag rustles a bit as I sit it down gently and peek at Dottie. "You're doing well so far. I got the feeling you wanted to come out and bite him, but with those two, it's *always* better not to engage."

She just looks at me curiously, and I sigh. It's only been forty-five minutes, and this day is exhausting. If I have to have the same fucking confrontation with Blake in AP Bio, I'm going to scream.

"We're going to huddle back here while I work, but if you stay under the desk, you can get some air. Understand?"

Dottie claps her hands, and I rub my hand over my face. The damn animal is cute as hell and I know part of what I need to do is figure out where she's gone missing from. But it makes me sad even though I've only had her around for less than a day. Talking to her instead of myself has been quite satisfying and I'm going to hate losing that.

I'm losing my fucking mind.

Once I have her settled under my legs, I log into the computer. I'm not worried about my paper; I finished it two weeks ago. But I want to find this Discordia place again and I need to see if I can find anything on local websites that tells me where my furry friend escaped from. I figure a zoo break anywhere in the surrounding areas will be on the news channel sites and if anyone lost a pet, they'll hit neighborhood boards. It's as good a place to start as any.

Time passes quickly as I scroll through tab after tab and screen after screen of information. I'm not finding anyone screaming that they lost their pet and no zoos are missing an exotic cousin of the raccoon, so I have no idea where Dottie came from. My luck with Discordia is no better—I can't even find a measly mention of them in any articles, blogs, or official college sites. The only thing I can find that references anything from the damn letter is *Dante's Inferno* and I'm pretty sure some rich dude thought naming buildings after rings of the inferno was cheeky.

Obviously, this damned place isn't sitting in Hell.

Huffing under my breath, I look down to see my stowaway curled in a ball, snoozing in my bag. I have no idea what I'm going to do if I can't figure out where she belongs. I won't be able to hide her for four more months of school and I know my parents won't let me keep her.

The bell for the next block sounds like a klaxon, scaring me to death and bringing me out of my worried thoughts. I log out of everything on my workstation with a sigh, and bend down to whisper to the animal I'm disturbing.

"Time to head to the next class, dude. We're going to the lab, so you *have* to stay out of sight. Shit could get messy if you get out in AP Bio. Blake's a loudmouth and there's dangerous shit everywhere. Just be cool like you were this time and we'll be fine."

I mean, it has to be true or we're going to have major problems.

Grasping the bag close to my chest, I speed through the hallways of the school. I want to get out of here as quickly as possible. The rest of the day was *not* as easy as the first period, and Dottie almost revealed herself in at least two classes, where the twins terrorized me in a much more direct fashion. The kinkajou seems to be imprinting on me and their bullshit made it extremely difficult to keep my secret. Once she had both of their scents, it was obvious she would not remain still and let me handle the idiots if they got too close.

The only time I took a deep breath was lunch, and that's because I rarely eat in the cafeteria. My preferred spots are in hidden corners or when it's warm enough, on sections of the lawn not taken by the cliques. I could take my secret friend to one of my spots, eat my lunch, feed her, and make sure she wouldn't make a mess in my bag later on. The last part was important because besides not having my stuff ruined, the last thing I need to add to my reputation is stinky.

"Just stay still until we get across the quad and down the street. I don't know if any of the morons will be watching. They have team activities after school and before the games, so we should be able to slip by. Once we get home, Brett and Allison will only be there briefly before they head out to the stadium. When everyone's gone, you can romp all you like while I keep trying to find your home."

A muffled hoot is my answer, and I hiss a curse.

There's only a little more to go and we'll be free, damnit.

I keep my head down as I make my way down the front steps of the school, not making eye contact with anyone around me. My steps quicken as I make my way down the walkway towards the sidewalk. So far, so good—no one is hollering at me, and I might be lucky enough to avoid my obnoxious foster brothers. It would be the first time all day, but my luck has to change sometimes, doesn't it? Those dipshits are working overtime to bully me about outshining their achievements, and little do they realize I might not have any prospects at all. My app hasn't dinged once since the night of the letter and my hopes are dimming slowly.

If I don't get to go to school, I'm definitely getting the fuck out of this town. I'll struggle somewhere else.

The lump in the bag presses closer to my body and I swallow hard because it feels like a hug. I can't remember the last time I had one of those, but it was before the incident in middle school. Both my aversion to being touched and my distant fosters made that possible, so I've never realized how much I miss this kind of support. And now I'm crying over a bear-monkey thing and I have to get out of here.

Jogging a little as I hit the main path, I move quickly enough to put the campus behind me before someone notices my weakness. Again, I don't want 'crybaby' added to all the other monikers the petty dictators in the high school ecosystem have tagged me with. I just want to keep my damn head down until graduation and escape this place as soon as possible. *Is that too much to ask?* It seems like it lately.

When I get far enough from school, I mutter softly, "Not too much longer. Stay quiet until we get upstairs. Then you can hide if anyone barges into my room while we wait for the house to empty."

Dottie moves a little and I take that as a 'yes,' continuing down the sidewalks past the businesses. My eyes are trained on the screen of my phone so people think I'm busy and don't stop me, but I'm observing the others. A lady getting out of her car gives me a weird look as I pass by, mumbling under my breath, but that's a small town for you. Everyone is overly concerned with everyone else's shit and even stopping in the store to grab something leads to possibly getting accosted by a well-meaning person. One wrong word or move hits the grapevine like wildfire, so despite my desire to get a few things for dinner, I avoid the open doors.

They won't leave anything tonight because they're going to the game, so I'll be on my own for food.

I cook a little, but I'll probably order takeout. My bank account isn't fat by any means, but I have some savings from living in prior homes where they weren't as strict with my time. I could work during freshman, sophomore, and junior years, including most summers, so I have a meager amount of money for emergencies. I try not to use it because it was always my safety in case I had to run away. Kids in my situation are always terrified of the next place they land and though I've had semi-rotten luck, I never knew if that would morph into a full-on unpleasant situation.

I'm almost free, so a night of takeout and trying to locate the goddamn university isn't too much luxury.

My stomach drops when I arrive at the Jamesons'. Both of my fosters are home before they should be, and I wanted to get Dottie settled before they breezed in. Now I have to trust the little monster to behave even if Allison gives me shit about something random. I don't know if that will work out and hell help me if Brett joins in on her nonsense. He gets loud quickly if he's forced to take sides, which is why I try to avoid stirring the pot when they're around.

Pausing at the edge of the drive, I hiss at the bag, not even caring that I'm talking to an animal like it knows what I'm saying. "Look. The parents are here and shouldn't be. You cannot be discovered or I'll have to kick you into the cold again. If they're being shitheads, hold your temper. Everything will be so much worse if you don't."

The bag doesn't move, and I sigh in relief.

Here we go…

I open the door, sticking my head in to see if my foster parents are in the living room. When I don't see them, I shrug and head up the stairs. As I get closer to the top, I hear voices and frown. That's not coming from *my room.*

"Find anything yet?" Brett asks in an annoyed voice.

"No. I don't know where she could hide it. The boys said she swears she has gotten nothing, but that man was here. We both saw him!"

I blink. Allison and Brett are digging through my room because they think I'm hiding… college letters? In what world is that worth violating my trust and privacy? And why the *fuck* does it matter to everyone so much? If I get in somewhere on a scholarship, they aren't expected to do anything for me. I'm eighteen and their responsibilities will end with graduation.

Pausing, I listen as they root through my things, hoping to figure out what their goal is.

"Ally, I don't know about this. Kat's an odd duck and she's done nothing to fit in anywhere, but she hasn't been in trouble. Digging through her things seems excessive," my dad says. His voice has an uncertain tinge to it, and I wonder how much of his behavior has always been about what Allison wanted.

A loud huff followed by a thump precedes Allison's response. "That girl has a *history* and you know it. We got more because we had to deal with her issues, but I won't stand for her showing up the boys. They've worked long and hard to gain their placements, Brett. We've worked hard to help them be poised for success and we'll be rewarded when they go pro. The last thing we need is to be tainted by weirdness, scouts and endorsement people would consider immoral."

That's her problem? She thinks the boys will be NFL players and I'll besmirch their name so they can't cash in on them?

I have to close my eyes and count slowly in my head. The history she's talking about is my assault and I didn't bring that on myself. Even saying it in that manner supposes I *asked* for it and that kind of shit is why young girls don't report things. I can't fathom treating another woman that way given the statistics on the topic; they're horrific and anyone who hasn't experienced it is the minority, not the majority.

My knuckles turn white as I back down the hall, avoiding the spots I know are creaky like the night before. When I get to the stairs, I move down a few so I can't be seen from the hallway and step hard like I'm coming up them for the first time. The sound of scrambling is louder than they think, so by the time I purposefully walk into the hallway, Brett and Allison are standing by one of the boys' doors. Their faces are red and they look disheveled, but Allison pastes on a bright smile.

"Kat! You're home!" she chirps excitedly.

Way to be smooth, guys.

Nodding slowly, I look at them before I speak. "Yeah. At my normal time. What are you guys doing here so early?"

They look at each other and it's clear they didn't plan on getting caught. Finally, Allison laughs nervously. "We had to grab a few things for the boys before we head to the stadium. You know how Bryce forgets things."

"Uh-huh." I arch a brow. "Didn't you find what they needed?"

Brett turns red and just stomps past me without a word. I suppose he's embarrassed. He should be; Allison's obsession with being a rich pro-player mom has revealed their bullshit even more than their indifference did.

"No, no... I didn't. He must have been mistaken," she says as she pushes the hair off of her face. "I'll call him when I get downstairs."

"Okay." I shrug and head for my room. I can't make myself care about this crap; I have too many actual issues to worry about greedy fosters who can't be bothered to even ask how my day was. "Have a good time at the game."

Allison looks relieved when I say nothing else as I open my door and head inside. Despite her consistent reiteration of the rules, I click the lock into place when I close it. If she and Brett are going to rummage through my shit when I'm gone, I'm sure as fuck not respecting that rule anymore. It will keep her from bursting in while I figure out what to do about Dottie and prevent drunken idiots from waking me up when they hit the wrong room tonight. I'd call it a win all around.

Looking around, I sigh. They were like a herd of elephants, and having to throw everything back into place at the last minute didn't help. Even if I hadn't heard them in my room, I'd know *someone* has been in here. Books are askew, clothes are poking out of the closet, and a bunch of my things aren't even close to where they were when I went to school. Hell, even the mattress is a little crooked.

They're the worst fucking burglars in history.

I plop down on the bed and open the bag, smiling as Dottie clambers out to perch next to me on the bed. "Well, we have to wait until they leave to get you a snack, but wander about and stretch your legs. I locked the door, so you'll have time to hide before one of them gets in."

The furry animal does what looks like a fist pump and goes careening off the bed to climb on the bookshelf. Shaking my head, I rub a hand over my face. I have to be imagining this shit because I'm so stressed about the college applications and the mystery school. Kinkajous don't fist pump and she can't understand a word I'm saying. I'm just looney tunes because my life is complete nonsense yet again.

"Speaking of which," I mutter to myself. "It's time to pull out the laptop and try again. I have to find this place or I'll lose my mind. It's impossible in this day and age to sit on a bench without someone recording something. There's just *no way* this place has zero digital trail, yet they found me through a misspelled application in an app aggregator."

Determined to succeed, I curl up on the bed while Dottie plays. When morons downstairs leave, I'll order food and come hell or high water, I'll find what I'm looking for tonight.

The letter is laying by my side as I surf through the internet fruitlessly, encountering dead end after dead end in the search engines. Discordia University isn't listed in any college directory I've found, nor can I find a whiff on any blogs or social media sites. It's like they truly don't exist—except I can feel the truth in my bones. This place is real and perhaps locating the information is part of my trials for acceptance.

That stuff only happens in books, Kat.

Flopping back on my pillows, I throw my arm over my eyes. I'm no hacker, so it's not like I can pull some crazy dark web stunt like the smart girl would do on a TV show. Being a loner means I don't have any friends—digital or otherwise—I can make a deal with to help me. As always, all I have is myself and my brains to help me survive. But I'm doubting that it will be enough.

Dottie drops from the ceiling fan, picking up the letter and waving it around. My eyes widen; I can't lose that to an animal tantrum. It's the *only* thing I have proving I'm not crazy! "Dottie, give me that."

The kinkajou makes the odd sound, continuing to dance around the bed with it. She clearly thinks she's playing, but my nerves are frayed and the fear of losing my one piece of proof makes me edgy. I dive for her, but she jumps to the other side of the pillow, waving it again. Eyeing her carefully, I dart forward with a frustrated growl, grabbing the paper from her tiny grasp. The side cuts my finger and I hiss as the paper cut bleeds on it, leaving a print on the snow white surface.

"No!" I wail mournfully as I suck my fingertip and look at the soiled sheet. "Dottie, what did you do?"

Hooting and hollering, the wide-eyed animal pounces on me, wrapping her arms around my neck to hold on. I can't stay angry; she's trembling with fear at my shouts. My head drops, shame filling me as I realize my desperation almost made me unintentionally hurt this creature—all in service of some stupid future that means nothing. I lay my cheek against her small head gently, being careful not to rest too much weight on her.

No college is worth losing a piece of my soul by acting like a monster.

Something in my head clicks, and I pause, feeling an odd change within me. Accepting that my vision of the future might not come to fruition without being bitter and resentful about why settles me in a way I haven't felt in years. It sounds 'new age nonsense' when I think about it, but it's like I finally admitted my path may not be completely under my control. Destiny plays as much of a role in our lives as chaos and butterfly wings; I have to allow myself to be open to possibilities I have never considered before.

"But what the hell does that even mean?" I whisper to myself. "If I'm not in control of my future, does that mean I'm also not responsible for my mistakes? That can't be right."

My brows furrow as I ponder the weighty subject and I sit down on the bed again, holding the paper absently. After a few confusing minutes of trying to figure out what the words in my head mean, I look down only to see the bloody print on the paper catch on fire. "Oh, shit, oh, shit!"

Leaping to my feet, I fan the paper like a maniac, terrified that I'll burn the entire house down and end up in jail. That is *not* the new future I'm making room for. The fire goes out quickly, leaving a blackened, embossed fingerprint just to the left of the Dean's supposed signature. I frown, unsure why none of it singed or burned; that seems impossible.

I study the paper as my little friend clings to me, settling back into my seat in front of the computer. Pulling the laptop closer, I put my fingers on the keys and wait. As if by magic, my hands move and the sound of typing fills the silent room. The air in my room thickens, smelling of sulfur and embers, making me swallow hard as I stare at the black screen. Suddenly, a blip on it opens and closes, then a large pewter logo fills the space, spinning madly in the middle.

It's the same logo on the fucking letter. I did it!

Nervously, I reach for the mouse, licking my lips as I move the cursor towards the wild icon. I have no idea how I made this work or why I suddenly felt the urge to play philosopher, but I know to the marrow of my bones that I *have* to click this link. Drawing in a shaky breath, I push the mouse button and my eyes slam shut, afraid to find out what I've done. Dottie bats her hand on my nose until I open my eyes again and when I do, I see the elegant website for Discordia University laid out for me like a pirate's treasure.

"No pictures of anything but buildings," I murmur as I slide the mouse around, letting menus drop. "A place to accept your invitation, I see."

I choose the section called 'About Us' but it doesn't provide much more information than the letter. A disclaimer at the bottom states that, for security reasons, Discordia's website is monitored and accessible only from the place you first opened it. I frown, realizing that means I *won't* be able to show that dipshit in Guidance what I found; it must be locked to the IP address somehow.

Grumbling under my breath, I continue surfing, hoping to find something, *anything*, out that would give me a better idea of what accepting their offer would mean, but I can't. "It's not like this is the fucking Pentagon; why all the security? And who the hell do they pay to keep it hidden?"

That thought reinforces my belief that it must be some sort of enclave for the rich and famous I've accidentally been given access to. If so, I'd be a fool not to accept the more than generous offer made in the letter. None of the Ivies have responded at all and I could get the hell out of this town and this house within weeks if I say 'yes' to their scholarship.

How big could the drawbacks possibly be?

I TOSSED AND TURNED ALL NIGHT, LYING AWAKE AS I TRIED TO CONVINCE myself to sign the paper and then alternately, not to. My cut mishap may have soiled the pristine document, but I doubt it invalidated it. And I'd gotten into their website where I could confirm everything, so it seemed like the answer to my sucky existence here was presenting itself handily, even if it was meant for someone they think is named Kit.

That makes me sit up in bed. The damn thing said elite boys' school and if I show up as Kat with boobs rather than Kit without, I might lose the sweet deal they offered. Single-sex universities seem archaic for 2024, but rich people are fucking weird. They love doing things in the stupidest way possible as long as it looks good in a press release.

I mean, imagine being a billionaire who claims they own seven sets of the same clothes because they hate decisions rather than saying 'I'm neurospicy, fuck off.'

Like I said, the wealthy are bizarre and an all boys university with a hidden campus and website is *not* a stretch at all.

If I'm going to do this, I'm going to need the right accessories to play a role. And since I've pretended to be a quiet, compliant foster kid for most of my life to survive, I'm sure I can live through four years of being Kit. As long as I look at it as a short-term annoyance for long-term gain, it will be fine.

Right?

But where the hell do I find what I need? The letter said all the uniforms and shit will be provided, but I'll need more than that to pass as a dude. I'm smaller than them, which can't be helped, but I also don't have facial hair, a dick, or the ability to run around naked in front of other guys. I'm going to need a variety of male shit, plus a very plausible reason to keep myself out of the bare ass zones.

Looking up at the ceiling, I let my mind drift as I make a list of everything from underwear to binders that I'll need to pull this off. There's a lot and it will eat up a decent amount of my secret savings. But if I don't have other expenses, it should be fine. I can do this.

I toss a bit more and finally reach over the snoozing kinkajou to pull out my phone. A few searches give me affordable ideas for some of the stickiest parts of my plan and I hit add to cart without hesitation when I find one of the more expensive items on sale. When the order confirmation for the chest binder comes through, it hits me—I'm really doing this.

I'm going to pretend to be a guy and accept this scholarship, even though it might be an awful plan.

The enormity of the risk floods my veins, and I swallow hard. I have no idea what might happen if I'm caught or what kind of education I'm agreeing to receive for this generous gift. All I know is that I'll be out of here soon and I won't have to worry about the twins making good on their threats or ending up working for a year before I can start my future.

Discordia University will be my escape and my salvation—that much I know for certain.

Now all I have to do is keep Dottie hidden until everything arrives, and I can click the right buttons that will tell them I've accepted. It's only two days and if I get up early, I should be able to sneak out to the library before any of them are awake. The twins attend parties after games and so do my foster parents—everyone should be hungover tomorrow. That will make it much easier to slip out and leave a note.

Flipping back on my pillow, I think about how Blake and Bryce behave. Obviously, I won't pass for a jock, and they're obnoxious as hell. But their mannerisms are very male and maybe I need to do some serious research into this role when I go to the library. I won't just have to fool the administrators who admit me; I'll have to fool all the fucking dudes who go to school there.

Shit. Maybe I can't *do this.*

No, I can do it. I don't have to be the manliest guy on the campus; all I have to do is to be a smaller, nerdy guy who keeps his head down and stays out of trouble. The research will help, but I'm thinking of archaic tropes and that's not how people operate today. Movies from the 90s and before showed girls pretending to be guys in a way that reinforced stereotypes; we don't have to do that shit anymore. Guys can be all types and flavors, so thinking I can't play this role because of my size or lack of care for sports is ridiculous and outdated.

Don't be an idiot, Kat. You know better than this.

A smile creeps over my face. I won't have to be in sweaty locker rooms or worry about getting pantsed in the showers. This will be easy as pie—we've evolved past that shit even if my Neanderthal foster brothers haven't. Besides, college is a completely different maturity level than high school. I won't have to worry about all the crap the high and mighty football players do to smart kids or 'freaks'. This is a place people go to expand their horizons and focus on their future.

My little internal pep talk comforts me and I close my eyes, satisfied that by Sunday, I'll be ready for my new life.

When I get up the next morning, I feel an excitement I haven't felt for a long time. My life isn't what I've been imagining for the past few years, but maybe it will be better. After all, a university so secret that you have to practically navigate the Labyrinth to locate even its website *has* to be a huge plus on your resume. No matter what happens there, attending alone will make my future brighter.

I roll out of bed, opening the window for a moment to let Dottie out into the tree outside to do her business. I know that she won't bolt; she's stayed close to me from the moment I discovered her and I don't think she's going to run away now. Before I get dressed, I walk over to the wall by my door and get down on my knees. There's a vent here that allows me to hear some of what's going on downstairs and though I don't feel the need to use it often, this morning I need to know where everyone is so I can work out how to go shopping without a lot of questions.

I also need to know where they're going so I can sneak my purchases back in.

Pressing my ear to the vent, I listen carefully, hoping to catch at least a few snatches of conversation.

"... boys are sleeping. We won't wake them until… Yes, I agree. Their success makes us…Even the Mayor was there…"

That's Allison, and she sounds so excited. I'm surprised she's not squealing. I don't know if she's talking on the phone or to Brett, though. It wouldn't do to decide based on half info, so I close my eyes and stay quiet.

"... well Brett is out playing a round with the City Council... Can you imagine? I know, Betsy, it's like we hit gold... even after they leave, we'll be the darlings. I'm beside myself..."

My eyes cross as I hear my foster mother go on and on about their climb to the top of small town society like she's ascending the throne of England. At least her babbling let me know Brett is out and the boys aren't, but that could change at any moment. Since she's distracted in the kitchen, if I get dressed quickly, I'll be able to sneak out the front with Dottie and she might not even hear me. That's good news for me.

Scrambling to my feet, I throw on jeans and a sweatshirt, working my feet into tennis shoes quickly. Dottie comes back in, climbing into my bag as soon as I open it. I close the window, murmuring praise for her as I run a brush through my hair. I don't need to bother with it much; part of my plan for today is chopping it off into some style that will help me protect my 'Kit' identity. After I grab my phone and open the door to my room slowly.

No one in the hallway—I should be clear.

I use my knowledge of the creaky areas on the floor to get around them without making a noise and then creep down the stairs. Pausing at the bottom, I listen for Allison, but she's still yammering in the kitchen. I wing a prayer of thanks to the universe, pull the front door open, and exit quickly. Heading down the stairs of the porch, I jog down the sidewalk and get as far from the Jamesons' house as possible. I need to call a rideshare to get to the mall because if I shop downtown, someone will tattle on me. People here have not enough to do and plenty of time to call one another to gossip. The last thing I need is Brett and Allison to sit me down to have a talk about my sudden penchant for boys' clothing.

Turning my phone on, I use the app to book one, checking the picture of the driver to make certain it's not someone from the neighborhood. Lots of graduates stay close when they can't afford college and gigs like this make it easy for them to continue their previous high lifestyle of partying it up with the locals. I don't want the older sister or brother of one of the twins' friends to recognize me. Sighing, I run my hand over my face.

You'd think I wouldn't have to sneak around to go get a haircut, but that's small town life for you.

I plop down on a bench in the park, peeking in my bag to make sure Dottie is okay. She chitters softly and I ruffle my hand over her head. This is the best behaved wild animal I've ever seen and I can't imagine she wasn't living domestically rather than in a zoo. But who would let an adorable creature like her go without trying to find her? I have found nothing online, which is odd despite her exotic status. Someone should be looking for my new friend, but they aren't.

Just another topsy-turvy thing in my world lately, I guess. Since the early admission day, nothing has been what I expected; why should Dottie be any different?

When the car finally pulls up, I look at the picture again, then hop in. "I need to go to Woodlawn Mall."

The driver nods, not replying as he pulls away from the curb. I look at him curiously, making sure I've never seen the guy before. He's older than most of the rideshare people I encounter with a severe jaw, smartly pressed suit, and classical music on the radio. I flop back against the seat of the black sedan, watching the scenery go by in the silent car as we head for the expressway. There's something odd about this ride, but whatever it is, it isn't dangerous enough to really set off my alarm bells.

That doesn't mean I'm not keeping 911 dialed on my phone in case I have to push it in an emergency.

My lip curls in a rueful smirk as I consider that. Men have no idea how often women and girls do shit like this. We have to be on guard all the time, watching and keeping our surroundings in mind so we don't end up in a real-life version of a *Criminal Minds* episode. Everything from jogging to fucking taxis is hunting grounds and we can't trust anyone we meet lest we end up trafficked to some Eastern European ring or a dude with lotion and a bucket.

Welcome to being a female in the year of our lord 2024, folks.

AFTER MY LOVELY INTERNAL MUSING, I'M ANXIOUS AS HELL TO GET OUT OF this car. Lurch takes the tip I hand him with a grunt and I scramble out of the car like my feet are on fire. Holding onto my bag, I head into the mall, not even looking back at the car. I'm probably paranoid, but hell, if I'm going to stop listening to my gut—the one time I did that, it was a complete disaster. No amount of therapy will ever change my regret at not following my instincts back then, so I'm much more cautious now.

Pausing at the map just inside the door, I frown. I doubt the places I'd normally go will suffice for this trip; I need to find an entirely new look to rock when I go to Discordia. That way, no one will connect Kit with the old Kat and figure me out. I find the basic salon inside, intent on getting the hair first so I can build my Kit character with that. Playing to a stereotype will make it easier to convince people I belong in a certain box and they won't question anything odd I do to keep myself from being discovered as a fraud.

Ugh. That means I'll have to create an entirely new social media to go with this shit. Shoot me now.

I'm not addicted to that shit like most people, but I also know it will help me keep my ear to the grapevine. If there are any rumors floating around, someone inevitably posts random, vague shit that eventually translates to figuring out what or who the problem is. Using social engineering, I should be able to pretend to give a crap and fake it until I make it. I'll have to claim my parents wouldn't let me on it to cover because it's brand new. There are people with parents overprotective enough for that nowadays, and it might even make me more sympathetic.

'Don't beat that kid up, his parents didn't allow TikTok' seems like a good sentiment to encourage.

Shaking my head, I make my way to the salon. I've never been here; Allison takes me to the one downtown where she goes. She always comes with me and I suppose it's making sure I do nothing that would embarrass her. It's not like she spends time with me while there—she drops me off and heads to the beehive of Woodlawn moms, *Common Grounds*, to chitter away with her friends. I've never cared; I prefer having the time to close my eyes and relax without being disturbed.

Today, I need to make my own decisions, though. I have to get something that will sufficiently put people off of my scent and leave no doubts. *So much bullshit gender role crap I have to do just to ensure my secret stays that way.* I'll just get it cut in a shorter, floppy looking thing that makes me innocuous and shy.

"Welcome to Short Cuts. How can we help you today?"

The person at the desk looks completely badass. Their hair is bright green and cut in a longer, angled undercut that's razored on the ends. The buzzed parts are a coordinating green that makes it look like a gradient and I can't help but stare. *This* is what I need to do—something so different and gender neutral that no one will even consider looking closer. It's the peacock effect.

"I want something like you have. I can't go with wild colors yet, I don't think, but the style is amazing. Is that weird? Does it make you uncomfortable? I'm sorry if it does." Babbling is all I can manage as I give them a sheepish look.

"Naw, it's cool. I'm Jayden and I think you'll look fantastic when you shear all that weight off. It's a bitch if you decide to grow it back out, but the freedom from gallons of styling products is rad. What if we take it dark with some bright undertones? No unnatural colors this time."

Allison and Brett will lose their minds when I show up like this, but luckily, it's fall. I can hide it under a beanie for a bit.

I grin at Jayden and nod. "Let's do it."

AN HOUR LATER, I WALK OUT OF SHORT CUTS FEELING LIKE A BRAND NEW person. Jayden took my hair dark, almost black, and used a dark burgundy to put lowlights underneath. If I pull the long part up, it will look amazing. Now I just need a basic wardrobe to match the persona of Kit—a little edgier and a lot tougher. I won't be able to go full on stereotypical scene kid, but I can look alt enough to fit in the right boxes.

I thought it was annoying to pretend to be more obsequious than I am by nature, but this role I'm going to create for Kit will drive me crazy if I can't settle into it. Frowning, I walk past more traditional stores, heading for the section of the mall that has darker stores full of anime and ripped denim. I don't need any spikes or leather, but I bet I can find the right things to make myself feel less fake. If I get enough to cover myself for the first bit of school, I can use scholarship funds for more later on.

The salesperson in the Raging Trends doesn't give me a stink eye for not looking like their typical customer, and I'm grateful. I have zero experience with this shit and I'm happy to let someone help me figure out what will look good, but not make me completely uncomfortable. Once I have an arm full of clothes, I head for the dressing room to try them on. I look at each combo individually with Dottie chittering her approval, then figure out which ones can be mixed and matched in other ways to maximize my expenditures. When I make my decisions, I head to the front to pay, wincing at how much trendy, ripped shit costs.

It's all in service of a better future, Kat. You had to spend your savings on life, eventually.

Now I have to sneak all of this shit into the house and hide it until my weird saviors clear my application and ride in on their white horses.

Simple, right?

unching on the pepperoni and black olive pizza, I grabbed at the food court. I walk through the mall with Dottie in tow. I convinced the workers at the bubble tea place to sell me some fruit bits in a cup that she's probably staining my bag with as I speak. Outside of the things I ordered on the 'Zon, I picked up some socks, a couple pairs of different styles of shoes, and makeup like I've never worn before. I figured if I need to lay the edgy look on more, I'll add the extra layer to my face.

"Dottie, do you think I forgot anything? I mean, they said a lot of things will be provided, but I just don't know what normal things I should get. I haven't paid attention to guys since… the thing… unless it's trying to avoid Blake and Bryce."

The kinkajou pops her head out a little, looking up at me with her enormous eyes. She has fruit bits in her fur and she looks happy as a pig in shit with her lunch. I arch a brow, waiting for her answer playfully, and she sticks a paw out, pointing.

Son of a bitch.

My unbelievably intelligent animal is pointing towards the discount store at the mall. I should pick up toiletries and underwear, as well as a few little creature comforts I don't know if I'll be allowed to take from Allison's home. I'd like to think that they won't try to take back all my shit, but who knows what people will do when they're backed against the wall?

"Good idea, little squeaker. I'm gonna get enough stuff to keep both of us covered until these weirdoes from the university show up. Hopefully, you'll eat dried fruit if we get in a bind. They should have that in the granola aisle and some energy bars. Who knows if I'll get caught and grounded?"

Speeding up, I head out the doors and across the parking lot to the Wally World. This will be a much cheaper trip and while I wait in line at the inevitably long lines because they are purposely understaffed, I can call a rideshare to get home. Lifting my bag, I look at it and mutter softly, "This place is *definitely* one you have to stay hidden in. From the front door to the exit, I could run into upwards of fifty people I know. In fact, give me that beanie."

I'd stowed it in the bag after I bought it and her tiny hand pokes out with the hat in it. *When did I start assuming my weird racoon bear comprehends English?* Shaking my head, I take it regardless and slam it on my new hairdo. Covering everything to the tips of my ears means no 'Nosy Nellies' will make a phone call to my fosters before I even checkout. All they can say now is that I look like a skinny boy—which I'd take as a compliment now.

After all, that's what I want.

Drawing in a deep breath as the sliding doors open, I look at the chaos embodied by this store. It's only eleven am on a Saturday, but it is packed to the gills with elderly people, families full of screaming kids, and employees in blue vests that look as if they're doing something but are mostly blocking aisles. Of course, if I had to work at this shining example of corporate greed going unchecked, I don't know if I'd be putting more than a quarter of my ass into it, either.

My bags from the store are getting heavy, so I grab a cart reluctantly. Carefully, I tuck or tie the tops of the bags that are already paid for, then place them in the cart right under a camera. Every teen in Woodlawn knows the lazy ass guards here would take great pleasure in trying to bust you for shoplifting, even when you absolutely could not have gotten the items here. Doing such a purposeful show in front of the cameras ensures they won't incur the wrath of Sheriff Bob and his deputy Wilbur by calling them down here. They should be in the same diner as Allison and her friends at the moment; interrupting their mid-morning coffee and biscuits would be suicide.

Plus, Wilbur is three years older than the twins, played ball with them, and came back to bully people from behind a badge.

He knows who I am and would make everything more difficult. I've met him at school events and that idiot can start an argument in an empty house. I'm not one to back down and if I'm unlucky, he'd end up arresting me. It would blow my plans all to hell and back. Pausing for a moment, I wing a prayer at the universe, hoping that going to school with snooty rich kids is better than judgmental small town sports worshippers. It won't be, but at least it will be a new challenge.

Pushing the cart across the threshold confidently, I head for the food side first. I need snacks and non-perishables for Dottie and me for the next couple of days. I hope whatever crap the people from Discordia are planning happens when they say, but I don't want to be unprepared. "Dried fruit, energy bars, granola, jerky, stupid meal bars from diet lands, nuts…" I mutter to myself. "Fake rations in case I get grounded Super Sayian-style."

I pass by the produce section on my way to the main aisle, snatching a couple grapes with my quick five finger lift and pushing them inside the bag for Dottie. My hands are fairly swift because I got engrossed in a book with a pickpocket and spent weeks learning to not set off bells on the coat hanging from my coat rack. It seemed fun, but now that I've gone a little nefarious; it feels like an amazing skill to have already. I can use it for so many things as long as I keep it a secret.

Kat Camponella, you've entered your villain era.

I blink, shaking my head. "No, *Kit*. Kit Camponella, you've entered your villain era."

"Hey, Katarina! What's this about a villain? Can't be. You're the quietest mouse in town!"

My eyes widen as I see the queen of busybodies, Becky Sanderson, in all her bright, fake red 90s hair bumped glory. She's waving her long bejeweled fingernails and the colors of the outfit she's got on threaten to blind me for life. It seems like it might be some kind of knock-off Lilly Pulitzer style—except the lizards on it look sickly, not sunny and happy.

"Hi…Becky…" I say with a weak wave. Her brows furrow and I add, "I mean, Mrs. Sanderson."

This is the worst possible person I could have run into carrying an illegal exotic animal and hiding a forbidden haircut.

AS PREDICTED, BECKY SANDERSON DOES NOT TAKE THE HINT THAT I'M NOT interested in a conversation. She immediately walks closer, her brows drawn together as she studies me. I feel Dottie press against my front, probably because she senses the tension building in me. I have far too many secrets to engage with a town gossip—bags of new clothes, a haircut I don't want her to see, and an animal hiding in my messenger bag. This is *not* optimal *at all*.

"I heard your brothers got into their first choice! You must be so proud of them!" she gushes, her bright red nails sparkling with tiny diamonds in the light as she claps.

Nodding, I give her another smile. "Yes, ma'am. They did and everyone is thrilled."

Her eyes narrow and I have to work not to squirm as she eyes me. Finally, she clucks her tongue. "Don't worry, dear. If you haven't heard from your first choice yet, there's always state school. You'll be perfectly fine there; no one is depending on you to play professional ball like them."

Wow. Just… wow.

I press my hand on my bag to keep Dottie from busting out to give this witch a piece of her mind. How I know she's going to do it, I don't know, but I'm dead certain the kinkajou wants to scratch Becky's eyes out for being so insulting. *Hell, I kind of do; who says that to a teenager?* Licking my lips as I work to clear the red fog of outrage from my mind, I stare at the tacky woman for a moment. When I get a grip on myself, I force a fake smile onto my face.

"That's exactly what I overheard someone telling Patricia," I reply in a sweet tone. "She seemed upset on early decision day and I was passing by her locker when one of her friends was consoling her."

Insulting her mean-spirited cheerleader daughter isn't my finest moment, but come on. I'm being nicer than I have to as it is.

Becky's face turns bright red, and she makes a strangled sound before she schools her features into the official 'polite society woman,' expression the moms make when they don't want to make a scene in public. "Yes, well, I have it on good authority that there was a mistake in the acceptance notification system. She should get her email soon, according to Jim's friend at Dartmouth."

That's beyond debatable—Patricia isn't stupid, but she doesn't have the grades or money to force an acceptance at that level of university. She's spent most of the time I've been here focused on the football team and dating every wealthy boy she can get her hooks into at the nearby prep school. I couldn't care less if she's boinking the Royal Navy, but it's obvious to anyone with a brain that she's looking for a rich husband, so she doesn't even have to go to college.

"That's great, Mrs. Sanderson. Uh, it was nice talking to you. I really have to get moving, though. I've got a lot of studying to do today." I let her bullshit ride because I really want out of this situation and I need to get home in time to stow my shit before the twins come back from films.

For a second, I think she won't let go, but she eventually gives in. "Have a nice day, Katarina. I will let your mom know I saw you today. She's always worried you don't get out enough."

Fuck. Me. Sideways.

"Thanks," I mutter before walking away. I have to control my posture and speed because I know that wasn't said to be helpful. She's going to call Allison and squeal on me, hoping I'll get in trouble for something. That's her passive aggressive way of getting back at me for the dig at Patricia—which I should have known better than to do.

Sometimes, I really think my temper is going to get me in real trouble. I've worked hard to curb all the anger and rage over my childhood and the incident with my therapist, but I can't always hold back. It's another reason I stayed as under the radar as possible this year. All I want to do is get away and start a life where I can be in control of my own decisions without worrying about what some random idiot is going to use against me. That's likely a pipe dream, I know, but a girl can hope.

When I get out of her view, I rush to a self-checkout and pay for my haul. Balancing the copious amount of bags in my hands isn't easy, but I carry huge piles of books. I can do this. I waddle over to a bench at the front of the market and sit them down while I call a rideshare. I have a lot of shit, so I may even have to bring it upstairs via the secret system I built when I first moved in. It's rarely used, but that's because I don't want anyone to find it.

Hiding a pulley contraption attached to the tree by my window wasn't easy, and the twins would dime me out in a New York minute.

All I have to do now is get home, get this stuff squirreled away, and survive until tomorrow. That original letter said they'd whisk me away pretty quickly; I just hope my online order arrives first. I don't want to start my new life worried that my boobs will be my downfall.

By the time my car shows up, my anxiety has taken the wheel in my head, but at least it's not Lurch. I let out a sigh of relief as I re-gather my bags and head to the compact sedan. I just wasn't made for high stress, high stakes situations like sneaking around with two terrorists and nosy fosters peeping over my shoulder all the time.

Hopefully, I do better with this when I get to Discordia or I might be screwed.

Lucian

"**I**s everything ready for the retrieval tomorrow?"

Standing behind my enormous mahogany desk, I glare at the staff gathered in front of me. We are way behind schedule with this recruit and it's because one of them got clever. Discordia University is not in the habit of accepting lost ones; that's a job for places like State U or Blackmoor Academy. However, the whispers from my seers told me I should allow this student, even if they have not been part of the supernatural world before.

My favorite divinator practically demanded I listen—something that seldom happens, as I don't take kindly to demands. I've been running Discordia since before the Crusades and even my demon brethren know better than to control my behavior. My assignment has always been to cultivate the most powerful demons and hybrids to keep the balance between above and below even.

Not that I believe there should be a balance, but as long as the Society rules, demons will keep their treaties.

"Your Grace, we sent Dank to monitor him until we arrive. The process of scanning, loading, and erasing records from human systems is in progress. Silvera is gathering all the things the new student will need and setting up their dorm. All is in place."

Something about Beccarus' tone tells me she's not being entirely truthful. I'm not foolish enough to think I have this minor demon's fealty; she's for sale to the highest bidder as most of her kind are. But when I ask a direct question, I expect the whole truth or I'll have her exiled to the barrens. Given her vanity and lack of skills, she won't survive a day before the ghouls or hounds take care of her.

"What aren't you telling me, Beccarus? You are rarely so cautious with your words unless you are trying to hide something." I look at her with glowing orange eyes, hoping to reinforce her fear of older, more powerful demon kin.

"A familiar felt the call. It joined him disguised as a pet and he kept it. I know you prefer the untrained without for the first year, but it was quite determined, and the hybrid had yet to accept their invitation."

Fire engulfs me as my temper gets the best of me, and I glare at the assembled fools. "That means he's partially a magic user—*dual* natured—and you missed it! I should exile you all to the wastelands for dog food!"

The group of demons from admissions cowers in front of me, dropping to their knees to accept penance for their failure. With a deep breath, I get control of my hellfire, straightening my tie as I work to calm the fury within me.

This strange freshman is already causing problems, and he hasn't even set one foot on campus yet. If the seers hadn't insisted he was the key to our future, I'd arrange for an 'accident' the moment he arrives. I had enough to deal with wrangling the grown children of my actual species, much less a mysterious human raised hybrid with no knowledge of our world. Perhaps that is the answer: put this Kit Camponella through such torture in the first semester that he either rises to the occasion or earns a one-way ticket to the wastelands.

I know exactly how to ensure that happens.

"I prefer those who have no companions or familiars to come to Discordia with a clean slate, but since you have failed, I will have to adjust my plans. Beccarus, fetch Jasper. He will need to be informed that we have no room in *Citadel*'s lower levels for our new student. Instead, we will pair him with Salem on the top floor owned by their caliphate."

"I don't want to question your orders, Your Grace, but…"

"Then don't. I expect Jasper within the hour. All of you… be gone. You have work to do."

With a flick of my hand, I send them hurdling out the door to my office, closing it with a loud click. I do not wish to be disturbed until the Prince arrives. He'll be angry because he dislikes being summoned, but if he wants to continue working at Discordia until his entire caliphate graduates, he'll bend the knee. His mother put me in charge of this place centuries ago and his father may be the current ruler, but I've survived many more kings of Hell over the eons.

I would have been, had I not been marked by my family's shame.

But that will change eventually. I've been waiting and watching for the right opening like a trap-door spider. Years in this place have given me access to many vulnerable demons and hybrids; that's a boon I have not wasted. My loyal followers are embedded in so many places that when the time comes, I will barely have to lift a finger to take my rightful place on the throne.

Until then, I need to keep developing my acolytes and ridding myself of anyone who dares to defy me. Jasper's caliphate is one of those problems, but taking him out would be a bad political move. The rest of his six friends have varying levels of power and their own mythos in Hell. I've been waiting for them to get to Discordia so I can determine how strong they are—both individually and together. Once I make an assessment, they will either be swayed to join me or they will die with their royal friend.

For now, I'm amusing myself by sticking them with the new student. Rich, powerful idiots like the caliphate will eat a human hybrid who isn't even aware of our world alive. They will resent being invaded and encourage the entire freshman class to punish Kit for the offense he had nothing to do with. Either this chosen boy will face the bullying and pain, or he won't. I'm no worse off regardless, but at least I gave credence to the strident advice of my seers.

After all, the devil is in the details and I'm a demon.

"YOU MAY ENTER," I SAY AS I FLICK MY WRIST AND UNDO THE MAGICAL tumblers on the lock. I've been waiting much longer than the Dean should when requesting an employee's presence, but Jasper is a prince, so he runs on his own timetable. I know how far I can push without angering his mother, and she is more formidable than his father. The Queen dwarfs the King of Hell's power, though she hasn't actively taken part in running this realm since not long after humans left their garden.

The demon in question opens the door, striding in with a look of annoyance on his face. Jasper Eversore is huge—not surprising given he's a dragon-demon hybrid. His black eyes flash with the emerald fire of his dragon as he glares at me down his sharp, aquiline nose. When he was a student, all the students and most of the staff, both for his lineage and the ferocity of his beast, feared him. It's something he enjoys and encourages by tailoring his appearance: dark green and black hair, septum and lip piercings, tattoos from neck to feet, and spiked plate modifications along his spine that are visible when he's not fully dressed.

Of course, it doesn't frighten me in the slightest, even when the little shit half-shifts, so his long, spiked tail is whipping about.

I arch a brow, waiting for him to speak. He's well versed in the power plays of shifters and demons alike, so we could sit here silently for some time, but the impatience of youth will win this battle for me. Steepling my fingertips, I lean back in my large chair as I watch him quietly. Jasper may be highly intelligent and calculating, but his dragon is impetuous by nature. If he gets irritated enough, he'll break the quiet because he cannot stand it any longer.

"By Azazel's horns, Lucian. What the fuck do you want? I don't have time to play games with you."

That didn't take long.

Smirking, I lift a file from my desk and hold it out. "*Citadel* is quite full this semester and I have a late arrival. Unfortunately, we cannot house him anywhere but on the top floor with your caliphate. Salem has a single room, so we will put young Kit with him."

"What?!" he shouts as he pops out of his seat. "That's unacceptable, Lucian. That floor is not available to anyone outside of our group—it has always been allocated to the strongest groups with the deepest bonds. You don't have the authority to change the university charter, old man."

"You'll find I do when it is a matter of necessity, which this is. Your new floor mate's details are in the file; I suggest you share them with your 'brothers' and prepare for his arrival within the next day. I have already sent my staff to make certain the room is ready for a second occupant. This wasn't a request—it is a done deal, Professor."

His rage is palpable as he stands in front of me, struggling to control both sides of his supe nature. Jasper knows he cannot attack me for an administrative matter—not without serious consequences he doesn't want. He wouldn't get punished in a traditional sense, but I'd be within my rights to fire him and ban him from campus. That would impact his access to his caliphate and damage his ability to combine powers and stamina.

His father would lose his mind if his favorite enforcer was weakened.

"I don't know what you're trying to do, Lucian, but this won't last." His eyes are slitted with the shadow of his dragon, and I have to stifle a laugh. "None of my brothers will accept some measly human freshman as part of the unit."

I shrug, dusting a piece of imaginary lint off my suit coat. "As a professor and representative of the university, I suggest you comport yourself accordingly. You are to ensure this new student learns the rules of the university, just as any floor monitor would be. His successes and his failures are yours."

My implied threat gets his attention and I know he's planning something, but he nods. "Fine. I'll treat this idiot exactly how I would treat anyone else on our floor—as you've instructed, Lucian."

"Excellent. I appreciate your attention to this matter, Jasper. I will note your compliance in my reports," I reply as I look at my watch. "For now, go back to *Canto IV* and prepare the others for your new student's imminent arrival. I trust you will ensure they receive a proper welcome when Dank retrieves him?"

His lips curve and I can *feel* the malice in his tone. "Oh, I certainly will. It will be a welcome he won't soon forget."

Waving my hand at the door to my office, I watch it swing open and push him out with a gust of wind. It closes quickly, preventing re-entry, and I smile to myself. I don't know why the seers insist the Fates themselves have sent this young man my way, but I have no interest in nurturing a weakling. If Kit survives the caliphate's torture, then I'll take him under my wing and discern what his true purpose is. If not, I will have lost nothing.

I'm a fan of win-win situations and this one seems like a no-brainer.

I could sneak in by shimmying up the tree by my window and though it went slowly; I hauled up the bags from my excursion. The house was quiet, which meant the boys were still at films and Allison left for her weekly coffee klatch with the other mothers in town. Since Brett always stayed for drinks at the club when he golfed, I knew I'd be able to get my things in order, so when the people from Discordia showed up, I'd be ready.

Like most foster kids who have been shuffled around a lot, I'm always prepared to be re-homed. I'm lucky enough to have bought a suitcase three homes ago, so I pull it out from under the bed and lay it out. It has some of my most treasured possessions still safely ensconced in the top zipper area— a trick you learn early on. If you don't need it every day and want to make sure it always comes with you, keep it in the go bag. It's hard enough to pack your shit while fuming or crying, much less remember everything you cannot leave behind.

Walking to my closet, I choose a few pieces of clothing that will pass for neutral and a few girly pieces, folding them for maximum space conservation. Next, I pare down my shoes, only taking what I absolutely need and leaving my boots for day to day wear. Inch by inch, I go through my meager possessions, from accessories to books to keepsakes, packing everything I can. I leave enough out to get through a week of classes if need be and make sure my day-to-day needs are all gathered on the top of the dresser in a compact group.

Finally, I empty the bags on my bed. Everything from my journey today is tucked in carefully and I make sure there's space for the few items that should arrive tomorrow. When I'm satisfied, I bite my lip. I should raid the bathroom, but I'm afraid to get caught having to take toiletries back and forth until my saviors arrive. With a sigh, I close the suitcase, leaving it unzipped as I slide it back under the bed. I'll go get the things I know I don't need in the next week to put inside, and I'll make sure I can grab anything else before I go.

Lord knows I'll need emergency tampons squirreled away until I know the lay of the land at this boys' haven.

Dottie scampers over from where she's been perched on the bookshelf, looking at me with her doe eyes. I can't tell if she's worried about me or if she senses my anxiety ramping up. Now that I've used up all my adrenaline from hiding all the activities I needed to complete, I can feel the wave of uncertainty creeping in. I reach over and run my hand over her head, letting the soft feel of her fur calm me down slightly.

I'll have to employ a *lot* of my coping mechanisms to get through the wait for whomever to get here. Logically, I know the chances of my fosters or even the twins paying enough attention to me to go rooting through my room a second time is unlikely. But Allison's never gone through it before— to my knowledge—and I can't figure out why she'd think I'm hiding some mind blowing acceptance letter that would eclipse the twins' D1 placement in a football town.

Even Harvard or Yale wouldn't matter to the sports people like 'Bama.

It's been a very bizarre week and everyone around me is making it worse by not acting as they normally do. Routine is integral to quelling my anxious demeanor, so even if the boys are being dicks, it's fine because I expect that. However, they're the only constant this week, so I'm left to deal with their shit and worry. Having mental health issues is a pain in the ass—especially ones you're fully aware of and can't control. People do not understand how upsetting it is to have a complete understanding of *why* you're behaving this way, but no ability to change it.

They'd rather poke fun at how you're 'triggered' or get frustrated you don't change to make them more comfortable.

"I have to distract myself for a while or I'll go nuts. The last thing I need is a big ass panic attack on top of everything else." The kinkajou makes a funny squeaky sound and I chuckle. "How about I go grab some snacks downstairs and we can watch a movie until it's time to face the firing squad?"

That gets me a resoundingly positive animal sound, so I point at the closet or under the bed. Dottie's head bobs and she takes off, scrambling under the dust ruffle where she won't be seen if someone from my family opens the door randomly. I tug the beanie I'm still wearing down, making sure I'm covered completely before I exit my room and head down to the kitchen.

There's still no one around when I raid the fridge and the pantry, which helps the thrum of tension in my veins. Based on what the letter and the website indicated, I shouldn't have to wait long before someone will show up to usher me into my new life, but they didn't give a timeframe. I know it wouldn't bother most teenagers, but my condition makes that far more stressful than it should be.

I decide to be careful with my choices—no coffee or soda. I don't need more restless energy. Grabbing a bowl of fruit for my secret companion and two bottles of water, I rustle up some cheese and meats, crackers, pretzels, and a yogurt. This should tide the both of us over until dinner, and once I get through that, I can bring Dottie a meal as well.

As long as she behaves until my new professors or minders get here, this may actually work.

"KATARINA CAMPONELLA!"

Sitting up quickly, I pause the movie and nod at Dottie so she scampers into one of her hiding places. I don't hear footsteps, but that doesn't mean they aren't coming. I wait for a follow up, hoping like hell I need to throw the rest of my shit in a bag to get the hell out of here, but it doesn't come. *Shit.* Sighing, I look at the clock, realizing I'd been so engrossed in my 90s rom-com that I lost track of time. Allison wants me to set the table for dinner and since I don't hear the grunts of the boys, they must be on their way.

Not much longer, Kat, I tell myself.

"I'll be back after dinner with your grub. *Don't* get caught; stay hidden." Dottie doesn't come out at my words, so I assume she got the hint. If I don't get down there soon, the bellows will start again and I'll be in trouble.

I jog down the front steps just as the boys burst through the door, smelling like sweat and jock straps from their practice after films. They barely acknowledge me other than to bump me out of their way, heading straight for the showers before dinner. Rolling my eyes, I head for the kitchen without comment. They never have to do any chores and the excuse is *always* football. I've given up on even trying to bring that tidbit up, and I'll be out of here soon.

Discretion is the better part of valor in this instance.

When I get to the kitchen, I pick up the stack of plates, napkins, and flatware. Allison is watching me and I'm not sure why, except for the beanie on my head. It's not like I haven't worn hats before and it's not cold for my chosen covering, so I ignore her in hopes she'll do the same for me. There's never been a 'no head covering' rule in this house because the twins so often have backwards caps on, so I won't be breaking a dinner tradition if I don't remove it. I just need them to focus on whatever bullshit Blake and Bryce are pulling, so they don't question me.

Brett is sitting at the table when I return with the dinnerware, and he narrows his eyes at me, too. Their inspection is making my gut tighten, and I feel the waves of anxiety roiling in my ears. I don't do a lot of shit. I have to keep it secret for a reason—it's an exercise in control for me to maintain normal levels of adrenaline, anyway. Having to hide things and wondering if people are onto me is almost torture.

A torture you willingly chose to endure for four years; grow a pair and practice before the time comes.

My brain is often both my worst enemy and my greatest ally, so I have to pick what advice I take from my inner monologue. Sometimes, I only make myself worse with criticism and nitpicking. It's a delicate balance, and it'd be a lot easier if I had even a *little* positive reinforcement, but I don't. I'm a party of one, and I will be at Discordia, too. College won't change that like I hoped—it's not in the cards.

"Kat, you seem out of sorts. What's going on with your college applications?" Brett says as he eyes me, putting down the place settings. "The boys are still celebrating, but you've heard nary a word. Did you mess something up?"

Swallowing a biting retort, I smile. "I've been told the sports programs announce before the intense academic schools and I shouldn't be worried. I'll let you and Allison know as soon as I do."

His eyes narrow as he huffs, crossing his arms over his chest. "Dan said his boy heard from Stanford. Are you certain your information is correct?"

"Doesn't Dylan row? That's a sports scholarship, Brett."

I couldn't care less about his work friends or Allison's hen party attendees, but I often have to answer to comparisons of their kids. These two aren't awful people, but their decision to house fosters *was not* purely out of good intentions. Our achievements elevate them among their friends and not measuring up is unacceptable. I memorized every single one of the people I'd have to be pitted against so I can answer without either of them getting pissy. It just makes life easier.

"Coach said the game Friday was our best," Blake says as he and Bryce bound in like thundering hippos. "What's for dinner? I'm fucking starving."

Allison comes in with a roast, jerking her head, so I go behind her to bring in some of the side dishes. "Hearty food for hearty appetites, boys. You'll love the potatoes and gravy."

Rolling my eyes as I gather four bowls, stacking them along my arms as I do at work, then walk out to circle the table. Placing them amongst the other items, I watch the boys heap food on their plates with no regard for anyone else. You'd think they're feudal lords and we're their damn serfs who get the scraps. I don't know why the hell Brett doesn't throw a fit about how much they hog at meals. It's shameful, though I honestly don't eat a lot of Allison's cooking, anyway. Her shit is full of high calories and high fat, something I have trouble digesting.

Maybe it works out that the boys vacuum up enough that they don't notice me not eating a lot.

"That's great, son. You two are going to be the biggest thing to come out of this town in a decade. Ally and I are so proud we could burst."

If I could shoot lasers from my eyes and kill that asshole, I would. He never says shit like that to me and definitely never calls me 'daughter' or any equivalent. Allison doesn't, either. I may not be looking at them to fill a parental role, but it would have been nice if they ever tried.

I huff quietly, staring at my plate as I push food around and making plans for the future that don't include assholes.

That's when the doorbell rings and we all look at one another.

"Who could that be?" Allison says with a look of irritation. "Everyone knows we eat dinner at this time; it's rude for people to just drop by without warning."

If it's for me, my guess is they don't give a fuck about her ingrained Southern mannerisms.

Brett drops his napkin next to his plate, a matching expression of annoyance on his face as he stands. "I'll make sure this rude visitor understands the rules." He turns to glare at me, then tilts his head at the twins. "No one is expecting company, correct?"

I shrug and shake my head, not wanting to admit my complicity with another dinner interruption if I'm wrong. The twins snort and go back to eating, which I suppose we should translate as a 'no.' Both of my fosters exchange a look and my brows furrow when I see it. It's like they know something we don't, but didn't want to address it unless we all claimed innocence. I'm not surprised by shunting the blame around, but their shifty glances make me wonder what they're hiding.

Other than that weird safe where I found Dottie. I still haven't been able to process that shit.

Pushing my food around my plate, I wait while he strides into the living room to answer the following ring of the doorbell. Whoever it is won't stand for being ignored and it makes hope flare in my chest. The letter was very clear that the person from Discordia would make certain I could leave and then take care of any paperwork necessary. Even if I'm trapped pretending to be Kit for four years, that's still better than any alternative I have now.

Suddenly, a shout comes from the other room and Allison drops her fork to push away from the table. She fixes a glare on me, and I have no idea why. I mean, sure, it's probably about me, but how does she know that? Maybe it's a fucking burglar.

"Way to piss off Mom, nerd," Bryce mutters as he heaps more food on his plate while no one is looking. "She's going to ground you forever."

I roll my eyes at him. "I don't think so. I haven't done a damn thing wrong and I have no idea what's going on out there. Get bent."

Blake grins and I don't like the look in his eyes. It's dangerous and they usually reserve those looks for the poor souls they torture at school. "If you ruin tonight and they don't let us go to the football party, I'll teach you a lesson you won't forget."

"Please. You wouldn't dare touch me," I scoff. My words are tough, but his threatening tone makes my anxiety ramp up and I have to put my hands in my lap to hide the start of trembles. I'm not scared of them, per se, but I know they can make my life miserable both in and out of school if this Discordia falls through. I don't know if my nerves could take having to watch my ass more than I already do.

Bryce arches a brow as he cleans the meat off a bone. "You'd be surprised what can be done without leaving bruises for people to see. We hear *lots* of shit at the team parties when adults are too drunk to think we're paying attention. You've been screaming for us to put you in your place, little kitty Kat."

Holy shit. What the fuck are the men in this town talking about over old films of glory days and booze?

My gaze narrows and I remember the stun gun I bought after the incident four homes ago. I haven't been carrying it at this one because the twins seemed like assholes, not sadists. Apparently, all they needed to flip that switch was some bullshit sport school to validate their egos. Now they think they're untouchable and whatever horseshit they've been hearing the adult men say in private has encouraged them.

I wish I was stunned, but I'm not. It's shocking but never surprising to find out what men are capable of. Women all over the world learn this shit every day and we have to navigate the fallout once it's clear. I fucking hate it and it'll surround me at this school. Schooling my disgust will be impossible, so I'm going to get a reputation as a snitch with so-called 'locker room talk' and stories about assault.

Oh, well. I'm not there to get popular.

"Get in here, you ungrateful snot!"

Blake smirks. "They're calling you. Remember what Bryce said."

I give him a cool look, smiling sarcastically. "Trust me, I won't forget it."

Rising from the table with as much grace as I can muster, I flip them both off, then head for the source of the rude-ass bellow. It was Brett and I haven't heard him shout like that in a long time. He's usually the calm, detached one of the pair, leaving most of the discipline to Allison. If he's this worked up, it's a huge deal.

The sight that greets me when I walk into the living room is puzzling as fuck—I get why Brett lost his cool. He and Allison are standing huddled together as they stare at a seven foot tall person dressed all in black sporting a fedora with a jaunty feather and a plague doctor mask.

Everything about the visitor reeks of money and power, but their posture is relaxed as they turn to look at me. The voice that follows tells me the person is likely male, but that's all.

"My name is Dank and I have the distinct honor of being sent to retrieve you, Master Camponella. If you will be so kind as to gather your things from your quarters, I will escort you to the vehicle post haste."

I'm sorry…what?

"You can't just… we're foster parents! I don't give permission for this," Brett splutters, as he stares at the strange-looking guy dressed like it's Halloween.

I think Mr. Scary Birdface is amused, but I can't tell because of the mask. His shoulders shift a little and he sighs, looking at me again. "Please get ready. I will handle this."

Allison lets go of Brett's arm, advancing on me as the twins get off their asses to join us. They're glaring at the guy as if I stole their birthright somehow, and I know for a fact they don't have a clue about Discordia. They just hate seeing me get anything they can't take and if Allison does something stupid, they'll back her play one hundred percent. I step away from her grasp, heading up the stairs as I hear crashes behind me.

Looking back is a bad idea and I will not do it—whatever happens, it's on them.

"Get in the bag!" I hiss at Dottie as I pull my suitcase out from under the bed. The kinkajou scampers over and does as I ask, relieving some of the pressure in my chest. I would never leave her behind and I sure as hell don't want her in the middle of whatever it's going to take to get me out of here.

Books, electronics, chargers, and anything I'd left out for a hasty retreat get slung into the big case. Moving quickly, I run out into the hall and to the bathroom so I can salvage the personal products I need from it. Dumping them all into a plastic bag, I tie the top and rush back to my room. That bundle joins the rest of the stuff and I go back to the closet, checking to make sure no one's followed me so I can pry up the other loose board. The rest of my money stash comes out easily, and I put it in the wallet in my bag.

Dottie moves so I can get the wallet back in my messenger bag and I whisper, "I don't know where we're going or how, but we won't be back. Just stay out of sight until I get us to a place where I'm sure no one will separate us, okay?"

A soft chitter is my answer and I stuff a few more things from my bookshelf into the suitcase because I have room. I think I have everything that I truly feel is mine and if that's true, then I can finally say goodbye to this place.

There's something very satisfying about that thought.

Taking one last look at the last foster home I'll ever see, I grab my shit and head to the stairs. I'm not one to be sentimental because I have had nothing to feel nostalgic about since the incident. I'm still surprised when I descend the stairs to see Brett, Allison, and the boys sitting on the couch stiffly. Both twins have a black eye and Allison's hair is a mess. Plus, something smells… burned?

What the actual fuck went on down here?

The way they're all glaring, I decide it's better to ask the creepy doctor when we're out of here. I'd prefer not to arrive looking like I've been in a brawl. I have no idea how fancy everything is at Discordia, and I'm self-conscious enough as it is. My lie is taking up every spoon I have and my foster family's woes will have to take a backseat.

"I'm ready, Dank," I mumble.

No one moves, nor do they say one word—typical. I can't see if my escort is surprised or not because of the mask, but he grunts when he takes my case. That might have agreed with my look of disgust, but who knows? Turning on my heel, I follow the mysterious dude out of the house without saying goodbye. No one there cared enough to speak and though I was never abused like some kids, I realize their neglect is part of the compounded trauma my therapist is always going on about.

Speaking of which…

Dank leads me to a large, dark SUV and when he opens the passenger door, I look up at him. "I have medication I need. I have enough for two months but… your letter assured me you'd be able to handle that and um… my doctor appointments?"

He lets out an odd, strangled laugh and my eyes widen. *What did I say?*

"Discordia has a full service medical facility and staff, Master Kit. You will receive information on your devices that allows you to book appointments with anyone you need to set up medicine or recurring visits with. Do not worry—everything you desire is provided for in your new home."

Nodding, I frown to myself as I pull the door closer. I'm not sure I'd phrase it as 'everything I desire,' but my anxiety meds and therapy appointments are necessary. One keeps me able to function, and the other is helping me process enough that I can sleep at night. I barely slept an hour a night when I got to the foster home after the one I was in when 'it' happened. By the time I got to the Jameson's, I was up to four hours and now I can do almost six.

Hooray for facing your deepest fears!

Dank gets into the driver's seat, not removing his hat or mask. That scares the hell out of me, but I just put my hand in my bag and stroke the soft fur of my extremely well-behaved kinkajou for comfort. How he's going to see the roads, I have no idea, and that's making my blood pressure kick up.

"I can keep us safe. You may allow your animal out of that bag, if you wish. No one will attempt to take her from you."

Jesus H. Christ on a skateboard; how did he know?

"While I am blind, Master Kit, I have many other senses to guide me," Dank replies creepily.

I guess mind reading is one of them because I *did not* say that out loud. My eyes cut to the plague mask, looking at it more carefully in the close quarters. There are symbols and sigils carved into it and it looks like the material is exotic. I hope it's not ivory; that would make me very sad and I'm sort of digging the weird chauffeur.

"It is ivory, but it is from an animal you would not be familiar with. I did not kill a rhino or elephant as you are imagining."

Thanks. What in the fuck did he kill to get ivory that I'm unfamiliar with?

"There are more things in heaven and Earth, Horatio, than dreamt of in your philosophy."

Okay, so if Dank is some sort of serial killer or weirdo animal hunter, he's a well educated one because he just quoted *Hamlet* at me.

"I wish I'd been able to convince my foster parents of that. They seemed to think I wasn't destined for much because I'm a foster kid," I reply softly. "They didn't get it when I told them 'The fault, dear Brutus, is not in our stars, but in ourselves.' It just made them think I was trying to make them feel dumb."

That odd laugh echoes in the vehicle as we speed along a road I didn't even notice us driving to.

"I like you, Master Kit. Be careful at Discordia." He pauses for a moment. "Many of the students are raised to be far more cutthroat and ruthless than your foster brothers. As they say, 'he who sups with the Devil should have a long spoon.' You should trust no one until you have thoroughly vetted their intentions."

I blink as I take that in.

Just. Fucking. Great.

My eyes flutter open and I realize that after Dank's advice, he was so quiet I fell asleep. It's not unusual for me to get wrung out when I face a lot of anxiety at once, forcing me to crash later on. The adrenaline wears off, making my body heavy until I have no option but to give it the rest it demands. How long I'm under varies by how stressful and prolonged the situation was, so when I awaken, I'm not sure if I've been out for ten minutes or ten hours.

Rubbing my face, I feel Dottie push her head against my chin and I smile a little. At least I know she's not another issue I'll have to disguise at this university. I shift in my seat, stretching my legs and back before I turn to the silent driver. "Sorry, I conked out. I have pretty gnarly anxiety and this whole thing tripped it."

I can't see his expression because of the weird ass mask, but he nods. "It is alright, Master Kit. The trip to campus from your location is longer by this method. However, there will be faster methods available in the future. The separation from your foster family was more arduous than my standard retrievals, so I understand your apprehension."

My lips curve up a little. If most of the students and staff speak with Dank's level of education, I'm going to enjoy interactions at Discordia. I'm not an intellectual snob, per se, but the people in my house acted as though I was judging their intelligence because I didn't dumb things down. It grated on my nerves more than I could admit; it's not my fault that I'm smart nor that they're average. I didn't dislike the twins because of that—their shitty attitude and bullying caused my distaste. Allison and Brett were no different; I tolerated their worship of the boys and disapproval of my academic pursuits, but nothing said I had to like them for it.

They made their insecurities my responsibility, and I fucking hated it.

"You said I should be careful who I trust at school. Is that because it's dangerous?" I cut my gaze to the driver, hoping to eke out some info before we arrive.

He sighs heavily, looking as if he's working out what he can say without getting into trouble. "It can be, Master Kit. Many of the students are children of generations of powerful alumni. Others are from powerful or wealthy families. The amount of students with similar backgrounds to yours in terms of… exposure… is very low, indeed. You will have much to catch up on, and it should be one of your priorities outside of your studies. History, politics, and general knowledge of the beings in residence are extremely important to your continued success at Discordia."

Brows furrowed, I tilt my head. "And where would I get this knowledge if not from other students? I tried to find things on this place before I signed my letter, but it was buried so deep I couldn't."

"I imagine many of the questions you have will be answered within the lowest stacks of the library and through using the school sponsored internet. I advise to be extremely careful with digital ventures, though. Things are heavily monitored both by the school and anyone with the technological know-how to do so surreptitiously."

Fucking hackers are everywhere, man. But why would they be watching me? I'm no one.

As if he could hear my thoughts, Dank chuckles. "There are strict hierarchies here, Master Kit. Your admission and placement was unexpected, so it has ruffled many feathers amongst staff and students. I cannot reveal everything, but when you ask questions that do not violate my contracts, I can help somewhat."

I frown as I stroke my hand over Dottie's fur. That's a weird way to phrase this, but at least he's giving it to me fairly straight. "Are people specifically going to be gunning for me? If so, are you able to tell me who I should watch out for?"

Dank is quiet for a moment as he thinks and he replies in a cautious tone. "I cannot name names, alas. However, I would be cautious of anyone in a position of power who is overly friendly or courteous. Not polite, mind—you'll recognize the behavior, I think. Human foster children have a good sense of false behavior, I'm told. Use your instincts, Master Kit. As for students? Your room placement has caused great distress among those you will be near. It will be an immense hurdle to overcome."

Fuck me. I was looking forward to living in a place where people didn't resent my presence.

"Okay. I don't want to get you in trouble for spilling to me, but I really appreciate your help. My anxiety makes it hard to juggle too many stressors, and this is a definite change. That alone will put me on edge for a while, but having students who hate me in a place where I should be safe will add another layer. It's not an unfamiliar layer because of my length of time in the foster system, but I was hoping to ditch that when I got to college." I scratch Dottie thoughtfully, looking at her as I adjust my expectations of my new environment, as I have many times before.

"You will survive, I believe. However, it will probably be difficult and you will need to use all the gifts you have at your disposal to do so—even those you aren't aware of yet."

Gifts I'm not aware of? This guy is full of riddles today and if I didn't know he's not doing it on purpose, I would be pissy. "Well, I appreciate the vote of confidence. I don't know if I deserve it, though."

Looks like I'm going to spend most of my first semester buried in research just to survive—awesome.

WHEN WE PULL UP TO A MASSIVE SET OF IRON GATES EMBLAZONED WITH THE logo from the letters, I lick my lips nervously. Dank has been silent since the not-so-subtle warning he gave me, and I have a knot in my stomach that is growing by the second. This place was my way out of that house, but everything about it is shrouded in mystery. Now I know it won't even be safe until I learn the lay of the land; it didn't take a genius to decipher the words behind my driver's encouragement.

Dottie scoots closer to my neck, burying her face in it as I fight not to tremble with the waves of anxiety that hit me when the gates open and we drive through. My brows furrow at the landscape surrounding the car —where the fuck are we? Black, craggy stone everywhere with no greenery to speak of, and some sort of dark bodies of water surrounding parts of our path to the huge Oxford-style building at the top of the drive. The place looks like a Darkverse version of the coveted English college campus and I shiver as more of the ominous landscape is revealed.

"Dank, why is this place so goddamn gloomy?" I ask as I look out the window.

The eerie masked man looks over briefly, and the silence hangs before he speaks. "I do not believe I can share that with you just yet. His Grace will want to address your concerns when we arrive at your dormitory."

'His Grace?' What twisted ass royal bullshit are people used to here?

"Great," I mutter as I rub Dottie's fur gently. "Some stuck up asshole is going to fill me in on whatever he deems necessary. I've been through that scene before."

"Perhaps you should listen not only to what is said, but what is not."

Nodding, I watch as Dank follows a road off the main buildings that leads towards a vast structure made of what seems to be black rock. When I give him a questioning look, he doesn't respond, but the sign in front of the odd statue in front says 'Canto IV.' As we get closer, I can see a tall imperious looking man with white blond hair and a pinstriped suit under a billowing cape.

Again, what the fuck is with this Bizarro-verse Hogwarts shit?

I desperately want to ask a version of the 'chicken or the egg' question to Dank regarding the wizard books and this place, but something tells me that would push it. My semi-friendly driver is notably less talkative since we entered this place, and I have the feeling the reason for it is standing in front of my dorm, looking as if he'd like to summon Zeus to smite me on the spot. I've never been a kid that caused trouble for administration besides Child Services and I didn't intend to here, but how can I respect someone who seems to hate me before I even arrive?

And why the fuck did they invite me and offer to pay for everything if I'm not wanted?

Biting my lip, I use all the tools in my long time foster kid tool box, shoving every ounce of emotion from my features. When the car stops, I allow Dottie to stay on my shoulder since I was told I could have her here. Dank gets out and moves to the back of the car to handle my bags, so I take a deep breath and let it out slowly.

This is no different from a foster home where you aren't wanted and you can survive this, Kat. As long as they don't find out you're not a boy, you can take what they dish out.

Once I feel ready, I open my door and step out of the SUV, looking at the cold yet impressive architecture in front of me. It's ten stories high, with an interesting dome and something on the flat part of the roof. I can't see it from here, but I'm determined to look at it until Mr. Eyebrows over there speaks to me. I get the impression I can't allow him to win at anything, or my time here might be limited.

No matter what this place is, I don't want to go back to my old home.

"Kit Camponella," the man says. "We are delighted to receive you at last. Was your trip smooth?"

I turn back to the man I assume is in charge, eyeing his cane and the Malfoy-esque look with scrutiny. "As much as expected. Dank was an outstanding escort."

You learn after a few different placements that praising someone can get them in as much trouble as complaining, so I purposely keep my reply lukewarm. Eyebrows gives me a wiggins for sure, and I can feel Dottie shaking a little on my shoulder, but I'm determined to keep him from knowing. He would likely enjoy her fear and my distrust more than I care to allow him to.

"Excellent. One of my assistants, Silvera, has sorted your housing and necessities outside of what you brought. Your original dorm, *The Citadel*, was unexpectedly damaged, and we had to house you in *Canto IV* instead. Unfortunately, housing is tight this quarter, so we've placed you in a vacant room on the top floor. It will be with one of the most elite caliphates in the university, though, so you should settle quickly."

My gaze shoots to Dank and I wish like hell I could see his expression under the mask. I have a feeling this whole 'floor sharing' shit is not a good thing. In fact, my nerves are singing with anxiety and I'd wager being placed here is more of a test or punishment than anything else.

That's fine. It wouldn't be the first time some asshole did that, either.

If they want to break me, they're going to have to work harder than placing me with hostile roommates. I haven't had a non-hostile roommate since I entered foster care. I'll be fine. So I nod at the man I assume to be the Dean, keeping my eyes level with his so he knows I'm not scared. "Understood, sir."

"Jasper!"

My eyes widen as a huge, glowering guy who looks a few years older than me steps out from behind one of the columns on the front of *Canto IV*. His frame is tall and bulky, but his features are sharp and beautiful. The green highlights in his hair are a stark contrast to all the surrounding gloom, as is the colorful ink on his exposed forearms and the steel of his piercings. He looks ready to murder me as he approaches, but I notice he's giving Eyebrows the same look of pure hatred.

"This is Kit. He's the new student on your floor. Please show him to the room he will share with Salem."

Room I'll share??!!

Jasper

Looking at the scrawny kid with a fresh undercut, I snort. *This will be child's play.* The entirety of his belongings seem to be in one ratty suitcase and he's dressed like an emo loving human. I'm slightly surprised by the familiar perched on his shoulder those are usually reserved for especially powerful demons and hybrids. A sniff tells me this interloper doesn't have even a hint of unlocked abilities; much like his cheap outfit, he mirrors the mindless sheep on Earth.

So what the fresh fucking hell is he doing at Discordia and in my dorm?

"Get moving. I don't have all day to play tour guide, shrimp," I growl darkly. The new kid looks unimpressed, as if my gruff manner doesn't bother him. That won't do; I need him to be terrified enough to go running to Lucian for a housing transfer. Grinning evilly, I give him my back as I allow my tail and spikes to transform in front of him. Showing him what the heir to Hell is capable of ought to do.

Lucian chuckles behind me and claps his hands. "Well, since we're introduced, I must be off. Dank, I expect you to report to me posthaste."

Coward.

"Thank you, sir."

The new kid doesn't comment or make a single noise as he follows me into *Canto IV* after they leave. In fact, all I hear is footsteps, the chatter of his lemur, and breathing as we make our way to the elevator. I wave my palm over the magic reader, letting it know where we're going by my signature. If he truly doesn't have access to his gifts yet, he's going to have a very rough first month using the steep stairs. There's no other way to use the lift beyond magical signatures.

When the doors open, I stride in, watching him as he stands perfectly silent and still next to me as it zooms upwards. It's fucking eerie and I wonder for a moment exactly *how* this guy learned to turn himself into a living statue. The effect is damn near unnatural because his facial muscles don't even twitch—it's as if he's trying to make himself invisible without having the actual power to do so.

"This is our stop. Hurry," I grunt as I walk down the hallway of my caliphate's floor. I reach Salem's door quickly, surprised again when I realize the little freshman kept up with me despite the heavy luggage he's towing. He doesn't look strong enough to lift a fucking fork, but maybe there's more underneath.

I need Zavida to do his thing and find every scrap of information on this kid stat.

Knocking on the heavy oak door of Salem's room, I wait for him to get off his ass and open it. He's smaller when in his humanoid form, but the panda shifter hybrid damn near embodies his family's demonic lineage. When he finally answers, I give him a seething look despite knowing he can't actually help who and what he is anymore than I can.

"Salem, this is your new *roommate…*" I pause purposefully, tilting my head as if his name escapes me and I can't be bothered to remember it. "… Kent."

"Kit. Kit Camponella," the shrimp replies without missing a beat. He doesn't look ruffled in the slightest, but his familiar is glaring at me like it wants to eat my eyeballs. "Thank you for making room for me. I won't take up much space."

You won't be here long enough for it to matter.

Salem leans against the door, his snow white hair and glittering black eyes taking the two of us in. He nods at me, then looks at the offending freshman. "Come in. That moron Silvera left your shit piled on the bed."

Again, no reaction from the kid except a nod before he looks at me. "Thank you for showing me to my room."

My eyes narrow as I work to get a read on him and fail. There's something not right about this late addition to the student body and I'm going to find out what it is. Blackmail will work just as well as intimidation, and I'm not above using any means necessary to protect my caliphate. "Didn't have a choice. Salem, we have a floor meeting in two hours."

"I'll have everything ready," he replies with a slow, sleepy grin.

I fucking doubt that, but stranger things have happened.

Nodding sharply, I turn on my heel, heading for Zavida's room. I want everything he can find before we have to face this weakling. It will give everyone more ammunition to send him scurrying away like the useless shit he is.

"Jasper, I was on a raid," Zav whines as I spin his chair around. "My team needs me."

Drawing in a deep, calming breath, I look down at the Kitsuné hybrid sternly. Zav's family is one of the seven powerful royal lines of hell, but they're at the lower end of the pole. He's fiercely intelligent and cunning, but his parents spoiled the shit out of him. Not surprising, given their demonic line, but his petulance sends me into overdrive.

Like now.

I ruffle his red and white streaked hair, then grab one of the spare gaming chairs he keeps for our tourneys. "Your caliphate and leader need you; suck it up."

He squints at me, spinning back to his screen, and typing like his fingers are on fire. His character disappears from whatever the fuck dungeon he was raiding and the login screen appears before he removes his headset. I'm about to get impatient again when he faces me once more. "What's the problem, Jas? You're only this pissy when it is Lucian."

Fire dances in my eyes as my dragon side flares up in anger. "That sly motherfucker gave Salem a *roommate*. A fucking newbie, magicless, *freshman!*"

Zav blinks, his face full of shock. "What the actual fuck? Salem? The only choice worse than him would be *you*."

"Glad you see my point," I chuckle wryly. "Salem is not meant to share space with anyone, but none of us should be forced to, given our status here." He nods, looking at me expectantly. "We need a full workup before the required floor meeting tonight. That gives you about…three hours."

"Shit," the Kitsuné mutters as he spins back to his monitors. "What's the name and where's this dead man walking from?"

"Kit Camponella… from the human realm." The last words are almost spit out of my mouth. While some demons find it amusing to gad about the human realm and play at making deals, royals like us limit our time there to dignitary visits with other supes. Humans are so insignificant in terms of lifespan and abilities; we don't need to consider them at all. We were here before them and will be long after.

Zav's fingers are flying across the keys again as all four of his screens fill with some sort of code and running nonsense. "Okay. I'll have the dossiers ready before the meeting."

"You have two hours," I retort.

Zav grins wickedly as he looks at me, then at his screens. "I can do it in one."

"Good man," I rumble as I rise to go visit my other brothers. "I knew I could count on you."

AFTER I LEFT ZAV, I HEADED DOWN THE HALL TO THE ROOM CLOSEST TO mine. Slash is the second strongest of our caliphate, both in terms of physical strength and power. His family lineage is paired with mine irrevocably because they serve the royal family as generals and captains of the King's legions. One day, I will rule over this entire land, and Slash will be my second-in-command. That's how it's been for millennia; neither of us has any reason to question it.

When his iron door opens, I find him watching an action movie with Xerxes and Anton. The two of them are curled together on the couch as usual, and the big shark shifter is sprawled in his huge recliner. Being part of the elite seven families comes with a multitude of benefits, but having staff to outfit our rooms to our specifications is one of the most useful. Everything in here is extra large to accommodate Slash's enormous bulk.

Of course, X and Anton look miniscule in comparison, but at least it's comfortable.

Slash nods for me to enter and I shut the door, heading over to the matching chair across from my old friend. No one will sit in this chair because they know by looking at it that he placed it here for me. The shark hybrid is surly and rude to most people, but his respect for our positions is unquestionable. "You look angry, Prince."

I sigh and rake my hand through my hair as I look at the silver-haired enforcer. "Because Lucian is fucking with us and I have to waste precious time fixing his bullshit."

X looks up, their eyes transforming to the golden slits of their lineage. They flick their tongue out, tasting the emotion on the air with a shudder of pleasure. "Very nice, Jasper. Your anger is as delicious as your other emotions."

"Stop fucking with him, X," Anton says as he squeezes their thigh. "You know, it only makes everything worse."

Arching a brow at Anton, I give Xerxes a dark scowl. "Your tastes run towards other emotions. Don't play games with me."

They throw back their head, golden locks spilling over their shoulders. "True. I enjoy making you look like a thundercloud on the horizon, though. It's tasty in a different way."

"Enough!" Slash growls, pounding his fist on the arm of his chair. "Tell us what you need, Jasper. We will take care of it. Whatever nonsense Lucian has put into place can be undone before the weekend."

My lips quirk and I nod at my most loyal brother. "I knew you would say that, but we have to be more… cunning about this task. If we are too overt, Lucian will know it bothers us and that will make him question why."

Anton shakes his blue hair, the rainbow tips falling over his eyes as he groans. He hates groveling for anyone and never admits when he's wrong—also the dominant trait of his family line. The peacock shifter is everything that's beautiful and compelling, which is why they sit fourth in the hierarchy of the seven. All the pretty things and pretty people owe their eternal gratitude to Anton's family, so his reach in every realm is immeasurable. "That means you've got Zav working overtime, I bet."

"Yes." I look at each of them, waiting for a moment before I relay the news. "Lucian gave Salem a roommate—a brand new, late admission freshman who seems to have no powers. Yet, somehow, the shrimp has a familiar. Do you see why I'm concerned?"

X's eyes widen and they unwind their body from the cuddle with Anton. "Where is this unlucky soul from?"

"Human realm," I grind out. It makes me sick to even say it and more angry when I realize the kid will be considered adjacent to our caliphate if we don't make certain to take care of this quickly.

Hell abhors a vacuum, and power keeps you out of the black hole.

"Shit," Slash says as he rubs his jaw. "Anyone told Oriel yet? He's going to lose his fucking mind. You know how that feathered bastard gets."

My smile is wicked. "He's my last stop. While Zav will dig because I asked him to, Oriel will pry into every crevice of this freshman's life because it amuses him. He's a more effective weapon when self-motivated and we all know it."

Plus, he finds humans fascinating and he'll prod the scrawny little shit to death.

"We're never going to hear the end of this," Anton says with a grimace. "O *loves* those meat bags, and he thinks everything they do is interesting. He'll be jabbering about it and every damn thing he steals long after we rid ourselves of this baggage."

"Guys…" We all turn to X, looking at them as they frown. Hell, even frowning, they're gorgeous. It's ridiculous. "I hate to be the voice of reason, but what if this kid isn't here to mess with us? Humans don't attend Discordia and they don't get chauffeured to Hell for an education."

Scratching his chin, Slash thinks about it for a moment and nods. "Xerxes is correct. I have never heard a tale of a human being recruited to our lands for schooling. The freshman must have latent powers that have not been unlocked. What's he like?"

I snort. "How the fuck would I know? After D-bag handed him over to me, the kid clammed up like a professional soldier. The only words he said were to thank Salem and me. I swear to brimstone, Slash, the fucker barely moved a muscle in the elevator. You might have thought he was a fucking sculpture."

"What did you do *before* getting into the elevator?" X asks as they tap a long nail against their fangs.

Frowning, I think about it for a moment. Lucian showed up, I walked out, there was an intro, and… "Shit. I was pissed at that motherfucker for violating the terms of our caliphate lodging, so I showed the tail and spikes as we walked inside."

Anton beams, clapping his hands. "Bingo, gentleman. We have a winner."

"What?" Slash and I say at the same time.

X and Anton look at one another in exasperation, then finally the peacock shifter answers. "You said the little guy is from the human realm with no powers, right?"

"Affirmative."

"He doesn't know!" X says with a wicked grin. "You scared the shit out of him as intended, but not because you're a bully… It's because he's a clean slate."

My eyes widen and roll my head back on the chair as I stare at the ceiling. Slash misses the ocean, so one of the most prolific artists has painted it in the royal court to make him feel at ease. It doesn't do a damn thing to help me as my mind races. "You think this… Kit… does not know he's at a demon school? Or in Hell? Or that anything supernatural exists?"

"Humans keep their young sheltered and compliant." The gravelly voice from the doorway makes us all startle, but Oriel just gives us a sneaky smirk. He looks a bit like the style the new kid is imitating—black eyeliner and black razor cut hair with ink and steel everywhere visible. "They tell them we're all made up stories; from shifters to demons to gods, human children believe none of us exist by design. So, yes, Salem's roommate likely shut down because he had absolutely no idea what the fuck was going on."

Kat/Kit

What the actual goddamn fuck is with this place?!

I thought maybe I was imagining shit because I'm tired when Jasper…transformed… but since he left; I realized I was wrong.

Salem guided me to the professional grade kitchen someone installed in his enormous dorm room without a word. That didn't phase me so much—rich people get many perks. But when he handed me a bowl and spoon to mix right before he grew five sizes and turned into a weird panda like reptile thing, it sort of clued me in that something is very wrong about Discordia.

Of course, I could be stuck in some Lost-esque fever coma, but I don't think so.

Wherever the hell Discordia actually is, it's not in some secret rich people enclave in a valley. There are people with magic fucking powers here and they seem to think I know all about it. No one's acting like it's strange or unusual for Jasper to sprout back spikes or Salem to become a giant furry bear thing. My secret is less shocking than theirs, but I feel they won't think so.

Swallowing hard, I put the bowl I've been mixing down as I watch the black and white guy. "Uh, so it's mixed. I'm gonna toss my stuff in that spare room and then I'll come right back?"

"Aces, dude."

He goes back to chopping something on the cutting board, humming under his breath as I slink away. I grab my duffel and go into a room I can tell held more of Salem's stuff before they gave it to me. It's small, like an extra office and the furniture is basic but livable. I can do something with this space, even if the circumstances of my attendance here are now in question.

The entire universe as I know it is in question, so it can't get much worse.

"Are you coming back?"

Cringing at the bellow, I drop my bag on the bed and pull out a snack for Dottie so she doesn't snitch things from Salem's cooking. He doesn't seem nearly as put out by me as Jasper did and I want to preserve what little leeway I have with the… whatever he is. "Yep, just feeding my kinkajou. One sec!"

I close my eyes, gathering my strength again. No matter what this place is or how much my world has changed, this is better than being at home with the twins and the Jamesons. I can do this; I've survived being violated and the foster system. All I have to do is maintain distance and focus on the task at hand—graduating with a damn degree. Dottie curls up on the bed with her dried fruit and I run a hand through my shorn locks, taking a moment to replace my freaked out expression with a blank one.

Now I'm ready.

"Hey, sorry. I just wanted to make sure she doesn't snitch any ingredients," I say as I rejoin the huge guy in the kitchen. "What do you need me to do next?"

His lips quirk, and he sniffs the air for a moment before winking at me. "You're not a terrible liar in terms of body language and expressions. But your scent gives you away immediately—you should know that by now."

I don't let his words affect me, but internally, I'm screaming. *How in the hell am I going to keep this shit secret if they can smell me?* "I don't follow. What am I lying about?"

Salem pauses his whisking, putting the bowl down to pad closer to me. "I'm not a mind reader—though there will be plenty here who can. But you're pretending *not* to be scared and freaked out; that scent is unmistakable, even though my shifter side isn't a predator. There's a hint of other things buried as well, but since I'm not as familiar with your realm, I haven't quite placed them."

"I was feeding my pet; I swear," I reply, rubbing my hand over my arm like he's making me feel badly. I know how to play with emotions, and this guy isn't as rough-edged as my so-called guide. "As for freaked out, this is a new place and I have an anxiety disorder."

That should ratchet up the sympathy, so he quits digging into me.

All it gets me is a snort. "Humans, man. They fuck up even the strongest of our kind, I goddamn swear. 'Anxiety,' my ass. It's your fight or flight in over-drive—likely since you hit puberty. And now I know your secret. Jas will reward the *hell* out of me for this."

Turning back to his cooking, Salem hums and I allow my mask to drop for a second. If he knows, I'll get expelled. That might be Jasper's goal, but it's sure as fuck not mine. I have to find out why this guy seems so pleased with himself. Why does he even care? I'm just a roommate, for fuck's sake.

"What do you mean, you know my secret now?" I stomp over to the counter, grabbing the bowl to mimic what he's doing as I glare. "What secret?"

"The secret is you don't know." He grins and pours his ingredients into another bowl, starting on that next. "You've been stuck up there your entire life, living with the meat bags, and no one's ever told you. Gotta say, not shitting your pants is kind of impressive. Jasper even had his spikes out and you didn't bat a lash."

"I don't know *what?*" I growl, hoping it sounds like an angry guy rather than a pissed off mouse.

Salem heaves a sigh, putting his bowl down to turn and look at me. "About the supernatural world, dude. Stop pretending. You had no idea Discordia was a demon college and everyone here is pure demon or a hybrid. Which means…"

Frowning, I stop as well, tilting my head. "Which means what?"

"Whether or not you like it, you gotta little D in you." He bobs his brows and guffaws at his own double entendre. "Of course, if that's your thing, there'll be plenty of rainbows to chase here. Supes aren't nearly as tight assed as the peeps you've been living around."

Rainbows? Demons? Supernaturals?!

I swallow hard and pick up what I was mixing, hoping my mini-panic attack isn't as…smelly…as my lies. Salem isn't being an asshole, but he's not being helpful, either. Figuring me out was probably his assignment for the cranky fucker who brought me here, and now he'll get a pat on the back while I'm having a heart attack. The universe really has something against me—it threw me in the deep end with the sharks again.

I DIDN'T KNOW HOW RIGHT I WAS ABOUT THE SHARK COMMENT UNTIL SALEM and I finished the cooking. Between the two of us, we made several trips to a room almost at the end of the hallway to set it up. When we were done, he flopped into an enormous chair opposite two other big ones—including one that looked suspiciously like a very comfy throne.

Within moments, more guys filed in, displaying many wild enhancements that would have made someone less capable than I gawp. A gorgeous, willowy dude with sharp serpent fangs and golden locks like a Greek god wandered in first, hand in hand with another beautiful guy with colorful chunks in his hair that made it look like a peacock's feathers with rainbow accents. They draped themselves in the middle of the gigantic couch, studying me with gold and sapphire eyes. Next came the ironic bit as a ridiculously large, buff guy with a fucking shark fin on his back and a mouthful of hungry looking teeth.

Shark guy eyed me like I was getting shit on his furniture, so I guess it's his room. A smaller, darkly hot guy with hair like a raven's wing and shifty eyes came in next, taking the seat closest to mine as he studied me in all his pop punk glory. No one said a word to me or Salem, and the anticipation was so thick I started chanting my mantras in my head to keep my blood pressure from spiking.

I know enough about biology to realize my temperature rising will strengthen whatever scents these fucknuts are getting from me, so I gather every bit of willpower I have in me to control my body's conditioned response to panic.

The surly older 'tour guide' with spikes walks in, immediately shutting his mouth when he sees me. His companion is significantly smaller than even emo dude and he might be the most adorably hot nerd I've ever seen. His red hair is streaked with artful white highlights and his emerald eyes glitter behind black frames that only make him more attractive. He's wearing a t-shirt that says 'Touch Some Grass' with a picture of a Minecraft block on it and I have to restrain myself to keep from laughing.

I've always envied people who can be serious gamers.

The closest I've ever gotten to being a real gamer was foster family number two, when I worked in an arcade for a year. I was in therapy hardcore for the incident and working there allowed me to lose myself in other loud realities that drowned out the noise of my flashbacks. I would have done it with family of three or four, but alas, arcades are few these days.

Grouchy Tour Guide, aka Jasper, looks over at me again, then at the table of food I helped Salem fill. "Good job with the refreshments, Salem."

My giant panda lizard roommate gives him a lazy grin, but jerks his head at me. "Kit here helped a shit ton. He's not so bad in the kitchen."

I feel every eyeball in the room move from him to me as he speaks, but no one says anything. I cough and shrug, keeping my gaze away from directly looking the crew of men in the face. "No worries. I'm used to helping."

That's all you get, you rich dickfaces.

It seems like the silence hangs for an interminable amount of time before the dark-haired punk grins broadly. "Good to know. These fuckers are useless at it except for Salem. We should test out the results."

His words snap the rest of them out of whatever trance the panda shifter's words put them in, and they shuffle over to fill a plate in small groups. I wait until everyone, even the dragon-dinosaur-whatever leader gets his, then I quietly walk over to pick a few items from the spread. I don't recognize some of it, which makes me *very* concerned about the ingredients—what the fuck do all these demons eat, anyway—but I take enough to tide me over until I can hit my stash in our room. When I sit down, they're studying me again and I wonder if I fucked something up by waiting. I don't have a clue what protocol people follow here, but I've never once been in a foster home where they didn't expect me to serve myself last.

It's not like every foster family in existence treats their fosters like unpaid servants, but I guess I was lucky to hit the jackpot four times.

I pop a weird, dough-covered puff thing in my mouth, chewing for a moment while they all stare at me like a bug under glass. It's not bad; in fact, it's tasty in a savory, meaty way. Once I swallow, I scrunch my shoulders and look at them. "What? Was I supposed to wait until you ate, too? If so, some-one's going to need to tell me the rules I need to follow."

The gorgeous fanged guy looks aghast as he turns to the golden god one and they seem to communicate without words for a moment. When they're done, he tilts his head eerily, moving in a *very* serpentine fashion. "Why would you need to wait to eat… or even to get your food, for that matter?"

Jasper rolls his eyes and huffs in his chair, looking annoyed that another person spoke to me directly. I clench my jaw, recognizing his regal asshole shit for what is, but I also don't want to be rude to the guy who asked me a direct question. *Fucking trapped. Great.* Pausing for a moment as I decide how much of my story I want to give them, I reply, "I've lived in a lot of homes. Every place has its own rules and expectations when there's a family unit. Things often go more smoothly if I am given those boundaries from the start, so I can respect the wishes of those I'm sharing living space with."

"Satan's balls," the gothic guy who spoke before mutters. "What the fuck are those assholes up there *doing* to our lost ones?"

That gets him a confused look from me, a glare from Jasper, and expressions of agreement from the two on the couch and the redhead. Big guy and Salem don't look surprised or concerned, but they don't look angry, either.

"Uh, I don't know what that means," I say with another shrug. "But when your home isn't really yours, you just go with the flow."

A light goes on in the eyes of the rainbow-colored handsome guy and he snaps his fingers. "Foster system. Of course!"

Giving them all a look like they're mentally deficient, I nod. "My entire life."

"Well, that explains *a lot*," Jasper rumbles as he narrows his gaze at me, then looks at the redhead. "You should have known."

Anger flares in me and I sit up, unable to continue listening to them all act like I'm barely present. "Why? Why should... whoever the hell that is... have known? Were you doing background on me or something? You moth-erfuckers!"

Jasper laughs darkly, arching a brow. "Of course we were."

That's when I really lose my grip.

Zavida

The ire that flares up in the new guy makes my gut twist in a way I'm unfamiliar with. His face flushes a lovely shade of pink and the heat that emanates from him is delicious. I love to watch people and the emotions playing over his body and aura are making my Kitsuné poke its head up in interest. That's not a common occurrence outside of gaming, so I tilt my head to keep my eyes on the meal not being served on plates.

"You could have just *asked* me. I might not be comfortable sharing everything about me with a room full of assholes I don't even know the *names* of, but I would have at least entertained your curiosity. What the hell is *wrong* with you guys?" Kit crosses his arms over his chest and it's like I can see invisible walls going up in front of more walls and more walls behind that.

This guy doesn't know his heritage, but he's been using some of his powers without knowing what he or they are for a long time.

Jasper snorts. "We don't ask permission, especially me."

"That is correct and you should remember it," Slash mutters darkly. "The Prince does not require your consent to do anything."

Kit bolts to his feet, setting his plate aside as his eyes blaze at all of us. "Bullshit. Consent is a cornerstone of every interaction and relationship, whether human or demon or whatever the hell you are. I don't care if you're the richest fuckwit in this place; you don't get access to *any* part of me I don't agree to."

He's shaking and trying to hide it—to his credit, he's doing it well enough that we wouldn't be able to tell if we were mere humans. The tremors are slight, his scent is mostly masked, and his expression is full of fire, not fear. *But I can almost taste the fear in him.* My eyes narrow when I recognize that behavior as well. People have done horrible things to this new student—unforgivable things—and he's learned to cover it so well even most demons wouldn't be able to sense it.

"Stop," I whisper as I notice Oriel and Anton about to interject, using some of their gifts. "Kit is right, though not for the reasons he thinks. We should have been more polite and at least introduced ourselves to our new floormate."

The Prince looks shocked, and he's not the only one. I rarely intercede on anyone's behalf and I don't take sides. Because of my sensitivity to emotions and auras, I endeavor not to abuse my powers around my brothers. It feels dirty and unless I have to do it, I'm keeping my counsel. Here, I can't help myself; Kit Camponella has been harmed so deeply he doesn't know *how* to defend himself outside of anger, snark, and distance. The human world twisted his perspective so completely that if they could see what I see, Jasper would cancel his plans.

Even the Prince understands abusive parents—both emotionally and physically.

"Zav, we can't just—"

I look at Jasper with a firm expression on my face. "No, we don't. Kit helped Salem without question and came to a roomful of people looking at him with suspicion quietly. Then he repeatedly asked what *our* rules were and how to make *us* comfortable. Does that remind you of anyone, Jasper?"

He frowns and looks over at Oriel. His family is the worst of them all, and his fondness for the human realm has always made it worse. The raging bitch he calls 'mother' has his father cowed to almost non-existence, while his siblings treat him like he has a disease because he's obviously *not* his father's child. He's a bastard because his pain demon mother slept with a crow shifter somewhere outside of her marriage to his weak, minor cross-roads demon father. All eight of his brothers and sisters are older than him, but the old bat named him the heir apparent because of his tie to their lines' affinity.

"For fuck's sake, Zavida," Oriel mutters before shoving food into his mouth.

Our brother won't remark further—he doesn't talk about his home life unless required, nor does he let his pain show in public. The true marker of it lives in his room—a horde of random stolen items and trinkets he fills his space with both on instinct and bloodline demand. His animal is a far better representation of his family power lineage than his siblings; the crow pushes him to steal, hide, and preen over the treasure trove of weird in his room-shaped nest.

You couldn't ask for a better avatar of greed, if you ask me.

Slash shifts in his chair, taking the attention off of O by moving his enormous bulk. "If Zavida is correct, Prince, then…"

"Fine, fine. Your council is noted, Zav." He turns to pin the angry new guy with a suspicious glare. "I will keep my eye on you. We *all* will. If you step out of line, even a millimeter, and cost us the reputation we have built so painstakingly, I will not hesitate to destroy you."

Kit puts his hands on his hips, then moves them quickly as if the gesture was second nature and he's hiding it. "Agreed. But I *will* need someone to give me the rules and regulations you expect me to follow rather than set me to fail by hiding them. And tell me who the goddamned fuck you are, unless you'd rather I call you my own names."

X looks amused, their beautiful face filled with joy. "What, pray tell, are those names? I find myself *very* curious, Kit."

His playful query seems to calm the tension in the kid and his lips curl as he looks at us one by one. Pointing to Jasper first, he makes the rounds. "Asshole Demon, Big Demon, Pretty Demon, Flirty Demon, Goth Demon, Lazy Demon, and Gamer Demon."

I'll be damned. That's spot fucking on. I might be jealous of his insightfulness.

That's par for the course, though, given my lineage. But I don't often truly feel it this deeply and my interest in this guy is puzzling as hell. The expressions on the faces of my brothers are varied, but I can tell they are just as fascinated by Kit as I am.

Which could be excellent or terrible news.

"Yes, well, I can't argue the logic," Jasper says smoothly. He doesn't look even a bit perturbed by his moniker, but that's because his persona is crafted to reflect exactly what he said. "You can use your own names, but I'd be remiss if I didn't introduce everyone."

Heaven forbid someone hear the Prince is as ill-mannered as he is ill tempered.

"That is Slash, my second-in-command since we were children." He points to the large aquatic shifter. "On the couch are Xerxes and Anton, who indeed, are pretty and flirty."

X winks at Kit playfully and Anton wiggles his fingers. They're the most outgoing of us all, and it's not just their affinity that makes them such. Both of them enjoy the company of others and their powers bring mostly pleasurable sensations. It's not surprising they aren't as cautious as the rest of us. Kit smiles a little, his gaze intense, like he's trying to memorize each person.

"You have the rotten luck of rooming with Salem and the darkly sarcastic one is Oriel." Jasper cuts his gaze to me, smiling softly. "Zavida, there is the opposite of my churlish personality, and that's the lot of us."

Nodding, Kit moves to sit, taking his plate to nibble on the food. A loud growl comes from his stomach before Jasper can continue and all eyes fly to him again. His cheeks flame and he mutters, "Sorry. Rude body parts. Continue."

Salem has been quiet mostly, but he immediately gets up and piles a plate full of the food we prepared. His expression is troubled when he walks over and hands it to our new roommate, growling in a low voice, "Less talking, more eating."

Jasper rolls his eyes and mutters something in the language of our people, leaving Kit to study the food. None of us speak until he eats again, his face not reflecting whatever is going on inside of him. Once everyone seems satisfied, our leader picks up the agenda he asked me for. He's done picking on the new dude and ready to get down to business.

"Our caliphate is special. Because of my family, we've been allowed to have certain privileges and exceptions made, so we must hold up our end of the bargain. The floor will remain spotless in public areas and presentable in private ones. All duties will be split as Slash and I see fit, with no questions asked. Grades will reflect the excellence of our group—this means *you*, Oriel —and every single person in this room will represent us in extracurriculars. *No one* will behave in a way that diminishes our image or it will be dealt with severely. Got it?"

His overbearing crap gets worse every year and now that he's on faculty, it's gone to his head. None of us wants to invite the intervention of our parents, so we are careful how we comport ourselves. Even when there's a coordinated campaign to teach a deserving rival a lesson, we know how to do it without leaving a trail. I suspect that's exactly what he has in store for Kit and suddenly it doesn't sit right with me.

The guy clearly has a shitty past in the human world and it feels wrong to compound that with a shitty future in this one.

"I'll need that damn rulebook if I'm expected to be a good little automaton," Kit interjects. "I cannot possibly read your mind to figure out what the hell you deign to be appropriate."

Oriel grins a little and tilts his head in a very crow-like manner. "I can shadow him."

"Beelzebub laughed," Slash grunts as he turns to Jasper. "That's the *worst* possible plan."

A smug, cunning expression comes over the Prince's face and I realize he's weighing the possible fallout of allowing Oriel to have permission to teach someone rules versus sparing someone more law-abiding for the task. He nods sharply. "Permission granted, O. You will be Kit's guide to everything Discordia, and the rules of our caliphate."

Of all the gin joints in all the supernatural world, this dude had to walk into ours. He's toast.

"We need to divvy up the extracurriculars. I'm *not* getting stuck with a sweaty sport this year, Jasper Eversore," Anton says as he preens a few feathers that have popped up. "I want to decide now so the fucking paths to captain or chair or whatever are clear."

"Dibs on student council," Xerxes says with a devious grin. "Planning events *full* of longing and well-dressed people is right in my wheelhouse. Plus, I'm the most social—you animals have reputations."

"Fine. Who else has a preference? Slash is clearly our demon in the Magic Battles." Jasper turns to the shark shifter, who nods. "His size, cunning, and magic are only matched by my own. Alas, I can no longer compete, but I will be heavily involved in coaching."

Of course he will. Jasper is the reigning champion of the Battles at Discordia, as his father and grandfather were before him.

Anton looks thoughtful before he hums. "I'll handle the arts—plays, music, and the like. Letting Oriel take them after our senior year would be a bloody disaster. He would steal half the props and pickpocket all the dignitaries."

Our dark friend chuckles softly, shrugging without a hint of remorse. "It's who I am, boys. You can't fight nature. I'll do the Thieves Guild. I'll learn more there than any other activity."

The Prince nods again. "Done. That leaves Zav, Salem, and Kit. Now is the time, gentlemen, or I'll assign you myself."

That gets the panda shifter's attention, and he sits up a straighter. "Leave the hospitality committee to me. I can get in tight with the staff in the office and the other house leaders. I'll behave; I promise," he says as he makes a pentagram in the air.

Slash and Jasper exchange looks that say they aren't convinced, but it is a fitting place to leave our least motivated member. He won't have to exert himself much and isn't likely to earn demerits for skipping shit to cook. Their gaze moves to me and I know what I want, but I'm worried about what will happen to Kit. He doesn't have a clue about this place, his powers, everyone's powers, or the politics. He won't be elected to a leadership position, and he looks as if he doesn't want one.

"I think Kit should try everything this first year. We will all be there to observe him and can appoint him as our seconds to monitor his progress. It's less likely to get us dinged by his lack of knowledge." I shoot him a sheepish look, hoping he knows I'm not being an asshole. He shrugs and continues eating. "And I should take on the academic clubs."

The silence hangs for another moment before the Prince finally sighs. "You can always see the entire chessboard, Zav. Your suggestion is accepted. Kit will join all of your activities and we can assess his strength—if he survives past the break."

From the look on his face, Kit will let no one stand in his way—even us—and that's yet another worry to file in my hard drive.

kät/kit

The rest of the meeting passes by in a blur. Most of what they discuss is above my head, but I figure I can ask Salem later. He and Oriel seem like the safest options based on their behavior so far. Anton and Xerxes are ambivalent; I'm not sure how to read them accurately yet. Zavida might be an option, but he's clearly very devoted to Jasper, so I don't know what will be shared with the ornery leader. It's clear Jasper and Slash would rather I fall off the face of… wherever we are. No one has mentioned it yet, but it feels safe to assume Hell is the answer.

I'd rather not make a fool of myself by asking to confirm though.

They referenced my being 'lost' more than once and my time in the foster system several times—I gather they believe my actual parents were hiding me or exiled from this realm. I've been keeping meticulous notes in my head of the terms and phrases I don't recognize so I can look them up in my textbooks. Worst-case scenario, I can hit the library on campus. The brochure had a map that showed one and though my phone isn't supposed to work here, Oriel asked Zavida to meet me later to do something that would give me access to their internal internet on my devices.

The devil is literally in the details, I suppose, because everything here is crafted to prevent humans from being aware of the truth about demons and other supernaturals. I can understand why; humans don't even treat their own kind well, much less people this different. If they knew all the creatures and beings from myths and stories were real, they'd lose their fucking minds. As a species, we're not the most adaptable, no matter what evolution suggests.

It occurs to me I said 'we,' but the guys were acting as if I'm not actually human, but some sort of hybrid like them.

Not calling myself human will take some getting used to. I'm not sure I believe it, anyway. In all my years on earth, I've never displayed any kind of weird powers. Even during my… incident… nothing happened. I couldn't stop him. Isn't that the kind of situation where some latent superpower should have taken over to help me? That's what always happens in books and movies, but it wasn't my experience. I was alone and helpless, like always.

Afterward, they moved me from place to place, year after year, until I ended up with the Jamesons. The excuses were all bogus and vague—as if there was some invisible stench coming off me to put the families off. I frown as I enter my new room, wondering if those people could *sense* I wasn't what they said I was. Was it my 'otherness' coming out and making them want me out of their homes? My anxiety always told me something was wrong with me, which is why I kept my distance. But now I'm wondering if this supernatural shit was the problem the whole time.

I'll never know; it's pointless to speculate. I need to focus on current Kat problems, not shit I can't fix.

"You okay, dude?" Salem looks up from where he's packaging the leftovers from the meeting in various containers. "You spaced out at the end and we couldn't get you to snap out of it."

My face turns bright red. Small fugue states where I'm unresponsive because my anxiety is so high aren't uncommon and I should probably warn him about it. It's normal because of the PTSD, but not everyone under-stands. It freaks people out to see me frozen like that and I don't want to be even more of a burden to guys who don't want me here to begin with. "Um, I'm sorry. I should tell you a few things about me since we're roommates. You know, so I don't cause problems."

The white-haired demon looks at me curiously, his dark black eyes shining. "Sure, man. But don't feel you have to reveal a bunch of personal shit because Jasper is a dick. He's used to being the big man because of his dad and it's hella easy for him to go overboard with it. Most of us just take it in stride at this point."

Good to know, but I doubt I can be so flippant about his edicts.

Licking my lips nervously, I drop onto the couch, leaning over the back of it to watch him work. "Understood. But this isn't because of him, per se, but it affects you as someone I share space with. I'd be a giant asshat if I didn't warn you about my shit. You'll be the most likely person to witness most of it and I don't want you unaware."

That gets his attention and Salem stops fiddling with the food to lean against the counter. His expression is serious as he nods. "Okay, shoot."

"I have PTSD and high functioning anxiety. There's other stuff, but those are the things you need to know about. My triggers are varied, so most people can't just intentionally work around them. I've been in therapy for years and I take medication, but my symptoms freak people out. The semi-fugue thing you saw at the meeting is one of them—I space and don't respond until it's over."

His expression softens a little—I think—and he rakes a hand through his locks as he blows out a long breath. I wait and wait, trying to control my rapidly escalating blood pressure while he processes my confession. Finally, the panda shifter looks at me again. "That changes things, Kit. I need to share it, and I want your permission to do so."

My eyes widen. "No, no! I don't *tell* people this. I'm *only* telling you because you might see me unglued in this room. I don't want anyone else to know; it's a weapon."

"Kit…" Salem groans as he rubs his hand on his face. "I can't keep secrets from the caliphate. We're sworn to honesty. Jasper will lose his fucking *mind* if he finds out I sided with you on this."

"*Please*, Salem," I beg, gripping the back of the couch as my hands shake in fear. "You don't understand. I can't tell you why I have this, but it's bad. And I *really* don't talk about that. If you tell them, I'll be interrogated and I won't be able to… function."

"Merciful Beelzebub, this is a mess. How did Zav miss this shit?" he grumbles as he crosses his arms over his chest. "He's slipping because of all that fucking gaming."

I frown and shrug. "Medical records are well guarded in my realm, and mine are registered with governmental services. I guess he'd have to be digging deeper than he's used to."

"You think he'll find them if Jasper is making him go deeper?" His expression is thoughtful. "If so, I can keep your secret until he uncovers it. That way, I'm not holding out for long and you're not being questioned. Your files should have the complete story."

It won't because they're looking for the wrong name, but I can pretend for now.

"I can live with that," I murmur as I let go of the cushions. His concession is allowing me to breathe better and I'm pretty sure I can survive the rest. "You have a deal."

AFTER I HELPED SALEM FINISH THE FOOD, I TRUDGE BACK TO MY ROOM AND shut the door. Dottie rockets towards me, climbing onto my shoulder, and wrapping her tiny arms around me. My eyes close and calm washes over me when she's back at my side. I didn't realize how much I depended on her presence until just now. Somehow, in the few days since she showed up at my window, the little kinkajou solidified her place in my life and I felt wrong without her.

I just didn't know it and now I have to adjust to needing her to be part of my routine.

"I'll be damned. Jacquelyn was right about companion animals. Too bad none of my homes would have accepted one," I grumble under my breath. "I might have had a lot fewer problems with people if I'd had you to help me cope."

Dottie chitters softly, and I walk over to the bed to sit down. This has been a hell of a day and my mind is full of questions and new information that I can't parse it. From the time we left the Jameson's to now, there's been this flood of *stuff* demanding I pay attention and respond with no time to process. My eyes close and I let Dottie scamper onto the comforter before I flop backwards.

"How am I supposed to deal with all this at once? Demons, shifters, magic... It's too much." Rubbing my hand over my face, I groan when I realize I have to unpack, so I'll be ready for tomorrow. "I don't even have time to work out how this changes things. I mean, if I make it through this, what happens then? I can't possibly go back there and pretend I don't know."

No one is here to answer that, so I sigh and push back up to look at the boxes of stuff that were here when I arrived. My meager suitcase is sitting there, too, and I chuckle. The crap the school provided more than triples what I brought with me and I have no idea what all of it is. This will take some getting used to—my advisor seems to think I require far more belongings than I've ever had before. I wonder how much of it is necessary and how much is typical rich people's junk?

"I have to dig in and find out, I suppose. I'll need the textbooks and uniforms for tomorrow." Dottie gives me a happy look I take as agreement, and I force myself to stand up. "Let's see what they put together for me and make my room less crowded."

The first box has five crisply pressed uniforms comprising dark pants, a white button-up, a tie, and a blazer. It appears freshmen wear black jackets and accented ties. If my research into private prep schools is correct, I believe the other levels will wear different colors to denote their years. Outside of Jasper, the other guys have the same blazer as me, but theirs are trimmed with cerulean blue because of their caliphate. Just another thing to make me stick out when I'm with them and piss Jasper off. I don't know what he'll wear as an adjunct, but I'm sure it will be fancy as hell, so everyone knows how freaking royal and cool he is.

I pause, hanging the pieces in sets when that thought flitters across my mind. *Why am I so angry? I barely know the douche.* Sighing, I finish my task and shake my head. I'm always prickly when I first arrive in a new home as a defense mechanism, but this is more than that. I'm actively pissed that he hates me for no reason, and normally, I don't give a fuck. His instant dislike rankles me because it's not fair. I have done nothing to earn the disrespect; in fact, I'm at a tremendous disadvantage.

I'm not a challenge to his power, so he shouldn't care.

"Stop being so needy, Kat," I mutter to myself as I unload stacks of thick textbooks. "You're here to get an education, not make friends. All you have to do is survive four years, come out with a degree, and this will all be behind you."

"Hey, are you talking in there?" The knock on my door is gentle, but it scares the shit out of me.

Breathing hard as I barely keep from shrieking, I wait until my heart stops thumping before I answer. "Uh, maybe? Who's there?"

It's not Salem, because I feel he would have opened the door without knocking. The person laughs softly and says, "I'm opening the door, Kit. I'm sorry I scared you."

Holy fuck, is this guy a goddamn mind reader?

"I'm empathic, yes," the red-haired demon replies as he peeks in the door's crack as it opens. "I can't hear your thoughts, but when you let your guard down, I can sense your emotions."

Gaping at him, I find a Discordia tee shirt on the top of the next box and throw it at him. "Rude!"

He catches it and shrugs before placing it on my folded pile. "I don't do it all the time because you're right—it's very intrusive. But I couldn't figure out how to approach you after the meeting. You seemed upset, and I didn't want to make it worse."

I blink, licking my lips as I study the quiet gamer. "What kind of… thing… Are you mixed with that gives you that ability?"

His eyes widen, and he shakes his head. "Oh, Kit. Man, *don't* ask anyone that. It's considered extremely rude—more than my little faux pas—and some people will lash out without giving you a chance to apologize. I don't care, so I don't mind telling you. As for the other guys, you'll have to let them tell you in their own time."

Frowning, I pick up my tee shirt pile and take it over to the dresser to stack it neatly. "Good to know. I'm still waiting on that damn rulebook."

Zavida smiles shyly. "That's why I'm here, actually. I sent you a bunch of files, but then I realized I need to get your tech settled or you can't access them. Salem let me in and told me you were in here unpacking. I could do it while you're working, if you don't mind company."

Shit. He's awfully cute when he's being nice. I have to watch this one.

"Okay. Just make a little noise. I can be jumpy," I mutter. I know I should tell him the stuff I told Salem, but one person's pity is enough for today.

"Great. And I'm part empathic shifter, by the way. My other line is portal demons because of how we're tied to the gateway. The Kitsuné is my mom," he says as he heads to my desk and starts pulling stuff out of his messenger bag.

Turning back to my suitcase, I pick it up and put it on the bed next to Dottie. "You didn't have to tell me all of that."

"I don't mind. You seem like you need a friend. Most demons aren't trustworthy, so I'm showing my belly first."

Huh. I didn't expect this at all.

Once I get the joggers, shorts, and other sporty gear in the chest, I take a deep breath. "I was talking to myself. I do it a lot because I'm used to being on my own. Moving from home to home and school to school means you don't have time to know people well. The people in the homes resent another kid taking up resources and in school, there are typical hierarchies. So I got used to being solo."

His brows furrow, and he tilts his head. "You have a familiar, though."

"A what?" I frown.

"Your kinkajou? It's your familiar, right?" Zavida pushes his glasses up on his nose as he rises from plugging in his gear. "It probably helped a lot. Not everyone gets one so young, especially since you didn't even know about our world."

Dottie leaps off the bed, using box stacks to get over to the desk, and looks up at him indignantly. I smile a bit when she seems to bitch him out in animal chatter. I guess she wasn't ready for me to know that yet. "I didn't know that was her function. Dottie showed up in my house, trying to steal stuff from my foster parents, a couple of days after my invitation to Discordia."

"That's really… odd." The cute red-head scratches his chin. "I need to think about that before I comment. Do you have your computer and stuff? I'll work on it while I mull this over."

I hand him my phone first, shrugging. "It's all really basic. I don't know how well it will work with whatever is going on here."

"Uh, try not at all." Zavida puts my cell down and pulls his out, pushing a few buttons before he says, "We have a problem with Kit's tech. None of it will—yes. I understand. I can do it before tomorrow if you—Yes. Thanks, O."

I give him a suspicious look as I pull my older laptop out of my suitcase and he shudders visibly. "What's Oriel going to do?"

His smile is wicked. "What Oriel does best. Just wait and see."

That doesn't seem ominous at all.

Z av knows my nature makes it easy to slink around unnoticed and tuck away trinkets that strike my fancy as I please. Of course, every single one of us could send for what we need—we're from the reigning families. Money nor power is an issue, so replacing Kit's tech would be little more than a blip on our radar. However, he knows Jasper would want him to have me deal with this, so if we decide Kit is a problem, there's an easy way out. Normally, I don't give a shit about following Jas' wishes because we have to do these things to protect our caliphate from spies and toadies.

But this feels wrong, and that's an emotion I'm unused to.

Jasper Eversore is my prince, but he's not my keeper. His will isn't mine and though Zav never questions him, I'm confident enough in my power to make my own decisions. I pause before I enter the bookstore, mulling over my decision before I enter. *No, I won't set this kid up; he's obviously had nothing but a bad hand his whole life.* Nodding to myself, I walk into the shop, feeling better than I did the entire trip here.

Heading to the counter, I give them the order for what Kit needs—a laptop, a phone, a tablet, and a couple other accessories to make his life less annoying. It occurs to me he's living with Salem and I toss a pair of wireless headphones in as well. The dude is slow, but he'll talk your ears off when he gets going. When they bring the shopping bags to the counter, I slide my card to the work-study student without remark. Jasper can be pissed all he wants, but I can spend my shiny dollars how I please.

Something in the avian part of my brain says this is the right thing to do and I always listen to the crow.

I take the bag from the cheerful guy, realizing I haven't responded to a thing he said outside of the question about what I needed. It's too late now, so I walk out secure knowing that I lived up to my reputation for being a rude motherfucker who thinks he's better than everyone else. That's not true, of course. I get lost in thoughts and often miss what's going on around me unless it piques the interest of my bird. Slinking around in the shadows helps me stay off people's radar, so I don't try to be different.

But I've been assigned to take this shit to Zav, which means I'll have to deal with Salem *and* the new kid as well. Salem is used to me drifting off, and Zav has his own issues. I'm worried I'll space out and make Kit think I hate him, too. *Why do I care?* I don't have an answer to that question, but it's rolling around in my brain like a pinball. There's an unexplainable interest in the one person Jasper seems determined to annihilate for being unlucky enough to get placed in our lair, and I can't figure out what the hell is making my mind focus on him.

My phone rings and I roll my eyes. This is the nervous Kitsuné. He's so hyper when Jas gives him an assignment and I know it's because he craves praise like he does air. His family has never given him so much as a pat on the head since we were kids because they were encouraging him to embrace his family heritage. The envy courses through his veins like fire whenever anyone gets so much as a thumbs up, so I guess they did a good job.

"What?"

"Oriel, that is not how you should answer a phone call."

I snort, heaving a calming sigh. "Zav, it's not the 90s. There's a fucking cornucopia of options that didn't involve a phone call."

"Fine. Did you get the equipment? Are you on your way back, or did you get distracted?" His voice is full of anxiety and it takes everything in me not to get curt with him.

"Yes. I'm on my way." I swipe the screen to hang up before he can get out a litany of questions that will be answered the minute I step foot in Salem's room. I'm almost there, so it's completely unnecessary to talk my ear off.

But that's Zavida for you. I'm sure Kit has endured his constant blather the entire time.

Pausing at the door to our dorms, I fire a brief text to the Prince so he stays ensconced in his room with Slash rather than coming to investigate. The two of them do best when they can hole up and plan the takeover of Hell without dealing with the rest of the universe. It's the only thing they think about when we're not in school or working on new schemes—at least, since the prophecies came true a few years ago.

Unlike my brothers, I'm unconcerned by a few coincidental events. Chaos being what it is and magic having its own effect means the vague ramblings of a bunch of crones in a cave on the surface aren't as relevant as they believe. I don't think the current king is on borrowed time and I definitely don't believe there's some powerful force gathering. Keeping that shit secret in the tech age would be impossible, and they're all over-reacting.

I shake my head as I exit the elevator, realizing I've done it again. I was so lost in my derision that I went inside, got on the lift, and headed for my destination without consciously thinking about any of it. This shit is why I stay off on my own; I'm not made for large crowds. Perching on the edges is much better. Walking up to Salem's dorm, I knock on the wood quickly, hoping the sound doesn't pull any of my caliphate from their rooms. Jasper might not follow up on the little details of my assignment, but one of the others might.

"Come in!"

Salem's sleepy tone echoes through the door, and I sigh.

Time to see if I can maneuver around Zav's rigid allegiance to Jasper well enough to help Kit get a tiny edge.

"THIS IS PERFECT, ORIEL. KIT WILL TRANSFER ALL HIS STUFF TO THE NEW equipment once I finish the set up and I'll let Jasper know I have added him to our chat."

I shoot Kit a look that I hope he can read as caution. My instincts tell me there are things Zav is installing that will let our Prince monitor him and putting all his personal details on these devices isn't a good idea. Deep in my gut, my crow senses he's hiding shit and for the first time, I'm not sure I'm on board with sacrificing someone to the plans of our leadership.

He tilts his head, giving me a tiny nod that I only see because I'm looking for acknowledgement. "I'll load it all up once you're done. Thank you for your help, both of you."

What little I know of humans in his situation from their television didn't steer me wrong —Kit is much more observant because of his background.

"I can make more food if we need it," Salem yells from the kitchen.

Zavida laughs and shrugs. "He's either asleep or cooking, Kit. You'll have to get used to Salem trying to pad your energy stores through constant snacks."

"I'm not used to that, so you may be right."

Squinting, I take in his lithe form in the baggy emo clothes and decide he's telling the truth. I doubt he was *starving*, but it doesn't look like he's had someone watching his health as a human, much less the enormous amount of calories he'll need once his powers are free. It begs the question of what shifter side he'll have and how that will affect his stature. Hopefully, something larger than his current size or the bullies will make mincemeat of him in physical classes.

"I have a question," I say as I lean against the dresser. "Call it another 'get to know you' deal."

Zav arches a brow, surprised by my continued presence and my voluntary conversation. "Not your normal style, O, but it won't distract me. Go ahead."

"The question isn't for you, man," I chuckle and look over at Kit, who seems to shrink into the background. "It's for him."

"Um, okay."

"If you were an animal, what would you be?" I hear Zav sputter a little under his breath, but I ignore it. The curiosity is fucking killing me and since Kit doesn't have a clue about our world, he can't help me figure out what to expect when his latent traits manifest.

His brows furrow as he strokes his fingers over the small mammal on his shoulder. "I've never thought about it before. It probably seems weird, but the only thing I imagined was going to college and getting out of that stupid town."

Not surprising. Living in survival mode prevents you from focusing on frivolous shit like day dreaming.

"Think about it while Zavida is working on your laptop. I bet somewhere in your gut, you have a word rumbling around, but you're not sure if it's right." His expression tells me I'm right. I don't push, though, because I don't want to make him more uncomfortable. Everything he said in the meeting made me believe people haven't allowed Kit to have any boundaries and since Jasper is intent on being a dick, maybe I can be the person who gives him space.

"Maybe," he says with a small grin.

My stomach flips and I turn away, blinking in surprise. *Is my reluctance to actively campaign against him actually attraction?* I don't have a damn thing to judge it against to know for certain; relationships aren't really my vice. I collect things—avidly and ferociously—but never people. My brothers were always a foregone conclusion because of our families; I never had to put effort into belonging with my caliphate. Except for Zavida and Salem, the others have had more than their share of trysts and paramours.

I'm not sure how to process this and I have no idea who I can talk to without it getting back to the Prince.

"I think that's an interesting question and very on point," Zav mutters. "Of course, you'll have to answer it, too."

I narrow my eyes at him, knowing he's paying zero attention to us, so it's not shade. However, it puts me in a difficult position. I'll have to answer truthfully, and that might color his opinion of me. Not everyone is a fan of clever, devious corvids, I've found. "Fine. I feel a great deal of kinship to crows."

Kit studies me for a moment, then smiles. "I can see that. Not because of the whole 'emo, goth' look and the movie or anything. That'd be a lame answer. No, it's more because you have this… curious and intelligent vibe. You know, like you're watching for things most people don't see."

"Dude, that's spooky. You nailed it in one try." Zav turns back to us with a cunning smile, his eyes dancing. "Oriel is always watching and waiting."

"You're harder," Kit continues, reaching up to give her familiar a piece of granola. "But I get fox—crafty, introverted, and a predator hiding behind a cute exterior."

Satan in a sling. This guy is good.

"Does all that insight come from being in foster care? I mean, the media makes it seem…like you'd need to be very good at shit like reading people." I ruffle my hair, feeling like I was insulting by mistake and I'm not sure how to reword it.

He shrugs and moves to perch on the corner of the bed. "Basically. I've had a lot of families over the years and being able to clock the situation quickly would have saved me a lot of grief. I had to train myself to do better as I got older."

"Did you figure out your animal?" Zav asks as he hands him the new phone. "You'll want to go down to the shop and get a case that suits you, by the way."

Kit rolls his eyes, looking very human as he sighs. "Aw, I'm sad Oriel didn't pick for me. But to answer your question, I'm torn between two things and I can't seem to decide."

That's… odd. And now I have to go find a damn case because I feel bad.

"Which ones?" I ask as I cross my arms over my chest.

"This is going to sound weird, but I feel like part of me wants to say a unicorn and the other part wants to say a dragon." Kit frowns and shakes his head. "Those things don't match up at all. They're completely different ends of the spectrum."

My lips curve as I meet Zav's eyes. They may not match up in *his* head, but his presence makes so much sense to me now. I know he's remembering the story we were told as kids; none of us could forget the nightly fairy tale mothers of royal lines in Hell tell their children. "Actually, it makes more sense than you realize. People, even demons, contain multitudes."

"Not me."

Oh, I very much disagree, Kit Camponella.

The next morning, I'm awakened by a weird sound that makes my veins hum. Looking around, I see the tech Oriel brought me lit up on the charging station on my tiny desk. All three screens show a different picture of what I can only assume are different parts of Hell, plus a pop up in the middle that says '*Tempus fugit, students. Arise and join your fellow demons for breakfast in the Triclinium.*' Frowning, I climb out of bed and walk over to pick up the phone. If this is something these assholes do every day, I'm going to be really pissed. It's fucking five a.m. and my first class is at seven; why in the…*here*… would I need to be awake now?

"Boys don't primp, so what's the damn deal?" I mutter to myself as Dottie climbs out of the small nest I made her at the end of my bed. She scampers up my arm to sit on my shoulder as I rub my eyes and yawn. "Let's go see if we have food here. I don't think I'm ready to eat in an enormous hall yet. We can look at it, though."

Dottie makes a soft trilling sound as we head into the main area of our dorm. I need caffeine like I need oxygen, and my stomach growls when the scent coming from the kitchen hits my nostrils. I have to hide a smile as I watch Salem shaking his very cute butt to some music as he flips pancakes. He's only wearing sleep shorts and his skin is covered in fascinating whorls of black and white that look like iridescent tattoos.

Of course, he's also unfairly hot with tons of muscles that would make an action hero drool, but we're ignoring that.

"Mornin', sleepyhead!" Salem says as he pushes a plate towards me. "You'll get used to the sleep schedule in a week or two. Hell runs on super early morning to early evening like what humans call a 'morning shift'? At least that's what Zav said when I asked him how to explain because you weren't up yet."

My brain struggles to keep up with his animated chatter. It doesn't seem like the Salem from yesterday, but I arrived later in the day. *Perhaps he's so used to that schedule that he turns into a lazy sloth when it gets close to bedtime?* I climb onto the stool at the island, sniffing the plate despite its delicious smell. "Thank you. What, um, what *kind* of pancakes are they?"

His grin is full of sharp teeth and I see his eyes flash white, then go black again. "Best not to ask that question until you're more used to this place, Kit. The answers will sound disturbing, and they really aren't. Culture shock, you know?"

Sighing, I nod. "Right. Can Dottie eat them?"

Another plate slides across the marble countertop, this one smaller and decorated with greens as well. "Guaranteed. Now eat up and get dressed. Jasper will expect us in the elevator at six fifteen sharp. The caliphate has to appear in the *Triclinium* even if we won't eat that garbage."

An appearance? That sounds… precarious.

"Okay, Salem," I say before I shovel his breakfast in. It's amazing, like yesterday's snacks, and I wing a little 'thanks' to the universe for giving me a roommate who doesn't seem awful and cooks for us. I'm not sure that uses up all my goodwill for a bit, but it's damn amazing.

"I'm heading for the showers in ten."

My eyes widen, and I thump my head on the counter once he leaves. Of course, our floor *shares* a bathroom rather than these fancy ass rooms having their own. How I'm going to deal with this, I don't know, but it looks like I don't have a choice. I look at Dottie as she's shoving greens into her mouth and whisper, "This is going to suck."

ONCE I'M DONE EATING, I GATHER MY UNIFORM, A TOWEL, AND SOME toiletries. My stomach is a nervous mess and I have to grip my things tightly as I follow Salem down the hall to the big double doors. I wondered what they were when Jasper brought me up here, but didn't get the chance to ask during my interrogation. Now I know they lead to what is surely my doom —a room full of naked, grouchy, and inexplicably hot demon guys who think I'm the enemy.

I suck in a deep breath and let it out slowly as we enter a vast room. My brows furrow as I look at the couches and chairs in the plush area. To the left, there are stalls I assume are toilets and to the right, mirrors sparkle over a bank of five sinks with plenty of room to get ready.

What the hell is this place?

The sound of water gets my attention and I walk a little further in, following my roomie towards it. Everything inside of me tightens until I see eight separate stalls with doors that stretch from ankle height to well over my head. I'm not short, but the coverage those outer doors give makes my gut unclench. I *should* be able to shower and change in here with no one seeing shit I don't want them to. Licking my lips, I pad over to one of the open doors and scurry inside quickly.

"You can do this, Kit," I whisper to myself as I turn the shower on. Salem is definitely naked in the stall nearby, and I have no idea who the other five shower rooms hold. Knowing they're all here, inches from being able to expose me for the fraud I am, makes me shiver. I don't want these guys to catch me because I'm terrified of being unbound around them, so I may have to figure out my shower schedule.

That decided, I step into the spray and get clean as quickly as possible. My hair doesn't need much now, so I reach into my toiletry bin and use the towel to dry it before I get out. It only takes me a few minutes to rebind myself and pull on my baggy, oddly fitting uniform. Having it on helps me breathe more easily, so I pick up my stuff and head out into the main room. I almost trip over my own feet when I see Jasper, Salem, and Zavida standing in front of the sinks, brushing their teeth.

Not a single one of them is wearing more than a tight pair of boxers that hide nothing.

It takes everything in me not to slap my hand over my eyes as my heart rate speeds for a reason that isn't anxiety. They're all different, but they have beautiful bodies, tattoo-like markings that must be species based, and various steel. Swallowing hard, I lick my lips as I try to get myself under control enough to go brush my damn teeth. When I approach, Jasper arches a brow at me as I pull out my stuff with shaky hands.

"Something wrong, new guy?"

Salem throws a tissue at him when I flinch at his tone. He scowls, but I straighten up, giving the emo demon a cool look. "Nope. Just brushing my teeth. Got an issue with that?"

Jasper's eyes narrow and he whirls around, stalking close enough for me to feel his breath on my face. The heat coming from him is choking me as he glares down into my eyes. "That's 'got an issue with that, *sir*,' plebeian."

I snort, turning back to the mirror. "If you say so."

Zavida snickers, ducking his head when Jasper turns on him. "Looks like you have your work cut out for you, Jas."

"We'll see about that."

Still irritated by the scene in the bathroom, I mutter to myself as I gather my things. Dottie is ready to go, her bright eyes watching me while I shove all the shit Zav and Oriel swore I'd need yesterday into my bag. It's heavier than normal, but luckily they assured me she doesn't need to hide here. Familiars, as they called it, might be rare, but they aren't relegated to ducking into bookbags or being locked up in our room. That makes me feel a lot better, but I still swallow back my morning meds and tuck the emergency supplies in the side pocket.

Anxiety is like a stalker that follows you everywhere you go, just waiting for the perfect time to strike.

I look around the room one more time, checking to see if I have forgotten anything. Nothing comes to mind, so I walk into the main part of our room to meet Salem. His eyes light up when I come out and he holds up a small package wrapped in paper with a string holding it closed. I take it, looking at him in confusion as I turn the bundle over in my hands.

"Um, thanks? What is this for?"

Salem runs his hand through his snow white hair and sighs heavily. "Sustenance, little dude. No one ever gets this shit, and I was hoping you would. Like, even demons gotta keep their energy bar filled, right?"

My eyes widen and I look down again, a smile curving the edges of my lips. "So it's like a care package? For me?"

"Duh. I mean, I might have included some tidbits for the furry gal, too, but…"

Before I can stop myself, I walk over and throw my arms around him in a tight hug. No one's ever given shit if I was taking care of myself, whether it was eating, sleeping, or even taking my meds. I've always managed that on my own as best I could. The big guy puts his hands on my arms carefully and I suddenly realize what I just did. My face turns bright red and I pull away, clearing my throat in embarrassment. "Um, sorry. It was just… really cool of you. And um… I hope it doesn't get you in trouble."

My roommate tilts his head, looking at me oddly as he shrugs. "Fuck if I care what Jasper wants. Only Zav and Slash are that far up his ass, Kit. The rest of us are less uptight; you should remember that."

I nod, wishing I could believe him. Gangs of boys and girls at my former schools have taught me *not* to trust anyone who promises to break from the fold. It's never true and the hierarchy never changes, no matter how hard people fight against it. Demons aren't likely to be any different from humans in that regard, and I won't forget Jasper's words. He doesn't want me here, so nothing Salem or anyone else says will convince him otherwise.

"Cool," I say as I tuck the provisions in my bag. "Should we get moving? I don't want to make the Prince mad."

"Then disappear into the aether, little dude, because that's the only way *anyone* can avoid making Jas mad," Salem snorts. He sees me blinking hesitantly and gestures to the door. "The *Triclinium* awaits."

Dottie chitters as I pass him, and I can feel his stare as I head for the elevator at the opposite end of the hall. Salem might be lazy and entirely focused on food, but he's not stupid. I have to be careful around him. The hug was an instinct and it may have given me away. My boobs aren't that noticeable and the binding garment is doing its job according to the mirrors, but finding out my secret would give Jasper the ammunition he needs to have me tossed out.

No more making nice with the adorable roommate or his less ass kissing friends, Kit.

"Nice of you two to join us," Slash growls as he stabs the button with a thick finger. The Prince's sidekick looks just as intimidating in his uniform as he did in the meeting, but this time it's more like an icy version of the big FBI agent in the Disney cartoon with the blue alien. He's even got sunglasses over his gray eyes and his silver hair buzzed short. My eyes drift over the dorsal fin he wears despite his human form, and I shiver.

"Something wrong, Kit Kat?"

Anton's dulcet tones bring me out of my meandering thoughts. His rainbow hair and gorgeous face make me pause for a moment, too tongue-tied to speak. When I finally get control of myself, Xerxes has joined us and the group is complete. Their golden hair and eyes are fascinating, but I'm suddenly poked in the side like cattle and I have to move into the elevator. Oriel's eyes crinkle at the corners as I meet his gaze and I duck my head.

I am in the worst fucking trouble of my life.

The surrounding men are all Milan runaway level hot, and I'm pretending to be a fucking dude to stay on a scholarship here. I don't know how I'm going to balance school, avoiding Jasper's machinations and my over-wrought hormones at the same time. Finding guys attractive has never derailed me this much before and I don't understand why I seem unable to find my brain cells every time I look at one of them. It's infuriating and I'm about to wear sunglasses of my own.

"Listen up, freshman." Jasper's voice carries in the small box we're crammed into and I feel Dottie wrap her tail around my wrist. "The *Triclinium* is the first step in re-establishing the pecking order for the year. Our caliphate rules this place and has since it was formed. You will walk in with your head held high, your gaze aloft, and your attitude befitting the royals of the school. Do you understand?"

In theory, yes. In practice? Fuck no.

But I can't say that to asshole Jasper, so I clear my throat. "I'm not stupid. Those instructions weren't above my comprehension level, *Prince*."

The mouth that led to the incident has reared its head and despite my suppression of the sassier side of myself, this place and his behavior are bringing it out. I know I need to keep my head down and make people ignore me, but I can't seem to stop taking the bait with this fucker. He's ten times worse than Blake or Brett—and I controlled myself with them most of the time.

Slash snarls, but Jasper raises his hand, waving me off like a gnat. "Good. I have no idea what nonsense humans taught you, so for all I know, you can barely read."

All my instincts tell me to slap the shit out of him, but my gut says to wait. I give him a cool look when the bell dings and it's time to exit the carriage. "At least they taught me basic manners and decency. Your demon education seems to have omitted the section on not treating others like shit to make yourself feel better."

The fury in the air ratchets up, but we're facing lots of eyes as we walk out into the atrium of the dorm. Jasper glares at me, but he turns on his heel and curls his finger for the rest of us to follow.

We've been summoned.

Jasper

I *don't know who that little punk thinks he is, but speaking to me in that manner is going to be his fucking downfall.*

Slash is close to my side, as always, and I know he's just itching to teach the runt a lesson, but now isn't the time. We have to appear a close knit, highly functioning unit to keep this place under our thumbs. All our *disagreements* need to be meted out in private, so none of the sheeple can witness our new dysfunction. It would draw attention to a weakness and I won't allow other caliphates to declare open season on us.

"Head for the coffee bar. We'll select drinks, then claim our usual table on the stage," I mutter as my tail twitches in irritation.

I don't look back to ensure they're following me; I know they will be. Even Kit wouldn't be stupid enough to disobey my commands in a cafeteria full to the brim with various demon hybrids he can't even identify. His lack of knowledge about our world is the only convenient thing about his sudden appearance; he knows he'd be demon chow if we throw him to the wolves. It makes it *much* easier to control him despite his smart ass mouth.

Frowning, I stride toward the coffee bar without glancing at any of the plebs staring at us. They're of no consequence—only the highest tier caliphates near the front of the room are worth checking out. I won't have to do so because Slash will take care of it and send information to Zav for analysis. We have to know who is in competition, even though I don't believe they truly have the power to compete. Demons are sneaky, underhanded mother-fuckers and we need to know who and what we're dealing with. Underesti-mating your enemies is how many rulers of Hell have died in the past and I sure as fuck won't be one of them before I even ascend the throne.

When we reach our destination, my group fans out and I blink when I see Salem helping Kit prepare a fancy ass coffee. He clearly does not know how the equipment works and the lazy fool is showing the new guy the ropes with a fond smile. *What the ever loving fuck?* My eyes cut to Oriel, narrowing as I catch him watching the scene as well, while X and Anton are chattering at them. I turn my head to see Zav making coffees for himself, Slash, and I quietly. Slash growls next to me and I nod, agreeing with his assessment.

We have a division problem, and this runt is causing it. I won't stand for it.

"Hurry it up," Slash barks and the group of traitors looks at him in exasperation. He glares, taking the drinks for both of us and cocking his head to our table. I nod and we leave them, Zavida close on our heels.

No one has dared to attempt taking the head table this morning—that bodes well for keeping the status quo. I sit at the far end and Slash takes his usual right-hand seat. Zav flanks my other side and I sip my morning caffeine as I watch the rest of my group filter over. It's short one chair at the other end and I smirk as Kit looks around in annoyance. His familiar hops on the table at the opposite end, giving me what I'm surprised to identify as a pissy glare while the new guy walks down the steps and calmly swipes a chair from the closest table.

Kit sits down, settling his things before he glances up at me defiantly, then pulls out his phone. The others are chattering as we establish our dominance at the head table, but this shrimp is making his own statement without a word. He will not go down easily and doesn't give a single fuck who I am. I'm almost impressed, but I can't show it. It takes a lot of grit to give the Prince of Hell the bird without actually doing it, but our newest member looks completely unconcerned.

"Should I deal with this insolence, Your Highness?" Slash asks, cracking his knuckles. Zav looks at us nervously, then down the table to Kit.

My crafty Kitsuné is too loyal to say it, but I think he's not comfortable with my plan, either.

"Not here." I shake my head and lean back in my chair, pretending to look out into the crowd as we talk. "The masses cannot see any dissension or my father will hear of it. You know that."

"He's such a fucking douche," my closest friend grumbles. "My father acts like he started the fires in the pits, but we all know he's the reason Hell is a disorganized mess."

I shrug, eyeing a table of athletes who will fill the varsity line-up of the Fireball team. Lettermen are usually part of the higher tiers and juiced up enough to cause trouble. That's why Slash always plays for the team; he's huge, well-trained, and keeps them in line when he makes captain. "Those new demons look mighty uppity, considering tryouts haven't happened yet."

"You know how the children of royal outliers and court suck-ups are, Jas." Slash shrugs and gives me a toothy grin. "I'll have them under my thumb in no time."

Rolling my eyes, I look at Kit again, feeling fury boil in my veins as he continues to ignore me. "I expect no less as my second."

"Jasper?"

"What?!" I growl at Zav, who shrinks back a bit. Huffing, I push the fury back so I don't upset the hacker. "Sorry, Zav. I'm edgy this morning."

He nods and tilts his head at Kit. "I don't really think he's going to be a problem. Kit seems like he just wants to get an education here. Everything I saw on the spyware after his import was geared towards getting out of the cycle he was in on Earth. He's not a troublemaker."

My eyes flash and I glare at him angrily. "Are you questioning me?"

"No, no. I'm… *suggesting* we give him a little time to adjust. Maybe he'll be useful if we don't send him packing right away. It's always handy to have a scapegoat, right?"

The smaller demon looks at me through his glasses hopefully and I sigh. He's always worried about the little guy, likely because without us, Zav would be mincemeat in every school we've attended. "Fine. We'll start in two weeks. If he doesn't prove useful by then, I'll have no qualms about taking him out. Fair?"

"Fair," he agrees quietly.

Thank fuck. I can't have my favorite bedmate upset or I'll have nowhere to work off my energy.

ONCE WE'VE ESTABLISHED THE ORDER IN THE *TRICLINIUM*, MY CALIPHATE HAS to split up for classes. I have combat classes to attend to with the Arms Master until lunch time while Zav, Oriel, and X are headed for Curses and Hexes 101 in the Magic Enclave. Anton and Salem are headed for the Library of the Ancients for Demonic Lineage 101, which leaves Slash to escort Kit to whatever class he has. The thought amuses me, so I nod at the others, dismissing them before I set my gaze on the intruder.

"Slash has a free period before his Weapons & Tactics class, so he will walk with you, Kit." It's not a question because he doesn't have a choice and I make sure he's aware.

Yet, there he is, waving a map at me immediately. "I can find my way to Intro to Demons & Shifters on my own, Jasper. Thank you for thinking of me."

The words *sound* sincere, but his expression tells me he's being a contemptuous little shit. I rise, striding down to his seat, and put my hands on the arms of his chair as I lean in. "That was a command from the Prince and leader of your caliphate. You don't get to opt out."

"Want a mint?" Kit says, blinking at me innocently. "Coffee can be a killer, man. Wouldn't want you to have girls laughing in your face all day."

Is he out of his fucking mind? Slash has killed *people for a less insulting statement.*

I raise my hand as I sense my second approaching with anger radiating from his form. There are better ways to mess with our problem child that won't break my promise to Zav. "Did you try Salem's pancakes this morning? They're the best brimstone bat and chasm worm flapjacks in the realm."

Slash chuckles and I think I've got the brat for a moment, but he shrugs as he picks up his shit and stands. "I did, and they were delicious; you're right. He mentioned teaching me the recipe later and now I'm intrigued."

"No concerns about your delicate sensibilities, right?" I grin at him smugly, taking my things from Slash.

Kit snorts, looking me right in the eyes as his familiar crawls onto his shoulder. "Only a spoiled Prince with no real troubles would ask an abandoned foster kid if they'd turn down a meal, no matter what the fuck is in it. Pathetic."

Gaping at him as he heads down the stairs with his map in hand. I look at my shark shifter friend, growling low. "Follow him. Make sure he's not tardy and we don't take demerits. And keep his sheltered ass away from anyone who will try to use him to get to us."

"Yes, Your Highness," Slash says. He's obviously covering up a laugh, which is unlike him, but I can't deny the fucker put me in my place.

I need more information and if I have to send wraiths to Earth to find it, I fucking will.

The Arms master has been shouting at the new crop of students in every class this morning and though I enjoy watching the plebs suffer, I'm tiring of my ears ringing. I haven't heard a word from any of my caliphate in our group text and I know those assholes aren't stowing their phones during class. Every time Ammon sends the class back to the beginning of the obstacle course, I take the time to walk back slowly so I can check. But none of them, even Slash, have filled me in on what the hell that damn unemerged kid is doing.

"Fucking disgrace, that's what they are," I mutter as we reset the course *again* because Ammon feels they were too slow off the line. "Both these idiots *and* my supposed brethren."

Sighing, I stand at the starting line with my arms crossed, looking intimidating as they line up. The bell rings and I watch the freshman stumble through basic traps like flat footed boobies. I hate that I'm required to be a TA for lower-level classes; it's beneath me and my skill level, so it's a misuse of my time. I'd rather be figuring out what that asshole Lucian is up to and how it will affect my caliphate. Instead, I'm watching boys who should have come here with a basic standard of abilities but instead, purchased their passing grades in the various secondary schools across the realms.

I give in and open the group chat, unable to resist.

> Prince: Why am I waiting for an update?

> Chef: Because I haven't had a class with him, man.
> Lineage, then Culinary.

> Hacker: Same. Hexes then Complex Algorithms.

> Thief: I think it's stupid.

> Designer: Lineage then Design Concepts. Sorry, J.

> Spy: Hexes. Then I headed to the Annex where he had
> Demons, but I missed him. Fucker's quick.

> Enforcer: He was quiet on the way to Demons.
> Thanked me for walking with him. That's all I got. He
> talks to the familiar and I don't know if it understands
> or not.

Prince: Fuck. I'm going to contact the wraiths, Slash. We need more info and Zav hasn't been able to locate anything we can use. We need to possess someone in the human foster system to get access to their records. I'll set it up and you manage them.

Enforcer: As you wish, Prince.

Growling under my breath, I walk along the course, noting several guys who will need to be transferred to remedial training. I absolutely refuse to work with recruits this substandard and I don't give a fuck if pushing them into that class will fuck up their entire caliphates. My father would have sent my brothers packing if they hadn't learned to keep up with the royal standards and they should quarter the parents of some of these freshman for their lies. No one should be this bad when they get here; they'll never survive the year in the royal army after graduation.

Today is not the day to mess with the Prince of Hell; it won't end well.

kat/kit

I'm pretty certain that fucking control freak has his people watching me.

As I sat in my *Intro to Demons & Supernaturals*, I felt eyes on me from all angles. Some of it is about being the new kid sitting with the badasses at breakfast. But I'm also being *watched*—something you develop a sixth sense about when you live in random foster families with other broken kids. I don't intend to break any of the school rules I pored over last night, so I won't get them in trouble purposefully. Of course, who knows what kind of complex social constructs this place has? I won't be able to avoid those until I've already sunk knee-deep into problems.

Honestly, I don't give a rat's ass about the broad spectrum of social bullshit in this place. The only things I care about are getting an education and avoiding a giant blowup with my unwanted caliphate of dickholes. I know from reading that private schools like this, even universities, are rife with caste systems set up to help keep the students in line because they police each other. It makes life easier on the staff and helps shift blame if some hazing or mistreatment goes horribly wrong. The entire structure is as much a cop out as the foster system and I know how to navigate that like a pro. I can probably use that knowledge to move through Discordia with little trouble—but only if my fucking group lays off.

Constant judgment makes my anxiety spike like hell and that's when I'm most likely to fuck up.

People who don't have that kind of chemically imbalanced loss of control don't understand what happens. The world loves to overuse psychological terms like 'trigger' or 'PTSD' or 'OCD' or even panic attack, but they don't truly understand how infuriating it is to lose control of your body and mind because of things completely beyond your control.

I may know a few things that will lead to my anxiety taking the reins, but there's also an entire universe of shit that could kick start it that I won't know about until it happens. It's the same with any of the spectrum disorders like mine and when people talk about that shit callously, it makes my teeth grind. Jasper Eversore and his band of merry sycophants are a walk-ing, talking *promise* of future breakdowns; I can feel it in my bones.

The only thing I can do to prevent a nasty scene I end up getting punished for is to keep my head down and do everything I'm supposed to. Unfortu-nately, I'm only good at the second part. The first part seems to have fled the building when I got whisked away to this place. I've never felt more willing to stand up to people and tell them to get fucked than I do here. *Is that because we're in Hell? Does this place feed my resentment and anger?* Maybe I can ask Salem. He seems to—

"Mr. Camponella."

I blink, looking up at the professor with wide eyes. After *Intro to Demons & Supernaturals*, I scurried as fast as possible to my next class so I could avoid Jasper's pets. *Deconstruction of Human History* was another large lecture, so I thought I'd be able to hide amongst all the other doe-eyed freshmen. Appar-ently, I was wrong. "Um, what was the question, Professor Lillabet?" The impossibly young looking woman at the front glares at me. I feel she's mad that I'm not lusting after her like the rest of the boys in the room. She's dressed provocatively for a classroom and moves like someone poured sex into a bottle. Given what little I learned in my last class, I think she's from the Cubi family, which means she's pissed that I'm not feeding her lust energy while she struts across the front of the hall. *Not much I can do about that.* She's hot, and I can recognize how sensual everything she does is, but... Professor Lillabet isn't my type and I might be the only fucking person at Discordia who feels that way.

This will be a terrible semester if she gets insulted by my lack of lusty thoughts the whole time. I smile as she stares at me, hoping to placate her enough to repeat what I need to know.

"I asked what the humans believe was the origin of evil. You need to pay *much* closer attention to my lectures, Mr. Camponella."

Frowning, I consider that question. It's far too basic to answer succinctly; at least from my years in the human world. "Well, different religions believe different things. You'd have to deconstruct what evil is for every subsect of those systems. Some Christians would point to original sin... Eve and the apple. Other religions will have a similar, but also different, moment in which they say evil came into the world—like Pandora and her box for the Greeks."

The classroom is quiet and I swallow hard, hoping she won't dress me down for stupidity. We all wait for another moment, but finally, Lillabet nods.

"Excellent answer. We need to break down all the mythos where demons became the symbol of the ills of the world and then rebuild those tales with the truth humans are unaware of. That is part of what this class will entail—learning where the narrative diverges and why."

Son of a bitch, I did it.

Sinking down into my chair, I focus on the rest of what she's saying as I type notes on the laptop Oriel got for me. I know I can't keep anything truly important on the devices Jasper's pet hacker set up for me, but class notes and things that he can check up on should satisfy his need to act like I'm a goddamn sea monkey.

If I can keep his attention on my *behavior*, he won't look as closely at *me*, and I won't get outed in some tragically awful version of a 90s movie where they strip the girl and laugh.

As if that isn't sexual assault—what a bunch of horseshit.

I swallow hard when those words flitter through my brain and only the motion of the spinning ring on my thumb keeps me from sinking into the past.

"Damn it, Kit. Keep it together," I mutter to myself. It gets me a weird look from the dude sitting next to me, so I hunch down more and clack at the keyboard.

Pretending is going to be even harder than I thought.

After my history class, my schedule says I need to head to the library. I have a class called *Demonic Lineage 101*, and I'm sure that's going to be another fresh hell involving shit I've never heard of. The students here probably started studying this shit when they were toddlers. I'm not only behind simply in knowledge of their existence, but also in the massive amount of general knowledge they have from their earlier schooling. In order to keep my grades up and professors happy, I'll have to catch up on more than just the two weeks I missed by coming in late.

I'm never going to have time to take part in whatever stupid extracurricular Jasper demanded the other day.

Before I can plan my protest in my head, a figure pops up behind me and I almost scream. I take a minute to catch my breath, but when I do, I glare at Oriel in annoyance. "You should know better than to sneak up on people like that! It could get you stabbed."

His brow quirks and he tilts his head, much like the bird he's named after. "You carry a weapon?"

My gaze narrows as I consider my answer. Will he try to take it away from me? Maybe he'll tell Jasper and they'll demand I give it up, which will leave me defenseless in this place full of shit I don't understand yet. "What if I do?"

"Then you're smarter than we gave you credit for initially, dude." He shrugs and I roll my eyes as he stays in step with me. "Definitely smarter than Jas gives you credit for now."

Dottie pops her head out of my bag, scrambling up the strap onto my shoulder to peer at him. I look up at her, smiling as she nibbles on one of Salem's snacks held in her tiny hands. "I don't know why he's here, either, Dot. Probably stalking me because Prince Dickface thinks I'm going to embarrass him by breathing in the same plane as he does."

Oriel snorts, shaking his head. "He seems unreasonable because he is, but there are good reasons."

"It's almost like he thinks we're talking to him," I coo at my kinkajou as I continue to the building marked on my map. "Do you know why these fucking douche canoes are intent on ruining my day with their presence?"

Dottie chitters an animated response, and that gets a full-on laugh from my emo shadow. He doesn't look at me this time, just asks, "Are those treats made by Salem?"

I suck in a deep breath, irritated that I have no more choice in what I do here than I did at home. "*Yes*, they are. He made me Dottie and I snacks to keep our energy until lunch."

"Smart panda. The magic here will tire you out more quickly until your abilities unlock. It will be hard for you to endure the entire day without bursts of energy from somewhere."

What the fuck? Was no one going to mention that shit until I fucking collapsed?

My anger increases, making me stride faster towards the immense library as if putting distance between me and the rest of the caliphate will fix my problems. Of course, I don't even know where the hell they are, so that's wishful thinking. "Yeah, I suppose it's a good thing he slipped these to me without telling me why. That way, he could defy your lord and master, but not be nearly as big a jackass as the rest of you."

Oriel stops, grabbing my arm, and I jerk away with a snarl. He sighs, looking at me from under his shaggy hair in frustration. "I don't agree with everything Jas does or I wouldn't be here walking with you."

"Oh, sure. Like you're not tracking me for him like Slash did when he 'escorted me' to my first class."

His lips curve and I see the handsome devil behind his mask of indifference. "I told him I was nowhere near here. Which was true, but now it isn't. He thinks none of us have eyes on you until the last class."

Oh, great.. They know my schedule, but I have no idea where any of them will be.

We walk again, and I hold back the growl of annoyance. "That makes me feel *so* much better. What happens in my last class? Do I get one of your super secret rings if I behave all day?"

He frowns as we approach the sprawling steps of the library. "We don't have rings. Besides, I only meant that Zav, Salem, and I have *Literature of the Dark Ages* with you."

Inhaling slowly, I spin the ring on my thumb and try not to let Oriel see how irritated I am. Opening my bag, I nod at Dottie, hoping she understands I want her to hide in it until I figure out what the next class' professor is like. "Got it. You'll all be able to observe me and report back whether you think I'm going to fuck up the caliphate GPA or whatever."

"Uh, no. I mean, we'll be lucky if Salem doesn't do that in a Lit class. He's more of a hands-on demon, and he gets *really* snoozy as the end of the day nears. You'll have to help us keep him alert more than anything."

I blink, licking my lips as I watch him fidget. He seems sincere and Oriel has said more words at once to me now than I think he usually does around people. "Okay, I guess. I'll try."

"Thanks. Um, I have to go to *EsTech* now, so… just…. fly under the radar, okay? That's the best way to keep Jasper from losing his shit."

"I'll do what I can," I reply with a shrug.

That all depends on what I run into before he sees me again.

Jasper is such a fucking bore sometimes. His obsession with our makeshift family being *perfect* so we can execute some nebulous plan in a far off future is tiresome. I get it; our parents are mostly garbage. He wants to oust them and do better for everyone. It's noble, but we've been hearing about it since grade school. Kit showing up has put a major crimp in his scaly tail and he's doing the usual dragon shit, but it's so much worse because of the *plan*.

Honestly, I've never believed it would work, but humoring him keeps things much more chill.

"Mr. Stryker, do you need to refresh your blood sugar? It's awfully early for you to be drifting off."

Turning my head, I look at Professor Basquez, the literal old bat of the culinary program, with an innocent expression. Before we came to Discordia, I took summer classes in the program, so they know me very well. Probably too well since Basquez is glaring at me like I shit on her carpet. "No, Professor B. I'm good; I was thinking about the spawned lamb and spider egg couscous I want to make for dinner. That can go bad if you don't plan every step, you know."

She snorts, the action making her nose hairs quiver, and I have to fight off a shiver. "Keep your attention on the projects we're making in *this* kitchen while you are in my class, Stryker."

I would, but her shit lacks imagination and flair, so I hate having to go through the motions.

My phone buzzes and I pull it out, sitting it on my thigh as I watch the messages in our group chat pop up. Kit has a free period and then lunch after this section, so Jas is driving himself insane figuring out who's on 'new kid' duty.

He'll be able to join the lunch at one, but he has to be in his office doing TA work for the first hour. It has to be chafing his tight ass something crazy, which is why he looked to see who else was free the first hour. O is, so is Zav, but Slash, Anton, X and I are out.

He'll pick Zav—they're thick as thieves and fucking like bunnies. O is a wild card.

"Mr. Stryker, will you fetch the ingredients from the freezer?"

I look up at my cranky professor, nodding as I rise. She's all of five-foot nothing and squat like a toad, so she does zero physical labor. Students constantly complain about her needing to retire, but she must have something *good* on old Lucian. I'm not a fan of having to be a hand servant for the woman, but if she's got the headmaster wrapped, it's likely she has hooks in the seven families, too. Bitching to our parents about the affront wouldn't do any good. Not that I'm unwilling to help people—just look at all the little shit I'm sneaking to my new roomie—I just resent being forced to.

"What do we need, Professor?" I call over my shoulder as I open the large walk-in door. It's filled to the brim with various premium ingredients, and I shudder to think how much Discordia spends on the supplies for the culinary program. It's top-of-the-line because many of the students go on to work for elite families or royals; my attendance in it is a bigger controversy than anyone admits.

The court heirs do not take commoner jobs—I've been told a million times.

As if I'll truly be *working* anywhere after graduation. None of us except Jasper and Slash will have labor intensive positions and we know it. I wait for my instructions, peeking at my phone again while the ancient bat shifter gathers her notes. Jasper is freaking out more than normal about Kit, and I don't get it. Yeah, our parents watch every damn move we make, but having this kid in our group will not change who we are. He seems like a decent sort, honestly, and I like the little familiar running around with him. Plus, I feel sorry for him—thrust into a new world, no powers, stuck with the biggest assholes around, and expected to catch up to keep a scholarship.

"We need beast meat, bat wings, pomegranates, root vegetables, fear fish, and a selection of fruits," she says.

I roll my eyes at the lack of creativity in whatever we're doing today, but I'll dress my version up on my own. Being as tied to food as the beast half of my demon form is, I've been cooking since I was old enough to reach the burners. I don't *need* these classes, but it's better than being forced to go through all the ridiculously boring business and governing shit I could be taking. "On it."

Using the basket inside to shop my way around until I have what Basquez needs, I think about what I've seen of my new roomie so far. He's very reserved and displays most of the signs human fosters do after a lifetime of being shuffled and likely abused in some ways. I know because I looked it up when I noticed Kit flinches when people get too close. You'd think it wouldn't happen with other dudes, but I don't know if his problem is sexual, physical, or both. It's clear no one's ever given a shit what he does or if he's taken care of, though, because when I handed him the snacks, I swear I saw both suspicion and a tear in the corner of one eye.

Poor kid doesn't know if he's coming or going and now he has to deal with all of us.

I rarely take sides in disagreements in the caliphate—Slash and Zav are *always* behind Jasper. Everyone else lands on whichever option suits them and since there's seven of us, I'm often the tie-breaker vote. I fucking hate that and abstain every single time. Discord isn't my jam, and neither is being forced to decide things I don't care about. It pisses Jas off something fierce because then they have to argue until someone else switches sides.

But I see how Oriel is looking at Kit and I think he's going to adopt the kid as one of his shiny trophies—the crow in him adores that crap, though it's usually objects, not people. Fortunately for him, I'm actually on a side this time and it is his—sort of. I'm getting fond of the floppy-haired little shit, especially the way he doesn't let Jasper and Slash push him around. O will not get Kit to himself, which he'll be pissy about, but I don't care in the slightest. He's my roomie and I like his little bear thing and his stupid messy facade. It's different and interesting—so he's going to be my project, too.

"*Mr. Stryker,*" the voice cuts through my thoughts again, and it's all I can do *not* to snarl in response.

Walking out with the basket of ingredients, I shoot Basquez a dark look. I don't care what blackmail material she has, this shit cannot go on all year. She's barely even spoken to the others in this class, yet she's focused as fuck on berating me. I might need to get Zavida to do some digging on her. Maybe someone in my family shit in her Cheerios recently and she's taking it out on the most accessible target. I don't know what's up her ass, but I refuse to have her interrupt my prime brain hours with her venom.

The panda part of me functions best from the time I wake until about four in the afternoon, then I get sleepy as fuck.

I'm not about to let this witch distract me several times a week during my highest brain function hours. That's a damn waste, and it annoys me. If I have to, I'll get Jasper on it, but right now, that's like using a hatchet to cut a slice of bread. It's overkill and I'll keep it in my pocket for later.

Once I hand her the basket, I give her one last withering expression and head back to my prep table. It won't take a lot of effort to make whatever she's got on the docket with the stuff I brought out. I tune out her voice as she talks about the dishes for today, thankfully assigning someone else to distribute the ingredients. My phone buzzes again and I pull it out of my pocket to see what fresh hell is going on now.

Thief: Giving Kit the snacks was a good plan.

I'll be damned. That's not in the group chat; he's texting me solo. Oriel *never* does this shit. So I consider my words, not wanting to set him off. When I figure it out, I respond.

Chef: No one has given him any information on this place and everyone else here knows what they need to in order to survive. It feels unfair and I don't like it.

Thief: As his caliphate, we should do that, you know.

Chef: I do.

Thief: But we're not, which sucks.

Chef: Yes.

Thief: I don't like it.

Chef: Me, neither. But you know what happens when Jas goes off on tangents—especially paranoid ones.

Thief: Yeah.

Chef: What do you propose?

Thief: Secret squirrels.

Blinking, I chuckle as he brings up the term some of us used as kids when Jasper and Slash would get ridiculous vendettas against something or someone that dragged us all into the fray. A few of us would band together to fix whatever was pissing them off and save whichever servant or teacher or peer was being savaged for no reason. Sadly, Zav used to be part of it before he and Jas hooked up and he's decided he has no opinions that aren't approved by the Prince.

Point of fact, I give less than a shit about sexuality.

X and Anton have been openly together since middle school and I've dabbled anywhere I feel the itch. Hell, Slash is the only one who's straight as an arrow. I think that's more a product of his asshole father than true preference. I mean, we're demons, after all. Sex is about pleasure and release more than procreation for us, so gender's not an issue like it is for humans.

What I care about is that our friend refuses to be himself now because he's into Jas. I don't blame that on the Prince, either. He's just a powerful personality and Zav has shitty ass examples of relationships in his family. His mom will sleep with anyone she pleases as long as they aren't older than twenty-five. That shit killed his dad, so they separated and he lives apart from Zav and his mom with some bimbette. Like I said, bad fucking examples of attachment are to blame for his bullshit, not sleeping with Jasper.

A loud bang disturbs me, and I stop shredding the devil's lettuce in my hands to turn and look at the source. Basquez is standing there with red-hot coals for eyes as her nostrils flare. Since I was doing my own thing, I don't have a goddamn clue what she's so pissed about. I put my vegetable down, turning to give a dark look at the hand that slammed on my prep table.

"May I help you, Professor?"

"I do *not* allow phones in my classroom, Mr. Stryker!"

I give her a slow, snarky smile as I hold up the phone, shaking it a little. "Perhaps *you* would like to tell Prince Eversore I can't respond to his questions? I'm sure that wouldn't be a problem for him at all."

Her eyes narrow and I can tell the bat shifter is considering what she's going to do. Jasper is a TA and a grad student, so she outranks him, but he's also *the Prince of Hell.* Any outright disrespect might get her called in front of the royals or their arbitrators, which I doubt she's prepared for. Truthfully, no one is, and this seems an awfully stupid reason to risk it. "Fine. Tell the Prince you need to finish your recipe and will be unavailable for the rest of my class, then get to work."

I snort, shaking my head. "Not in a million years, Professor. If you want to tell Jasper Eversore to fuck off, you'll have to do it yourself."

That said, I go back to my prep, laughing to myself as she stomps away.

I mean, can you imagine? I sure as fuck can't.

kät/kit

I don't know if I've ever sat for two hours with my mouth hanging open before, but my *Deconstructing Human History* class had me looking like a wide mouthed bass. Students around me snickered constantly, and it made the hairs on the back of my neck stand up. Seriously, though, I *just* landed in the giant pile of dog shit; what did everyone expect?

Absolutely nothing *in history is what humans think it is.*

Most of the wars have to do with factions of supernaturals—especially rogue ones—and demons definitely influenced them to take up arms. Deities exist and they played their parts as well, which is another smack in the face. Both sides are neither good nor evil, only playing their parts in the wheel of Fate like they are intended. Images of three old crones who weave the threads in their various forms are also burned into my retinas, and let me tell you, I'm having a bit of shell shock.

If I thought my world was rocked when I arrived here or in the Intro class, this is so much worse.

Interestingly, demons play by a more distinct set of rules than the mainstream supernaturals. They have treaties with this mysterious Society group, as do the deities, mythicals, and the Fae. But they don't have to play by *all* of their rules. I don't have any powers which, according to Professor Alabaster, means I'm something the other groups called 'unemerged.' If I were anything but a demon, Fae, or deity, this world would get hidden from me until my gifts show up. Some of them *never* have gifts show up because they're mixed species, so they never know. That concept is utterly wild and the resources they exert to track those people are immense.

Luckily, even if I'm a 'hybrid' demon, the royals of Hell want their brethren trained and educated. Hybrid is the word supes prefer over mixed race and it makes me think of stupid boxy trucks made by megalomaniacs. But no one asked me and honestly, I don't have the spoons left to debate it. I'm two classes into my first day, and reality has tilted so far that I feel like I'm slipping off the edge of the planet.

"Do you think I'm a demon, Dottie? I have to be if that stupid letter system found me, right?" I whisper to my kinkajou as we walk towards the building where the cafeteria is located. She chitters, grabbing my thumb and hugging it as we walk. It makes me feel a little better, but that's only because I'm struggling to let go of the very human idea that demons equal bad guys.

Like I said, my head is jam-packed with things I have to re-frame and deal with—that's one.

Loosening my tie a bit more, I take a deep breath as the panic tries to take over. It's a lot harder to do with my binder on, but I'm training myself to breathe correctly. I read this article about actresses who have to train in corsets for movies and shows. They have to wear them as often as possible when they start because it restricts their breath in unnatural ways. Especially if they have to sing in a musical, the actress might wear one for months during rehearsals to get used to it. This is kind of like that, so I focus on calming my mounting anxiety while not hyperventilating.

"Headed to the cafe?"

I damn near scream when a voice behind me catches me off-guard. "Holy *shit*," I gasp, putting my hand on my chest as my heart hammers. Being scared out of my mind is *not* a good thing when I'm already fighting an attack and bound around my chest.

Oriel comes up next to me, his brow creased in what might be concern. It also might be confusion, though, because he's hard to read. "Settle down, Kit Kat. It's just me."

Using the name Kat makes the color drain from my face and the attack ramps up, making me white knuckle my messenger bag. *Shit, shit, shit… does he know?* I have to find out, but the words are sticking in my dry mouth. Finally, I force out a huff and squeak, "Kit Kat?"

Great. That was not a dude's way of answering. Way to go, Kat.

"It suits you, man. You seem soft on the outside, but you get crunchy when you break off a piece."

I blink, digesting that statement for a moment before I smile. It's actually kind of nice. "Oh. Well, yeah. I had to learn to stand up for myself in the system."

"Why?"

My head whips around and I see Zavida joining us, his eyes curious behind his glasses. "Because the human foster system is like *The Most Dangerous Game* for predators and abusers. Kids fall through the cracks and those people are good at catching them when no one is looking."

Oriel tilts his head in a bird-like fashion, studying me. "Did you fall through the cracks?"

"No," I say as Dottie scampers up to my shoulder. "But bad shit happens there even when you don't fall into the cracks. That's all you've earned of my story, by the way, so stow any more intrusive questions."

"See?" Oriel grins a bit, looking much different from his emo persona when his face lights up. "Crispy as hell. I like it."

I shrug and squint at the gigantic building ahead. It's swarming with students and that makes me want to crawl in a hole. "Speaking of questions, what the hell are you two doing? Is His Royal Dickface making you stalk me to lunch, too?"

Zavida tries to look chagrined, but Oriel shrugs. "Of course he is. But that's not entirely it—whenever we have overlapping lunch or dinner we eat as a caliphate. Dinner is in the dorm sometimes because Salem cooks, but sometimes it's in the hall. Lunch is almost always here, so people can see us."

"We have to make sure our table is always representing us," the smaller demon says as we approach the steps. "So make sure you behave so we don't have to calm the Prince down later."

"*We*," Oriel snorts as he shakes his head. "That's rich, Zav. Everyone knows *you're* the Jasper-whisperer."

Oh.. Oh…. Zavida and…

I swallow hard as that image fills my brain and I realize it's hot as fuck. Sucking in a slow breath, I work to calm the heat that travels over me as the little movie plays in my mind. This place is affecting me—I need to get some food in me. Maybe that protein bar wasn't enough? Oriel said something about energy.

"Hello? Hell to Kit? Hey, man," Zavida says as I come back to reality. He's waving his hand in front of me and I flush bright red. "Where'd you go?"

"Nowhere. Just lead the way inside. I think I'm hungry or something," I mutter as I look away. Dottie pulls a lock of my hair and I can tell she knows I'm struggling.

Who knew attractive, rich demons were my fucking Kryptonite?

"DO YOU EVEN KNOW WHAT YOU HAVE ON YOUR PLATE?" ZAVIDA SQUINTS AT me, his soft eyes watching me as I dig into the plateful of delicious smelling food I piled high.

"Nope," I say between bites. "Don't care, either. The little card things were in some fucking language I don't know, and I was too hungry to bother with seeing if this phone you gave me could translate it."

Oriel's laugh makes Dottie sit up and glare at him, looking like she wants to go over and shake her tiny fist in his face. "Don't worry, little furry. I'm not judging; I find it hysterical that someone else eats like Slash. He's a fucking trash compacter."

Ha. Shark, garbage compactor, Jaws…

Looking at the guys, I realize they have no idea why I almost snorted food into my sinuses. "Um, there's an old movie called *Jaws* about this killer shark. There's a couple of them, really, but they were made in the 70s and special effects were pretty basic. So, like the huge ass great white in the movie was made from a trash compactor and people didn't know."

Zav's eyes light up and he immediately whips out his phone. He's checking my facts, but it's true and it's funny. "I'll be damned. He's right. That *is* kind of funny, Kit."

I give him an eye roll as I wolf down some kind of sugary pastry thing, then wipe my mouth. "Of course I'm right. I'm not an idiot, despite what your asshat prince thinks. Just because I'm new to this world doesn't mean I wasn't smart enough to get a scholarship here, jackass."

The nerdy hacker has the grace to turn pink and Oriel laughs again. I enjoy seeing it because I feel like he doesn't do it much. Being the one who makes him crack a smile is satisfying. After fumbling a bit, Zavida finally clears his throat and looks at me again.

"Sorry. I didn't mean to imply that. Sometimes, I don't have a good filter."

Oriel huffs another laugh and nods. "He's telling the truth, Kit Kat. Zav doesn't have the best social graces when he's not focused on it."

"He doesn't need a good filter. He's fine exactly how he is," a deep, rumbling voice says as a tray slams down in the seat to my right.

My lips curve as I see Jasper seethe at my position at the head of the table. I sat here specifically hoping that fucker would show, and he did. "Something wrong, Your Highness?"

If he could shoot fire from his mouth indoors, I'd be burned toast right now. His eyes are dancing with flames as he glares. "You know what's wrong. And stop making Zav feel bad."

"Uh, reality check, Prince Chud. I didn't make Zav feel bad; he made *me* feel stupid. But he apologized, and I accepted—it's what non-shitheads do."

My answer doesn't help the rage building in him at my rebellion. I can tell because he's gripping his silverware like he's contemplating driving the fork into my eye socket. His teeth grind and he cracks his neck, looking frustrated as hell.

I have news for him—me, too, buddy.

"Fine. Everyone report, then."

Arching a brow, I go back to cleaning my plate. I don't work for this mother-fucker, and he is not my goddamn supervisor. This is my lunch and I've already been imposed upon enough to entertain Zavida and Oriel.

"*Curses* and *EsTech* were fine. Nothing I can't handle," the dark-haired boy says with a shrug. "I could probably teach *EsTech*. It'll be a GPA boost."

Jasper nods sharply, turning to the ginger across from him. "And you?"

Zavida grins, and I think I see a hint of what his animal might be. I've only figured out Slash and Jasper so far, but they gave me enough physical hints. Zav's animal is intelligent, small, and crafty. "*Curses* was fine. Not my forte, but O and X can help me. Complex Algo will be useful to us, and Turing will allow me to focus on my work because I'm so far ahead."

Dottie scampers up my arm, tugging on my hair, and I pick up a piece of fruit. My eyes dart to Oriel before I give it to her, and he shrugs.

Guess we'll find out; I just hope if she barfs, it's on Prince Ass-sore.

"What about you, Camponella? Report." Jasper digs into his food as he waits for me to answer. I would never have thought a dragon would cut every damn thing into perfect squares, but he's doing it before each bite.

When his glare doesn't let up, I sigh heavily. "Intro was like being put in a goddamn reality show where you're the only one who doesn't know it's not real. And History was even worse. People snickered at me the whole time, even when I answered questions well, despite having *no fucking clue about any of this before two days ago.*"

"We seem to have different definitions of 'don't make the caliphate look stupid,' Kit Camponella," he growls as he dabs a napkin on his lips. "You're going to embarrass the shit out of us by the end of the day."

"Look, asshole. It's not *my* fault I didn't grow up in Hell with rich parents and perfect lives. I'll catch up, so don't worry about your precious reputation." Crossing my arms over my chest, I push back in my chair, needing space from his judgment.

This shit sucks and I don't even get to make friends who aren't dicks because I'm stuck with all of them.

"You'd better or there will be consequences."

Dottie chitters again, bolting across the table before I can stop her. My eyes widen as she climbs right up the Prince's arm to get in his face and when he turns to brush her off, my kinkajou shocks the shit out of everyone at the table.

She promptly shoves the grape-like fruit I gave her right in his nostril, then prances away before he grabs her.

I guess that's one way to end a conversation with the Prince of Hell—I just don't know what it's going to cost us.

Jasper

As if it wasn't humiliating enough to have that smarmy little bastard defying me, now I have to deal with the *jokes* about his rodent jamming a grape in my nose. Removing it was utterly demeaning and Oriel damn near pissed his pants. Zav had the grace to pretend he wasn't laughing, though I suppose the thought of my blistering his ass was enough to keep him compliant.

Not in any permanent, non-consensual way, of course, but my temper can be an issue.

Kit sat there, cradling the damn thing and cooing at it happily as I gathered the tattered remains of my dignity. His eyes danced with merriment as he watched me clean my face, shoot to my feet, and stomp off to my office until my next class. Not once did it look like he was going to attempt an apology, which is why I left before I did something that would set the tongues wagging.

I am unused to people refusing to bend to my will, and it infuriates me.

What is this kid made of? He comes here, gets hit with our world and my caliphate, yet is still standing? I can't imagine what chaos he grew up in for none of this to even phase the little shit. Kit is small for our age and has emerged no powers. Regardless, he juts out his chin and practically dares me to come at him. It's baffling.

Zavida needs to get his tight ass on more research. I don't understand why he's running into so many blocks in the human world, nor why he's found dick amongst supernatural contacts. The Demon Registry doesn't have his file as a registered hybrid. Even more suspicious, Zav didn't find dick in the shared Society archives the royal family can access. So neither the demons nor the supe councils know about Kit— which is weird as fuck.

I suppose that's how he ended up in the human foster system rather than Hell or an enclave.

Unfortunately, that means there's a big, fat question mark where the names of his parents should be. Since he has zero physical traits to use as tells, it also means there's a blank space regarding his powers. Kit Camponella could be a hybrid of any demon and any damn supe on the planet, in Hell, or even in the Veil. We won't know until something fucking appears.

I don't like unknowns, and the balance in this realm is tricky enough as it is. The only beings who would so thoroughly bury a child *have* to be powerful and very forbidden. That's the *only* explanation I can come up with. Otherwise, why not drop the squirming bundle at one of the Society enclaves like tons of supes do? I assume it's because unlike the Demon Registry, the testing done at Society enclaves determines where and who the damn brats go to. We take DNA to classify and adopt out hybrids to families who can support them.

The Society uses their testing to decide who goes to what enclave or if they're ruled entirely human, they get sent to another version of Hell right there on their own terra firma.

"And they think *demons* are bad," I mutter to myself as I get to my office and unlock the door. "At least we don't send human descendants of supes and gods to some criminal factory on a tropical island in the name of keeping them 'safe.' My father isn't even that cruel, and he's fucking awful."

Raking my hand through my hair, I drop into my custom desk chair and lean back. I don't know why Kit has me so twisted. Normally, I find a target, destroy it, and move on. Something about the wimpy asshole makes me want to poke and prod just to see what he can take. It's not healthy, I know, but what demon can claim actual mental stability?

None I know.

I shake my head to clear it, then scoot forward to open my email. There's a damn deluge in the box—something I can't stop but rage over constantly. I've been gone for forty-five minutes and the build-up of nonsense is back to pre-lunch levels. Being a TA was never my dream, but I'm older than the rest of the guys by three years. Taking the stupid job gave me a way to stay here, take graduate classes, and be around them with no one whining.

The less attractive part is teaching a bunch of morons who didn't grow up with as stringent physical, mental, and academic standards as those of us from the court. Discordia might be the top tier university in the pit, but that doesn't mean tons of lazy, entitled fools don't get in. Anyone can bribe that sleazy asshole in the Dean's office; he's determined to elevate himself within the ranks so he can come to court.

It's boring as fuck, so I don't know why, except he has a hard-on for it.

My eyes narrow as I consider Lucian for a moment. He and Alecto are thick as thieves, but I don't think old Horatio is as corruptible. He swears they choose the scholarship students by stones and fire like they have been every year since fuck knows when. I'm inclined to believe him because the portly old seer hates controversy. I doubt Lucian could have convinced him to use his authority to bring in some rando just to fuck with me.

No, Lucian took advantage of the situation as it came up. He's crafty and willing to do anything to advance himself—especially if it fucks with me. When I started at Discordia, it disrupted his little fiefdom and he hates me for it. He even tried to block my position here, but my pull is far greater than his.

But placing this kid on our floor, in my sphere, is purposeful—I can feel it in my spines.

I delete most of the emails—I don't respond to bitching parents one day into the damn term. They can complain to whoever the fuck they want, but I'm not cutting their precious darlings any slack. If the former human can handle the pressure, these lifetime demon hybrids need to up their goddamn game. My father won't accept any of these weaker fuckers into the capital jobs if I tell him this shit. They'll get relegated to the outer provinces and shitty lives if they keep this up.

Sucking in a quick breath and blowing it out my nose, I close the email program and open up the VPN to the royal network.

If I'm going to compare people to this puny fucker, I need more information and it has to be buried in the system somewhere.

I PUSH AWAY FROM MY DESK AFTER AN HOUR'S WORTH OF DIGGING. MONDAYS and Wednesdays are my day with a lot of free periods between my duties and actual classes. I could sit here and sift through shit for at least another hour, but it feels like a waste. Zav could write programs to do this without batting a lash and they'd be faster and more accurate. I'm spinning my wheels, just trying to justify my suspicions, so I feel comfortable handling the situation in our usual fashion.

What if I'm wrong?

That's not likely, but I'm not so egotistical that I discount the possibility. I growl as I get up, walking to the couch in the corner and flinging myself onto it. The only members of my caliphate *not* in class right now are Salem and X—neither of whom will indulge my need to rage about the new guy. Xerxes and Anton prefer to be the middle balance in our group—tempering the hot natures of Slash and me while keeping Salem and O from being too emotional. Zav would side with the two softies if he wasn't my pet—which I mean in the best possible way. Having varied personalities helps us stay united, but until now, everyone eventually got behind my decisions in the end.

Kit Camponella is changing the vibe two days in and I don't like it one bit. I pull out my phone as I stretch out on the cushions, opening the caliphate chat. None of them are busy enough to ignore me, even if they are in class.

Prince: Updates.

Thief: We just saw you an hour ago, man.

Prince: Not you.

Enforcer: Gym. Warfare. Gap. Won't see him until dinner.

Designer: Same, Jas. Painting, then Studio. I'm booked solid.

Spy: Me three.

Chef: Dude, you're losing it. You know O and I will see him in Lit next. Then I've got him in Hospitality Club and we all meet for dinner.

Thief: I tried to tell him...

Prince: I can't operate like this. Zav, we should tag the little shit.

Hacker: I can see him in Demonic Lineage with the one on his phone, Jas. Kit isn't moving.

Thief: See? He's not doing bullshit to undermine us. The kid's just trying to survive his first day.

Prince: I want to know if he goes anywhere near Lucian's office. I don't like him being involved.

Enforcer: No one does, Prince. Salem, we need to know how he behaves in the extracurricular. It is more social than classrooms.

Prince: Thank fuck someone is thinking with their head on straight.

Chef: Fine. I'll take good mental notes and you can
quiz me after dinner—that is, as long as the scary kid
with an emotional support familiar doesn't take down
your empire while in Lit class.

Frowning at my phone, I close the chat. It's obvious he thinks I'm being ridiculous, and Oriel agrees. Dissension in our ranks will leave us open to attacks from the other assholes who attend this place. I need them all to get on board, and fast. This semester sets up the basis for my caliphate's ascension and I don't need this goddamn shit to fuck it up.

I'm still waffling over my course of action when my phone pings and a new chat window opens.

Thief: Kit Kat, this is the caliphate text chat. You can
use it to get info or ask questions.

Oh, that sneaky son of a bitch. And what's with the nickname—O doesn't like people this much.

KitKat: As if I need you nosy assholes more in my
face.

Prince: You'll have us wherever I see fit for as long as I
see fit, pleb.

KitKat: Please, please don't tell me Hell is literally
where they invented the whole 'academy caste
system' trope from books. Wait, that makes sense,
actually.

Prince: What?

KitKat: Nevermind. Obviously, you're not in the know
with human shit anymore than I am with demon shit.

Anton: I got the reference. It passes the vibe check.

KitKat: **smirk emoji**

Prince: What the hell are you two talking about?

Chef: He's gonna lose it if you don't get back on task
in three... two... one...

Enforcer: SHUT UP, SALEM.

KitKat: Yikes. Well, this has been appropriately
terrible, so I'm going back to class. Jasper, as always,
get fucked. Everyone else have a good day or
whatever.

The chat window blinks as Kit removes himself and I have to grit my jaw not to throw the phone against the wall. A glance at the screen shows the guys laughing their asses off, even Slash. He doesn't put up with much shit regarding me, but I think this punk's fire is amusing him.

That's why I have to get this shit under control before his antics encourage anyone else.

Rolling to my feet, I grab my messenger bag, shoving everything I need for my last class of the day into it. I can go to Royal Diplomacy, then head over to the kitchen area and spy on him and Salem during the Hospitality meeting. It might give me the insight I need without relying on the panda shifter to give me the full story.

I'll get what I need to know, even if it kills me.

kät/kit

By the time I get to Literature of the Dark Arts, I'm stewing in my irritation with the royal ass clown.

How dare he add me to some ridiculous group chat—without asking, mind—and then treat me like a fucking serf?

Blowing out a huff of annoyance, I stomp into the library lecture hall with Dottie chattering her agreement in my ear. I've been fuming since I exited the chat and despite having to take shit from every family I've lived with, Jasper's attitude rankles me more. I get how the power trip of bringing a 'meal ticket' kid into your house goes to your head—especially since most kids in the system are so damaged they don't fight back. But to be born with every fucking advantage and *choose* to act like that makes you better is foreign to me.

But for a random snip of the threads of Fate, Jasper Eversore could be me —anyone could. Nothing in life is forever and though I don't believe the universe gives a shit about balance, at least some asswads get their due. You can't predict if you'll be that person. It's stupid to build up shit on the bad side of your ledger.

Of course, I doubt anyone's ever told the Prince of Hell he's racking up karma demerits.

No one's here yet and I sigh in relief. I've arrived early to every class today, meaning I get to choose the seat that makes me feel safest. Licking my lips slowly, I take in the room, noting exits, aisles, views, and windows. Once I find the optimal place to sit in the upper right corner, I settle in to get comfortable. Dottie climbs up on my shoulder, her little paws brushing over my head as if she's comforting me.

"We've got a bunch of company in this class, girl. Hopefully, they won't make it impossible to concentrate, but I appreciate you trying to help." The kinkajou hugs the side of my head and her tail curls around my upper arm.

I could have been so much calmer a long time ago if anyone had let me have a damn animal for support.

My face scrunches into an even angrier expression as I open the laptop Oriel got for me. I've been taking notes in classes, organizing everything in folders so I have what I need to study. On my break, I downloaded a bunch of books to my reading app on my tablet after doing a deep dive into the demon layer of Google. It's fucking weird that all these creatures have their own sub-layers of the dark web, but I guess it makes sense. They can't have their shit getting out to humans or there'd be chaos.

If I'm going to catch up to my classmates, I need to read as much as possible—fast. I don't want Jasper to think he's responsible for my motivation; his ego is big enough as it is. But I'm not stupid; I have to catch up before I fall further behind. This scholarship is my chance to make a future for myself—even if it's in Hell—and fuck if I'm going to waste that opportunity.

"Well, hey there, Kit Kat."

Salem's voice brings me out of my hyper-focus moment and I blink as he drops into the seat to my left. He looks exhausted, so Oriel's comment about keeping him awake in this class checks out. "I didn't hear you come in."

He chuckles and shrugs. "I'm not a quiet dude. The guys say I sort of lumber… but not as much as Slash. I don't know how you missed me, except you looked like you were totally zoned."

"I might have been," I mumble as my face heats. "It happens sometimes when I'm anxious. Luckily, it wasn't a bad one or I wouldn't have noticed you sitting down."

His brows furrow, and he tilts his head. "That's some serious dissociation. I'll keep my eyes out for that look. Thanks for telling me."

Nodding, I stare down at my screen again, not feeling comfortable saying more. I don't share this shit with anyone; I've already told Salem more than I tell anyone outside of my therapist. It's weird, but my brain keeps saying if he has to live with me, he needs to know. Finally, I swallow hard and whisper, "You're welcome."

"Oh, good."

I jump, whirling my head around to see Oriel approaching from the right side of me. He frowns when he sees I'm sitting on the aisle and Salem has the seat next to me. My heart hammers for a moment and I press my hand to my chest. "Jesus, did you guys take a fucking class on creeping?"

Oriel tilts his head in a bird-like manner, his eyes glittering as he smirks. "Not that asshole, but me? Absolutely."

Well, I asked, didn't I?

"Scoot over, Kit Kat. I don't want to be stuck next to some rando and you're in charge of keeping the big guy awake." He sweeps his hair out of his eyes as he looks at me expectantly, and I swallow hard.

Like all my new floor mates, Oriel is gorgeous in his own way. I've never been so impressed by anyone's looks that I felt the need to obey mindlessly, but when his dark, liner rimmed eyes find mine, I want to comply. Wrinkling my nose, I give him a dirty look. "Don't make a pretty face at me; it doesn't work. I don't… enjoy being trapped."

Salem lays his hand on my arm and I almost jump again. "It's okay, little dude. O won't let anything happen—he's the most observant person I've ever met. It's in his blood."

I lick my lips, feeling my pulse kick up and clench my fists to fight off what has to be another anxiety wave. "I just met you guys and everyone is threatening me. What about that says I should trust you when Prince Cockwaffle says I can't trust anyone?"

A slow smile spreads over Oriel's face, and he claps softly. "Very good, Kit Kat. That suspicion will serve you well with the rest of the fuckers in this school. But Salem is correct, too. What can I do to prove it before a bunch of idiots flood this room?"

"Tell me something *real*," I counter as I look at one demon, then the other. "Something risky. I've shared far too much with strangers in the past two days and I shudder to think what the hell Jasper has Zavida doing to prove I'm some sort of spy."

He looks surprised, but he nods. "Fine. This stays between the three of us, yes?"

"Fuck yeah. Jasper is already annoying enough right now. His control freak shit is making my tail twitch," Salem says.

His what?

I shouldn't be surprised since he's a demon *and* a shifter, but when I look down, there's a long black and white tail curled around his leg. "But didn't you say… he's a panda? Pandas don't have tails like that. In fact, they eat bamboo and Salem eats—"

"Everything?" Oriel snorts. "He does. This is the demon form. You'll learn about that as you go through Intro to Supes, man. Demon hybrids are weird as fuck—you should see what happens when he multi-shifts because he's horny."

My eyes pop open and my face turns bright; I know it. "That… Too much information, Oriel!"

Salem chuckles and bumps my shoulder with his playfully. "It stays like this but gets furry and poofy like a fucking panda poodle. The guys give me hell over it, so now you have *my* something real."

I have no idea what to do with that, except now I have the strongest urge to look up panda… equipment.

Argh!

Oriel winks at me, and I swear to fuck he *knows* what's going through my mind. "Then my secret is I sort of lied to Jas and Zav about your computer shit. I know a little about tech, too, because of my skill set, so after he planted all his spyware, I turned a few levers off. Not enough to raise suspicion—he'd know if he couldn't track you, for instance. But you should be able to surf the supe web without worrying if they're laughing at you."

"You did? Won't His Royal Assface be furious if he finds out?" I pretend it's no big deal, but getting a modicum of my privacy back is *huge*. Oriel has no idea what that means to a kid who lived in homes that didn't belong to them under rules that kept them from having any secrets.

"He will if he finds out." The dark-haired boy shrugs, his lips curving a bit. "But Jasper Eversore isn't the king yet, and he needs to quit acting like he is. I'm no simpering courtier, and I never will be. I have my code."

Salem grins and holds his fist up for a bump. "Word, dude. Zav and Slash might be jammed up his ass, but the rest of us are mostly free agents. Although, I feel Zav is struggling with that with you, Kitten."

I bristle, glaring at him. "Kitten is *not* a nickname for a guy. Kit Kat is bad enough."

His eyes roll back and he rises, looking down at me with his hand held out. "I'll think of a better one then. Can't have the same one O's using, right? Now, will you let that bastard sit before this becomes a public scene, please?"

Pursing my lips, I war internally. Salem's adorable with his enormous frame, ruffled hair, and that interesting tail. Plus, they shared things with me as promised. So maybe… I huff, picking up my shit and let him tug me to the seat he was in. Once I sit, he plops into the open one on my left and Oriel does the same in my vacated chair.

"Much better. The caliphate always sits together in shared classes—or we did this summer at the orientation and Jasper says that's how it always is. You'll see other groups who are *always* together, by the way. Lesser caliphates and all. Watch them."

I frown for a second. "Aren't you guys sophomores? I thought by the way you talked…"

Salem shakes his head. "Jasper is three years older than us. He graduated last year and got this TA thing so he can be here while we go through school *and* take grad classes. It means he doesn't have to go home to the palace without his caliphate—a good thing, trust me—but also gives us time to cement that bond before we all have to get royal positions."

"While he was here, we were on campus a lot. But we also came here for summer classes so we could get settled into our dorms. That's why it seems like we know what we're doing more than other freshmen," Oriel explains as people file into the classroom in loud groups. "Anton, X, and Zav took the most classes, so they have higher level stuff this semester. Slash spent the summer taking a few intros and training for Fireball next semester, plus Magic Battles this one."

Shit. The extracurriculars Jasper mentioned.

"Um… Jasper said I have to do… all the activities this semester to see what I'm good at?" I bite my lip, knowing I have to give them another truth. "I don't exactly have any experience with those. My last foster brothers played football, but um… I worked and studied, that's all."

"Did you ever go to their games? Fireball is a bit like football on magical steroids," Salem replies as he digs for his book, then yawns. "I doubt they'd put you on the field 'cause you're scrawny. No offense."

I shake my head. "No, they didn't want me there. Trust me, that wasn't a bad thing, nor is hearing I'm too small to get fielded for a contact sport with magic. I don't have any and um…"

"You will, Kit Kat. But I'm sorry to say he's going to make you come to Magic Battles and that will get painful until yours emerges. You'll have to be tough or Slash will give you hell. No one can stop that fucker but Jas, and he won't lift a finger."

Drawing in a slow, steadying breath, I nod at Oriel. "Tough. Okay. That's not at all terrifying. Got it."

His hand covers mine and he squeezes. "You can do it. I have faith in you."

Thank fuck someone does.

The free period between Demonic Computer Languages and our first Quiz Team meeting is perfect for the project Jasper wants me to complete. I still feel like he's taking this Kit thing too seriously, but I don't want to push him. It took years for Jas to admit how he felt and even longer for him to be comfortable with everyone knowing.

It had nothing to do with my being male and everything to do with his fear that his father will target anyone he cares about.

He's still skittish about presenting a united front—especially with me. Slash has been his second since they were born, but I'm a recent addition to the closest confidants of the Prince. I hate being tested with this issue because I have such a strong feeling that Jasper is overreacting. Kit got put with the wrong people and now our leader is going to make him suffer for it.

Fucking Lucian. That asshole is up to something—*that* my prince is correct about. The headmaster has been trying to get in with the seven royal families for centuries, though I doubt it's for cache. He's far too cunning for that, so I know he's got plans for Kit. Untangling all those threads is what Jas wants me to focus on, and I'm perfectly happy to comply.

I just don't want to give him a bunch of ammunition to destroy Kit while I do it.

Scrubbing my hands over my face, I sigh and then look at the multiple screens running programs on my system.

I have a scraper harvesting information from the internet on the human level hoping to piece together more about Kit. In another window, code flashes across the black background as my sniffer searches for vulnerabilities in the royal archives' system. That one will be hard—my father and uncles set it up and we're the best. I've got another pen test running on the human foster care records from Kit's state. I need to see where he's been and where he came from. My final monitor shows Kit still sitting in class with Salem and Oriel via the HPS data I installed on his laptop. He's not using it at the moment, but the signal is still strong.

Being the tech guy can be exhausting, especially since most of my caliphate aren't hugely tech oriented. Anton, X, and Salem mostly use it for school and socials. Slash is practically allergic to his phone and the Prince mostly hands down edicts with his. Only Oriel is good with this shit and I'm not sure exactly *how* good because he's so tight-lipped about his skills.

Having a professionally trained thief in your family is a pain in the ass.

I don't envy Kit having to concentrate on class while trying to keep Salem awake. It's hard as fuck and he's stubbornly resistant to people's efforts. Not to mention, Oriel's silence is enough to drive you wild. The poor kid is trapped between them while hoping to learn things he's not remotely prepared for. Shaking my head, I whirl my chair around to scoot over to my gaming system. The programs are doing their things, so I can go back to my group and quest away.

No one will know…

"COVER THEIR RIGHT FLANK!" I GROWL INTO THE MIC, MANEUVERING INTO place for an AOE attack so our tanks can penetrate the horde. My usual companions aren't online, but I was jonesing for a little release after classes today. The Discord chatter in my headphones distracts me for a moment— I'm not sure why humans feel the need to fill our channel with irrelevant noise when we're in the middle of a raid.

A hand on my shoulder almost makes me scream in surprise and I whip my chair around to look at the intruder with wide eyes. Jasper looks down at me with an arched brow, his expression full of reproach. "Is this what you call 'on the case,' Red?"

Uh-oh. He only calls me that when we're alone.

"Yes?" I reply as I pull the headphones off and click the button to log myself out. I'll have to explain to the group later, but it's not the first time I've had to jet quickly. The humans think I'm a trauma doctor who's on call and now they don't question my disappearances. "I mean… the code is running for everything I promised, Jas."

"Mmm," he murmurs, his hand cupping my jaw as he bends towards me. "And you think that freed you up to play around instead of focusing on my tasks?"

I lick my lips, looking into his dark eyes that flicker with a hint of his dragon. Jasper is hot as fuck as a humanoid, hotter as a demon, and fucking nuclear when he's multi-shifted. The shit he can do with his tail is enough to convert a saint. "Well, I… I thought it was okay to take a break while it… ran…"

The Prince smirks as he brushes his lips over mine. "I doubt that's true. You know better."

All resistance in me melts at his touch, and I groan as my dick hardens. "You're right, my prince. I was bad. I should be punished."

That makes him grin wickedly. "Oh, you will be. But for now, I want you to give me a quick run down before you go to the Quiz Team. I told X to take our new member to the Drama Club with him, so I'll be able to go over what you found before dinner."

Swallowing hard, I nod. "Yes, Sir."

Jasper pulls back, giving me room to slide my chair over to the various codes I have running on my other system. My fingers fly over the keys as I attach files and paste links into the email I'm sending him. I'm not worried that I haven't gone through any of it yet; Jasper wants all the raw data so he can make his own conclusions. Then he'll speak to the caliphate and we'll either be in concert or there will be a huge fight until we can come to a compromise.

"Good job, Red. That's a lot of information. Doesn't get your ass out of the fire, but perhaps it will earn you a reward as well."

My body shudders as he wraps his hand around my neck from behind, his fingers dancing over my pulse lightly. His praise makes every cell in my body sing with happiness—I'm an absolute slut for it and he knows it. "Jas, I have to get to the practice in ten minutes. You don't want me… unpresentable, right?"

He chuckles darkly, scratching one extended claw over my pulse lightly. "True. I'm fine with sharing unless it's outside of our family. Oddly, no one takes me up on it. I wonder why…"

"Because you're a scary, possessive motherfucker that we don't trust?" Oriel scares both of us, making Jasper snarl at the doorway. "I mean, I'm just guessing."

"Oriel, you've been warned to stop using your skills to eavesdrop or frighten the rest of us." The Prince gives him a narrow-eyed glare, but doesn't stop stroking my neck.

The crow hybrid laughs, shrugging as he approaches. "And you know I don't always follow your high-handed edicts, Eversore. I won't have an option when you're king, but I do now, and I am exercising my right to free sneak."

I don't know why O always has to taunt Jas until he loses his shit, but it never fails.

"Guys, don't fight. At least keep the peace until dinner. I'm sure we'll have a grand argument when Kit gets grilled," I whisper. "Save the vitriol for then, please?"

"Oh, fine, Zav. I'll stop poking the bear for a bit." Oriel grins and jerks his head at the screens. "I want access to that, too. I'm going to read through it while I watch Kit and Xerxes flounder about on the stage."

Jasper lets go of me, turning to square off with him. "Why? What is *with* you and this kid, Oriel?"

"I don't like snap judgments, *Your Highness*. You know how people treat me and I refuse to be part of doing it to someone else. I'm fine with bullying a bunch of rich dickholes in our way, but I just don't have a good feeling about doing it to Kit." He steps closer, getting in Jas' face and tilting his head. "Are you scared I'll convince the others your vendetta is an overreaction to Lucian being involved?"

My eyes ping back and forth between them, watching our unusually aggressive friend stand up to the prince. Oriel has always rebelled, but this… this is *not* his M.O. He creeps around and pulls secret pranks when he's feeling ignored, but he doesn't go toe-to-toe with the big guys. If someone else told me they'd seen this, I wouldn't have believed them. But I'm here, witnessing it in real time, and it's fucking surreal.

"Don't say my name like that, asshole. None of us asked for our family lineage, and you know it." Jasper's body is taut as they stand inches apart, glaring angrily at one another.

The emo thief snorts and pushes his hair off of his face. "No, but you're the one who uses it to exert your influence over everyone else."

"Of course, I do. I'm the leader of this caliphate, you dipshit." Jasper huffs in irritation, giving me hope he will not lose his temper and set my room on fire. "I'm only trying to *protect* all of you."

Oriel's lip curl up a little and he scratches his chin. "Dude, you know you can do that *without* torturing the new kid until we know he deserves it, right? He doesn't even have his magic yet. Kit might not bow and scrape for you, but I've watched him trying to do what little he's been told without you realizing it."

Wait, what?

"Hold on," I cut in as I stand up. "What do you mean by that, O?"

He rolls his eyes and waves his hand. "Kit spent most of his first day doing the best he could in his classes, downloading an asston of shit to catch up, and despite giving you shit, doing exactly as told at every turn."

I blink, then my eyes light up. *Oh, this will be fun.* "He's a brat."

Both of them whip their heads towards me and I shrug. It doesn't matter whether they agree or that Kit hasn't said a fucking word about preferences. Once Oriel put this in the right frame for me, I know exactly what's happening.

Of course, no one *in this room but me is going to admit that I'm right, but at least I'll get them thinking.*

"Kit enjoys pissing you off, riling you up, and walking off with the upper hand. Maybe an alpha brat and granted, I have no idea which way he swings, but... I'm sure." Pushing my glasses up, I grin at them knowingly. "And both of you like it."

Jasper growls, his hand shooting out to grab my arm. "Watch it, Red."

"Oh, please," Oriel huffs.

Their crappy denial makes me laugh and I shake my head as the humor in this situation washes over me. I'm curious about the poor kid. Jasper and Oriel have some sort of attraction, and Salem probably does, too. If he can enchant Anton, X, and Slash, he'd have a full fucking set. I'd bet my last loot drop that Kit has absolutely no clue about any of this.

This is rich.

"Why the *hell* are you laughing?" Jasper grumbles as he lets go. "What's going on with everyone today?"

I shrug and give him a smug smile. "I'm enjoying the irony of the situation and being the first one to see shit for once. It's pretty satisfying, TBH. I know why O is always gloating about it."

"Fuck off, Zav," O says as he backs away from the Prince. "Just download that shit and send it to me. I want to be prepared for this stupid discussion."

My gaze flicks to Jasper, and he nods, so I go back to my computers, forwarding the same info I sent Jas to Oriel. "Done."

"Good," the crow shifter says when his phone pings. "Now you two can go back to whatever while I sift through this and monitor Kit and X."

"Why do you need to do that?" I ask curiously.

He snorts. "You've *met* X, right?"

Oh, that's *why.*

kat/kit

Keeping Salem awake was a challenge—Oriel was right. Professora Romero is lively and engaging, if not a little snooty, but the minute she turned on the screen and dimmed the lights, it was a battle. I wanted to focus on her lecture about the history of verbal storytelling at its earliest roots—especially since I didn't grow up attending schools that teach this material. I *needed* the review of the oral and pictorial origins of demon lore and the subsequent literature. However, the hulking, cuddly panda next to me kept laying his head on my shoulder. His face buried in the crook of my shoulder, a rumble of happiness setting in when he dozed.

My body couldn't decide if I should panic at the touch or warm from head to toe with fuzzy, sparkling sensations that made me squirm in place.

Every time I had to elbow him awake, my mind went cuckoo with relief and regret. My anxiety spiked and I could barely hear the lecture to take notes as I worked through my exercises mentally. Oriel seemed to notice, though he did nothing to stop it, but I saw him taking diligent notes. I highly doubted someone as smart and observant as he needed to, and when he handed them to me at the end of class, I gave him a relieved smile. He reminded me that the caliphate takes care of one another and sauntered off with my roommate, leaving me to head for the amphitheater to meet Xerxes.

I know little about them other than they focus on design and clearly have a *very* intimate relationship with Anton. The two of them are stunning separately, but together? I don't know how I'd handle seeing anything more than PG shit. It makes me feel weird because I've never been overtly sexual since the incident—in fact, the opposite. My new 'gang' is brimming with smug, entitled rich kids, but I can't deny how they affect me.

Even that fucking asswad Jasper's bullying control shit is hot and I hate feeling that way.

"Get your shit together, Kit," I mutter under my breath as I speed walk across campus. "You're not here to be a giggling twit fawning over hot dudes. This place is a means to an end. You have to survive it—that shit will only lead to trouble. Besides, you're a *boy*, and the few that seem interested in that menu are taken."

Dottie pops out of my bag, climbing onto my shoulder and chitters softly. I reach into my pocket to pull out one of the small snacks Salem sent for her, smiling to myself. Her tiny hands grab it quickly and I chuckle. The panda might not stay awake in class after three p.m., but he definitely got the reserve food idea right. I'll thank him when I get to dinner—if he's even awake and present.

The Discordia Arts & Creative Pursuits Amphitheater Complex comes into view, and my eyes widen. I know there are big cities at home with huge outdoor performance spaces like this, but I've never seen one. It's glorious and the building behind it is massive. I'm a little surprised a demon college has a serious presence in this area of study, but I suppose humans are always saying arts are the work of the devil.

Maybe they're more accurate than they know?

"This is going to make my ass clench for an entire hour," I tell my kinkajou. "I can barely do person-to-person interaction, much less be asked to pretend I'm a cow and moo on stage."

She makes a high-pitched sound that I take as a laugh. It makes me feel a little better—who cares if only my companion animal thinks I'm funny? That's good enough for me. She's a hell of a lot better than most of the people in my life up to arriving here. I'm reserving judgment on the stooges I'm tied to—except for fuck knuckle Jasper—until I've had time to figure them out. I'll be able to get a better read on them when I have one-on-one time with them over the next week.

Then I can plan for the rest of the year, be it acceptance or dismissal.

Letting out a slow breath, I get moving, descending the high stone stairs to join the group of people waiting on the sunken stage. I recognize a few in passing—I saw them throughout the day in the hallways. People didn't approach me when I had glaring escorts, which helped my anxiety at meeting unknown people a lot. Unfortunately, the other symptom of that comfort was that I've talked to *zero* people at this school who aren't employees or the caliphate. Every eye is on me when I approach, and that makes this whole thing worse.

A flash of gold catches my eyes just as I'm about to count backwards in my head to ease the pressure. Within seconds, Xerxes is smiling at me in all their glory. They prefer what I heard termed as a 'partial shift,' because a hint of their fangs show in the grin. X is wearing the uniform, like me, but you can tell someone with a flair for fashion added their spin. Sparkling golden piping is sewn along the lapels, sleeves, pockets, and hems of their jacket and skirt. The tie is shimmering with a glittery gold sheen that can't be anything but magical, and they tailored their Oxford to outline the impressive muscles underneath. I note the look is completed by black and gold thigh high fishnets and matching knee-high combat boots with a chunky heel.

"Damn," I say as I blink. X is fucking amazing, and they had to have changed after breakfast this morning because I'm slow in the a.m., but I would have noticed *this*. Who knew I could have had a skirt if I pretended to be gender fluid? I pause for a moment and chastise myself internally for that. I don't mind pretending to be a boy to attend—despite how annoying it is—but I would never fake a truth I don't own. That's shitty and I'm not that kind of girl.

X arches a brow when I don't follow my statement up with anything else. They look at me for a second, then roll their eyes. "Kit, you have to actually *speak* to people here. It's pretty obvious you've got trauma and baggage, but you don't have to take it with you everywhere. Put it down sometimes, man. That's why I take this EC, you know? Our life in Jasper's boy band is so serious; I enjoy being able to leave that at the steps a couple of times a week."

Holy shit. X isn't just gorgeous and talented; they're perceptive as hell. I need to watch myself.

"Sorry," I reply as my face flushes. "New things can be overwhelming, especially crowds of people. I'm better now than I was years ago, and once I get more comfortable, I'll be less awkward."

They tilt their head, frowning for a second, then realization lights in their eyes. "Oh, shit. You've had *severe* trauma. Humans are the fucking *worst*." I swallow hard as an arm twines through mine. "Don't fret, baby demon. I'll introduce you to people and make sure you know who to avoid and why. That will make Prince Pissypants' edict about this activity less terrible."

Dottie peeks around my face, looking at X curiously for a second, then lifts her tail towards them. I lick my lips, understanding that she's approving of the golden demon's offer. "Okay. That would be really helpful. I don't want to be a burden, though."

Snorting, X shakes their head. "I do *not* offer crash courses to anyone I don't want to. If it was a burden, I'd let you flail about on your own like the awkward trout you are."

Well, okay then.

As promised, the flirty demon helps me survive the first drama production meeting without having an attack. If I thought they were talented when I arrived, the ease X had with keeping me calm was almost god-level. I've never met anyone able to soothe my internal voices the way they did. It's a goddamn miracle.

"Now we'll head to the *Triclinium* to eat dinner today, but we'll only take the evening meal a couple of times a week at the beginning of the semester. Jasper says we establish a powerful presence to start, then we can taper off. On the nights we don't go there, everyone will meet in *your* room because Salem makes the meals."

My brows furrow as I look at X in confusion. "But he falls asleep at four?"

The laugh I get is rich in amusement. "Yes, he does. I forgot you had to deal with that before you showed up at the Circle. Our snoozy bear is awake instantly if food is involved, trust me. His passion in life is cooking, despite how parents like ours see it, and it's one of the few things that will keep him from being the lazy bastard he is."

I can see that. He's very intense in the kitchen and enjoys sharing it with others.

"I see. So… you guys always eat together? Like… all the time?" I wrinkle my nose. This group does a *lot* together, and I don't want to feel claustrophobic right off the bat. I'm used to keeping to myself unless I absolutely have no choice. Now I have a pet, a roommate, and seven other people breathing down my neck. It's going to make me paranoid and nervous to have so many eyes on me constantly.

They stop at the door of the *Triclinium*, grinning broadly. "Baby Demon, you're adorable. Yes, we stick together as much as possible because that is what caliphates do. It's a built in support system, a brotherhood, and a promise to band together as one against all enemies. You should… *oh, shit.*"

My eyes widen as X gives me a panicked expression. "What? What? What did I do?"

Xerxes' head shakes, and they squeeze my forearm. "Don't get all twisted. I just realized you don't get this stuff because we're mega assholes and didn't induct you or explain."

I do not know which of those terrifying words to address first.

"You *are* mega assholes," I mumble, going with snark first because it's my go-to. "But I'd be lying if I didn't admit that every word in that sentence scares the fuck out of me."

"They don't need to." X pauses, then reconsiders. "Okay, maybe a little because you're new to this world, but I promise no one will let Jasper do anything awful. This is important and even he won't fuck it up by being a dick—it would be like pissing on an altar."

"That serious, huh?" I squeak out, trying not to let the fear of weird closed door rituals make me fly off the deep end. "What does it entail?"

X tilts their head at the open door, and I sigh, walking inside of the elegant dining hall. They follow, taking my arm again to steer me towards the food service area. "Virgin sacrifice. Blood. Screaming goats. That sort of thing."

I blanch. "*What?* Humans were *right?*"

That earns me another rollicking laugh, and I have to force myself not to pout in irritation. When they stop snorting, X leads me through the line, suggesting various oddly named dishes. When we take our trays to the expansive table from this morning, they speak. "I was *joking*, Baby Demon. Yeah, there's some chanting and ritual shit. A little bloodletting because we're fucking half-demons. But no one is ever a virgin by the time they bond with their caliphate and farm animals would be smelly."

My face heats with my embarrassment at my naïveté. I don't want to tell Xerxes that in terms of consensual sex, I'm most definitely a virgin. That's a truth I'm not comfortable admitting to someone I barely know; hell, I can't even discuss it with my therapist without having a PTSD flare-up for weeks. So I nod, giving them a weak grin. "Ah, I see. And I need to do this?"

"Absolutely. It might even help us get your magic to come out." X pats my arm. "Just let me do the talking with the big guy, okay? I can usually make him see sense, and even if not, I can get Zavvie to do it for me."

Sucking in a deep breath, I nod again. "Okay. I'll try to trust you."

"Now we're off to the races." They wink and guide me to the table where Salem, Anton, Jasper, Zav, Oriel, *and* Slash are all waiting. "Evening, gentleman. I have a proposal for the table."

Why do I feel like this is a firing squad?

slash

When X struts up with their proposal, everything in my gut tightens. This new kid is a distraction we don't need, and it's eating at my Prince. His focus is shot because of a scrawny little shit who doesn't even have magic. If anyone thought that asshole Lucian was neutral in the silent battle for the future of Hell, they were wrong.

This just proves it.

Our parents have ruled for far too long; they've become corrupted by their own wealth and fame. Jasper's father has been in place for a millennium—a testament to how long our kind lives because our demon side doesn't hit school age until we're a century old. I bet telling this new kid that despite appearing to be what humans would gauge as nineteen, we're older than the country he came from. Time moves differently down here, of course, but this is part of why we stay separated from the supe community. Their petty squabbles are mere blips on our radar. We live long enough for them to consider us immortal, like the Fae or the deities.

But that doesn't matter when the ruling families have fallen so far. The longer it goes on, the worse shape Hell is in and it's ripe for some terra dwelling fuckheads to return to the fold specifically to take over. There are plenty of gangs, covenants, and criminal enterprises in Kit's homeland that would *love* to make a run for the crown down here. The only reason demons like that leave is so they can find a power vacuum where they can conquer. My caliphate has been biding our time as we finish schooling. Then we'll wrest control of our kingdom from the generation of leaders who are currently failing.

That's why I'm going to make certain this kid doesn't fuck up hundreds of years of hard work and sacrifice.

"...so we need to induct Kit formally or he'll never truly be part of the group. I think it might goose his magic, too. That'd be a good thing since he has to join Slash in Dueling later in the week. Magic battles will be a bitch with nothing in the tank, even if he can fight."

My eyes narrow as I watch the expressions of my caliphate. I need to judge their response to this carefully. As the second to the Prince, keeping my eye on the pulse of our group falls to me. If someone is faltering or struggling, it opens us up to danger. I don't want to believe any of them would betray us; however, it's not intelligent to assume any demon is swayable in the right circumstances.

"I agree," Oriel says as he holds up his hand. "It would help him learn about our ways, too. That will help with his catch-up."

Soft as an old shoe, the crow is. I need to watch him.

Salem plucks a fried thing off his plate with an irritated expression, then shrugs. "I think so as well."

"Me, too," Zavida adds as he pushes up his glasses. He looks at the Prince fearfully, but Jasper wouldn't deny him anything. He pretends otherwise to appear hard assed and big Dom vibes, but he's wrapped around the Kitsuné's finger.

Anton shrugs. "I trust you guys. No offense, Kit."

The kid in question is glaring at the entire table as if we've offended his ancestors. His arms are crossed over his chest as he seethes in place quietly. I have no fucking clue why *he's* mad, but it's amusing. He doesn't reply to Anton, only keeps his narrow-eyed gaze on Jasper. It's hard to take it seriously because of his size and the cute monkey on his shoulder, but he doesn't know that.

That means the decision is down to the Prince and me.

Jasper sighs, rolling his eyes to the ceiling as if he's exhausted by the entire conversation. When he finally looks at our caliphate again, I feel the tension radiating from the dragon inside of him. "I assume you're giving me a dirty look because you think I'm going to forbid it?"

Kit snorts. "Wrong again, Inspector Clouseau."

That gets a snicker from Anton. He loves mysteries, so even if he was on the fence about Kit before, he's probably in now. Satan help us, they're all so damn easy to convince of shit.

"Then *why* do you keep staring at me like I pissed on the carpet?" Jasper roars. I grunt, jerking my chin at the room and the Prince cools down a little. "I'm unaccustomed to being treated like a naughty puppy, Kit Camponella. You'd be wise to remember who is in charge here."

The kid waves his hand dismissively, which almost makes me laugh. He seriously has *no* instinct for self-preservation. "I'd get right with Jesus, then, Prince. I will not follow *anyone* blindly and you deserve my disdain. Not one of you fuckers has asked if I *want* or *am willing* to be inducted, much less explained the process of significance. My body, my choice, assholes."

I'd intercede, but I honestly want to see where this goes.

X blinks. "We discussed it in class, Baby Demon. I thought we were a go."

"I said I'd trust you with it. I didn't give explicit consent to do it. You just assumed," he says with a shrug. "I also didn't think you'd be advocating for some mysterious magic bullshit that you're going to do before Thursday."

The cobra demon hybrid looks aghast, grabbing Kit's arm. "I am *so sorry*. You're right. I did *not* mean to cross your boundaries."

"It's okay." The new kid looks a little green and I'm not sure why, but he doesn't elaborate on what's causing it. "I know *you* didn't mean to. Everyone else here is guilty AF, though."

They all look at one another for a second, then a flurry of apologies starts. Jasper pinches the bridge of his nose, looking like he wants to teleport to the furthest region in Hell to let his dragon rage out. That's not a bad idea, actually, and I'll suggest we go after dinner. The rest of them have homework and the thorn in our side will accompany O to his Thieves Guild meeting. No one will question our absence, so he won't look affected by the human.

Note to self: Insist the Prince find an outlet that is private and not Zav's ass for this irritation.

"Enough!" I say in a commanding tone. My fist hits the table as I issue the order, and every head swivels to face me. "Your Prince has not yet weighed in, so any personal slights should be tabled until he extends his decision."

"Excuse me?" Kit says as he stands and puts his palms on the table to lean forward. "No one died and made you General of my emotions. You can fuck right off if you think *his* decision means anything to me if *I* say 'no.' We already had the consent discussion and I'm not in the habit of doing emotional labor for free multiple times."

I hate *when people go to fucking shrinks.*

"You will respect the edict of your Prince or—"

"Slash."

I turn to Jasper, giving him a quizzical look. He never stops me when I'm disciplining the troops. "Yes, Your Highness?"

"Knock off the formal, man." He sighs and leans back in his chair as he watches our problem child. "It's hard to decide whether I'm more furious at you for the disrespect or glad to see you have a backbone. Slash intimidates damn near everyone and his input usually makes lesser demons crumble. He isn't called the Annihilator on the field for nothing."

The harsh snort from Kit makes my gut clench again. "So? I've dealt with bullies and abusers before; I'll do it again if you force me to. Maybe you win, maybe I survive… either way, it fucks up your little boy band image, right?"

Shit, fuck, damn… he's figured it out.

"I mean, you could have done what human jerks in your position would have done. Rejected me, beat me up, spread rumors, sent other students after me… all of that would be par for the course in this kind of situation at home. But you didn't, and there *has* to be a reason. Whatever it is, it's more important than your stupid royalty flex."

Oriel's eyes widen as he turns to look at Jasper and when I survey the table, the others are failing miserably at hiding their own shock. "Well, fuck, Jas. Now the shit has hit, eh?"

"Shut up, Oriel," I growl as I send a targeted stream of water magic to hit the bird in the face. "You don't have permission to chitter chatter."

Kit looks even more irritated now. "You can torture the others if you want, but they didn't tell me, nor are they disobeying you when they speak up. Stop being a dictator, Jasper Eversore. It's tired."

"You think so, hmm?" The Prince grabs his glass, sipping at the batberry wine I brought him calmly. What Kit doesn't know is that calm Jasper is much more frightening than raging Jas. His dragon is hot-headed and passionate—that can be handled. His detached sociopath demon protected him from his father's behavior his entire life. And that is the scary mother-fucker—even to me.

"Everyone does, man. Rich royal bullies being dicks to the new poor kid? I mean, it's like some dumb movie from the 90s. Be more original than that."

Zavida chuckles and I sigh internally. Now this little shit has him on board —at least for this conversation. He loves human movies and is likely planning an entire marathon in his head.

Fuck.

"For the love of crunchy crab puffs, J, just ask him if he wants to do this!" Salem stands, looking more awake than he has the entire meal. "If your plan was to approve this, then you're being a stubborn shithead for no reason. I'm going for dessert, but this better be done when I get back. Ire fucks with my digestion, and I'll make you all suffer with me if you don't calm down."

"His digestion?" Kit whispers to X.

They grin and whisper back, "The panda side. He'll nuclear fart us out of the entire floor if he doesn't digest correctly. Honestly, speaking from a solely evolutionary standpoint, it's amazing that pandas and their shifter counterparts haven't gone extinct. Everything about them is delicate, with no care for preservation on their own."

A soft chittering sound distracts us and I'm surprised to see the rodent familiar jump from Kit's shoulder, skitter across the table, and sit at Salem's spot as if waiting. Kit tilts his head, a small smile playing about his lips as he takes note. I'm not sure what that means, but I doubt it's good.

This fighting is a threat to good order, and our recent addition is the cause. Jasper and I have to get it under control. If fear and our normal tactics won't make him fall in line, maybe X is right about the induction. Magic has a way of corralling us to its will, and the ceremony certainly focuses on group cohesion.

No one speaks until Salem ambles over with three plates full of sweets balanced on his arm. He puts them down, then smiles in his sleepy way at the animal waiting for him. "Hey, girl. I didn't forget about you."

When he pulls the baggie of fruit out, Jasper growls. "Don't feed that rodent at the table."

Oriel glares at him. "Her name is Dottie, and she's Kit's familiar, Jasper. You know how that works; don't pretend to be dense."

"I don't care what its name is," the Prince says, waving his hand. "But I suppose Xerxes has a point. If Kit is this perceptive, it makes him even more dangerous to us. We should induct him as soon as possible. Since you're so keen, O, you can explain to Kit what it entails while you're at the Guild tonight and get his *consent.*"

I don't think that word has ever sounded so disdainful as it does coming from my angry Prince.

I don't think that word has ever sounded so disdainful as it does coming from my angry Prince.

My dinner isn't sitting well and I'm having trouble following the shit going on at Oriel's meeting. This is the longest fucking school day I've ever experienced, and that paired with the constant acrimony with my new 'friends' is making my entire body lock up. Dottie is pressed close to my neck, which helps slow down my pulse, but it doesn't prevent me from feeling trapped. I'm not claustrophobic, but the walls are closing in on me. It's so much to handle all at once; I don't know how to keep it together.

"Kit, you're wound so tightly you feel as if you're going to explode," Oriel murmurs in a very low tone. "Does the purpose of my activity upset you?"

I shake my head, giving him a small smile. "Hell no. I couldn't care less about stealing; it's hard to have black and white morals like that in the system. Sometimes, you have to do things others would judge for you to survive. How often that happens depends on the time you spend in group homes or with bad fosters. I've never given a shit about conventional ideas of right and wrong."

"Interesting," he murmurs. "Your flexibility is very appealing, Kit Kat. Morally and mentally, I mean."

My brows fly up when he hurriedly adds that qualifier. *What the hell does that mean?* Licking my lips, I try to figure out what I'm going to say in response. I find my tongue, keeping my voice soft as the people in the guild continue their speeches. "Thanks, I guess. I'm an odd duck, I know. Most people avoided me at home, and it's because I purposely kept them at arm's length. How is this thing X and Jasper agreed to going to change that?"

"I can't tell you much beforehand; it's a… rule. But it *will* help you fit in and it *will* protect you in a lot of ways. Plus, if you've never had a family who'd jump in front of a rabid were before, you will now. Does that help?"

I wrinkle my nose as I stroke my finger over Dottie's tail. No fucking way am I jumping in front of *anything* for Jasper Eversore. He can choke on a werewolf *dick* before I do that. "I don't know if I believe that part. Jasper and

Slash obviously hate me. I don't know about Anton and Zav. But you, Salem, and X seem to be pretty cool."

"Something to add, Mister Camponella? It's unheard of for an unemerged hybrid to attend a Thieves' Guild event." The pointed question from the huge ass red-skinned demon at the lectern makes me wince. His smile is mocking and his mouth is full of sharp fangs—I don't think he's a hybrid like my guys based on the way he said the word.

Awesome, I've found the demon racists.

"Uh, nothing to add. Thanks for checking, though." I paste on a friendly expression, hoping the vengeful bitchiness I feel about being publicly called out isn't showing. Oriel snorts, covering his mouth as he looks away.

Guess I was wrong.

"Perhaps if you have nothing to add—and your uselessness in every aspect makes that a foregone conclusion—you might keep your fucking mouth closed, then? The adults are speaking and you shouldn't even be at the table, human."

Before O can stop me, I shoot to my feet, glaring at the ugly, horned motherfucker. I don't know what's gotten into me since I arrived at Discordia, but I'm not willing to let people trample on me in public like I was at home. This jackass is spoiling for a fight and he's going to get one, even if it kills me. "Last I checked, every person at this school has a seat at some table, asshole. Given you sit with the knuckle-dragging morons, I'm okay with not being invited to yours. But this group isn't *your* table until you win this vote—which you'd all be fucking tools not to elect Oriel. He's a million times more skilled than you."

I don't know that, but it sounds good and by the surprised noise next to me, I think I'm right.

"Oriel hates people. He's not even running, scum." The demon stands tall, assessing me as our gazes lock in stubborn confrontation. "The crow half-breed has no interest in being a leader."

My lip curls up at his nasty words and I feel my hands shake in the fists by my waist. "Even unwilling, he'd be a better leader than you. I doubt you could steal an apple from a tree. You're a loud, pompous dick who overcompensates for his... shortcomings... by being a bully."

"Kit..." Oriel says, his hand touching mine. I jump a little and he frowns. Within seconds, he's on his feet, smirking at the guy I'm berating. "What do you know, Bastion? All it took was a new guy to remind me how woefully shitty this guild is because it lets fools like you take charge. I guess I have no choice but to toss my wings in the ring."

Whispers break out in the crowd as the demons and hybrids react to his declaration. I've likely fucked up this entire meeting because I refused to let one dipshit be nasty to me. Kat Camponella is not a troublemaker, but I can't say the same for Kit. My dude persona is out of control. I lean closer to O, muttering under my breath. "Sorry about that. I didn't mean to corner you."

His grin is *gorgeous* and lights up his darkness. "Don't be. I enjoyed the fuck out of you going at it with that shitty example of an *avaritia daemonium*. He doesn't deserve the title or the attention it would bring him."

"Jasper would be stoked if you win, too," I mumble, hoping to make myself feel better for forcing a less extroverted person to take the spotlight. "You can leave out my part in it."

"Why would I do something stupid like that?" Oriel winks at me. "I can't *wait* to report this shit."

Me and my fat mouth really appreciate that, dude.

To no one's shock, Oriel wins the damn vote and now I'm stuck following him to what he calls 'the workspace' in Jasper's room. I have no desire to go into the Prince's room, much less be trapped there with the rest of them, but I did this to myself. My thieving escort is more excited than I've seen him so far, almost having a pep in his step as we exit the elevator and head down our hallway. He winks at me as he raps on the heavy mahogany door in a weird pattern.

"You have a secret knock? Demons are way lamer than humans realize," I grumble. "All my reading didn't prepare me for you guys to be just as sucky as us, but with magic."

"Don't be a hater, Kit Kat. The knock was my idea."

I snort. "That doesn't make it any less lame. I don't like you *that* much, Oriel."

His eyes dance as he leans in closer than I'm comfortable with, his expression unreadable. "Maybe I don't believe you about that. What would you say then?"

The oxygen is sucked out of the hallway as I look at him inches from my face in panic. I'm not afraid of him like I am most males who get close; no, my PTSD doesn't even raise its head. However, I *am* feeling itchy and hot with his lips near mine in the dim light of the dorm hall at night. Swallowing hard, I try to figure out what to do.

He knows I'm a boy. I mean, I haven't fucked it up already, right?

Oriel tilts his head as he watches me struggle, studying my face as if he's memorizing it. "You don't believe it, either. Good to know."

"I… Who said that?" I blurt defensively.

"Your face did. I don't need the words when I can see it in your eyes, man." The door opens, and he pulls back, giving the grumpy-looking shark shifter standing there a cheerful smile. "Wait 'till Jas hears what happened!"

Slash glares at me, his gigantic frame blocking the view of the room. "No one said to bring him here."

For fuck's sake…

"I'll go. I don't care about the victory lap, O. I have studying to do anyway," I say as I back away slowly.

"But Kit Kat…"

Shaking my head as I ignore the satisfied smirk of the big demon in the doorway, I turn on my heel and walk towards my dorm. I keep my head held high and my spine straight as Dottie and I disappear into the room. Once I'm inside, I lean against the wood, closing my eyes as my heart races in my chest. The rejection paired with the weirdly intimate moment with Oriel beforehand has me barreling towards an awful night.

I don't care if they won't let me into their stupid royal club house.

But I know that's not true because they want me to do some demon binding bullshit. *How can I be tied to them if they're going to exclude me?* I stomp over to the fridge, pulling out a container of what Salem told me was fruit earlier in the day. Sitting at the counter, I watch as Dottie nibbles on it, smiling softly. At least I have her with me—that's more than I've ever had before.

The kinkajou offers something that looks like a fucked up version of a raspberry, and I take it. Popping it in my mouth, I'm surprised to find it's delicious, but I can't identify exactly what fruit it's like. I grin at Dottie, leaning down to take another. "It's like a party in my mouth. Good choice, girl."

"Well, that's the first time I've heard anyone describe crunkleberries that way, and I don't know if I'll survive it."

Whipping around, I hold my fists up at the intruder. It might not help, but if someone's come to take me out, I won't go down easy. "Show yourself!"

An exasperated sigh echoes through the room and I'm shocked to see Zavida appear out of thin air. "You're no fun, Kit. I wanted to pretend to be some all knowing deity voice like in a game. Now I'm just me and it's far less impressive."

I put my hand on my chest, letting my pulse slow as I stare at the nerdy Kitsuné. Perhaps the others know he can be invisible and appear without a damn portal, but I didn't. That scares the *hell* out of me. Luckily for me, I hadn't started getting undressed or said anything that would reveal my secret status. "Zav, you can't just *appear* in my room without being invited and hide while you creep on me."

He frowns, walking over to the island. "I wasn't *creeping*. You seemed lost in thought and I actually came to bring you to the study session. O said Slash scared you off, and that bothered me. You can't be part of our caliphate if you aren't *part* of our caliphate, you know?"

"I don't think Jasper and Slash agree," I murmur as Dottie hands me another berry. "Fuck, these things are good. Why didn't Salem lead with them?"

Zavida flushes a little and I don't get why, but he ignores my statement. "They're suspicious, but that's just because of who and what they are. I promise you won't have to deal with it for long and the ceremony will actually help with it."

"Oh goody," I reply with an eye roll. "Just what I wanted for Christmas."

"Kit, come to the study session. Seriously. We can help with your questions and um, Jasper doesn't believe Oriel about his meeting." The redheaded gamer shrugs, looking sheepish as he pushes up his glasses. "He could use your help, if that matters."

Damn it, why did he have to go there and why the fuck is it actually working on me?

Lucian

It's been two days since I dropped the new student on the Prince, but I haven't seen the payoff I would have expected. Based on his reputation both at school and in court, I would have thought I'd see Camponella in my office either whining or beat to a pulp by now. But I haven't and it's making it hard to focus on all the levers I need to pull to keep my end of the bargain.

Of course, Luca demanding I attend his ridiculous gathering on the other side of the Mouth took precious time I didn't want to give up.

Looking around the room full of simpering demons, hybrids, and a smattering of other supernaturals, I see nothing that warrants my attendance. Face time can be important when you've been planning things for eons, but I have duties to attend to, unlike him. He's an earth dwelling recruiter who's living it up on the dime of our benefactors. For the fistful of years he's been up here, he's shown very little progress for the amount of resources he drains on a monthly basis. And his sons are even worse… seeing them with a lowly Fae that works for the Society made my stomach turn.

Even lesser Princes of Hell shouldn't be slumming it with hybrids.

My real employers agree with that sentiment and they'd be very interested to know his progeny are gallivanting with scum. However, that would require me to put in significantly more effort than I deem Gemini's downfall worthy of. I don't want to replace him here; my school is the perfect location for my tasks. It would be considered a promotion, though, and I wouldn't be able to turn it down without revealing my distaste for being topside. So the lazy ass vengeance demon will survive to live another day, I suppose.

I watch the newest Gemini heirs flirt and flaunt their relationship with the girl, noting their useless friend floating about as well. The Dark Fae is certainly seductive—she's built like a more solid version of the human model from the fifties who wore lingerie all the time—but something about her is off. My instincts are rarely wrong, but I can't put my finger on what makes her different from all the other hybrids at the party. She's not even comparable with the Unseelie slinking around and that's certainly in her heritage.

I should warn Luca, but I'm not eager to help the bastard, either.

"Lord Darkstar…"

Beccarus is dancing near me, gesturing for me to approach her. I dart my eyes to a shadowy corner, hoping the simpleton realizes I don't want people to see us together. She works at the school, so it wouldn't be unusual for her to attend as an assistant, but she's not one for humanoid form. Gemini prefers no or half-shifted demons at his Earth events, so my sniveling toadie will stick out like a sore thumb. I don't want the quorum meeting to begin with a lecture on how human and supe paparazzi sneak into these events.

We shouldn't have to hide and his security should be far better—unless he allows it to maintain his celebrity mobster status.

Making my way over to the spot I indicated, I peer down at the lesser demon impatiently. This had better be good. Silvera joined me on this trip above because he's good at cloaking his form, even if he loses his temper and shifts. "What is so important that you dare interrupt me at this event? We have a quorum, and the meeting will begin in the next hour."

"I am sorry, Headmaster. However, the watchers we recruited have brought some news. I knew you'd want to hear it before you go into the meeting." Beccarus ducks her head, obviously thinking I'm going to lash out despite what she said. I would, simply for the impertinence, but this is not the time or place to discipline my staff.

"Spit it out," I snarl. "You're wasting time."

"Camponella survived the first day with a few bumps. However, our spies in the activities witnessed a few irregularities you should know. He accompanied Xerxes to the drama meeting and during, they discussed induction. Then, after the evening meal, he went to the Thieves Guild gathering. Kit stood up to Bastion, and the crow got elected to lead the Guild."

That's… not what I expected in the slightest.

"The boy might not have magic, but he has a spine," I murmur as I consider the possibilities. "Perhaps we can use this. After all, the Prince is predictable; he'll force Kit to take part in everything his caliphate does until he finds the activity where the human shines. Jasper is skilled at making certain to dominate every aspect of life at Discordia."

Beccarus gives me a crooked, toothy grin. "If he makes the human join Magic Battles, we can use our allies to eliminate him. The bad feeling you have about him will be taken care of when he's killed. Plus, if they induct him beforehand, it will harm the Prince's power base."

"Yes, it will." Glancing around the room, I note Lola holding court with a group of easily swayed young demons. She's the key to getting Luca to vote the way I want him to in the session. I need to approach her before it's time to convene. "Beccarus, I must attend to things here. Find Silvera and apprise him of the news, then head back to the school. Whatever you've done to turn screws on students so they'll comply, intensify with a reward they can't resist. We need anyone we have on our side hungry for blood during Battles this week."

The demon grins again, doing a small curtsey before she disappears in a puff of sulfur. I sigh as I walk away from the hidden alcove, moving through the crowd toward the redhead Luca married. They aren't fated mates, but demons don't find them as often as we used to. I don't blame the blowhard for claiming a woman as ambitious and vicious as himself to help rule their empire here.

I blame him for being weak and lazy, but that's not my call.

"The King and the families are not interested in coming to the table," Luca says with a smirk. "We will have to take more definite action to force the negotiations. Perhaps aligning ourselves more fully with our new sponsor is best."

Of course, he thinks we should get in deeper with the mysterious benefactor—Gemini is little more than a thug.

"I don't believe that's our only option," I reply as I observe the others. The Geminis may have control over the West Coast, but the Midwest, Southern, and Eastern families don't look convinced. We'd need their support here, plus unconditional support from traitors within the seven families below to fully commit. "And we do not know enough about the group to pursue additional partnership."

"I think they're makin' a bigger play than y'all understand," Cornelius Rhodes says in his lazy drawl. The bulky crossroads demon runs the

Southern United States, and he's sharp as a tack. His down-home demeanor purposefully conceals his intelligence—a fact that aids him in tricking most people into underestimating him. He's a necessary ally in any decision. "I don't cotton to being used for some hot-headed numbskull's plot to take over the world. My people don't care about the top-side unless it affects our allotment."

That's the rub with demons; they don't give a damn unless it impacts their comfort.

"Dethroning the current monarchy *would* impact them," Lola says sharply. "We'd re-negotiate terms with the Society and it would be from a position of power. Remember, our benefactor is working on both the supernatural and human realms with other partners."

I shake my head at the same time as Phelps Brewster, the head of the Midwest sector. He's similarly doubtful that any group can accomplish infiltration with supernaturals, humans, and demons. The landscape is too big and there are too many species to consider. "I don't believe that for a second, Lola. You're naïve if you think anyone can manipulate that many groups at once successfully."

"Not to mention it would start another 'world war' scenario," Constance Braithwaite adds with a disapproving cluck of her forked tongue. The woman is a pit demon, and she seems to get uglier every time I see her. She's forsaken Luca's humanoid decree in our private quorum room and the results are not pleasant. "Disrupting the power structures of *all* the various species across the globe will only foment chaos. Someone like Lola might covet that outcome, but it won't end well for business."

Finally, someone making sense. It's about time.

"Those of us with interests that require *live* humans, supernaturals, and the like will suffer far longer than those who feed off of atmospheric conditions," Phelps agrees. "My folks need crises of faith, greed, lust, and all the rest to function. Hell, Luca, your woman would be okay, but you need living beings for vengeance, too."

The onyx demon leans back in his chair, considering the input. "That's true. But none of us are getting what we want or need at present. Perhaps we need to use what we can from this secret contributor and break ties once our realm is in play?"

"That would mean we have to figure out the prophecy," I interrupt. "No one's done it so far and it's been millennia. Not even the fucking Fae know what the hell the damn thing means. There are parts scattered all over the globe, and we don't have a full version to get scholars working on. The Society has parts, the Fae have parts, we have parts, and we believe somewhere, the humans have pieces. Those damn seers the supes and deities use won't give anyone a clue—and they're immortal, so we can't torture it out of them."

"Not to mention they have powerful magic directly from the Source," Constance mutters. "If you screw with them, they find ways to re-weave your tapestry that no one wants to experience. I've seen it happen; I won't be party to it."

Suddenly, her horrendous appearance makes a lot more sense; even for a pit demon, she's hideous.

"Well, this has been enlightening, but if we don't have other business to discuss, I have things to handle at the university," I say as I stand. I will not sit here and contemplate our navels all night. No one has anything usual to add and we can't agree, so I want to get back to my minions to find out what they've arranged.

The door pops open, and every demon at the table whirls around to glare at the intruder. A smartly dressed succubus looks at us in fear for a moment, then clears her throat. "Apologies, my Lords and Ladies. Mr. Gemini, we have a situation you need to deal with."

Luca stands, looking infuriated as he stomps over to the assistant. "I *said* no disruptions!"

"Y-Yes, my Lord. But… I believe this is too important to ignore."

Hold on, I might be interested in staying if I get to see Gemini humiliated at his own altar.

"What could *possibly* be that urgent?" Lola sneers at the girl.

She swallows hard as she looks back and forth between her employers, dreading her duty to report the incident. "Your sons… just announced the Fae girl is their mate to the entire party. It's chaos out there."

The Geminis both look stricken and I have to stifle my laughter behind my hands. This is *delicious*. They were hoping to marry this set of twins off for political connections. If the sparkling hybrid out there truly is their fated mate, it will tarnish their image in all the circles we run in. It might even get him recalled if he's not careful.

"Well… I suppose that *is* pretty urgent," I say as I arch a brow at the other leaders of the movement. "Especially since the girl is not even partially demonic. Rotten luck, Gemini. The Fates definitely aren't feeling kindly towards you and Lola today."

His sneer as he stalks out is the best thing I've seen all day.

Perhaps I should come to these parties more often.

Kat/Kit

Zavida pulls me into the room and every eye lands on me. I grit my jaw against the swell of anxiety that brings up, staring back at the six demons in irritation. At least some of them have clued in about my issues, so this silent gawping is ridiculous. How am I supposed to gather my thoughts and speak if my chest is caving in? Dudes are the goddamn worst and I signed up for years of being surrounded by them.

Past Kat is an idiot.

"Look, I don't know why you're all looking at me like I'm the Holy Grail, but that idiot at the Guild was taunting me. With my background, I'm not likely to back down when challenged because it made everyone around you think you were weak, so… I refuse to be a victim. If it's a problem, that's on you, not me," I babble as I cross my arms over my chest, hoping to look defiant, not nervous.

Jasper's eyes narrow, but he says nothing and Slash mimics him. Anton studies me quietly, like he's working out a riddle as he leans against X. Oriel and Salem both grin, obviously pleased by my outburst. I turn to look at the Kitsuné still gripping my wrist and he lets go as if burned, his face flaming. Their continued silence makes me even more pissy, and I suck in a breath before letting it out slowly.

Fine, be a bunch of judgy fuckwads.

"Anyway, the dude got all 'my shit smells better than yours,' so I let him have it and said Oriel would make a better leader. People were all whispery shocked for a minute and then Oriel shot back at His Ugliness, then they did a vote. Imagine that I was right about Oriel beating this shitstain without even trying. The End."

The demons exchange looks again, then all eyes go to Jasper. Prince Assface strokes his chin, and his slitted dragon eyes glitter with unsaid opinions. I'm about to fuck all the way off and leave them to it, when he deigns to speak. "You actually told off Bastion and then influenced the Guild to elect him? With little more than a few statements?"

I blink, then give him a look as if he's lost his mind. "Are you hard of hearing *and* rude? Yes. That's what I just said, Jasper."

Salem snorts, covering his hand with his mouth as he tries to hide his amusement from the angry-looking Prince. The rest of their reactions vary, but only Slash follows his leader's flash of annoyance. It seems he'll be the toughest nut to crack on my way to the Prince.

That is, if I give a shit about getting these guys to like me and I don't.

"Kit, I'm surprised by your bravery. Bastion could have easily taken you out without raising an eyebrow—even if he had his minions do it. Yet you confronted the dipshit in public and raised the caliphate's profile by getting Oriel elected to a position of power. And he didn't decline out of laziness, which is also fairly astounding." The dragon pauses as he looks at the other demons. His lips quirk up in a sardonic grin. "The rest of you should take note and ask for his help in your activities. Perhaps his newness is more of an asset than we expected."

Huffing, I shake my head. "I'm not your damn PR rep, Jasper. I'll defend myself and people I care about when needed, but I will *not* pimp myself out to increase your market share. You can go fuck yourself if that's the price of admission to your little club."

Slash opens his mouth and I get ready for the big, bad bully to tear into me, but Zavida cuts him off. "Kit, we don't expect you to do a bunch of work for free—"

"I'm also not for sale," I spit back before he can finish. "Being poor isn't a precursor to being up for purchase by rich dickheads."

The Kitsuné flushes bright red, stammering as he tries to apologize, but he's saved by Anton. I have had little interaction with the gorgeous designer, but he's mesmerizing to look at and it distracts me. "Kit, you misunderstand Zav. I'm certain what he *meant* to say is that we do not expect you to do a bunch of unpaid emotional labor for people you don't know. The Prince often forgets that not everyone is his staff and being royalty doesn't mean he can push everyone around with impunity."

"Anton—" Jasper's voice holds a warning that doesn't intimidate the peacock hybrid in the slightest.

He waves it off as he gives me a brilliant smile. "I believe you can be very helpful to us, but it's understandable that you want to get to know everyone before you take up their mantle. Clearly, Oriel has done his part on his own, which led you to speak up. We should *all* do the same if we expect you to be part of our world throughout university."

Holy shit, one of them has emotional maturity on par with an adult. I'll be damned.

"That's… fairly accurate," I mumble as I nod at him. "Thank you for saying it, so I didn't have to explain."

X winks at me as they snuggle with the rainbow demon. "Anton's always the grown up in the room. He's good at translating dickhead boy ranting."

I snort, finally smiling a little. "I'll say."

"Plus, he's fucking beautiful," X continues. "None of these idiots can hold a candle."

Uh, no way I'm answering that. *They're all far too good looking for me to keep focus when I'm not panicking.*

"Stop fawning over your boyfriend," Salem says with a yawn. "We know how you feel about each other."

"Jealous?" X purrs with a smirk. "You can always—"

Rolling my eyes, I sigh loudly. It really doesn't matter what species they are —some people's children are insufferable at this age. "As much as I'd love to hear about all your sexual escapades, I have homework to do. Are we done with this conversation? Can I sit down and read?"

Slash crosses his arms over his chest, looking bigger somehow when his muscles bunch up. "Who said you could stay here and study?"

For fuck's sake…

"I did," Zavida says stubbornly. "Anton's right about getting to know each other and it's not fair to send him packing when we do normal caliphate stuff. We can't use Kit when it suits us and treat him like shit when it doesn't."

"Finally, man," Oriel mutters. The Kitsuné looks at him quizzically and he shrugs. "I wondered when you were gonna take your entire head out of Jas' ass. Good for you."

Jasper looks infuriated, suddenly morphing into the spiked, fanged mother-fucker that brought me to this floor the other day.

This will not end well…

I take a step back, feeling the tension rise inside of me as the dragon advances on his friend. Oriel doesn't move despite the aggression, so Jasper stalks closer. Swallowing hard, I shut my eyes, focusing on breathing. The very first foster house I lived in was one where fists were used to make a point to the boys by the seemingly perfect 'dad' and it brings up bad memories. He never hit the girls—his words were the preferred method of dealing with us. But I watched the rotating door of boys who came in either take it and end up bruised in inconspicuous places or run away when it got to be too much. Violence doesn't bother me as a general rule, but coming from someone older, in a position of power, smacks a trauma button hard.

I need him to stop.

"What the *fuck*?!"

Jasper's roar of anger brings me out of my self-induced meditation and when I open my eyes, he's frozen in place with Oriel lifted in the air by his collar. The other guys' eyes widen as they look at their leader, so I know they aren't doing this. Slash jumps to his feet, yanking Oriel out of his grip and tossing him to the couch. The Prince is still unmoving, his eyes full of fury as he glares at the room.

"This isn't funny. Whoever is doing it, fucking let go," he growls low.

They all shrug, looking helpless, and I watch as it unfolds. Oriel brushes himself off, smirking at the dragon as he tilts his head. "Maybe the Fates taught you a lesson about using your words, Jas."

Frowning, I note he's not upset or worried in the slightest. *Maybe he knew Jasper wouldn't have actually hurt him?* I lick my lips, feeling the panic inside of me subside as the negative energy in the air decreases. Within a few minutes, each of the demons has denied their involvement while the Prince grits his teeth, and my shoulders relax. I might have misread the situation because of my past, though I think Oriel is right about their leader reining in his temper.

"Don't look so worried, Kit Kat," the crow demon says with a grin. "He does this all the time. Not the frozen thing—that's a puzzler—but losing his shit and acting like a dick. Our Prince has to work through some poor, learned behavior from our benevolent ruler."

I wrinkle my nose. "That's not an excuse. You can grow up with shitty people and not be a shitty person. He needs to do better since he's supposed to become a fucking ruler." My eyes flick over to the spikes on his back and the tail held in place. "You probably have way too much magic and power to go off the chain at something as small as Oriel mouthing off. Get some discipline or do some yoga, man."

Anton snorts, then X follows, and before long, everyone but Jasper and Slash are howling with laughter. Salem gets up, walking over to me to bump fists then slings his arm over my shoulders. He leads me to the couch where he and Oriel have their stuff spread out, giving me a little push until I sit down. I look at them all, feeling the heat rise to my face at the acceptance that move shows.

Then Jasper's tail twitches, and he's free. His gorgeous face is twisted in irritation as he scrubs a hand through his hair. He looks at O with a half-grimace. "Sorry, dude. It's still hard to control the scaly part when I'm angry. I shouldn't have grabbed you."

His apology feels sincere, but I'm keeping my eye on him; I don't need to be triggered by anything else.

"No worries," Oriel winks, as he bumps my shoulder. "I know better, but you should apologize to Kit for scaring the piss out of him. He looked like he'd seen a damn ghost. Your tantrum must have brought up terrible stuff."

That gets the Prince's attention, and he whips his gaze to me, intensity coming off of him in waves. "Did it, Kit? Were you in a home where someone hit you?"

I give Oriel a dirty look, unhappy that he brought the focus back to me, especially about this topic. It makes my anxiety spike again and I have to count backwards for a few seconds before I can answer. "It bothered me— not just because I'm a poor foster kid, but because it's unacceptable to treat anyone you care about that way. But to answer your question, I was not in a home where anyone hit me."

That's as close as I want to get in a room of people I don't yet trust, but it's not a lie.

"Mostly true," X says under their breath. "No one hit him."

Jasper nods, then turns back to me. "I will try not to use violence with those in our caliphate in the future. Salem is an asshole for telling you without my permission, but he's not wrong. However, I am not my father; I refuse to be. You're right about treating people appropriately."

"I'll be damned," I mutter. The Prince narrows his eyes at me and I shrug. "I accept your half-ass apology. If you do better, we won't have a problem… at least, about this."

Oriel laughs and leans his head back, staring at the ceiling imploringly. "Thank fuck. Can we *please* fucking do our work now? I have shit to do at night and we're burning moonlight."

Slash grunts, giving me a suspicious look as he ambles back to his seat and Jasper nods. "We should. Everyone has to keep a sterling grade point average to make the caliphate stay on top—and Kit has so much catching up to do."

Looks like our damn truce is only about his stupid fists, then.

Breakfast the next morning is unusually quiet.

Jasper is in a *mood*, which is normally preceded by calls or visits with his father. This time, I think it is about our new floormate.

Kit and his adorable familiar behaved last night—in fact, I think he studied harder than anyone. He reads at a ridiculous speed; I know because I monitored him as he worked. It's unusual for Xerxes to land on the same side as O and Salem on any topic, but he's vehemently in favor of the new guy becoming one of us.

My lover, much like me, prefers to placate from the middle ground, not take a side.

That means I have to figure out why the guy is causing a divide in our group without even trying. Kit's past is still eluding Zavida—another anomaly—and he's so closed off that it's hard to suss out what his game is. Though, to be fair, he might not have any nefarious notions at all. It's obvious he genuinely doesn't know shit about the world he belongs to. I highly doubt Lucian or the King would pluck a semi-human spy from Earth who truly has *no idea* what the fuck he's doing.

I'm left with no solid conclusions, just vibes. Vibes are X's thing, not mine. The vague feeling of helplessness pricks my very core—I am an avatar of pride, after all. Out of anyone, I should be able to use my superior intelligence and social skills to coax this kid to talk. I can't seem to make myself do what I normally do to 'encourage' people to spill their innermost machinations, though.

This entire situation is fucking weird, and I don't like it.

My irritation ruffles the bird inside of me, making my shifter side prance and fluff impatiently. I'm sure my eyes are flashing with the rainbow of my tail—a sure sign I'll need to fly it off at some point. The silence is unbearable as I look at my friends eating their food and basically ignoring one another. We only come here to set the expectation and being up this early won't be required in a few weeks, but our obvious discord isn't doing us any favors.

"Curses and Hexes is going to be a *bitch*," I comment casually. Kit looks up at me curiously as his little bear thing nibbles on fruit. "Elias Wormwood is a stuffy, prissy little shit who uses the professor's title to abuse students."

Slash grunts around a mouthful of meat. "I'd like to see him try me."

"You know he will," Salem says with an enormous yawn. "He thinks battle magic guys are 'wasting his precious time' because they don't care about anything but offensive spells." He reaches over and scratches the tiny animal's head, earning him a chittery sound and a smile from Kit.

That damn panda is never *this chummy with people.*

Xerxes leans forward, looking past me to where the new guy is sitting with a serious expression. "Be very careful, Kitten. Elias won't care that your magic hasn't emerged yet. He's a fucking sadist and he'll let dickheads fuck with you on purpose. Trust me."

Kit lets out the most human sounding growl I've ever heard, stabbing his Cantu berry toast with his fork. That gets a guffaw out of the crow shifter on one side and a chuckle from the lazy chef on the other. "Just fucking peachy. Another professor who wants to see me fileted for their amusement."

"Perhaps you should head back home, then, if you can't take it?" Jasper finally acknowledges the rest of us rather than stewing in whatever bullshit he's been lost in. "You're not getting inducted with a piss poor attitude like that."

A palm slaps on the table as Kit pushes out of his seat, glaring at our leader. "I didn't ask to be part of your stupid boy band. You guys think I need to and X made good points, so I agreed. Don't hang that shit over my head like a punishment; it won't work."

If I didn't know better, I'd think his kinkajou was shaking a tiny fist at the grumpy dragon.

"Excellent point," Xerxes says as he looks at the more hostile end of the table. "It's unfair to act as though we're going to yank this away every time Kit doesn't react the way you expect."

All eyes land on me, and I feel the bird flutter with pleasure inside of me. He likes when we're important; the warring sides making us the swing vote does just that. I press my lips together, pretending to contemplate the situation. Of course, I know Jasper's full of dragon dung; he will not let some uninducted rando live on our floor all year. This is him flexing his muscles at the guy to regain control; unfortunately for him, Kit Camponella seems to be made of sterner stuff than that.

"I think it's tawdry to threaten someone with shit you're not willing to back up," I say as I look at each of them. "That shit is beneath us."

Slash glares at me like he wants to rip my head off of my shoulders, but I could give a fuck. He never pries himself out of Jasper's ass long enough to see when the Prince is being ridiculous. Zav used to, but that's taken a hard left since they started fucking. It leaves X and I as the eternal arbiters of the previously uncommon disagreements. Now that Kit is here, it's plain to see that unless he's inducted, the balance is going to hinge on us continually.

I enjoy being important, but not that *important; it feels like work.*

"Thanks, I guess," Kit mutters as he gathers his shit and stands. The familiar scrambles up his arm to his shoulder, giving the other end of the table a glare. "I'm going to head to class."

Salem nearly knocks his chair over as he stands up, and I observe. He's really into befriending his roommate. Normally, he stumbles around like a half-drunk frat guy unless he's in a kitchen. "I'm coming with, Kit Kat. We've got this one together."

"Maybe don't crowd me this time?" Kit says, but there's no bite to it. "I can't take notes and poke you awake all the time. Suck it up, man."

It only takes me a second to grab my stuff and stand as well. "Me, too. We all have this session together."

"Slash."

The one word from Jasper gets the big guy to rise, but he gives us all a pissy look. "Fine. Since I'm in the class, I will escort you."

"Gee, thanks, dude," Salem snarks as he rolls his eyes and slings an arm over Kit's shoulder. Somehow, he misses the kinkajou, but the animal runs up his muscled arm to sit between the two of them. "What a kind and not at all forced offer."

Kit snorts, and even I have trouble keeping my expression straight.

Semi-conscious Salem is pretty amusing.

"Perhaps you could tell us the fundamental difference between a curse and hex, Mr. Camponella."

Kit's eyes widen as the sharply dressed mage-demon hybrid glares at him intently. His mounting anxiety is palpable as he fiddles with a ring on his thumb that spins around as he strokes it. "Um... I..."

Slash makes a sound that I assume is satisfaction and irritation from the other side of Salem. The shark shifter's unnecessary dislike of our new member stems solely from Jasper, and it's grating on my nerves. I know he can think for himself, but he's not right now. He and the Prince pride themselves on differing from their asshole dads, but they're acting *exactly* how their parents would.

It's a goddamn shame.

"Find your tongue, Mr. Camponella, or you'll find yourself in a much worse situation."

Glaring at Wormwood, I remember why mage hybrids have been relegated to my family's territories. They're a stuffy lot whose greatest downfall is their own ego; it comes from their more humanoid appearances and ties to human supes. Ridiculous if you ask me, but for some demons, the more or less you look like humans defines your place in Hell. The King could give a fuck less, but he indulges both sides, so they spend all their time fighting each other rather than the ruling class.

That's a trick demons taught humans a long time ago and they've no more wised up than our own people.

"Professor, I... I don't... know." Kit says in a low voice. He's looking at his hands and I can't decide if he's angry or upset.

Salem, however, looks more awake than ever. Flexing his bulk a bit, I note his tail slipping out from under his seat to wrap around Kit's ankle as he gives the smug-looking dick at the front of the hall a filthy look. "Must feel good to pick on someone who can't fight back, huh?"

"Salem..." Slash hisses under his breath.

I roll my eyes because he'd do and say much worse if someone was this combative with any of us, particularly the Prince. "Let him talk, man. How often does Sleepytime speak up?"

"Don't… it's okay," Kit says softly. "I'm used to this shit."

That hits a button inside of me. Whatever the fuck he's gone through top side is bad enough that he'll fight Jasper like a wet cat, but he won't stand up to someone in authority when they humiliate him in public. I press my lips together, unsure what I'm going to do now. I despise bullies in positions of power; it's why I willingly became part of the caliphate. We're working to take our corrupt, shithead parents out so we can make things better for our territories. Sure, Jasper's got issues, but it's *nothing* like his fucking parents.

Wormwood is a scum sucking bottom feeder for treating a student this way—especially one he has *to know the background of.*

"Bullshit, Kit Kat. This asshole is purposefully calling you out, despite knowing you're new to this world." Salem crosses his arms over his chest, looking much bigger as he sits up at attention for once.

"Mr. Stryker, I don't believe I requested your input." Wormwood gives him a stern look, but the panda demon is unswayed. "Mind your words before you lose marks for the day."

Salem sure as hell doesn't need to lose points in *any* class that isn't about food. My decision becomes much simpler when the professor turns his ire to my unusually verbose friend.

Closing my eyes for a moment, I let the bird spread out, pushing its way to the surface and through my skin in a half-shift. Gasps echo off the walls of the room—it's typical for those who have never seen me transform to behave like this. Ignoring them, I smile as a soft, feathery blue fluff that matches my hair covers my frame. My tail goes from the typical demon to a cascade of peacock feathers that mirror my eyes and the tips of my hair, while my features sculpt themselves into an even sharper beauty. When it's done, I look at the mage-demon with my head cocked to the side.

"Your pride is outweighing your brain, Professor," I say. "Perhaps you should reconsider this course of action."

Unlike Jasper, I don't need to make myself enormous and threaten to breathe fire to make my point.

"Ah, the heir apparent," Elias sneers as he gives me a look full of disdain. It's clear he's one of the extremist magic hybrids who covet a more human appearance by his lack of awe at my glory. "I'm afraid your little display doesn't impress me. This is none of your concern."

"That's where you're wrong," I reply. "You should remember that we are all students, here to learn, and your mandate is to teach us, not humiliate us."

The asshole snorts at me as if I've said the dumbest thing he's ever heard, and I make a note to personally end his career once this year is over. Taking steps now will make a lot of waves and unless he becomes dangerous, we'll survive his bullshit for a year. That's nothing in terms of time in Hell and I'm more likely to garner my mother's support for exiling this fucker if I've shown restraint.

"You may be the next ruler of the House of Pride, but you're not my master yet—maybe ever." His eyes convey a suspicious smugness that I don't like as he looks at our group. "None of you hold the power you imagine. Now be quiet or I'll—"

I don't have time to be shocked at his insolence before Slash stands up. He's much bigger than Salem and his sharp teeth and razor sharp dorsal make people gasp again. If demons coo and admire my beauty and X's allure, they cower in fear at the sight of the Prince's enormous second-in-command before he even shows his genuine power.

"No one speaks to the Prince's caliphate in this manner, Wormwood. Your treasonous implications aside, I would advise you back the fuck off all our members."

Wormwood scoffs. "The *powerless* human isn't one of yours, Scrum. You're out of line."

The silence is so thick you could cut it with a knife as his statement hangs in the air. I sense Kit shrinking further into his seat as we wait for the huge shark shifter to reply. Finally, he shifts into an even more combative stance and barks a laugh. "Shows how little you know, Wormwood."

"Excuse me?"

My lips curve when I realize what Slash just did. He's a demon of few words, but if you know how to translate them, it doesn't matter. And he just claimed Kit as part of our caliphate without actually saying it out loud. "You heard him, Elias. Kit Camponella is ours and anyone who comes for him will be handled accordingly by our Prince's decree."

Jasper's going to shit a gold brick, but for the first time today, I feel pretty fucking good.

kat/kit

The whispers in the hallway aren't surprising—Slash's proclamation has zoomed all over the farthest corners of Discordia by now. Wormwood had to confiscate a dozen phones by the time class ended; that's, apparently, how big a deal it is when that fucking shark speaks.

I'm getting a lot of sneers and I'm not sure if it's jealousy, competition, or plain bully shit.

"That was a rather eventful class, mm?" Anton says as we head for the library lecture halls. "I dare say it'll be hard to top for at least a week."

Rolling my eyes, I try not to let that frustrate me. I don't want to be in the damn spotlight for the next week or more. I just want to get a goddamn education and a job so I'm not living on the edge of precarious ruin like half the damn world anymore. "I suppose so. If you guys have to defend me in every class, I'm going to have more enemies than I want by the end of the week."

Anton tilts his head and I marvel again at how bird-like it is. Most demon hybrids have a tell about their animal—I'm figuring out my floor mates. "I doubt you'll be able to stop some of our guys. You seem to be an acquired taste, Kit Camponella—though once tasted, you make people yearn for more. It may indicate some Cubi blood. We'll have to monitor it."

"I am *not* Cubi," I protest. "I can't make *anyone* do what I want and especially not in *that* way." A shiver runs over me as the past floods back and I stop in the middle of the open space when my vision blurs. Swallowing hard, I chant in my head, hoping to get this damn attack under control before I make a bigger spectacle of myself.

Dottie scrambles out of my bag and up my arm, positioning herself next to my ear as her small paws run over my hair. Anton studies me again, opening his mouth to speak when I hear a familiar voice in the distance. It sounds concerned, but I can't divert any energy to recognition; no, I need every molecule focused on *not* losing my shit in a flashback in the middle of the damn quad.

"Kitten," the voice says as it gets closer and in my head, I want to admonish X *not* to call me that.

But I can't, so I just lick my lips and continue working through the steps to push back the fear. The voices around me sound worried, and I wince when a gentle hand takes my arm. It pulls a bit and I work out that they want me to move. My legs feel like lead weights, but I move after I put a lot of willpower behind my internal commands to my body. Oddly, I often feel like I'm not even in my frame when I get like this. But I suppose a lot of trauma victims let their minds float away when they can't stop nasty shit from happening.

At least I didn't end up with a fractured psyche and multiple people living in my brain.

"Kit, we're just leading you to a washroom near our class, okay?" That voice is the adorable, yet gutless gamer. I had such high hopes for Zavida on the first day, but his devotion to Jasper makes him unreliable. That makes me tense up and I stop short, knowing I shouldn't follow someone I don't trust when I'm only half-conscious.

Another hand lands on the opposite shoulder, and I hear Dottie chitter. She likes the owner of that hand, so out of the three demons I know are here, it must be X. "Don't worry, Kitten. We won't let the pasty hacker take you to Jasper's sex dungeon."

Blink. That will not make me move.

"X, you've made it worse, for fuck's sake. His eyes are *more* glazed now." That was Anton and his irritation is laced with worry that sort of shocks me. "It's obvious what triggers this response now, so can we all behave as though we're not morons?"

X tsks under their breath, murmuring, "Oh, Kitten. I *am* sorry to hear that."

My lips press together, but I still don't speak. It's hard to claw my way out of this and though I stayed semi-aware this time, that's not always the case. Sometimes it's damn near a blackout and I need to trust that someone other than a three pound exotic pet will be around to help. I just don't know if it's the demons I'm supposed to join or if that's another trick by a clan of assholes with bad intentions.

After all, my judgment on what's safe has been faulty in the past.

The hands urge me forward again and I obey—if only to salvage what little dignity I have left. I don't want to miss a class and incur the wrath of another Wormwood -type professor. The name wasn't listed on my schedule and I'm utterly convinced they're all going to be like Wormwood or Lillabet.

Missing my first session won't win me points no matter who it is, so I have to snap out of this shit.

My hands curl into tight fists and I let my short nails bite into my palms. *Nope, not enough.* I rake my teeth over my lower lip, splitting it slightly. The tang of blood helps a little, but it's still not enough. A soft grunt escapes my mouth as I try to knock my brain loose from the fog of trauma, but it's not there yet.

"Stop." The voice echoing around me is Zavida's, and I tense up. "He's doing shit to himself and I bet it's to shock his system into rebooting."

Okay, maybe he is smart when his head is removed from Jasper's ass.

"For the love of Satan's furry goat pants…" X makes an annoyed sound as I hear rummaging. "Here."

The cool hilt of a blade touches my hand, and I recoil.

I need a shock, but I am not a cutter.

I'm not judging, of course. It could have been how I dealt with the PTSD and anxiety, but for my absolute cowardice with my hide. I frown, knowing it's more complex than that and feeling bad for doing exactly what I was saying I wouldn't until… a sharp pain on my wrist snaps me into the present like a rocket.

"What… what the fuck…" is all I get out as I look at the slice on my arm with wide eyes.

X gives me a little shrug, licking a long, curved snake fang protruding from his mouth. "You wouldn't use the knife and we have, like, two minutes to get into that class. It was an emergency."

I don't know that I've ever heard of a 'Cobra Emergency,' but I guess it'll do… for now.

THE LECTURE HALL FOR MYTHOLOGY IS HUGE, AND I SIGH A BREATH OF relief. I'm still recovering from one of my 'mid-tier' attacks, but I'm up and mobile. That's better than my usual routine of holing up in my room or the basement for days while I try to avoid calling the therapist. I know that's counter-intuitive to healing, but I learned not to trust *anyone* assigned to me by the system a long time ago. I give up just enough for them to not have a reason to make me do more—or, at least, I did.

I'm still not used to admitting my life has taken a total three-sixty and I'm free of that.

Of course, I'm trapped in a whole *new* system with people I don't trust. Being surrounded by assholes is par for the course, though. My eyes cut to the demon dudes guiding me to a section on the back right side of the room. At least two of them seem like they *might* be okay, but it's too early to be certain. Zav is a question mark I wish I could solve, but until the Prince gets his swollen head out of his scaly ass, that will not happen.

"Now, Kitten, just sit between Annie and I. Zav will take excellent notes just in case you have trouble focusing."

I frown as they settle me into a cushy chair. "Why are you being so nice to me?"

"Because a panic attack bordering on a flashback is not normal," X murmurs as Anton plops down on my other side, then Zav takes the end. "You don't have to bother denying it, but I've seen it before. So sit down, relax, and work on whatever helps you get right."

"But I—"

Zavida pushes his glasses up, his expression earnest as he leans over the pretty peacock. "We're not judging you, Kit. Every single one of us comes from less than auspicious families with varying levels of abuse. I know we seem like spoiled rich kids with no problems and maybe a little, we are."

Anton snorts and rolls his eyes. "We definitely are. But that doesn't mean our home lives are remotely within levels of acceptable. Being part of the royal family or their court is a bitch in ways no one wants to publicize… even when it's as plain as day."

My brow furrows. "People ignored when some of you looked… abused?"

They do in my old life, but not with rich royalty and shit—just us throwaway orphans.

"The King and the General are less than subtle with punishment," Zav mutters as he sets up his laptop. He doesn't look at me, but I get his drift. He wants me to know why Slash and Jasper act like they do.

A loud squeal from the front gets my attention and my eyes widen when I see the person at the front of the room. His dark eyes and menacing look make every single demon in the room shut up without being told. I guess everyone's afraid of the Headmaster—not just me.

"Attention, students." Lucian straightens, focusing his glare on the entire lecture hall. "Because of a change in sabbaticals, I will cover your intro level Mythology course. You are expected to be on time, engaged, and not break

Discordia's codes while in my presence. Punishments for failure will be severe."

Son of a bitch. I'm zero for six in the 'Professor Games' so far.

A wave of ice hits me, and I lift my head to find the asshole staring at me like he's trying to make me implode. My eyes narrow as I hold his gaze, trying not to let it affect me. I don't want anyone here to believe they can intimidate me since these guys can't be with me twenty-four-seven. When he finally looks away to organize the smart board, I let out a slow breath.

"Why does he look at you like that?" Anton whispers. "Did you do something stupid when you got here?"

I shake my head, reaching up to pet Dottie's head. "No. He was impersonal and abrupt. Then Jasper showed up angry about having to deal with me. I have no idea what I could have done."

A low whistle comes from X as they bump my shoulder. "You've got a talent for pissing people off, Kitten. The headmaster, the Prince, the Enforcer, that dickface Bastion… and let's not forget all of your professors."

Scooting my foot over, I grind my heel on their shiny, gorgeous shoes. The outfit today is fucking impeccable and though I might not smash their toes, I can scuff them up. For X, that's probably just as bad. "Shut. Up."

The Kitsuné leans forward again, looking at me with concern. "It's only your third day in Hell."

"Yeah, I've been this way my entire life. I attract winners everywhere I go." They all give me disbelieving looks and I smirk. "Just watch. This will only get worse as the week goes on—guaranteed."

As every caseworker I've ever had said, I was born under a bad sign—and I highly doubt that will be any different in the underworld.

Kindervelt is a pain in the ass, but at least Demon Lineage is over. It's one of the classes I have with none of my brothers in it, and to make it worse, I found myself piqued. I didn't have the new kid in it, either. It made focusing on the lesson easier, but surviving a two-hour lecture from that jackass harder.

But it's lunchtime now and hopefully, one of those dicks brings him with them to our table.

Squinting as I cross the quad, I try to remember who shares their free period and lunch for this block. Today it should be Kit, Slash, X, and his royal dickface-ness. It's not the best combo I could imagine, but Jasper has his TA time afterward, so maybe he'll order lunch at his office.

"What am I saying? Of course he won't. He won't miss a chance to clash with Kit again."

Rolling my eyes, I consider how all the chips are falling. Slash's declaration yesterday has whispers floating around the school, but it's unlikely someone will approach Kit directly until they figure out what it will cost them to do so. Saving face for their families is paramount, so lower tier demons should steer clear. Unfortunately, morons like Bastion who have always thought they should be included in our circle are going to gang up together.

Hell is rife with politics, even at this level.

"O! Wait up." The deep growl makes me pause, and I turn to find the shark himself ambling toward me. "You move too fast."

I arch a brow at him. "I'm part crow, dude. We zip around as quickly as possible to snatch what we desire."

"You're going to lunch, not a job," he huffs. "Or is there some reason you're in a hurry?"

Waving off his obvious attempt to gather info for Jas, I slow down so he can get even with me. "Hungry. Didn't eat a lot at breakfast. Too much bullshit."

He grunts, matching my gait as we climb the steps to the *Triclinium*. "You're too easily thrown off. I don't know how you do the shit you do when you're so sensitive."

"Slash, thieving is in my blood. It's like the air I breathe—sort of like battling is for you. I don't get thrown off breathing. See what I mean?" I look at him hopefully, thinking he might understand this time.

"Nope. I just do what's necessary. No deviation."

Satan, save me from the single-minded focus of sharks.

He's not wrong about how he works; Slash is a machine with no off switch when he's set to task, just like his animal. That's why he's such an excellent weapon for Jasper and a perfect team member for the Magic Battles. Absolutely *nothing* stops him once he's on the trail. "Fine. But to answer your unasked question, I am curious to see how Kit's last class went. He seemed to have it rough yesterday before you… said things."

"Hmmph."

The big dude also clamps his mouth shut like a vice—figuratively and literally—when he doesn't want to discuss things. Now is one of those times because he opens the door for me with a narrow-eyed glare that would make lesser demons shiver. I wink at him playfully and he rolls his eyes as we head for the royal table, only to find Kit and X already waiting for their food.

Kit's familiar is sitting on the table between them, munching from a small bundle of food that reeks of Salem. It makes my lips tip up, glad he's taken to our new member so easily. He's a good dude, but his food obsession and panda-style narcolepsy make people get angry with him for no reason. So far, he's done better with the raven-haired guy beside my colorful friend than anyone in the past.

"How was Mythology?" I ask as I plop down on the other side of the small, frumpy guy. "Make any new enemies since we saw you last?"

Xerxes snorts, and Kit groans as he buries his face in his hands. "Our teacher is on sabbatical."

"So? A substitute will be a much easier grader." Slash sits in the seat next to Jasper's favorite one carefully. The furniture here isn't made for a demon quite his size, so he has to make sure we don't have a repeat of the elementary school incident.

Let's just say he's not allowed on any aquatic teams after he got his revenge and leave it at that.

"You'd think, right?" Kit mutters in irritation. His hand reaches out to pet the kinkajou and I realize he's using it to calm his nerves, so I don't comment.

X lifts one sparkling, fingerless gloved hand lazily as they hold up a finger. "Unless the sub is the Anti-Christ himself."

My eyes widen, and I shoot a concerned look at Slash, who pretends not to care. Huffing, I turn back to Kit and my glittery friend. "Lucian? Lucian Darkstar, the Headmaster of this college, is teaching an intro level Mythology course for a semester?"

"I didn't stutter, Oriel, darling. The man himself is our teacher, and it's absolutely wretched." X wrinkles their nose as they look at themself. "He gave me demerits for 'altering the uniform unsuitably,' which is ridiculous."

Kit looks like he's going to chuckle as we both examine the rips, bedazzling, and alterations X made to their uniform today. The changes today are as striking as the ones yesterday, and I doubt it will get better as the semester rolls along. This will definitely be an issue going forward. Jasper will lose his shit if our caliphate falls behind in points *or* grades, so it has to be rectified quickly.

"What did you say to him?" I ask curiously. "Did you refute the validity?"

"Nope."

Before I can ask why, Kit elbows me in the ribs. "I did. Fuck that guy and his arbitrary rules. I saw at least ten guys in the hall with modified uniforms and theirs have to do with bullshit, not identity. A group of…" he pauses and thinks for a moment. "…wolf hybrids, I think, were roaming with shredded shirts to show off some stupid tattoos. So I told the Headmaster he would have to apply the rules equally or not at all—anything else could be challenged in student government or something."

I blink, impressed as hell. "I think you're right, but how did you know that?"

The small animal chitters, making a gesture like it's rubbing its eyes and Kit laughs. "Dottie's right. I stayed up late reading stuff online about all these stupid activities. I'm so far behind in studies, but catching up on the rules of all your outside things was easier than decades of classwork."

I'll be damned. That dude is a smart little son of a bitch.

"WHAT THE HELL IS GOING ON HERE?"

The first half of our lunch/free period is almost over when Prince Eversore shows. I'm not sure if he did his teacher shit, but he's obviously had a shower. His hair is wet, and he's got on a fresh uniform as he stalks to his spot by Slash. His eyes rake over the group, zeroing in on Kit as he stifles the laughter from our previous conversation.

"What's so damn funny?" Jasper presses when no one answers quickly enough.

The new kid rolls his eyes, slouching in the chair as he shrugs. "Nothing. You had to be there."

Jasper's eyes flare with anger, lightning dancing around his pupils as he grits his jaw. "Enlighten me. Perhaps I can enjoy the revelry despite not being present."

He's being such a tool, and I don't think he even knows why. It's going to be hysterical when he gets his head out of his ass.

"Fine...." Kit sits up and looks directly at the pissy dragon. "So yesterday in Lit, the guys said I had to keep Salem awake. But that's like... fucking impossible at five p.m. To make it worse, O was getting fidgety after sitting so long and the professor hates me. So I kept moving back and forth between them with the invisible orb to get them back on track."

"Invisible orb?" Jasper parrots as he frowns. "You don't have magic. Or did that change and you forgot to inform me?"

"He does not have magic," I confirm with an innocent grin. That's not true, but none of us need Jasper having a tantrum in the cafeteria in front of all these eyes. Besides, I'm not sure if Kit even knows he froze everyone the other night when he was upset.

"Then what the hell is the invisible orb?"

Flipping his dark hair off his face, the new kid holds up his hands like he's framing a crystal ball at the top and bottom, then moves them around like it's forming and reforming between his palms. "This is the invisible orb. A shrink taught it to me because I had a foster sister who couldn't focus long enough not to get her ass kicked by her drunken dad. I asked for something to use to capture attention without words or props so I could help her."

The Prince makes a face like it's the dumbest thing he's ever seen, but I'm transfixed by Kit's hands moving. Once he stops, I shake my head and grin at the rest of the table. "Stupidly simple, but it seems to work. I get focused on his hands and the movement, which pries me away from whatever I'm hyper-focused on. Salem sort of wakes up to pay attention."

Kit shrugs as he picks up a berry and hands it to his familiar. "I didn't know it would work on demons, too, but I guess it makes sense. The funny part is that I did it in Mythology today and X kept swaying with my hands like I was playing a *pungi*."

Xerxes snorts again, shaking their head. "Trust me, I was less than thrilled, but I couldn't stop. Annie says he has to remember it for… reasons."

The cobra shifter gives us a sultry eyebrow bob and Kit elbows them again. "Don't be gross at the table."

That's when I see Jasper's eyes glow for a second, as if he's just had an idea. He sniffs, tilting his head as he studies Kit. "Well, it is funny, I suppose. X is a good dancer and I imagine it was very novel for a *human."*

"It was novel for anyone, you asshole." Kit rolls his eyes and stabs a piece of lettuce with his fork. "Leave it to you to ruin a good time."

Our leader's smirk only deepens, and I sigh internally. Whatever he's going to do now will be shitty, and he thinks it's brilliant. I'm not sure what will happen after he lashes out, but I doubt it will be pretty. "I doubt his dancing was as exciting as the dance I got from the visiting auditor for the weapons cache. She was… delectable."

Tilting my head back to look at the ceiling as he licks his lips lasciviously, I consider whether I should just grab Kit's arm and ask him to head to the library to study with me. We both have an extra long free time today. I doubt he'll waste it screwing around; the kid is fucking dedicated as shit.

"Jasper," Xerxes says reprovingly. "You're too old to wave your conquests in people's faces. Button it up, man. Kit just asked us not to be sexy at the fucking table two seconds ago."

"Why? Is he some kind of prude? We're all guys here. I'm sure you'll find my story just as amusing as his little tale, unless you're some ridiculous virgin. She was a pleasure demon, and I know how much Slash *loves* their kind."

"You know what?" Kit pushes to his feet, slinging his bag over his shoulder in a blink. The kinkajou scrambles up his arm as he shrugs. "Please continue with your tale of male prowess. I have years of knowledge to catch up on, and I don't need to dampen the fun for the rest of you. I'm out of here."

Even Slash looks a little chagrined as he stomps across the cafeteria towards the doors. I whip around, giving Jasper a murderous look. "Not cool, man."

His pleased expression doesn't quell my anger. "If he can't take the heat, he shouldn't jump into the fire so often."

"You're being a grade-A knob, Jasper Eversore. I will not remind you again that behaving like your father doesn't make you him, but it makes people dislike you as much as him." X pushes to their feet and tilts their head at me. "Coming, Oriel? I think we should check on our new friend to make sure he's not being cornered by some dumb fuck."

"I'm game."

Stew in that, Prince Fuckknuckle.

Kat/Kit

I don't know why Jasper waving his sex games in my face bothers me. It shouldn't. I'm not stupid; I know how guys talk to one another when girls aren't around—for better or worse. The twins spent many a night loudly describing their bullshit to one another on the other side of thin walls, plus the guys at other homes weren't exactly angels. I'm not eager to be part of it, but I've always been able to shrug it off as dumbass boy hormones.

Then why does it bother me so much now?

Growling under my breath as I stalk across the quad toward the library, I keep my eyes on the ground while I stew. Maybe it's because the fucker was *obviously* trying to get under my skin? That was the twins' way of punishing me for existing though, and I could ignore them most of the time. Do I just want his approval? My social life has never been very active, but I want these guys to accept me, so that's possible. It's odd because I've spent a long time not giving a fuck about what people think.

"I feel so damned *drawn* to these dickfaces and I wish I knew why," I mutter as Dottie clings to me. "Normally I would have figured out how to completely avoid Prince Asshole by now. But I don't know the rules here and I'm not sure I can survive without people in my corner, even if they're likely to stab me in the back."

I climb the steep stairs to the hulking building with anger still vibrating through me. I have plenty of time to read during this long break and I'm going to use it. If I can learn the basics of this world, I can pull away from the toxic men who amuse themselves by being hurtful.

Wait… hurtful?

Frowning to myself, I yank the door open and stomp inside, flashing the stupid ID at the desk before I head as deep into the library as I can go. I need to lose myself in school work; it's always been the best way to deal with the chaos of my personal life.

I'm sure it will work just as well in Hell as it did above ground.

THE COMFY CORNER I BUILT MY LITTLE NEST IN IS SECLUDED ENOUGH FOR ME to read the children's books without someone seeing me. I used my laptop to search the library's files for curriculum at the elementary and secondary schools for rich demons so I could mimic the education the rest of the students received. It might look stupid to be reading such basic materials, but starting at the beginning has always been the best way for me to build a foundation.

Dottie is curled up with her snacks in my bag as I move through the sixth grade subjects while I chew on my granola bar. She's been quiet and well behaved—something that helped me focus immensely. I think she tries to mimic the mood I need, but I haven't gotten to familiar education just yet. It's not mentioned in any of the young reader texts or books so far.

"I haven't found that fairy tale the guys mentioned, either. Could it have been a verbal tale?" Sighing, I shake my head. I know verbal storytelling is big with humans and it might be with demons or other supernaturals too. That means sizeable gaps in my knowledge base will stay open until I figure out where I can go to get the urban legends and old wives' tale type shit.

A rustling sound distracts me and I'm instantly on alert. I've caught the whispers in the hallways that I'm sure that idiot Bastion is responsible for. I know being the next member of Jasper's stupid boy band isn't making me popular with others who were hoping for the chance. It's not the prize those guys think it is, but you can't convince people about something they've already decided. So random noises coming from vague locations I can't see could be nothing or a major problem.

"If I have to stab someone and get expelled, I'm going to be pissed," I whisper to Dottie. She bobs her tiny head and shakes a fist as if she's going to help. "Well, at least I have your support."

Moving slowly, I put my book down and crawl out of the nook I created. There are a lot of fucking places someone could lurk in this section, and when I picked it, I was hoping I'd be the one doing it, not some psycho shit-head playing a prank. Looking around, I find a large enough piece of furniture to crouch behind—if I can get over there without being seen. It would give me a good view of the space while I try to formulate a fucking plan.

"Here goes nothing," I murmur to my kinkajou as I scramble across the pathway to the oversized armchair and duck behind it. Once I'm there, I press my lips together, closing my eyes so I'm listening for the sound of movement more carefully. If I made it, I'll be safe for a few more minutes at least.

Normal people don't hear sounds in a library and assume it's someone who wants to do them harm, Kat.

Of course, my life has been nothing remotely normal and my experiences have my gut telling my brain to get fucked. Hyperawareness is a symptom of my trauma, but like the baseball player said, it doesn't mean they aren't out to get me. The quiet finally settles and I turn, opening my eyes so I can peek out of the crevice between this chair and the wall.

An eyeball is staring directly at me when I do, and I let out a high-pitched scream that makes Dottie go running for cover.

Who the fuck is that??!!!

"HOLY *FUCK*, KIT, STOP!"

The breathless sound of Oriel's voice brings me back to reality, and I suddenly feel my limbs thrashing around. My limbs feel heavy and my brain is full of cotton—it's almost impossible to focus on anything. Breathing hard, I put a hand on my chest as I mentally run through the 'five things' exercise slowly. I have to get the 'fight or flight' brain to disengage or I'll hurt someone by mistake.

The one thing I know for sure is my hand is wrapped around the knife I carry in my pocket like a vise.

"Damn, man. This is not a normal response—he's having a flashback. Or… he was and maybe he's coming back? Don't touch him."

That's X's voice. They're right; touching me now would certainly lead to someone being injured. It wouldn't be the first time an innocent bystander was treated to a left hook, but this time, I'm armed.

Breathe, Kat. Just breathe in and out, do your exercises.

"This is bad, X. It's just like when…"

"I know."

I frown a bit, wishing Oriel had completed that sentence. They all have such a long history and I don't know any of it. No one will tell me, either. It makes me feel like I'm ice skating uphill to prove myself—and I hate that I seem to care about proving myself at all.

Oriel's energy moves back a bit and the pressure on my lungs decreases. I guess he was close enough for me to sense him, but not actually feel his touch. That was for the best, but now that he's further away, my senses are calming a bit. I blink, forcing my eyes to focus little by little so I can at least *see* what the fuck is going on.

"Kit, we didn't mean to frighten you. We came to apologize… well, no, not apologize." X pauses for a second, then continues. "O and I came because we weren't okay with Jasper's behavior. He was being a douche—a disrespectful douche who needs to make his own apologies."

O snorts and I want to smile. *Jasper Eversore will* never *admit he was wrong, much less apologize—even I know that.* My right arm untenses and I can stop the knife hand from flailing, so I do. Both of them let out a relieved noise, which makes me want to smile again. The two of them aren't bad, honestly. Add in Salem and I feel like I have at least three people who I believe would help me if I needed it. I'm not sure about Anton yet and I know Zav and Slash only do what serves them or their Prince at the moment.

Jasper can sit on a fucking cactus and spin.

My vision adjusts as my pulse goes from a brass band to a lower tempo, allowing me to see the elegant Xerxes and goth-y O sitting on the ground on either side of me. I loll my head to the left, giving Oriel a grateful look— at least, I hope it is—and then to the right to do the same for X. The room is quiet as they give me space to regain control of the rest of my faculties. I swallow hard when I know it's time, then gingerly push myself out of the supine position to sit up.

"So…" I croak in the raspy post-episode tone I know so well. "That happened."

Oriel tilts his head at me, his brows furrowed. "It did."

"For fuck's sake, O," X mutters as they shake their head. "Kit, it's okay. You did nothing wrong."

My lips curve a little because I know that. Part of my therapy was accepting I can't blame myself for these reactions. I have a condition—several, in fact —just like people with epilepsy or diabetes. It doesn't matter that mine is caused by my brain anymore than it matters their pancreas causes a diabetic's sugar crashes.

"I know," I rasp. "But I'm… sorry… you had to experience it."

A fiercely determined look comes over Oriel's face as he practically growls, "Do *not* apologize for something you can't control. I scared you and I should have known better. It was obvious you have trauma from your past life up there. My silly stalking caused an attack and I'm the one who should be embarrassed."

Uh… what. No one has ever *said they were sorry for triggering me; I always have to hang my head in shame.*

"Kit Kat, I don't know what the hell the fucking humans do when people have issues, but at least *some* of us down here are more evolved than that." X gives me another gentle smile, holding a hand out. "You don't have to talk to us about what causes this but if you make sure we know what triggers you're aware of, we can try to accommodate you."

Swallowing around a dry throat that's closing up with emotion, I nod slightly. It takes a lot of effort, but I reach out to take their hand and squeeze a little. The touch sets off a round of tremors and I have to bite the inside of my cheek so I don't cry. This dude thing is hard as fuck when I'm up in my head like this, but I know it will be really suspicious if I burst into tears right now.

"You look like you're going to fall apart at the seams," Oriel says softly. "Can I come closer? I don't want to make this worse, but you seem like you need… reassurance?"

Nodding silently, I continue to hold on to X's hand as the broody crow shifter scoots over until he's within centimeters of me. I bite my lip, then look up at him through the strands of hair flopping in my face. He groans, then carefully pulls me into his arms for the best damn hug I've ever experienced in my entire life.

Oriel feels safer than a fucking armored car, and I have no idea why.

Chuckling, X lifts our twined hands, watching me closely before they put a light kiss on my knuckles. "You, little Kit Kat, are an interesting bit of trouble for our group."

I turn bright red at the kiss, not sure how to handle it. X is with Anton, for one, and I'm not a damn guy, for the other. There's so many complicated layers involved in this situation and I do *not* have the brainpower to parse it out.

Then again, I'm clinging to the loner like a monkey and I have no idea what rules there are around that.

"You guys are being really nice and I hate you have to see this, though." I sniff, pushing back tears again as I pull back from Oriel's shoulder. "Everyone keeps saying how cutthroat this place is, and I *can* handle that. But I also have this *thing* I have to keep people from knowing because it will make me weak in their eyes."

More than one thing, right, Kat?

I'm not sure if I imagine the soft brush of lips on the top of my head, but my body warms just the same. After a moment of the two of them looking at one another, Oriel finally speaks. "Kit Kat, X and I are on your side. You can trust us; I know that will take time, but you can. I think the others will be on your side, too, but they need time. Most of them don't... *vibe*... like Xerxes and I do."

"He's right. Annie is a softie once he's in and Salem seems to dig you. The rest? We'll work on after the induction." X grins a bit and shrugs. "Who the fuck knows when Jasper will remove his head from his big dragon ass, but we'll cross that bridge when we come to it, okay?"

I nod, letting out a slow breath. "Okay."

"Now, how about you tell us what you learned while we were searching for you? I don't give a shit if I miss a class or two and you don't have any for a bit, right?"

My eyes narrow as I look at the fabulously dressed cobra shifter. "Are you using me as an excuse to skip?"

"Maybe. But you're a fantastic excuse, Kit Camponella, and don't you *dare* suggest otherwise."

If they put it that way…. How can I say no?

O f *fucking course, the next class after the new kid's long free period is mine.*

To make matters worse, every single member of my caliphate except my second is in this period and I'm the goddamn professor. Oriel and X look as though they want to rip my head off—a dangerous emotion in a weapons class—and they started whispering to Anton and Salem immediately. Only Zav is standing close to me, but I can see the furrow in his brow as he watches our friends.

I can't bitch about Kit, though, because unlike everyone else in this damn session, he's sitting on a bench near the outdoor locker bank quietly with his head down. He's not looking at me, nor is he gossiping with the rest; no, he's stroking the little monster he calls a familiar as he stares into space. The vibe in the room is off and I dislike not knowing what's going on—especially with my own fucking people.

That's it; I'm done with this shitshow.

"Listen up, baby demons." All eyes turn on me as I don the mask of the hard-ass instructor. "Welcome to Weapons & Tactics 101. Your performance in my class will decide if you can continue to the next level in battle classes at the end of the year. Attendance is mandatory—no exceptions. If you're injured, you're here. If you are sick, you're here. If you are dead, it's because you were *not* here. Do you understand?"

The doubtful looks of some stupid first years give me change in a flash when I allow more of my shift to give me fangs and spikes that show my dragon. Out of the corner of my eye, I see Oriel snort, then turn to check on Kit. The new kid is still zombied out, and it infuriates me that even when he's not spitting at me in fury, he *still* doesn't fear me enough to follow directions. I can't allow it and I sure as *fuck* won't allow my caliphate to baby him.

"Kit Camponella, do you have some special exemption from paying attention I wasn't made aware of?" I stomp over to the bench, glaring down at him until he looks up at me. Something in his expression makes me feel a hint of guilt, but it passes when his eyes narrow and fill with the fire I'm used to.

"Sorry, *Professor*. I tune overgrown bullies out. Something about your *lecture* must have triggered my selective hearing. I'll try to do better when you actually teach."

His answer brings a chorus of gasps, chuckles, and whispers in the crowd of guys. Before I know it, my tail is whipping and I'm holding back the legendary Eversore temper. My father is known for roasting people who question him alive before they can finish sentences and unfortunately, my dragon's ire is a hair trigger like his. If I don't quash his public insubordination quickly—despite the consequences I'll face with my brothers—I might as well hand in my resignation as a TA. That would make my father call me home and ruin the plans we've been concocting for years.

Villain it is, then.

"Put that mangy thing down and get changed, you little worm. If you think being assigned to our floor in a dorm gives you special privileges, you are *sorely* mistaken. I want you running laps around the weapons field for the entire class. If I see you stop for more than a few seconds even once, I'm sending you to the Headmaster for punishment."

A mixture of defiance, terror, and fury fills Kit's aura as he stands. The bear creature scampers to sit on his bag, glaring at me and I'm glad there's no fruit to be shoved at me anywhere close by. He's a scrawny kid, but I can *feel* the push of his emotions as he slowly steps into my space. When he speaks, his voice is calm and flat, almost robotic. "He who wishes to be obeyed must know how to command."

I blink as my brain finally grasps the quote, sneering a little at his fairly accurate usage of Machiavelli. The fucking guy is book smart as hell; I'll give him that, but his street smarts are shit. "Are you saying I don't know how to lead, first-year?"

The blank look on his face disappears for the first time since he arrived, shrugging. He walks over to the locker with his name on it, opening the door to pluck out the Phys Ed uniform kit quietly, then flips me off. "I suppose that's a judgment only *you* can make. There are mirrors in the bathroom, I imagine. Reflection is good for the soul, Prince."

Kit jerks his head and the furry beast skitters after him as he heads off. I make to follow his snarky ass and make a *real* example of him, but a strong hand grabs my arm.

"Let it go, Jas." Salem, who barely stays awake most of the day, is gripping my limb as if he'd happily break it if I fight him. "You don't have all the information this time. Just move on."

What the actual goddamn fuck is going on with my friends?

"We'll discuss this later," I snarl under my breath as I shake him off. Striding to the front of the room, I look at the rest of the class with anger in my eyes. "The rest of you strip off and get warmed up before I call this entire lesson a fail."

That threat gets people moving and I stalk away to the weapons cache to pull the basic staffs out for once they've all gotten ready. I have no idea how the fuck I'm going to keep all my students in line if our newest member won't stop baiting me in public, nor how our caliphate will survive their time at Discordia if they allow this kid to bring them to mutiny. Slash would have *crushed* this shit for me and I'm cursing his placement in Dueling during this period. That's what happens when I don't throw my weight around and insist my people always get placed in the basic classes together—I won't make that mistake next semester.

That is, if Kit Camponella hasn't destroyed us with this bullshit by then.

BY THE END OF CLASS, MUCH OF MY THIRST FOR VENGEANCE GOT SLAKED BY watching Kit run endless laps around the large practice pitch. My perception of his intelligence proved accurate when he didn't run full steam for two hours, but paced himself evenly. Sweat soaked his black P.E. shirt, and he looked ragged as fuck for the last half, but not once did he stop for more than water or a few stretches before starting up once more. Even curiouser, he didn't complain or sling insults.

He did what I ordered until I called the class.

Baffling, to say the least.

As soon as the rest of the class and my floor mates trudged off the field, Kit rounded the last bit of his current lap and then headed for the bathroom like before. The exhaustion radiated off him in waves, but he just disappeared into the latrine without a word. Shaking my head and I turn back to the class, I watch the rest of the first years whine as they put away their weapons and re-dress. Seems like a fair number of them could benefit from extra training, and more than that, need the type of cardio I used as a punishment for Kit—not that my gambit worked.

"On Thursday, we'll test your stamina and overall fitness. If you're not in the shape to run with brief breaks like our newest delinquent, expect extra assignments to be completed until you are in fighting shape. Our kingdom needs no more pathetically lazy assholes occupying space when they graduate from Discordia. Dismissed."

The groans that follow my proclamation are music to my ears, so I grin as I exit the area. Normally, I'd stay to chat with my errant brothers, but I doubt that conversation is one that should be had in public. From O and X's disobedience before their free period to the gossipy shit at the beginning of my class, I have almost an entire goddamn caliphate to get back in line. Hell, even Salem dared to gently correct me today.

I don't know what's in the water since that kid arrived, but I'm going to find the antidote quickly.

"Jas! Jasper, wait."

Whirling around, I see Zavida rushing to catch up to me and though I'm pissed as fuck; I feel myself soften. "What?"

"I know you're pissed, and I get why." The nerdy ginger catches his breath as he looks at me from under his glasses and I sigh. He's one who needs serious catch-up on their physical skills. "But maybe there's more to this than we know. Salem hinted at that, but… I think we need to find out why the guys were so freaked out before you tear into them."

I grit my teeth as the strains of '*et tu, Brutus?*' drift through my head. "Why in the hell would I care what bullshit they swallowed from the little spy Lucian sent us?"

Zav tilts his head, scratching the back of his neck. "Because you're not a ruthless dictator who doesn't give a shit about the people in his care? I mean, Jas, the mean dragon front is supposed to be for outsiders, man. I know we don't trust Kit yet because of the trouble I'm having finding out who he is—but does that mean you have to torture him?"

Fuck. Now my bedmate is defending this kid. Is he wearing some sort of charisma charm?

"Zavvie, we need to have this conversation away from prying eyes and ears." I look around, noting most of the students are gone, even our brothers. Since we're alone, I walk closer and yank him close, bending to a hair's breadth from his lips. "You have influence over me because of our relationship, but I cannot allow my fondness to override my instincts."

The Kitsuné shifter whimpers a bit as his gigantic eyes meet mine. "I know, Jasper, *sir*. But… I have this *feeling* I can't shake. We're missing something and I don't know what it is. Maybe that's why you're so suspicious of a guy who seems to only want to go to school and get a job."

I roll my eyes, not wanting to admit how cute his naivete is. "Spies are trained to behave as though their agenda is not the one we expect. Oriel would be the first to say that if he wasn't somehow enchanted by this dickhead. And you, my darling boy, are a demon who sees the good in others. You're not programmed to believe the worst."

"True," he rasps as a shiver runs through his lithe frame. "But I also have a different perspective that you value. Unlike our king, Jasper, you allow us all to contribute equally and listen when we speak. You haven't been doing that since Kit joined us."

My fucking father rears his ugly mug again—as if I already don't measure everything I do against his evil bullshit.

Sighing, I lean my forehead against his, closing my eyes. "I know. And I can't seem to stop myself because he rises to every bait and fights back without fail. Something inside of me cannot abide his total lack of fear when he deals with me. It's… unprecedented. How can he truly be a normal human who will emerge if he isn't scared of the demon dragon Prince of Hell?"

A soft coughing sound makes me spin in place, pushing Zavida behind me as I look for the source of the unexpected sound. My eyes widen as I see Kit pick up his bag, sling it over his head and wait for the small monkey to climb on his shoulder. He looks tired as fuck, but his eyes are piercing as he looks at us.

"You could try not being a fucking jackass and *talk* to him."

He stares at me for a moment as I fumble for words. I'm not comfortable with him seeing my vulnerability with Zav, nor hearing my innermost thoughts. I open my mouth to roar my indignance at him eavesdropping, but pause when I remember I didn't clock his bag or the damn animal. I was so eager to find a little solace in the Kitsuné that my perimeter check was far too cursory.

I suppose that's not this idiot's fault. Maybe.

"Look, Prince Fuckhead," Kit says as he approaches. "I have no affiliation with that dumbass principal guy and he fucking hates me as much as you do. Ask the others about the class he's covering. But I'm never going to let you treat me like dogshit because you were born from the right cum splattering the right egg. Life is far too difficult to worry about assholes like you disliking me. There's bigger shit and you're not at the top of the pile."

I blink again and Zav chuckles, earning him a swat as we both watch the new guy leave without another word. I can't decide if I'm going to kill that motherfucker or send him after someone I really hate.

Luckily, I've got time to decide.

kat/kit

I was so angry and tired that I completely ignored the demon assholes from my floor during Supernatural Law and sprinted out the door as quickly as I could to avoid them at the end. Dottie and I went back to our room, skipping dinner to shower in peace while they were all downstairs. My phone blew up when I also refused to leave my room to attend their stupid ass meeting, but I turned it off.

I belong to no one and certainly not these fucking pricks—I don't give a shit who their families are.

My eyes open for a moment as I look up at Dottie as she sits on the top of the bookshelf, nibbling on her snacks. I grabbed her food and some hydration before I locked myself in my tiny room for the night. I'm too anxious to eat and I have so much to catch up on ensuring the Prince of Ballsacks will leave me alone. The kinkajou chitters and I sigh. "I know it's not *all* of them, but right now, I'm so fucking exhausted. I can't deal with any of them, even if they aren't the ones being a shit."

The look she gives me seems disapproving, and I fling my arm over my eyes as I groan. Now I've made my freaking pet mad, and she's the only one in my corner. How the fuck is this worse than living with those meathead twins and their Stepford parents? I mean, it's Hell, but foster care has always been worse than the concept of lakes of fire. Human high school is a gauntlet full of traps and pitfalls created to punish anyone who doesn't hold the special secret to being popular. Living here should one hundred percent be easier than all of that.

And it would, if not for Jasper Eversore's shitty attitude.

A loud knock sounds on my door, and I grab a pillow to scream into it. I told all of them how important boundaries are to me and I don't want to see or speak to them.

Why can't they accept that?

Dottie hops down from her perch, skittering over to look at the door expectantly. She thinks I should let the person in, but I still don't want to move. My stiff, achy body is as comfortable as it can be in my brooding spot.

"Go. Away." I call out in a firm, yet emotionless voice.

Another pounding knock rattles my door in its frame, and I grunt angrily. "Are you deficient? I *said* 'go away,' so get fucking lost." The idiot at the door doesn't answer and my temper finally sparks, forcing me to roll up to sitting and gingerly push to a standing position.

Let it never be said that my stubbornness will not outweigh my common sense; showing no fear of Jasper damn near crippled me.

I take a hot minute to shuffle to the door and when I yank it open, my jaw drops. The enormous frame of the Prince's snarling enforcer is standing there rubbing the back of his neck like he's unsure what the fuck he's doing. His other large hand has a large shopping bag with delicious scents emanating from it and despite myself, I salivate a little. We're both silent as we stare at one another in a battle of wills until he rolls his eyes to the ceiling, as if pleading for help. When his gaze returns to me, he makes an annoyed expression.

"I brought this. Eat it." His growl comes out like an order and I immediately bristle, opening my mouth to shoot back where he can shove whatever it is. "I mean… Look. It's fresh, Salem said you'd like it, and… you should eat. The running burned a lot of energy."

My brows furrow as I study the typically ass-kissing shark demon. How did he know about that? I sure as fuck didn't tell him in the Law class and I know Zavida didn't get a chance, either. And why the hell is he here? I know for a fact that jackass Prince didn't send him. He's probably still stewing over my witnessing him behaving like someone with a modicum of emotional depth. So what's going on here?

"Why?"

Slash presses his lips together and I get the impression I'm trying his patience, but I don't care. He sets the bag of food at my feet, then crosses his arms over his chest. "You're small—undernourished and undeveloped. That amount of training should be assigned to someone with the stamina and physicality to survive it without possibly damaging themself. Not refilling your energy and hydration is dangerous and irresponsible, especially for someone as frail as a human."

I frown. "So eat because I'm weak?"

"For fuck's sake…" The big demon shakes his head and his bulk flexes in a way that my body notices, despite the bone-deep ache in my frame. "Yes, but not how you said it. Eat because your body is a complex machine with extremely sensitive maintenance requirements in non or new supernaturals. You are here, and that means you will change at some point. It is not advisable to continue such poor self-care, as it will make your transition more difficult."

"Eat because I'm a machine that needs fuel. Got it."

This time, a low rumble comes out of the big man and his eyes flash with a deep blue light. His teeth seem to have sharpened and are gnashing as he breathes a slow breath out. "*No.* Why must you insist on twisting my words, human?"

Tilting my head as I watch his face, I shrug. "Why can't you decide if I'm human or not?"

"Fuck!" Slash says as he throws his hands up, then moves like lightning to cage me against the door. "You are purposefully irritating and we all rise to the bait every time. When we do, you get angry and spit like a cornered cat. I do not understand it, and I dislike it. This food ensures your health and you will eat it or so help me, I'll feed it to you myself."

Swallowing hard as he presses against me, I feel the tremble of fear that he'll discover my secret. I'm not worried at all about the aggressive way he came at me, or even the controlling bullshit he's spewing… only that he'll find out what I am and they'll send me back. So I look up at the angry shifter demon through my lashes and, for the first time in a long time, I agree willingly.

"Okay."

He blinks. "Okay what? Am I feeding you, tiny human?"

I snort, then shake my head. "No. I will eat it."

"Good. See you at breakfast."

Slash pushes away, turning on his heel and heading out of my dorm without another word. Dottie pokes her head out of the doorway, chittering as I pick up the bag full of tasty smells. I lick my lips as I stare at the space where the last demon I'd ever have expected to show up—outside of the Prince himself—just stalked off.

What the hell got into him?

THE NEXT MORNING, I SKIPPED OUT OF THE 'REQUIRED' BREAKFAST AND headed straight to Intro to Demons & Supes. None of the guys were in that class, so I didn't have to do any explaining or listen to bullshit excuses. Unfortunately, that also meant I was fair game for the other idiots and my skeezy professor. Lilabet all but crawled over the boys, making my skin crawl. Dottie stayed pressed to my stomach under my shirt as she struggled to help me keep my horror at the lack of consent in check. With my past issues, it made me more of a mess than my floor mates' shit would have.

I expect the four hours a week I have this class to be some of the worst of the entire semester, without a doubt.

"Mr. Camponella? A word, please."

Gritting my teeth, I rise from my seat in the back of the hall and make my way down to where she's posing at the lecturn. The curvy succubi bats her lashes as I approach and my stomach turns. Sure, men are the fucking *worst* with this crap, but it feels like a bigger betrayal when it's a woman doing it. I don't care if it's in her nature to feed off others or if it's part of demon culture... I'm not okay with it.

"Yes, Professor Lillabet?" I stand a good three feet out of range, hoping it will keep her from doing something I can't ignore.

Her lips tuck into a small pout as she rounds her podium, stalking towards me with intent. "You seem distracted in class. Is there something I can do to tempt you into participating like the others?"

Is this bitch actually asking me how to seduce me so she can feed off my sexual energy? The fucking gall.

Arching a brow, I shrug. "I'm behind in this arena, Professor. I have to focus hard on the material while many of the others do not. It means I can't joke around; I have to take notes."

"You'd learn *so much more* if you loosened up, though, Kit," she purrs as she comes within an inch of me and places her hand on my arm. The way she bit the 't' off in my name makes my jaw tighten and I narrow my eyes as I work out how to get her away from me before I do something stupid like stab her in the goddamn thigh.

Dottie scrambles up to my shoulder, shaking a tiny fist at her as she perches by my head. I smile a little, knowing that she'd try to scratch the woman's eyes out if I let her. "I think my anxiety prevents 'loosening up,' but I will keep that in mind. Is that all?"

"Oh, dear," she gasps, tightening her grip on my arm as her eyes widen. "You poor thing. Maybe I can convince the Headmaster to allow me some one-on-one time with you. Private tutoring *always* helps the new students in my class."

I'll just bet it does.

She presses closer, looking down at me with her gorgeous face and perfect hair angled to accentuate every feature. "I know I could help you release some of that tension… just keep looking into my eyes…"

Shit, shit, shit… now I get it.

I try to yank my arm away, understanding what the professor is attempting to do in a flash of horror. Her nails dig in hard and Dottie makes a loud, screechy sound as she holds on with her back legs. My limbs lock up when I realize I can't break free despite my self-defense classes because my body is frozen in place. This must be magic and that makes my throat swell in panic, causing my breaths to come out in soft pants.

"That's it, little one… You'll feel so good if you just give in…."

"L-l-l-l-lettttt gooooo of meeeeee," I slur as the fear gets a hold of my brain for the second time in two days.

Sweet Lucifer, I was a fool to think I'd be able to defend myself in this place, even with a weapon.

Professor Lillabet smiles sweetly, but I can see the hunger and malice in her gaze. "Don't worry; I'll be gentle. It's your first time, right?"

No, no, no, no….

"Kit, you're going to be late for Deconstructing History and Jasper will… *What. Is. Going. On. Here?!*"

My head swivels and I look at Oriel with a frantic expression. The look he gives me conveys his fury, but also concern. The lead weight on my chest lifts a little more as he bounds down the stairs in a blur of black magic tinged with the scent of lavender, geranium, and patchouli. A black feather floats by my face, catching my focus until it hits the ground. In fact, I'm so entranced that I barely feel the hard grip release my arm and a warm pair of arms envelop me as I shake.

"Shhh. She's gone," he says in a low tone. "I took care of it. And the caliphate will make sure it doesn't happen again. That slutty predator won't get her dirty hands on you again. Come back."

I must have checked out for a few minutes while he did…. whatever he did. That means Oriel is seeing me in the absolute most vulnerable state he possibly could and yet… I feel safe. It takes a few moments for my breath to regulate and my heart to stop thumping so hard it makes my ribs ache. Once I'm calmer, I lift my head and look up at the beautiful, dark demon boy. He arches a brow, smiling a little when he realizes I'm fully present.

"There he is. Damn, I was worried for a second. You were so gone that your eyes glazed like you were in a coma."

Ducking my chin, I pull back and shrug. "It's one of the symptoms. I… uh, I can't control it if the trigger gets flipped really hard. Her freezing me with magic was… not good for me."

"Freezing you with magic without a secondary chaperone is against school policy." Oriel flips his hair out of his eyes, looking annoyed. "Jasper will have her fucking job for this."

I snort. "He'll get her a raise, I'm sure."

Oriel shakes his head. "If he hadn't upset you yesterday, you would have come to the meeting and we *all* would have shown when your panic hit the bond. This is partially his fault, and I'll be damned if he doesn't need to make up for it."

Turning to grab my bag and let Dottie climb back to my shoulder, I swallow hard.

Pretty words, but I'm not sure they'll mean anything when they're flung at the Prince of Dickness.

Kit skipped the caliphate meeting last night, which was for the best. Zavida said he skedaddled from Supe Law like his pants were on fire, and Oriel showed up positively fuming. Apparently, our future inductee got cornered by the well-known staff predator and a quirk of curiosity lead O to find them before something terrible happened. The thought makes me shiver, as I've had similar experiences throughout my life with nasty little shits who secretly want to mess with my sexual identity without people finding out.

Bigotry looks the same whether it's human or supernatural—shitty and close-minded.

Anton and I were suitably furious that Jasper's suspicion pushed off the ceremony, even by two days, and it got the kid assaulted. I like him, and Annie does, too. In fact, I think everyone but Jasper does, even our resident ass-kisser, Slash. I noticed he stomped out of the fiery tempered meeting with a scowl that usually promises death and destruction. We didn't see him again for hours and he refused to tell anyone why he left the meeting so abruptly.

Unfortunately, nothing got resolved anyway, and first thing this morning, Zav, Annie, Kit and I share Arms & Battle with our pouting Prince. Kit wasn't at breakfast, either, so Jas was even pissier and Salem refused to tell him why the new guy was absent. I feel he doesn't know, which is concerning, but hell if I'm going to coddle Jasper more by intervening. He made his bed and he can damn well lie in it until he gets his head out of his ass.

"He's not going to skip, is he?" Zavida whispers as we huddle by our lockers. "That would be terrible."

I shrug as I strip down and put on the drab phys ed uniform with an annoyed sigh. "Who knows? He had Lillabet torture him Wednesday, then yesterday he was a ghost all day until Jasper ran him into the ground in Weapons. Kit doesn't seem like a quitter, but this first week has been rough as hell."

Anton pulls his class armor over his shirt, shaking his head. "I have to admit, he's irritatingly good at hiding in plain sight. That must be a human foster kid thing, too. We had classes together before Prince Dumbass fucked up, and I didn't see him. I'd think he knows an invisibility spell, but his magic isn't emerged yet."

Zavida elbows me and I turn to watch Kit slink into the room with Dottie on his shoulder. He looks like he didn't sleep well for the past two days, and I curse Salem internally. Either his heavy sleeping ass didn't notice or he gave our new member too much space. Oriel told us Kit was having a much worse attack when he bum-rushed the Intro classroom and I hate to see him suffer. Honestly, I hate to see *anyone* who doesn't deserve it suffer, but somehow, I've developed as much of a soft spot for the fashion challenged guy as Salem and O have.

I sort of love that he's not once asked about who I am or how I present myself.

"I feel bad for him."

Narrowing my eyes, I look at Zavida reprovingly. "Then stop letting Jasper's dick lead you. He's not going anywhere and you're allowing him to behave like a fucking tool by not saying anything. Between you and Slash, he feels justified because the closest people to him aren't speaking up, man."

The Kitsuné winces, but I don't feel bad about calling him out. He's small and less powerful magically than most of us. Zav got through lower school because of our protection and he's denying Kit that same benefit. His discomfort at confrontation isn't more important than doing what's right and he knows it. The dude is far too goddamn smart to accept whatever rationalization he's come up with in his head.

My lover shuts his locker, turning to look at our brother. "X is right. You and Slash accepting this nonsense weighs more heavily than all the rest of us put together. It shouldn't be that way, but Jasper struggles to fight the way he was raised, just like the rest of us. Segregating counsel to serve your own aims is very much straight out of his father's playbook and he can't see it right now."

A door closes quietly, and I see Kit slink out of the bathroom. His damage is so obvious—he never changes in front of anyone, even those who aren't hostile to him. His familiar stays within reach at all times, and he spins that anxiety ring on his thumb like it will save his life. I've even seen him mouthing whatever shit a therapist probably taught him to control his emotions when he thinks we're not looking.

Whatever happened to him wasn't one incident, and he's worked very hard to appear totally normal to the rest of the world.

"Man, I know we're rough in Hell, but I'm kind of shocked at how fragile he seems," Annie says softly. "Humans are idiots, but whatever Kit experienced is bad enough that he's developed a ton of habits to power through."

I smile, oddly happy that he noticed. The best way to pull my guy into the fold completely is to involve the soft heart he hides under his fancy exterior. "Definitely. It took O and I awhile to fix the accidental triggers in the library and I'd wager even longer for Kit to get over Lillabet."

"She needs to be dealt with," Annie says resolutely. "Zav, you can redeem yourself by adding that to the Prince's task list for you. Find out how we launch that bitch out on her ass and it'll be your first step to fixing your mistakes."

The relieved expression on Zavida's face is almost funny. He did *not* want to go up against his bedroom buddy full tilt, but if he starts small, it will give him time to gather himself. "Okay, Anton. I'll work on it while I'm continuing to research Kit. The systems are stubbornly resistant to all my usual techniques."

"*You* can't hack human systems? That's blasphemy," I joke as we head out to the field.

Zav pushes his floppy red hair away from his face with a grunt of frustration. "I've never seen blocks like this in their world. Part of why I haven't been able to argue with Jasper is the inconsistencies in getting all Kit's background. The things I'm encountering almost feel like a techno mage helped write this code."

Well, that explains why the Prince refuses to listen to us—he thinks he's got the scent of betrayal.

"None of you would last a minute in an actual battle! I want to see *effort*. These tactics could save your life one day. Take it seriously," Jasper yells at a group of jocks fucking around with their weapons as if they're in the space cult movie.

I don't know why he's acting surprised. It always takes a semester of beating the new blood into the ground before they realize that even if they don't expect to be conscripted by the families, they have to pass four years of this class. Since a great deal of them have been allowed to slide their way through the lower schools on their sports rep, it's a rude awakening. Or… that's what Jasper told us as he was going through his time here. I assume he won't treat them any differently than he got treated, especially because the caliphate has members in this section.

We shouldn't be called up except for Jasper and Slash, but war has been brewing in Hell for a century.

My eyes skitter over to where Kit got paired with an Invictus demon. To my surprise, he's not doing poorly despite how wiped he looked. I assume he's imagining our rigid leader with every thrust of the dulled swords we're using for practice. I wouldn't blame him if he was, but since he seems to have other shit haunting him, I could be wrong. Regardless, Jasper can't complain that he's shirking; he's holding his own, even though Roquefort is much higher in status than him.

"Roquefort, stop fucking around. You're better trained than this… you'd have to be with acceptance into the Thieves Guild and the Underground. Why is the new kid kicking your tail?"

"Don't be a dick, Eversore. Just because you're royalty doesn't mean you can insult students."

The growl from the Invictus is vicious and I pinch the bridge of my nose as I pause my sparring with Zavida. Jasper just painted an enormous target on Kit's back by hitting the drug dealing shit's pride. Given his family operates within Annie's family line, I highly doubt it was a mistake. The Prince is doubling down on his bullshit.

"Jasper, for the love of sweaty fireballs," I say as he passes us. "You're going to get the kid killed. I don't care if you think he's suspicious; this is stupidity."

His glare could slit throats as he looks at me. "You don't run my class, X. Keep your eyes on your own paper."

"I'm fine. Leave me out of your shit," the grunt comes from Kit and I blink. He hasn't spoken to any of us since he walked in. Now he's pushing himself as Roquefort puts his back into sparring like our leader intended.

"See? He says he's fine." Jasper looks smug now and I want to deck him— something that is definitely *not* my preferred method of handling conflict. "Everyone has to learn how to take responsibility for themselves at Discordia."

Beelzebub's nest, Kit's pride and Jasper's stubbornness rival one another for idiotic behavior.

"Maybe so, but caliphates protect one another. It's part of the commitment," Anton throws over his shoulder. "Loyalty dies when trust gets broken."

Kit snorts as he clashes with the demon, and I pause again to watch. I doubt he ever picked up a sword before this morning, but he's moving extremely well for the uninitiated. I would assume his demon comes from Slash's line with that innate facility, but his damn pride points at Anton.

Then a howl rents the air and everything stops.

Roquefort is grinning like a maniac and I see blood dripping from the sliced shirt at Kit's shoulder. These damn things got dulled prior to class, and I'd bet my favorite kimono that the Invictus used magic to sharpen his blade just enough to be dangerous. Poking a sociopath like Roquefort was a mistake; he has a reputation for shitty behavior ranging from drug distribution to espionage to soft whispers about how he treats the demon girls from our sister school in Purgatory. Invicta usually prey on those who have lost faith in their beliefs, luring them to certain doom by bargaining. They're higher in the hierarchies than crossroads, but lower than vengeance or fear demons.

Jasper screwing with his ego lead to this without a doubt because he'd behaved beforehand.

"Your sword is sharp." Kit stomps up to the delighted demon with eyes full of fire. "You're a cheating asshole who couldn't handle a human keeping up with him. Admit it, fuckface."

I wince as the smaller kid pokes his opponent in the chest hard, ignoring the blood dripping on the ground as he does so. Not only is Roquefort more powerful, but better connected and blood-free. Letting that flow in a room full of demons is like asking to be mobbed, but Kit doesn't know that. All he knows is that yet another demon is picking on him for existing. His fury is almost palpable in the air as he breathes hard and stares up at his opponent.

"Kit, you can't…"

"Shut it, X. If he starts it, he'd better be willing to finish it." Jasper stands back, crossing his arms over his chest like that settles the matter.

As if he's not part of this… he's got fangs and spikes again, so I know he's watching with the same demonic hunger the rest of us feel. The difference is, he's pretending he wants our new member to get squashed while Zav, Annie, and I are hoping he backs down. Kit would lose face, but joining our caliphate for real will negate that. If he doesn't, we're going to be rushing him to the hospital wing soon.

"Who cares if I did? This isn't some kiddie campus where humans party and guzzle kegs, newb. Get your fucking head on straight—you're in *Hell*. Demons lie, they cheat, they steal, and they will fuck you up if you challenge them. It's who we are." Roquefort's smile turns nasty as he looks at the rumpled picture Kit makes. "Even the Headmaster will agree that this is *not* a school for the faint of heart. You've been surviving off the popularity and fear of the idiots living on your floor, but now that you pushed me—that ends."

My gaze cuts to the Prince, arching a brow. His surrogate is crossing a line in terms of respect and he'll look weak if he lets it go to spite Kit. Jasper shrugs and I grit my teeth. I'm going to shove a fucking poker in his eye soon. Annie snorts, picking up my emotions nearby, and I shrug.

I can't help being irritated at how damn stupid the dragon is being.

"I don't care who the hell you are or who you're planning to conspire against me with." Kit straightens and holds his head up high. "I survived bullies and worse up there; I'll survive whatever the fuck you douchebags want to throw at me. You need to get it into your bony skulls that I'm not going to bow to anyone… *ever*."

A gasp echoes in the room, and Roquefort throws his head back to laugh. "Oh, what do the humans say on the social media? 'Touch some grass'? Yes, that's it. Kit Camponella, you need to touch some grass. Only someone delusional would believe they could survive being enemies with someone like me. I have infinitely more power and popularity than you; I'll crush you."

Pushing his hair out of his eyes, Kit shrugs and drops his sword. "Do your worst, asshole. I'm no one's bitch." He strides out of the ring with a trail of blood behind him as he grabs his bag and the cheering kinkajou from the bench.

That was both brave and stupid—he'll have to sleep with one eye open after pissing off Roquefort.

kät/kit

I'd like to say I can't believe Jasper would allow that little prick to fucking slice me, but I'd be lying. Jasper Eversore *enjoys* torturing people, especially me. And all that pretty talk X, Oriel, and Salem have been filling my head with about how I'll be 'one of them' once I do this stupid ritual thing is bullshit. I'll never be one of them and their Prince is determined to make sure I get that.

Mission accomplished, asswipe.

Luckily, I have the next period free, so I can follow this stupid map in the school app until I find the goddamned infirmary. I'm going to need stitches and I'm in no mood to have a bunch of demon assholes sniffing me when I go to my forced Dueling activity in the next hour. Grumbling under my breath, I stomp across campus toward the Admin building I haven't visited since Dank dropped me off. Maybe I'll see the guy when I do—he was the first person to be kind to me without some twisted agenda and I could use an ally who isn't my non-verbal kinkajou.

"Not that you're lacking, girl," I whisper to Dottie as my non-injured hand brushes over her head. "It's just that you don't speak, and I need someone to curse those fuckers out with me. Or at least agree that they're a bunch of crusty dildos who deserve to get scabies."

Dottie chitters angrily, and I grin. *Perhaps speaking is overrated.*

I glance at the map again, noting the infirmary is in the damn basement. Not a fan of underground levels in places I'm not familiar with, but my whisper of claustrophobia will have to take a backseat to pain relief. It doesn't look like I'm hurting outwardly—a lesson from my past—but I need to numb this bitch before I pass out. That blade was much sharper than it should have been and I'm going to blast Roquefort into the next ring of Hell when I get the chance.

I fucking hate bullies, especially ones like him.

Being a foster kid *and* a nerd *and* the new kid so often, I learned a lot about the shitty humans who decide to lord their perceived fame and influence over others. Most of the time, their meanness comes from their own insecurities—mommy or daddy issues—and they punish others because they have to make themselves feel good. All the classes they give at schools get that part right. However, there's also a vein of cruelty that's not about their crappy self-esteem in a lot of them. Call it borderline personality disorder or psychopathy or even sociopathy—some people are just born assholes and never evolve past that behavior.

If you happen upon a person who is a combo of both? You gotta run, and run as far as possible, or they'll never leave you alone.

There was a chick like that at high school number three, and I didn't see it until it was too late. She spun a great spell about being one of the good guys and inviting everyone to her table that the bullies cast out. That lasted for about two months before she showed her true colors, and by then, I was trapped. I had to endure her daily verbal abuse and shitty takes on everyone else in the school until one day I lost it. I told her off in private and cut that bitch out of my life like a tumor. It was the most healthy way to deal with her, even my therapist said so, because I had too many issues as it was.

Unfortunately, she was infuriated that I refused to be her punching bag. She spent the rest of my time there working to get me expelled and publicly humiliating me. It affected me so badly that I almost had a mental break and was off to a new foster family in a new town for the next year. That last year with the Jamesons, I remembered the lesson of never letting someone get close to you well. I kept to myself and didn't make waves unless directly confronted by the asshole twins' cronies.

No one will stand up for you if they're afraid the bully will turn that ire on them, so you're on your own—might as well act like it.

"Which is why you have to quit acting like the few decent guys in this group are ever going to help you, Kit," I mutter to myself. "They'll never turn on their boy, and you'll always be walking somewhere while wounded and alone."

"I don't think that's accurate."

Whirling around, I clutch the bleeding arm as I look for the deep voice behind me. I was so consumed with reviewing my past mistakes and applying them to here that I let my guard down. It was only for a minute or two and now I might be in big trouble. Cursing mentally as I see the hulking shark shifter, I scowl as he comes closer. "Fuck off, Slash. I'm not in the mood for bullshit."

He arches a brow, crossing his bulging biceps over his chest with a smug look. "Clearly. However, you're going the wrong way."

I blink, then my eyes skitter to the phone in my hand. The damn infirmary is marked on the map with a caduceus, so I'm not crazy. "I am not. So go away."

Rolling his eyes as if I'm the most trying being in Hell, he sighs. "Your app is wrong. Don't ask me how; that's not my thing. But the infirmary is not where we go."

What the fuck does that mean?

My expression must amuse him because he lets out a rusty bark. "Our caliphate doesn't go to that dirty, ill-trained staff of washouts. You need to go to the top floor and see Dr. Danckwardt. He's the physician used by the elite families."

"How would I know about some super secret doctor you rich dicks keep on retainer?" I glare at Slash, suddenly feeling both grateful and pissed that no one mentioned this shit. My app was supposedly set for being on their floor, which I assumed meant whatever I needed was in it. What other bullshit are they hiding from me? "And why are you here? Didn't you have some other class this morning?"

His toothy grin only makes me madder, and I spin on my heel, stalking up the steps to the Admin building with my head held high. I can't stand around and argue with this shithead. My arm is killing me. I only have an hour before I have to go get my ass kicked in Dueling, and I'm going to rage out if I don't get away from all the testosterone floating around this stupid school.

Too bad it's all male and I'm fucking trapped in a sea of the shit.

WHEN I FINALLY LOCATE THE OFFICE BELONGING TO THIS PRIVATE DOCTOR, I'm even more irritated and getting drained. I don't think I've lost enough blood to be dangerous, but definitely enough to get lightheaded. I raise my hand to knock on the door and almost fall over when it opens to reveal the very person I'd been thinking about earlier.

What the fuck is Dank doing in Dr. What's-his-fuck's office?

The mysterious chauffeur tilts his head, gesturing for me to come inside and I hesitate for a split second. He just looks at me, and I sigh heavily. I don't have the energy to fight about this. Grunting as I trudge in to flop into the first chair I see, I wait until he closes the door and comes to face me. To my utter shock, Dank reaches up and pulls the plague doctor mask off, revealing a face burning with embers stretched over a skeletal avian visage.

"I cannot go to Earth in my true form," he says. I assume that's my explanation for the creepy appearance, so I nod slowly. "However, an old friend designed this mask to withstand my powers so I can make the trip when it is necessary."

Frowning, I cross my arms over my chest, then wince when I hit the wound. "Why did they send a fucking doctor after me?"

"I do not know, though if I were to guess, it would be because I could sedate you for the trip. My training includes hybrids, so I am familiar with the needed drugs and correct dosages. Anyone else might have harmed you unintentionally."

I hate when I'm geared up to be angry and someone talks sense—it's very unsatisfying.

"I agreed to come here. Why would I have resisted once you arrived?"

He shrugs and walks over, taking my arm with a gloved hand to study it gently. "Those raised by humans are unpredictable in the best of times. Stressful times such as leaving your home can cause wild reactions. But you didn't come here to question me about that; you've been harmed."

I blink, remembering why I came, then growl softly. "No, I was attacked, but that doesn't matter a hell of a lot in this place."

The gentle smile is weird coming from the burning skull of some hellbird, but it's still comforting. Dank turns to walk over to a cabinet marked 'human,' and busies himself with gathering supplies. Once he has what he needs, he comes back to me, gesturing at the exam table. "Please be seated, and I'll stitch you up. I am concerned with your pallor. I don't know if it's a sign that you may be gravely injured, but I recognize we must act."

It takes a lot of effort not to be snarky since I'm so damn angry. But Dank is trying to help, and no matter what Jasper did, it's not this demon's fault. "Okay. Don't worry about being gentle, though. I can take it; just get it done so I don't miss class."

Dank frowns as he cuts the sleeve of my ruined shirt, pulling the bloody garment away to clean the wound. The damn stuff he puts on stings like a motherfucker, so I assume it's close to alcohol. Once he's satisfied with his work, the demon threads a sparkling line through a needle and looks at me sympathetically. "This will hurt a lot, but if you can get through it, I will give you a special blend to take once you get dismissed from lessons."

"How did you know I won't take it until after class?" I watch him yank the knot with his teeth, fascinated with the fact that his thread shit doesn't catch on fire by his face.

"Your spirit is strong and you are stubborn, Kit Camponella. That much is obvious, even to an old demon such as myself." The first puncture makes me gasp, but I get it under control before he puls his thread through to the end. "I am pleased you ended up with those who could give you access to my services. You would not have enjoyed the treatment in the infirmary."

There's something worse than being stitched up sans anesthesia with magic floss?

"I'm grateful you can help, but trust me, the demons I ended up with are *not* good people."

His laugh is rusty and full of rasping smoke. "No one here is a person at all, much less good. This is Hell and all its inhabitants behave as you'd expect. You may need to adjust your perception of the boys and staff at Discordia with that lens."

Sucking in a breath, I blow it out of my nose and think about that as I grit my teeth against the pain. For demons who live in Hell, Oriel, X, Salem, and even Anton have been decent. I can't imagine they often coddle anyone like they have me, and they don't even know I'm a damn girl. Plus, some of them are even standing up to their Prince when they can. They wouldn't classify as good 'people,' no, but they're probably on the high end for demons.

Shit.

"Maybe I am being harsh with *some* of my floor mates," I admit begrudgingly. "The others are assholes, though."

"Is one of the better gentlemen the person who sent you to me?" Dank asks as he continues stitching in slow, even movements.

"No," I groan. "The guy who sent me here is a giant asskissing dickwad. He always lets the worst of them act like a shithead and never once steps in."

"Mmm, I see. So your bully sent him to make sure you didn't suffer at the infirmary? That seems odd for such an evil dictator." The fiery demon chuckles, then coughs dusty embers again. "But what do I know about being the Prince of Hell?"

That crafty old fire chicken… he knows exactly who my roomies are!

Looking up, I squint at Dank with curiosity. "You're *only* here for the royals, right? That's how you know who I'm talking about. Someone in Prince Fucknut's group had to give me your info, or I wouldn't have ever known."

His smile is terrifying, but I don't care. Dank is the only staff member here who isn't actively treating me like garbage. "Yes, I serve the palace. I still do not know why the Headmaster sent me, as it was not an edict from my masters, but I didn't complain as I get to see the colors of your world so infrequently."

"Well, I'll go to the surface with you sometime; I promise. I don't give a rat's ass if anyone up there *or* down here like it." Dank closes the last bit and I tilt my head as I look at his work. He stitched an oddly beautiful lattice pattern that will scar, but in the prettiest way I've ever seen. "Wow. This is like… a medical work of art."

Again with the creepy grin, but I'm happy to see it. I doubt he gets a lot of appreciation for his talent from the caliphate idiots. "Thank you, Mr. Kit. I will fetch the pouch of tea for you to use later so you can sleep. Mind that it will have very unusual effects on you. Make sure you're not totally alone, and I don't mean the furry friend in your bag."

Dottie sticks her head out, chittering at the demon before ducking back in.

"Okay. Watch the magic tea because I'll be really wacky. Got it."

He shuffles over to procure a velvet pouch from another cabinet, then comes back to hand it to me. "Also, try not to come back to see me unless it is social. I dislike seeing someone as kind as you injured. Perhaps you might reconsider your opinion of the person who led you to me rather than the butchers in the basement."

Ah, fuck. Now I've got to decide if Slash is really a bad guy or just shitty at standing up for himself.

I can't decide if I'm surprised or impressed when Kit strolls into our Dark Magic class. He's clearly been to a physician, but he doesn't smell like the pit that is the general infirmary. Someone must have blabbed about the good doc, which will infuriate Jasper. His extreme ire towards the poor guy is troubling and I'm trying to get him to relax, but it's slow going.

It would be easier if Kit would stop antagonizing him purposefully, but that will never happen.

The guy is tough, I'll give him that. He's taking everything thrown at him and lobbing it right back to anyone who fucks with him. Amazingly, he's not even concerned with how much bigger or more powerful they are than him —he just stands up for himself. I'm a little jealous, actually, because that's something I've never been able to do. Having the caliphate kept me from getting trampled most of my life—not giving everyone who messes with me the finger.

"Do I have something on my face? Are you deciding what to report to your master?" Kit hisses out of the corner of his mouth as Salazar passes out the syllabi.

I blink, ducking my head as he hits me where it hurts. "You don't pull any punches, huh?"

Rolling his eyes, Kit bends to grab his tablet out of his bag, wincing briefly. Once he straightens, he rolls his sleeve up, revealing a bandage that he looks at carefully. "I hardly think stating facts is akin to punching you unless you have something to feel guilty about. Do you?"

Again, with the rough treatment. Jasper truly fucked up this morning.

"How could I have stopped Roquefort from being a cheating fuckwit?" I ask with a sigh. "The answer is that I couldn't, so I don't feel guilty. I felt bad that you got injured, though, because I'm not a sociopath."

His head turns slowly, and the weight of Kit's glare is palpable. "You stood there and said nothing while Jasper let him act like a goddamn psycho. At least Anton and Xerxes spoke up, but you? You cowered behind your lover like a simpering belle. *That* you should feel very guilty about."

Salem's eyebrows pop up as he strolls in late—as usual—and overhears our conversation. Once he plops down in the seat on the other side of Kit, he leans forward to give me a shocked look. "Zav, you let him encourage a bully in public? What the fuck, man?"

Until one of the others arrived, I could pretend I didn't know why Kit was being so pissy. Now I have to see it through the lens of someone who was around when Jasper and the guys saved me from the bullies as kids. "He was teaching, Salem. Questioning him in public is bad enough, but while he's doing professor shit is worse."

"Coward," Kit mutters.

My old friend continues looking at me, his gaze burning into the flush on my skin. "Kit Kat isn't wrong, buddy. You're afraid if you stand up to Prince Asshat when he's being a dick that he'll drop you. I get why, but I also think you're underestimating what you mean to him. Because of that, you're letting him get away with being an abusive prick."

"I'm not..." I protest, but Salem shakes his head.

"No way, man. You *know* he's punishing Kit because he doesn't trust him. Jasper thinks he's a spy for old Lucian, or maybe even his dad, and he's taking out his rage at both of them on someone who didn't do shit." Salem leans in again, brushing the injured arm, and Kit makes a strangled sound.

I didn't realize it was that bad.

"Fuck, sorry," the panda demon says with a doleful expression. "Gimme your tablet and I'll take the notes. It looks like it hurts."

Kit gives him a grateful smile, only hesitating for a moment before giving my brother the device. "Stay awake, though. I'm so far behind and I can't afford to miss anything."

"*Gentlemen,*" the loud voice comes from the front of the classroom and we all turn to look. Professor Salazar is standing with his arms crossed as he leans against his desk, his expression thunderous. "Since you've seen fit to force me to pause my lecture, would one of you like to recite the ten basic tenets of dark magic and what they do?"

Kit winces because he doesn't have a clue, and Salem gives me a sheepish look. Unfortunately for them, this is *not* my forte and I don't have the answer we need. But I was an asshole earlier, so I gather myself and respond.

"Sorry, sir. We don't know."

"Then I suggest you *shut your yaps* and listen, because that is exactly what we are discussing," the chaos demon says wryly. He turns to the class and gives everyone a creepy smile. "You'll find that I do not give detentions or send people to the Headmaster in this class. I find it much more effective to let you know I will use my powers to punish you as I see fit for the timeframe I deem fair."

Son of a bitch. Having a chaos demon mark you is worse than being stabbed.

"Understood, Professor Salazar," I reply. Once he finally looks away from our corner, I lean in to whisper to the others. "I get why you're mad, but… I'm…"

Kit rolls his eyes, flipping me off before he speaks. "Zavida, if you want to be someone's lackey for the rest of your life because they have a fine ass dick, that's your problem. Stop making excuses and don't act like you have no control over your bullshit, though. At least then I might respect you."

I wince, and Salem has to cover his mouth as he snorts. "That's not fa—"

"Life's not fair, dude. If it was, I'd be at an Ivy League college in *my* world, living my life without a bunch of bullying demons trying to stab me, but here we are. You pampered dicks just don't get that sometimes… we don't get what we want, and we have to play the hand we're dealt." Kit shakes his head in frustration and turns his shoulders so he's leaning closer to Salem.

That's a cue for me to leave him alone if I've ever seen one.

AT THE END OF CLASS, KIT LETS SALEM LEAD HIM OFF AND NEITHER OF THEM say a word. Running my hand through my hair, I curse under my breath. My anxiety is spiking; I hate conflict and the Kitsuné in me wants to burn it off with mischief. That will only cause more problems, so I fight my natural urge to be self-destructive by heading for Intro to Fae a few steps behind them. Everyone but Jasper and X are in this section, so it's going to be a pain in the ass.

Slash will be on my side, though. He never questions the Prince.

The hall for Professor Cedar's lecture is enormous—one of the biggest on campus. Rumor has it the administration created the damn thing for him years ago because he refuses to teach over two Intro classes a semester, so they have to get the freshman into four sections split over two semesters. He's a hybrid like my caliphate—part Reaping Fae and part incubus—and uses magic to shout his lessons over the giant crowds.

I wasn't looking forward to this large a crowd anyway, but with Salem and Kit snubbing me, I'm worried I'll end up getting pushed to the end of the row. Much like the new kid, I have my own quirks and issues, but he doesn't know it. Crowds are one of them, and if the guys force me to be on my own, I'm going to lose my shit halfway through.

The trail of people headed into the enormous room is long, but I see Oriel standing in a perfect position to let us know where he is. He's not the one I would have expected to be a beacon since he prefers the shadows, but the inconsistency gets explained when my sharp, fox ears hear Kit tell the panda they should head for Oriel. Slinking along behind them, I see Slash has taken the end seat—which I'm grateful for—and Oriel has the other end of the row. There should be plenty of room for all of us to sit together, so I wait for Kit and Salem to settle in. Once Anton drops in place next to Salem, I hop over the row and take my place between him and Slash.

Thank fuck. This will help a lot, actually.

Slash frowns, leaning forward to look down the row. "Doctor?"

"Oh, for fuck's sake," Kit grumbles as everyone shifts back so he can lean forward, too. He holds up the bandaged arm with a huff. "Yes. See? You don't have to lurk like you did with the food."

My eyes widen as I take in the exchange. What the hell is Slash doing bringing him food and getting him to *our* doctor? Jasper is going to freak the fuck out when he finds out. I turn to look at the shark shifter with an arched brow and he just glares before settling back into his seat silently.

There's quiet in the group for a moment before O braves the question. "What the hell are you talking about… when did he lurk?"

Kit sighs, and I swear, you'd think he's about to poke his own eyes out in frustration. "The night I missed dinner. This asshole stomped up to my room, brought a bunch of food packed up from the kitchen, and demanded I eat because the royal fuckwad made me run a bunch earlier. As much as your leader hates me, most of you guys act like you're my freaking keepers."

You know what? They really—oh, shit.

Putting my hands on my face, I make a soft sound of pain as I realize what's going on—they're all into this kid. Even straight-as-an-arrow Slash has fallen victim to the new guy's vulnerable yet feisty schtick and honestly? It's a goddamn feat. I don't know if I've ever seen over two of us agree on a person in decades, but Kit Camponella has united almost the entire caliphate in their desire to protect him.

I'm not sure if they all get that they want to fuck him, but that's a later issue.

Professor Cedar's voice echoes through the room like a damn loudspeaker, and I cringe as we all stop to get our notes ready. I'm pretty fucking familiar with their kind since there are a decent amount of their hybrids within our family group. Fae usually gravitate to the demons in me, Anton, and X's lines when they're looking to have fun. It makes sense, given their natures, but it also means I can focus on something else besides this lecture.

Scratching my chin, I type information into my laptop furiously as if I'm taking notes, but really, I'm working on the code for the background information. Figuring out five of the seven demons in our caliphate have a crush on this guy means I need to resolve this shit *now*. Jasper won't stop torturing him until I do, and the protectiveness will only escalate if Kit reciprocates with any or all of them. I don't think he's ready for five lovers, but he's definitely soft with Oriel and Salem. They seem to have the most imminent chance of getting him to date them.

My resolve deepens as I run into more and more wormholes, and I frown. I swear, I've never in my life seen information so thoroughly locked down in the human world as Kit's. I have to code magic into my hack and I was hoping to avoid it. It will leave a trace and whoever did this will probably know the intruder came from Discordia's servers. They won't be able to trace *me*, but it will give them the location where the breach originated.

Is this important enough to raise flags outside Hell?

It doesn't take me long to decide that it absolutely is. The infatuation with Kit will only drive a wedge deeper into my group of brothers, and we have to be united. We can't go up against the current king, and our parents, if we're split over a random kid who might not even be here by then.

Taking a deep breath, I start coding spells and hexes into my code as I attack the server denying me.

Here's hoping this doesn't lead to some bigwig crashing into Discordia this weekend or Jasper will have my ass—and not in a good way.

No fucking way am I attending that Hackers Collective bullshit I'm supposed to go to with Zavida. Until he gets his head out of his ass, I refuse to go to some stupid extracurricular where I will know absolutely nothing about what to do and be forced to appeal to him for help. He wasn't an asshat during Intro to Fae, but I could tell he had shit running through his big brain.

Hell if I know why; I didn't bother him.

Since I have four damn hours until dinner and I know at least three of the guys do as well, Dottie and I avoid the dorm. Instead, I give them the slip via a bathroom excuse and take off on my own. Using the map on my app, I take a spin through the academic building, finding all the offices, the laundry, the athletic facilities, and everything else I've missed this week. Knowing how the buildings work in terms of layout calms my anxiety a little, and once I'm done there, I head for the library building to go through all of its nooks and crannies as well.

Looking around carefully, I dart outside, headed for the Arena. It's near to the freshman academic area, and I'd like to see where I'm going to be expected to perform like a fucking monkey, eventually. As I walk in, I take the first set of stairs, monitoring my surroundings with each step. I won't forget that douche Roquefort's promise or even the taunts of Bastion soon.

I know for a fact cocksuckers like them mean it when they promise to come after you.

"But we have an emergency button, right, girl?" I murmur to Dottie. She chitters, but her big eyes don't look sure about it. "I know; I need to carry more than just a knife. I have to find magic or whatever they think I can do. Otherwise, I'm toast."

Dottie holds onto my neck tighter and I sigh softly at the comfort it brings. I'm pushing my own boundaries by doing this, but I'll be damned if I'm going to be some sheltered idiot who can only survive with the bad boy demons watching me. Since my… assault…I've been determined to never let my condition rule. It's no different in Hell than at home.

But this place is dark and goddamn huge—like it's built for a division one football program above ground. I'm climbing for what seems to be forever when I finally reach the top. I'm winded and I grumble because I might have to go to that stupid gym in the dorm's basement. That means I'll see my floor mates even more. I know they're down there a lot, particularly the spoiled royal and his second banana.

Definitely a con for the gym.

"I have to, though," I pant a little as I stand still while I catch my breath. "Running is also an option if the twenty-one feet from knife to stab isn't enough."

My self-defense instructor would be proud of me for remembering that, but not for staying somewhere I know I'll need it. He was adamant about not letting shit get out of hand in my homes following the attack, but I'm a stubborn bitch. I don't like to let bullies win and I don't like admitting when I need help. It makes my anxiety even worse.

When I feel steady again, I open the heavy door to walk out onto the top section of the weird ass seating. The arena is every bit as gigantic as it appeared, and the field is a little bigger than a standard football field. It's covered in obstacles—pits, trenches, lava pools, mini bunkers, targets, and weird embedded symbols. It's like some sort of demon-style American Warrior course that we… duel magically on?

I am in so much fucking trouble.

"What the fuck are you doing here alone?"

The angry voice startles me and I jump about fifty feet in the air, shrieking in a much too girly way. "Back off! I have a knife!"

The shark shifter gives me an annoyed look as he wipes his dripping face off with a towel. "Yeah, well, my teeth are knives, but you don't see me screaming like a little princess about it. Don't make me repeat myself, human."

I hold up a finger, trying to quiet the racing of my pulse and my hammering heart so I can breathe. If I can do that, I can answer him. He taps his foot, looking like he might show me those damned teeth if I don't hurry. Once I have my shit together, I lick my lips. "First, you assholes keep saying I'm not human. Make up your mind. Second, you're not my goddamn keeper, Slash. None of you are. I can go where I please."

His hand comes up to pinch the bridge of his nose and he sucks in a breath before gritting out, "You agreed with the others that it was dangerous for you to wander about without someone. Did you lie to them? I *hate* liars."

He means that.

Pausing as I consider how to say what I need to, I ignore the smug look on his ruggedly handsome face. He's not my usual type because he's a fucking monster—literally and figuratively—but I can't deny the dude is stacked like a brick shithouse. It's even more obvious in the small running shorts and shredded workout shirt, so combined with the scare, I'm having trouble focusing.

"I didn't lie. But…," I rush to continue before he can cut in. "…I can't feel like a pillow prin…ce." Shit, I almost blew that one. His frown lets me know he's not familiar with the term, so I expound. "I don't want to feel like a protected, precious little weakling that has to be with an escort. I'm already smaller than most of you muscle-bound demon meatheads; if I'm also unable to be independent, the bullying will get so much worse. And I don't mean from Prince Prickface, either."

The laugh Slash barks out surprises the hell out of me, and I grin a little as he doubles over. "Prince Prickface. You sure like to take your life in your hands, bantam."

I frown at him, fighting the urge to put my hands on my hips and demand he explain. That, however, would not be very dude-like and I've spent all my bullshit tokens for today. "He pisses me off on purpose. I'll call him whatever the fuck I feel like. If he pulls his head out of his lower intestine, I might use his name."

My grumble gets another bark and I feel pretty damn good. Slash is quiet and non-emotive—outside of glowers—most of the time, and I'm making him laugh. Score one for Kit, baby. Dottie squeaks and tilts her head as I look at her with a small smile. I can't tell if this makes Slash okay, but maybe he's working towards it?

"Okay. I get not wanting to seem like a wimp, so idiots don't bother you more. But it's still not safe until the ceremony. So… if you sit here while I finish my stairs, I'll walk you to the next place. Deal?"

Given he's speaking more words at once than ever, I nod, walking over to one of the odd stadium seats. "Deal. I've got work to do."

He looks relieved and turns to the steps again, calling over his shoulder, "Don't think I missed that you're avoiding Zavida, by the way."

Damnit. Busted.

IT TAKES ANOTHER HALF-HOUR FOR THE HUGE DEMON TO FINISH WHAT LOOKS like a *grueling* workout. He rifles through a gym bag, wiping himself down with a dry towel, then cleans up quickly. By the time he walks over to me, he doesn't stink—no, he smells like the damn ocean breeze and looks irritatingly lickable. Smacking myself internally for noticing, I gather my stuff and get Dottie perched before following him as he lumbers away from the door I entered through to a different one.

"Where are we going?" I ask as I try to hide my fear that he's going to turn on me and take me somewhere to get my ass kicked.

Slash grunts as he stabs the button to an elevator—how did I miss that—and looks over at me. "I'm taking you down the easy way, but also I thought you might like to see the locker room. You can grab your things and shit."

Oh, right. My uniform is about to get whipped to death in magical battle ball or whatever.

"Great," I mutter as we step into the metal cage. "Super excited about that, by the way."

Giving me a toothy grin, the big guy shrugs. "Sometimes we only find our strength when it's born in fire."

I give him a sour look. "Being philosophical will not save my ass when I have to battle people who have magic and the knowledge of how this works. I'll be about as useless as a dildo in a cookie baking contest."

That earns me a slow blink, then another shake of his head. I feel he has no idea how to deal with my sarcasm or my attitude. He's not the first to have that issue and that difficulty is why I didn't bother with making friends at home.

Kat Camponella is weird, off-putting, and unfriendly was perfectly fine with me.

"I'll send you the handbook. You like to study, right? That should help."

Another damn thing to catch up on. I'm never going to get any sleep at this rate. But I know he's trying, so I nod as the doors to the elevator open. "Thanks. That will work."

Slash strides out of the carriage with the confidence of a dude who can wreck damn near anyone in his path and I tag along like the little Looney Tunes dog. We come to a huge set of double doors, and I cringe at the stink emanating from them. Yanking one open, the shark demon smirks and waits for me to enter.

"This is the locker room," he says as he squints at the various guys in states of undress. "I did not think there would be this many people here now."

My eyes widen and I have to find a place on the floor to stare because there's an enormous—both in size and shape—amount of dick dangling about. I'm sure my face is heating, which will be a sure sign that something is wrong. I have to get the attention off of me and out of this haven of nut sacks before I'm even more scarred for life.

"Uh, great. Can you point me to… what I need?" I mumble as I quell the panic in my chest.

"Helpless," he mutters before stomping over to a locker next to his in the corner. He grabs a garment bag out of it, then comes over, shoving it at me. "Here."

"Get your fuck toy out of here, Slash."

The sneering voice makes me raise my gaze and I see a *lot* more of Bastion than I ever wanted to—not that there's much to see. My eyes flick back to his twisted face, then over to the guy who insisted on bringing me here. He says nothing and I almost facepalm when I realize I just chastised him about people assuming I can't handle myself.

Way to go, Kat.

"Get bent, Bastion. That is, if you have enough to bend. I don't have my magnifying glass with me, so I'm not sure. Sorry, man." I paste an evil smirk on my face, hoping that's enough to get the other dudes to look away from me.

Unsurprisingly, my gambit works because the asswad splutters and the other demons howl with laughter. Slash nods at me, and I take that as approval. It might not be, but I'm claiming it, regardless.

"Let's go, Kit. We have dinner to get to and then a meeting."

I frown, squinting at the shark, but I don't ask him about this new meeting here. It's obvious the caliphate works hard to keep their shit under wraps, and it's the only thing I can think of that would require a meeting that late. "Gotcha."

Together we head out of the locker room and I can finally inhale without vomiting. We walk through a few more halls and out another new set of doors without speaking. When we're finally in the fresh air, I suck in cleansing breaths and my companion chuckles.

"It's rather rank in there."

I snort. "It smells like the inside of a kraken's asshole—I think. I've never met one, obviously."

His lips twitch and he leads me away from the arena toward Canto IV. "It's not an entirely inaccurate description."

That makes me grin and I decide to try talking since he's in a good mood. "Why don't we go to the other dorms at all?"

"The classes only intermingle in common areas, sports, and at mealtimes. The douchebag in charge believes it eases interpersonal conflict." He shoots me a look over my shoulder. "He's full of shit, obviously."

"No duh," I reply as I shake my head. Adults are so ridiculously short-sighted with managing young people, even demons, it seems. They totally forget what the hell they're doing the minute they cross thirty, I swear to fuck.

It helps nothing that people are putting off kids until around then now.

"You're always thinking, aren't you?"

I blink, considering his question, before I nod. "Yep. It's because of my conditions. There's a big fucking ratatouille-style mess in there because of my past. I've got enough letters to make alphabet soup."

"Mmm," he says as we walk up the steps to the dorm. "You have much in common with all my brothers in that regard—both the thinking and the issues. We all come from… unfortunate situations in various ways. But here, it's considered a weakness by the elder demons to do the talking thing humans are addicted to."

"Therapy?" I ask. "Like no one in Hell gets therapy? Or medication?"

He holds the elevator open and I step inside as I wait for him to respond. "Medicine for injury or illness, but not… head things."

Well, that explains Jasper fucking Eversore and all his merry men.

"I'm sorry. I know how much it helped me and it feels criminal that you guys are just supposed to deal with it."

He shrugs as the doors open again, gesturing at my door. "It's the way here. We're used to it. Now put your things away. Salem will need your help in the kitchen as he cooks, and we eat in the main room on Fridays. His class is almost over."

"How will I know what to do?" I ask anxiously.

Slash shrugs and gives me one of his shark-like grins. "That's not my problem, bantam. Figure it out. I've got to shower before dinner."

That said, he stomps off and I sigh, digging for my key so I can get into my room.

If I'm lucky, Salem left me a damn note or something—but I'm never lucky.

P rofessor Viscounte is literally the worst. He runs his Kitchen Lab as if he's that screaming human from their cooking channel, and when I didn't submit to his suggestions on my dishes, he locked me in the fucking freezer for an hour. When I got out, he'd taken over my station and completely ruined the shit I was planning on serving for the caliphate's dinner. I wouldn't serve a hellhound the trash he left simmering on my stove, so it all had to be tossed at the end of the session.

Unfortunately, that means whatever Kit did in our room will dictate how late dinner is— something Jasper will blame him for despite my protests.

I'm muttering under my breath angrily when I use the runes to open our door, but it stops when I see what's happening inside. I shake my head to clear it quickly, then shut the door behind me, leaning against it as I watch. Kit's standing on a chair with his back facing me, wearing a dark baggy shirt tied at the spine, baggy shorts, and one of my aprons as he peers down into the pot to stir carefully.

Nothing about that image should be attractive—I can barely see a stripe of pale skin at the knot—but the way he's humming under his breath with the headphones in his ears, oblivious to everything, is cute as fuck. It helps that the scents wafting from my kitchen smell as if he's completing his work to the letter, which means we have some of dinner salvaged.

That's surprising given the ingredients, but Kit isn't phased by shit like that, it seems.

I watch for another moment or two, grinning to myself as he shimmies on the chair. That's when the kinkajou spots me, chittering and waving her tiny paws at my roommate and blowing my cover. I wait until he pulls off the headphones and whirls around, looking at me with narrowed eyes. "Hey, dude. Having fun?"

"Sort of," he mutters with a shrug. "I did little cooking at the last house; my foster mom, Allison, was a control freak. At some prior foster homes, I did a shit ton of work, but nothing fancier than burgers or whatever. This is oddly soothing—I follow the instructions, I watch the food, and I get results."

Nodding at his assessment, I drop my bag near the door and head over. "You seem to be doing okay for the first time alone. Mind if I go change?"

Kit shakes his head. "Nope. I'll hold down the fort with my stuff and when you get back, you can see if I fucked it up. It's possible, you know."

It is, but my nose says it's not the case.

I head into my room, closing the door as I strip off the sweaty clothes from the hot lab. After Gastronomy this morning, I used the break to change and set up all these lists for Kit. I knew the guys would be hangry as fuck after the long day and when I heard through the group chat he stormed out of Arms class, I figured he might hide rather than come here or the cafeteria. Jasper's bullshit and that idiot stinky cheese kid probably pushed the kid's boundaries well beyond his limits.

At least Slash found him and set him up with the Doc. I couldn't decide if I was surprised or not when I found that out during the lectures, but I'm glad about it. Kit looks like he's recovering well; if he hadn't, I would have held our Prince to account myself. His behavior is getting increasingly erratic and illogical with our new initiate; I'm tiring of it.

"Enough brooding, Salem. You'll turn into Oriel," I tell myself as I rummage through my drawers to find a pair of university sweats and a vee neck tee. Leaving my feet bare, I tousle my hair a little and apply some much needed deodorant, then head back to the kitchen.

Kit looks up, smiling as his hair flops in his eyes. "Took you long enough. I was going to send Dottie in to check on you soon."

I chuckle as I walk up to the counter and his familiar rushes over to offer one of her grapes. The guy next to me doesn't know it, but that's one of the best things that a bonded animal can do to show trust—present you with some of their food willingly. It means his little beast likes me and wouldn't make a fuss if I get any closer to her person than I do now.

Shoving the grape up Jasper's nose doesn't count; it was a deliberate snub, and he knows it.

"Thanks, shorty," I say to the small rodent as I pop the fruit in my mouth. "You're the bomb."

"I made everything you said in the notes—which really helped, so thanks—but you didn't come in with trays from your class." Kit tilts his head curiously. "What happened?"

My rueful expression makes him groan and I throw my hands up. "I know; I know. But the fuckface little weasel running my lab ruined all my shit while I was being punished by freezing my nuts off."

He frowns, thinking about it for a moment, but then he does something I couldn't have predicted. Kit jumps off of the stool, rushing over to me before he runs his hands up and down my arms. His expression is full of concentration as he nudges me until I spin, lifting my shirt up to look at my inked back, then turns me again to grab my hands. I stand there, letting him inspect my fingers, my toes, the tips of my ears, and everywhere he wants until he finally steps back.

Then I see the panic and fear in his eyes and I know; he's known someone who got punished that way before.

"I, uh, I'm sorry," he says, flushing bright red as his pulse slows from the hammering thrum it was as he examined me. "I didn't mean to overstep; I just…"

"You were worried about me," I say in a low voice, moving closer as he backs away. I'm not sure what I'm doing, but the primal parts of me have plans. Kit swallows hard, continuing to back up until he's trapped against the counter with nowhere to go. "Because you know what happens when someone's locked in a freezer."

"I…I…" He blinks up at me and I can feel the fear rising from him, but the scent that comes with it doesn't match. Our new floor mate smells like pheromones, which the demon *and* the panda both like. "Yes. I know. But… um. It wasn't… me."

At least I don't have to hunt anyone down now. That's comforting.

"Was your… friend… hurt afterward? Is that why you learned where to check?" I lean, whispering my question in his ear as I inhale the scent of food and desire with a rumble of happiness.

Kit's hands land on my chest, provoking another growl that makes him squirm a bit. "Yes. I… He got hurt because they didn't take him to a hospital when… But, um, they removed him not long after. I just… I had to know what to check afterward."

Pulling back, I smile softly at him. He acts like he has a stick up his ass, but it's a front. Kit Camponella cares a lot about people, but he's learned they aren't permanent.

Being one of us is, and I'm going to help him realize that if it kills me.

"You're an odd duck, Kit Kat. Yes, I know Annie and X use that, but I like it." I smile as he looks up at me with wide eyes full of uncertainty. My hand comes up to push the hair out of his face, tucking the longer part behind his ear. "Am I making you nervous?"

His head shakes, then he nods, then he shakes it again. Finally, Kit croaks, "I don't know."

"Hmm," I reply, humming a little of the song he was singing when I came in. "Good to know. I'd prefer it if you didn't get scared when I touch you, but trauma is a funny master. It pops up even when you don't want it to, huh?"

Kit's lashes flutter as he looks down and I'm slightly entranced by how thick they are. I'm certainly pan, so this attraction isn't weird, but I rarely get distracted from cooking by… anything. I watch as he swallows, then licks his lips slowly. When he lifts his gaze to mine, I *almost* push forward. But the slight tinge of confusion on his delicate features gives me pause.

No. it's definitely not the time to rush and make him panic.

"I think we should get to prepping the meat, don't you?"

The disappointment that flitters over his expression before he nods makes the demon inside of me purr with happiness. Whether he knows how to deal with it or even wants to admit it, my new roomie is interested in exploring with me. I'm not sure he has a damn clue about what we'd explore—other than a clinical knowledge because he's not an idiot—but he wants to find out.

"Y-Yes. Yes. We should, uh, check the sides, and um… what we'll be… making now?" he almost squeaks as I pull back to give him room to collect himself.

A low chuckle escapes my lips and I wink at him, turning to walk over to the fridge. My tail is doing its thing behind me, sleek and duotone in demon form because I'm aroused. I know it will intrigue him because of how he acted in class earlier in the week, so I don't hide it. Curiosity is a good thing when he's going to find out a hell of a lot more than how big my cock is if we go any further in the future.

Demon hybrids come with a lot of surprises in the bedroom.

"Salem?"

I look over my shoulder at him before answering. "Yes, Kit Kat?"

"Did you think the ingredients were going to make me freak out?"

His lopsided, knowing grin hits me in the gut, and I have to swivel back to the fridge before he sees the flashing of my eyes. Kit is ridiculously adorable when he's frumpy and mussed like this—something I have a hard time resisting, no matter who evokes the feeling. The guys say it's part of the panda thing, but I'm not so sure. Non-shifter pandas in Kit's previous world aren't super bright, despite being very good at looking cute.

"I did, but I wasn't being mean. I hoped that you'd get over it so we could cook together. It's nice having someone in my space to talk to." I look at him again, my cheeks flushing this time. "I didn't actually know I felt that way until you were here, by the way. The guys have always given me a private room because I'm impossible to live with."

Kit frowns, his face screwing up in confusion. "That's weird, man. You've been cool to me the whole time. In fact, you were the first one to *not* be a super dick."

Pulling out several types of meat, I walk over to the counter and spread them out on the cutting boards. As I work, I consider his words, glad he didn't press for me to respond right off the bat. The various slabs of meat get sliced and ready within minutes, so I move to gather up some shit to make quick marinades.

"Well, I probably deserved the label the other times," I admit. "I'm a tyrant in the kitchen, though I guess since you've been so easily taught and respect-ful, that didn't come out. I snore like a buzz saw—they say—and I have trouble staying awake, so roomies in my classes get mad about alarm clock duty."

Kit scratches something on his face, smearing some of the flour from his bread duty on it. He doesn't notice, just keeps kneading the dough as he replies. "I don't hear the snoring 'cause I wear sleep headphones. I can't sleep without the silence, though, sometimes I can't sleep with it. You haven't noticed my insomnia pacing, which is pretty cool, and I'm fine with you running your kitchen. Being a foster kid meant nothing was ever really mine in common rooms, so I'm used to following other people's rules in that regard."

This fucking guy… he's like a giant of ball of contradictions and mysteries. I fucking love it.

"Then we make a good pair, Kit Camponella," I say with a grin, and he ducks his head to study the dough intently. "But then, you do well with my friends Oriel and X as well."

His head jerks up and he looks surprised, then the red color intensifies on his face, spreading to his neck. "They're, um… They're nice, too. Not like the fuck faced Prince, I mean."

Laughing as I plop the meats in the various bowls to soak, I arch a brow. "No one in the history of Hell has *ever* called Oriel 'nice.' He's even more reclusive than me, normally. X might be a different story—he and Anton are our social butterflies."

Kit rounds the counter, then bends to get into the cabinet with the baking sheets. "They're very welcoming, even when they're trying not to look like it. I knew at the first meeting they wouldn't be as bad as they tried to project."

Huh. That's unusual—Annie and X are fucking fantastic at shielding.

"Who did you worry about afterward?" I ask curiously as I watch him pop the breads into the ovens.

"Jasper, of course. Slash. I wasn't sure about Zavida, but he's shown his true colors." That sentence is punctuated with a sniff of disdain as Kit moves back to his chair, standing on it to get a better view of the shit he's working with. "Though maybe I was wrong about the big guy, too."

I blink, my jaw dropping as I stare at the half-human methodically peeling and chopping fruit for the dessert. "What?"

"He's been a decent being to me now three times, and statistically, seven times can change an opinion. I'm half-way to thinking he's not a goddamn mindless toadie. Only time will tell."

Slash only mother hens people he really likes… and it's never dudes. Hearing he's been secretly doing shit for Jasper's least favorite floor resident is like giving the dude a fucking medal. I'm shocked as shit and I have no idea what to do with that information.

All I know is…Kit Camponella must really be something special.

I've never been so glad to huddle at the end of a table and pretend I'm invisible during a meal as I was when Salem and I finished cooking. The entire experience made me hot and nervous and unable to figure out what the hell to do. This damn school is full of shit that makes my emotions tilt off the scales, and I don't know how to deal with any of it. I've never actually wished for therapy sessions before, but I'm kind of missing it now.

That's never a good sign.

"Kit helped me save dinner, you know," Salem says with a smug expression. "He's a pretty good protégé."

My eyes stay on the plate as I pretend not to choke on my meat. I was hoping everyone would leave me alone while they talked and ate. It would give me time to figure out my feelings about the moment Salem and I had in the kitchen, and maybe I'd know what to say if he brought it up.

But no…

"You never use that word and you swore you'd never take one." Jasper's words are tinged with venom and I duck my head again, unwilling to engage with the asshole while I'm so jumbled inside.

Unfortunately, the lazy panda laughs and says, "I know, right? But he's doing so well, I might let him apprentice next semester. He's joining the team, so it works out great."

The room gets so silent I can hear the Prince's teeth grinding—at least, I think I can. It's probably my imagination, but given the searing glare I can feel on me, he's definitely pissed. I stay quiet, stabbing my Hell veggie things with my fork and shoving some into my mouth to make sure I won't provoke him. Dealing with his bullshit while I'm trying to figure out how Salem didn't trigger every single one of my trauma buttons is asking too much for Friday dinner.

"We've only been here a week," Zavida says softly, and I have to chomp the crunchy root veggie to make sure I don't bitch him out, too.

Spineless little shit—making me think he was cool at first and then turning out to be a simpering sycophant.

"But what a fucking week, man," X interjects gleefully. "Admit it, we haven't had this much fun in a long time."

"Fun?" Jasper sneers, the disdain in his tone practically dripping onto the table. "You've lost your mind, Xerxes."

Oriel scoffs, and I look up, meeting his eyes briefly before I go back to staring at my dinner. "He's right. I've enjoyed having things to do that are not simply plotting for our... future. We've been focused on it for so long that I've gotten bored with my own distractions."

"You're always bored," Slash notes in a flat tone. "That's nothing new, O."

"True, true," the crow demon says. "But I think fresh blood is invigorating us. There's more... *feeling* than we've had in forever. And I don't just mean the hate for the Big Bad."

Must... be small and quiet... say nothing...

"Are you sure it's not that you enjoy having a new toy to figure out?" The Prince drawls lazily. "You enjoy taking things apart and putting them back together again more than anyone I know."

"Stop."

I blink, raising my gaze to the huge shifter sitting next to the asshole taunting me. His dig hurt and definitely hit a trigger because I was immediately spiraling out. But now I'm looking at a person who I thought would never challenge the bullying dragon in public with shock on my features.

"Excuse me?" Jasper grinds out as he grips his fork like he's going to stab someone with it. "What did you say?"

Slash crosses his enormous arms over his chest as he glares at the dragon. "Oriel is a sneaky motherfucker, but he does not manipulate people. His line is avaricious, not angry or desirous."

Now I'm chastising myself for thinking the big guy is dumb, too. This day truly sucks.

"He's right," Anton says as he shares a look with X. "We certainly are capable and have done such things in the past to protect the caliphate, but Oriel's curiosity for knowledge isn't based on hurting people."

Salem bumps my shoulder, but I stay quiet as I process this conversation. It feels like I'm missing clues because of my lack of knowledge about this world. I'll need to study lineage more so I can figure out what the hell they're talking about. I hate being in the dark, and even though there are bigger things going on here, it's annoying the shit out of me. Of course, that's probably just me compartmentalizing my fears about the sexy moment with Salem and the fact that Slash just hit his fourth action that makes me question my preconceived notions.

"Thank you for weighing in, but you aren't here for your intellectual observations."

Nope. That's enough.

Slamming my hands on the table, I rise to my feet and look the dickhead right in the eyes. I hate how he keeps making me do this shit, especially when I'm not ready for it. "Fuck off, Jasper. Leave him alone."

Every head in the room turns to look at me as I growl softly. I won't let him be shitty to the rest of them because they feel sorry for me. Except for him and Zavida, the others have been decent to me when I needed it, and they don't deserve to be paid back by him shoving pointy sticks in their own traumas. I can handle myself; I have been for a long time.

"I'm sorry. Did you think someone was talking to you? How embarrassing."

I stab a mushy potato-like thing on my plate, pull my fork back, and fling it at the smug looking royal. It smacks him right in the face—thank fuck—splattering on his handsome visage in a way I couldn't have predicted. My hand flies to my mouth, preventing the howl of laughter from escaping as I gape at my work.

He's going to murder me.

Slash snorts, then leans back in his chair, tilting back as loud, deep laughs fill the room. Oriel is next, followed by Salem, and finally, Anton and X join in like a chorus of basses to tenors harmonizing in their humor. Zavida keeps rubbing his lips and I feel even he wants to snicker, but he can't bring himself to defy the Prince.

"You'll pay for that, Camponella."

"What a cartoon villain thing to say," I reply drily. "Very scary."

Jasper picks up the cloth napkin on his lap, wiping his face off with an evil smirk. "Yes, you will. You've fucked up my caliphate—something I didn't think possible—and I will make you sorry for that."

Rolling his my eyes, I sigh heavily as I ask, "And how do you plan to do that, Prince Dickface?"

He stands, his face cleaned of the vegetable mess as he straightens. "By inducting you tonight, of course."

Somehow, I don't think the guys told me everything about this—the Prince looks far too gleeful.

Fuck.

"WHAT THE HELL IS GOING ON?" I WHISPER TO ORIEL AS HE AND SALEM flank me on either side. They exchange a look and I elbow them in the ribs hard.

"Fuck, ow, Kit Kat," Salem mutters as he rubs his side. "Jasper and the others are setting up the ritual shit for the induction ceremony. I thought you understood that when he made his whole 'scary cult leader' declaration."

I lick my lips, chanting the five sense mantra in my head so I don't freak out. "You realize that since I didn't grow up in Hell, I haven't caught up to your however fucking many centuries of knowledge, right? I don't know what the fuck that means, except I know Jasper wouldn't be happy about it if it wasn't going to *suck.*"

Oriel cringes and scratches the back of his head. "Yeah, it's rough and the adjustment period can vary, but…"

My eyes widen, and I grab his arm. "I'm going to need more than 'a bit rough,' Oriel. I do really badly in situations where I can't control things and I get scared."

"We won't let you get hurt," Salem says with a yawn. "I swear on a stack of Anarchist Cookbooks."

Tilting my head, I squint at him in confusion. "Those are… for making bombs, not food, Salem. And how is that supposed to make me feel better?"

"Because he knows the chaos demon who encouraged the human to write it and he'd never lie about his mom." Oriel shrugs when I gape, his dark eyes watching the door the rest of them are behind. "Plus, he's fantastic at making exploding food *and* I'm agreeing with him."

Putting my face in my hands, I scrub my palms over it to quell the sparkling sensation under my skin. My anxiety is ramping up despite their reassurances, and it feels like the attack coming is going to be a doozy. "Even if I did trust you—which I don't—I still need to know what is going to happen when they come out of there. If you don't quit dancing around it, I may not be upright when they come to get me."

I raise my eyes, waiting for the looks of pity that usually accompany this admission, but neither of them even blinks. "Stop that, you weird ass demons. Say something."

"Kit Kat, we know you have anxiety. If you think admitting you need something is going to make us turn into Prince Prick in there, you have another thing coming." Salem grins and I feel my cheeks heat at the softness in his expression. "I meant the apprentice thing and they're right, I never say that."

Frowning, I scrunch my hands in my short locks. "After I helped you twice? That's nonsense."

Oriel rolls his eyes. "Shit, fine. I never let anyone come to the Guild with me. They knew that when Jasper assigned it to you. He thought I'd kick you out and humiliate you in public just like he thought Salem would pelt you with food like he did his past roommate attempts."

"What? When did… I mean, past attempts?" This information makes my gut clench in anticipation of something terrible. I don't know why, but I feel like I'm hanging off the edge of a cliff by my fingertips.

Salem grins, shrugging as he grabs my hand. "Do you think this is the first time some fuckhead like Jas' dad or Lucian have tried to infiltrate the caliphate by putting some loser on our floor? I mean, maybe not *exactly* this, but there have definitely been a bunch of hare-brained schemes to join us over the years."

"Is that why Jasper hates me so much? Because he thinks I'm just another plant?" Somehow, that actually makes it worse and I don't know why.

"Hell, no," Oriel growls. "We mostly froze the others out until they gave up. But I knew you were different the minute our illustrious leader dropped you off to Salem and stormed all over the floor in fury. He sucks ass at hiding his emotions."

Neither is making any sense, and my heart rate is escalating by the moment.

"What the fuck does that even mean?" I ask in frustration. "Jasper hates me for no reason and has since he picked me up from that frigid asshole in charge of this asylum."

The panda demon gives me a look that mirrors my own, then shakes his head. "Obviously, the dude is determined to be obtuse. Let's just tell him whatever you think we can get away with, O."

"Thanks," I grumble.

Oriel sighs, leaning back in his chair with his fingers steepled in front of him. "The ceremony isn't the part you need to worry about. There's chanting and weird languages and candles and shit. You know, everything your people stole so they could pretend to be worshippers."

My brows furrow and I purse my lips. "I don't think that's at all accurate."

"Whatever. The point is, that part is pretty normal, but once the chants gather our lines' powers, that's when the weird shit begins," Salem adds as his fingers thread with mine. "There's a light show and everything gets super intense, then normally the inductee's powers would join to bind it all together."

"I don't *have* any powers," I grind out as I glare at them one at a time. "What the hell will happen when I fail to 'merge' powers or whatever?"

"We don't know," they say in unison.

My jaw drops open, and the only sound that comes out is a high-pitched squeak.

"I went to get Dottie from our room when I said I was going to the bathroom," Salem says before making a soft chitter sound. My kinkajou comes scampering in, climbing my leg to wrap around my neck immediately. "We really don't have a fucking clue what will happen, but I know having her in the room can't be a bad idea."

It's sweet, but I'm still stuck on the 'we don't know' part.

"I appreciate that, but I don't get why you'd push this if you didn't know what would happen. It's not doing wonders for my trusting you, either."

The two demons look at me seriously, and I'm surprised when Oriel grabs my other hand. They're both squeezing my shaking palms in theirs, but the warmth isn't comforting. It just makes me worry that I'm being tricked. No one does shit like this unless they want something, and somehow, in the confusion of the relocation to Hell, I forgot that.

"X suggested it first, but we got on board because otherwise, you wouldn't be able to withstand what's coming, Kit Kat."

Arching a brow at Salem, I snort. "Uh-huh. And what the hell is that?"

"War. Hell is headed for a war, and you were determined to stay here for school, so… You need to be ready for war." The panda grimaces, but stops when the door opens and Anton pokes his head out.

"We're ready."

I'm sure as fuck not, but here we go.

Jasper insisted we set this damn ceremony up in the most formal, ridiculous way possible. I have no idea where the fuck Zav got all the shit to have it so quickly, but the Kitsuné are a resourceful species. Paired with his demon side and off-the-charts smarts, I guess he was the best candidate for the job. X and I got tasked with the atmosphere once we had the supplies—not surprising, either. What made me arch one of my perfectly sculpted brows was the heated discussion our fearless leader and his general had in the corner—it was obviously contentious.

By the time we finished the set-up, the room looked sufficiently like a human horror movie set with Satanists and witches. It's a bit much, honestly, but our Prince wants to terrify the plucky new kid. Nothing here will harm Kit, which was X's biggest concern. He might punch Jasper when we're done—and I'd pay to see that—but nothing he planned will scar his psyche. I think that's what Slash was arguing with the dumbass about, and I'm glad he won.

"We're ready," I say as I poke my head out the door to look at Kit as he sits with Salem and Oriel. They each glare at me and I hold my hands up as Kit rises to join me at the door to the altar room. "Stop acting like this was my idea, assholes."

Kit sighs, patting Salem on the arm. "It's okay, guys. Anton isn't to blame for this spectacle."

How did he know?

I must look shocked, because the dude grins and shrugs. "How could it not be some convoluted bullshit that's far more intricate than necessary? Prince Prickface wants to punish me, and he's making all of you take part. I'll take my lumps like a good…boy… and then maybe he'll leave me the fuck alone."

The stutter makes me blink, but everyone's anxiety is different. Not knowing what is in store for him is probably excruciating, and I don't blame the guy for having brain blips. As he passes by me, I feel a 'plink' on my shirt, and my mouth drops open. Kit's little rat threw a seed at me and it definitely has a smug expression on its face. "What the…"

"Not on the inside yet, dude," Salem says with a chuckle. "Dottie's very protective of her owner. At least you didn't get that stuck up your nose."

I shudder, backing away a little to give the beast a wide berth. "Good to know."

"Come on, man, just take us to the big room and let's get this over with," Oriel grumbles as he follows behind Kit. "We know Jas has some ridiculous shit planned, and it's going to piss everyone off, so let's get it over with."

Stopping at the double doors to the main area, I pause, hoping to figure out what I can warn the guy about without Jasper freaking out. "Just know that this isn't how it's done anymore, and there's a reason it's being done this way today."

"No shit, Anton. It's because your Prince is a fucking psycho," Kit retorts drily. "Open the doors. I'm as ready as I ever will be."

I nod, tugging the huge wood and iron door open to reveal the dark rooms full of candles. We set the corners, the circle, the pentagram, and the normal trappings first, but that's where normalcy ended. Jasper insisted on turning the room into a dank cave of mystery with skulls and horned imagery Zav pulled out of storage in the basement. There are incense burners hanging all over, emanating spicy scents like basil, amber, musk, frankincense, myrrh, and mastic. It's over the top, especially since the last time we did this as a group, it was in a fucking locker room in elementary school.

The place smelled like dirty gym shorts, and it worked just fine.

"Enter, supplicant," Jasper says from beneath the stupid robe he's got everyone wearing. "But know that…"

Kit snorts, covering his mouth for a second as he gets a grip on himself. "Fucking *Christ*, man. Tell me you don't have '*spes omnes relinquite, o vos intrantes*[1]' in your speech or I'm gonna have a real hard time keeping a straight face."

"You speak Latin?"

That voice comes from under the hood with black lace quickly glued on it, so I know it's my Xerxes. His excitement makes my lips curve up despite the ridiculous situation the Prince has us in. I bet his question has more to do with Drama Club than this nightmare.

"I do not," our new inductee says flatly. "But I definitely know Dante's Inferno, and one ex-family member was Catholic, soooo…"

Everyone pauses for a moment as that admission hangs in the air. Even Jasper didn't think to ask because obviously, *Kit is here in Hell*, but maybe someone needs to pose the question. Before I can open my mouth, Salem grabs his hand and blurts, "They didn't baptize you, right?"

"Uh, no. Why?"

Jasper flips his hood off, his face a mask of fury that his dry ice filled fever dream is ruined. "Because, you little twerp, if you were, this would really fucking hurt. It wouldn't kill you, but you'd be sorry for quite a while."

"I *told* you we rushed this," Slash mutters as he pulls his hood off as well. "Zav couldn't find—"

"I can find anything. There's something very wrong with his files. We all know what I found and—"

"*Excuse me!*" The in-fighting stops and all eyes fall on the rumpled guy standing in the middle of the circle, looking ready to stab the next person who speaks. "I don't *care* about any of that. I wasn't baptized—probably good if you assholes think I'm a demon—and I have no idea why whatever file Zavida is looking for is hard to find. What I know is that I want this damn ceremony over with so I can go back to my room and be *left alone*."

Blinking, I stop forward, hoping to press pause on #TeamJasper before they start again. "Kit is right. It's getting late, the set-up took forever, and it's been a long day. Let's do this shit."

"These capes are hot as fuck," X says and we all know that's their way of agreeing.

"Fine!" The Prince says, throwing his hands up. "Kneel in the middle of the circle, Kit. Close your eyes and place your hands palms up in front of you."

"Uh, *fuck no*, because that sounds like the start of some terrible frat prank that will go very wrong."

The dragon growls and looks at the rest of us impatiently. "One of you, please help me. For fuck's sake, we're never getting out of here."

"Look, you damn diva, I wasn't—"

Oriel walks into the circle, putting his hand on Kit's shoulder. I frown, because that's two of them who seem to be allowed to invade his space without the slightest reprimand. "Kit Kat, we won't let him do something awful. That really is how it starts."

He looks up at the crow shifter, gauging his face before sighing. "Fine. Here I go, making a *Pretty Woman*-sized mistake simply because I want to sleep on that damn cloud you rich dicks called a mattress."

"Do the chanting and shit, Jas. Get this over with," Slash commands as he rocks from foot to foot.

Sharks don't like to stay still, and all.

"*Hac nocte portam lunae aperimus.*[2]" Jasper's voice is powerful as he holds his hand up to the open ceiling to look at the pitch black night. "*Sub Regis oculo Sanguinis, Ossa, Cineres, et Flammae, sanguinem novum tenebris deferimus.*[3]"

I can see Kit trembling as he listens, but the booming Latin sounds scarier than it is. Finally, Jasper asks who presents the new blood to the gate, and we all respond. "*Caliphatem Principum et Furum facimus.*[4]"

"Be nice if I fucking knew what anyone was saying," Kit mutters, but he keeps his eyes closed.

"Quiet," the Prince growls before starting again. "State your name, supplicant."

"I can't very well state my name *and* be quiet. I don't know sign language, Jasper Eversore."

Salem and Oriel have to cover their mouths as they snicker and even Slash has the hint of a grin on his face when our leader stomps his foot like a kid.

"Don't ruin this or I swear I'll…"

"What? You'll what? Refuse to let me in the 'Ancient Society of No Homers'? Be fucking for real," Kit says as he stays perfectly still in the position we asked him to. When no one answers, he sighs heavily. "*Fine.* My name is Kit Camponella and I'm super excited to join the Rancho Carne Toros! Go Toros!"

"Lucifer's sweaty ball sack, I didn't think I could like this guy anymore, but now…" X leans in to whisper in my ear and I bite my lower lip.

Yep, I definitely have to get to know Kit better. I see where this is headed.

"Are you done with the smart mouth, human? Because we could have finished already if you weren't determined to be a smart assed little shit."

I'm pretty sure if his eyes weren't closed, Kit would roll them. Regardless, he zips his lips as he waits for our dramatic royal to continue. Salem is holding the familiar, and I have to admit, it's kind of cute to see the little thing perched on his enormous bulk.

"This step requires you to repeat after me. It's in Latin and it has to be, so if you're worried about translation… it means you swear loyalty above all others to the caliphate and no matter what, you will strive to ensure the happiness and safety of your brothers for all eternity."

"Someone who speaks Latin give me a clue if he's lying about that?" Kit says and Salem grunts his response. "Thanks. Go ahead."

"*Testor fidem fratribus, caliphate nostro, corde et mente, in eternum.*[5]"

"You're good," Salem says softly.

Kit repeats the phrase almost perfectly, and it makes me grin. There's definitely more in him than a fragile human, even if he isn't ready to admit that yet. He's struggled a little since he arrived here, but not like he should have if that were the case. The air alone should have had him coughing and wheezing, but other than his anxiety and PTSD, the kid's right as rain.

"*Tenebrae factae sumus omnes, quae pandimus in umbris. Ut in unum, extendemus potestatem nostram ad omnes mundi angulos prout intendimus.*[6]"

"Still okay," Oriel interjects. "It's the whole made of darkness, spread it around shit."

His lips purse for a second, but our new initiate repeats the phrase. The floor shakes as he finishes and I flash a concerned look at Jasper. He's not paying attention, though, because the dumbass is half-shifting. I don't know if he meant to or not, but that question is answered when Slash lets out a snarl as his body gets bigger and his massive set of teeth drop in his mouth.

Shit.

"Maybe we should…"

"*Virtus omnis lapsae per venas fluitant Donec desinat tempus. Sanguine signamus hunc daemonium nobis; in perpetuum teneamur!*[7]"

Neither of my brothers give Kit the go ahead because they're busy dealing with feathers and a poofy tail, so I look over at X, but they're similarly afflicted. The soft hiss of their cobra lets me know I don't have long, so I yell, "Go, Kit!"

I barely get the words out before my tail feathers sprout and my body forces me to half-shift into my demon hybrid form. We all have three forms and I have no idea how much Kit was told about us, so I worry that he's going to lose his shit when this is over. Unfortunately, none of us seem to have control over it, and that's immensely bad.

No sooner than the words leave his mouth, it's like someone yanked the poor guy off the ground by a string. He's suspended in air, legs akimbo and palms still up when a bolt of magic pulses through the opening in the ceiling. My eyes cut to the others and we all stare with jaws slack as Kit crackles with the energy like he's a fucking X-man. The room is silent for a brief second, then a loud roar echoes through the room and a light so blinding I can't keep my eyes open fills the altar chamber.

That can't be good.

I PICK MYSELF UP OFF THE GROUND, GROANING IN PAIN AS I DUST THE DEBRIS off of me. The first thing I do is check for the rest of our caliphate—but the bond is intact. In fact, I'd almost say it's *stronger*, which is odd. X grunts and I reach down to help them up carefully. We're all still half-shifted and I have no idea what happened after the bright light, so I don't even know how long we've been out.

"Fuck me," Jasper mutters as he flicks his tail behind him in irritation.

"How 'bout you go fuck yourself, dickwad?"

The sound of Kit's voice makes me let out an enormous sigh of relief, but I don't know where he is. Leaving Xerxes to get Zav on his feet, I stride over to an immense pile of rubble that is shifting slowly. Motherfucker, that pile could kill a skinny dude like him. "Salem, Slash, get the hell over here."

The two huge idiots lumber over pretty quickly once it occurs to them why I'm yelling. Both pick up rocks, hurling them aside as we dig through the mess to find our newest member. When we finally get to the bottom, I can't help it—I literally fucking choke.

Kit Camponella is lying there covered in dust, ash, blood, and injuries, but that's only because he has patches of scales that have appeared on his skin.

He's definitely going to lose his shit; I was right.

1. abandon all hope ye who enter here.
2. Tonight, under the moon's light, we open the gate.
3. Under the eye of the King of Blood, Bones, Ash, and Flames, we bring new blood to the darkness.
4. We do, the caliphate of Princes and Thieves.
5. I swear fealty to my brothers, our caliphate, in both heart and mind, for all eternity.
6. We are all made of the darkness that unfolds in the shadows. As one, we will spread our power to all corners of the universe as intended.
7. May the power of the fallen and all his children flow through our veins until time stops. With blood, we seal this demon to us; forever may we be bound as one.

Bright light fills my eyes when they crack open and pain explodes in my head.

Ugh. I feel like a fucking dump truck hit me.

Swallowing past the dry ache in my throat, I take a slow, even breath in, wincing when it hurts. Damn, I was hoping if I moved a little, the dull ache covering my entire frame wouldn't kick up a notch. Unfortunately for me, whatever bullshit happened to me isn't on board with letting me get my bearings. I let my eyes close so the burning in my eyeballs stops and the throb recedes a little.

"Kit? Kit! Oh, shit, man, he's awake!"

The sound makes me cringe, and despite the excited tone in the speaker's voice, my brain is far too fuzzy to even place it. Obviously, it's one of the seven fucking demons who are responsible for this nonsense; I just can't make my mind sharpen enough to figure out which one. That's a problem for later, I suppose.

Thundering footsteps echo in my ears as someone responds to the call, and I wince again. I have no idea why they're stomping around like goddamn Shrek, but it's gotta stop. Preparing myself for pain, I open my mouth to croak, "Shhhhh."

A blast of worry rolls over me, blanketing my emotions with fear like I'm being mummified. It's so trippy. I blink rapidly as I try to cope with the intensity of the feeling battering me. Whatever I'm lying on dips and a soft voice says, "Dude, chill. I think… I mean, I'm not the expert, but I think your emotions are hurting him."

"They are? How?"

Not another argument. These dipshits argue constantly, and I don't have the spoons right now.

"Look at him. He's shrinking into the bed. Get Dottie. Maybe it will help."

The comment helps me, because I'm pretty sure it narrows who is talking despite their voices sounding like they're coming from the bottom of a well. I don't think Slash, Jasper, Zavida, or even Anton know enough about me to remember my girl's name. It has to be one of the remaining three. I feel safer with that extrapolation given my current physical condition, so I let my body relax against what I now realize is someone's bed.

Please let it be mine or I may have an issue when I get a better grip.

My throat works again, and my eyes flutter as the dry ache slices into me again. I feel movement, and suddenly, a straw is being placed against my lips. I suck gently, grateful for whichever one figured out what I needed, and when the cool liquid slides downward, I almost cry in relief. I don't know what the shit happened, but I don't know if I've ever been this physically hurt since the incident freshman year.

"Kit, I think you can hear me. Maybe you're hurting a lot and that makes sense, but blink once if you can hear us."

I can do that. My eyes do as instructed, and I hear more than a sigh of relief. It helps me to know there are at least *three* people in the room, but it could be more. My senses are haywire—much like my brain—and I'm getting a lot of weird emotional feedback, sort of smashing into my consciousness right now.

Of course, I could have a concussion or something and none of that would even be real, so who knows?

Another voice creeps in, low, but quiet. "You're likely in some pain, though we had the Doc come give you things to help with that. I realize that might creep you out because you weren't awake when Dank checked you, but no one other than him was in the room. You can ask him when you're doing better."

Good catch, whoever. I would have had a fucking panic attack on the damn spot if I thought those guys were all leering at me when I was out cold and…. *oh no.*

Oh, no, no no no no.

He said Dank examined me. That means their doctor has to know my secret. Did he tell them? He couldn't have or I'd probably have awakened in a human hospital, not in Hell, right? They definitely wouldn't keep my secret, even if some of them kind of tolerate me. Their vengeance would be swift after the whole induction thing we just did.

I can't help the rising feeling of dread pouring through me like a wildfire, and my breaths get shorter as it increases. Digging my hands into the soft material under me, I squeeze my closed eyes, chanting in my head to hopefully curb what I know is coming. I count; I recite mantras. But nothing helps as the spiky anxiety continues to mount, tensing my body and jacking my heart rate into the stratosphere.

You can do this, Kat; fight it.

But my mind is too weak and my body is weaker, so my words of encouragement to myself don't help. A fierce itch starts on my hands and feet—as usual—and I'm too exhausted to scratch it like normal, so it just burns uncomfortably as I lie still. My gut clenches, then roils like it wants to heave the water up and maybe more, but it expels nothing… yet. The pounding in my ears gets louder and bright spots dance beneath my lids as the vibration in my body pulses with my blood pressure. I pant softly, shaking as I struggle to get the reaction under control before it knocks me out cold again.

"Kit, calm down."

As if that phrase has ever, in the history of humanity, helped anyone actually do such a thing.

I swallow again when I notice my fingers are trembling. That will move through me like a seizure and I'm too frozen to explain that to my watchers. My panic attack is going to lead to a flashback; I know it now. My injured state—whatever it is—is keeping me from preventing the progression. These guys are going to get a crash course in what's it really likely to have Kat Camponella tied to you and they will not like it.

Figures this shit would happen when I have the least ability to stop it—that's my life in a nutshell.

"Fucking hell, Salem, get the familiar over here. I don't know what's going on, but I think he's getting worse."

Dottie is sitting on my stomach within seconds, then she chitters and climbs up my chest to curl up in the crook of my neck. Her tiny paws and soft nuzzles work like a magic I've never known. I almost wind myself from the shock alone when my limbs untense and my heart rate slows slightly. Oriel— I think—was right to ask Salem to bring her in to me.

"His blood presssssure is going down. Good plan, O," the other voice says.

That tell just identified it as X, but they rarely shows their shifter side, I thought. I frown as the fear and panic subside slowly, realizing I need to see what is actually going on around me, even if it hurts. Dottie burrows closer, rubbing her tiny face against my skin, and I sigh as warmth fills me. My little thieving friend is one of the best surprises I've ever had and this just clinches that opinion.

I give my body a few more moments to wind down, then I force my lids open to squint around the room. There's not a lot of light, despite what I thought earlier, but I'm surprised to see four half-shifted demons staring at me with various expressions on their faces. When I look at each one, a feeling forms in my gut, and it's like I'm sensing how they feel. Oriel is the one whose worry is gnawing at him. Salem feels guilty, X is afraid, and Anton is confused.

What the hell is with this shit?

"What… happened?"

They look at one another, then at me, and finally, Oriel takes my hand gently. "You said all the words. Then after the last bit, this tremendous wave of power sort of crumbled the fucking ceiling, and we all shifted. By the time we got control, you were buried under a shit ton of rubble."

"If you could *not* do that again, it would be great," Xerxes mumbles and Anton takes their hand, squeezing it. "Freaked me out."

"Samesies," Salem pipes up. "Slash and I had to dig you out since the rocks were so damn big and I was worried you were a Kit Kat-shaped pancake. Cute in theory, bad in practice."

I think I'm smiling sheepishly, but I honestly don't know for sure. "Sorry."

"You sure as fuck didn't mean for that to happen," Anton says with a scoff. My pulse jumps when I think he's being an ass, but he follows it up with an explanation. "Jasper pushed that damn fancy ceremony with the Latin and shit, even though we do not know what powers or forms you have. It was a dumb risk to take."

Wait, what?

"But I'm not—"

"Kit, *you* brought the ceiling down," Oriel says, as his dark eyes scan my face. "You said the words and this big… burst of energy yanked you off the ground, then you sort of… exploded. The ceiling came down, and we all had our animal forms come out without us intending it."

"I did not."

Salem gives me a lopsided grin. "Sure did, Kit Kat. I've never in my life had the bear come busting out when I didn't want him to. But it was pretty badass."

Frowning, I try to sit up and my body creaks painfully. "I…"

"Is he awake finally?" The deep rumbling voice is loud, and my eyes widen. I tense up, gripping O's hand when the door flies open. The rest of the clown car piles into the room, sucking up the space and the air as they assemble along the walls.

"Shhh!" X admonishes as they glare at the three demons. "His head hurts and he's having trouble. If you act like dicks, Annie and Salem will toss you out on your asses."

Annie will? What don't I know?

Jasper rolls his eyes, huffing as he stays in the corner with his tail whipping in irritation. "Coddling the little shit won't help."

Dottie pulls out of her small ball and scampers down my body, standing on my stomach as she shakes her tiny paw at the dragon. Oriel laughs softly, holding a finger out for her high-five, then turns to his grumpy leader. "Jasper, shut the fuck up for once, man. Admit you made a goddamn mistake. We shouldn't have gone so hard, especially in an unshielded space with someone we had zero knowledge of what might emerge if it got triggered."

Salem points at him, making a finger gun as he says, "Bull's eye, man. O nailed it."

The Prince throws his hands up and snarls, "Zav, *please* tell these dipshits that absolutely nothing we did, even in Latin, should have caused that kid to go nuclear."

The red-headed Kitsuné has been silent so far, but he rubs the back of his neck and his tail flicks before he says softly, "You might think I'm just saying this, but Jas is right. The induction is the same regardless of the language and whether we do it fancy or plain. That shouldn't have happened and he wouldn't have known it would. I didn't or I would have stopped him."

I blink. *He would have?*

"That is true, *bantam*," Slash says.

It's the first time he's spoken since they entered, and I study his face carefully for deception but don't find any. The weird gut feelings agree with my eyes, so I nod. "Okay."

"But now that it has…" Zavida says as his brows furrow. "We need to figure out what you really are. Not knowing how to help you will cripple you at Discordia and it's too cutthroat for you to wander around without powers for long."

Licking my lips, I gesture for Salem to bring the water closer. I take another sip before I ask, "I thought you said the induction would help?"

"It will and it won't," Jasper says with an eye roll. "It will take you off the lower level morons' lists. But being associated with us gets you onto other lists that are less… obvious and more dangerous."

Mother. Fucker.

"I don't understand how this helps, then."

Oriel grins at me, squeezing my hand. "Because even if that asshole fucked up, it got something inside of you to loosen the hinges. We need to finish prying the lid open so you have access to all of whatever it is you have locked away inside."

"I think it's a snake like me," X says with a grin. "Did you see the scales yet?"

Scales?!

Panic grips me again, but Salem scoots closer, pressing his leg against mine as he sighs. "Well, I'd hoped to ease you into that part. But since the excitable enby other can't keep their pants on…"

"Fuck you, Salem," X chirps good-naturedly. "I look fucking amazing in skirts. You couldn't hack it."

"That's a bet for later," Oriel winks at me, then arches a brow. "You ready to see a piece of this? It's not in a private place."

Great, that means they've all seen it.

"Yeah. Not fun being the last one in the room when it's my skin."

He lifts the hand he's holding, then pulls the clip off the gauze on my forearm. It unravels slowly, and as it does, my eyes turn to saucers. Every so often, an eruption of iridescent scales in jeweled hues graces my skin as if someone tore open my human skin with claws to reveal them.

Holy. Mother. Forking. Shirtballs.

"Do you even know what day it is?"

The lanky kid blinks out of the trance he's been in since Oriel showed him the eruption of scales on his arm. "What day is it?"

For fuck's sake, what did those two tell him before we came in?

"You were out for two days. That's why they brought Dr. D in to speed up the process." I frown, hoping they at least conveyed that part of the equation. "He said he believes once your form completely emerges, such measures won't be necessary most of the time."

"Two days?!" His eyes flicker to each one of us, looking for the truth, and even Jasper nods. "So I missed the entire weekend of studying? Fuuuuuck."

"*That's* what you're worried about?" The Prince snorts and shakes his head, looking dangerously close to losing his temper.

I whip my gaze to his, crossing my arms over my chest as I stare. "Don't."

"What is *with* all of you? First, that fuckwad Lucian sends in a spy, then half of you decide to fall for his bullshit, and now we're all tied to this weakling." Jasper is fuming and unfortunately, I know why. Fear of his father and our end of the line goals being fucked up has him drowning in his own paranoia and angry misery. Kit is simply the convenient target for him to use as an outlet.

"Man, you've been the biggest asshole in the universe since Kit Kat arrived. This year was supposed to be about… our plans and our caliphate tightening the bond," Oriel growls softly. "I get we didn't plan for this and you hate that, but you have *got* to cool it."

Jasper throws his hands in the air, looking completely unhinged as he stalks over to the bed. When I move quickly to step in his way, his eyes flash with gold and I let mine flash icy blue back.

"You will not hurt him. He's already injured because you were in such a hurry to prove his treachery when the induction failed." I've never stood up to my prince so publicly, but he's allowing the abuse of his past to dictate his present. I know he doesn't want to become his father and if I don't stop him, he'll do something he regrets. "As your second, I must prevent you from making a mistake that cannot be corrected."

The four demons sitting closest to our new member narrow their eyes almost in unison and I know that despite Jasper's nasty dig at dinner, I'll have to show the side of me I rarely allow people to see. Turning to pin Zavida with my gaze, I bark, "If Kit was not meant to be in our caliphate, if he was fully human, would he have survived that nonsense?"

"No." The Kitsuné has the grace to look ashamed. He should, because while Jasper and he must have discussed this, no one else realized the possibilities. "I'm sorry I stayed quiet, Kit."

"You're not forgiven."

His angry words make me chuckle and I look behind me. "That fury will serve you well, little demon."

"Don't call me that. The only people allowed to call me things are Oriel, X, and Salem."

Such fire for someone so clearly abused.

"I have helped you several times," I remind him and he rolls his eyes. "Not enough? Then keep listening."

"Fucking Lucifer's hairy goat legs, not you, too," Jasper snarls as he steps back. "What is going on with my *people*?"

"We're not people, Eversore. Thinking we'd behave like them is not a good strategy." I shrug, giving him a toothy grin before I continue. "And you're one to talk about strategy—being nicer to Kit would have gotten a lot more cooperation than your campaign of terror. Look at your brothers who chose better methods of learning about him."

"Jesus fucking Christ in a hentai cartoon. What the hell do you assholes want to know so badly?"

We face Kit when he yells in frustration. His face is pale and his hands are shaking, but he's sitting up in the bed with the little rodent clutching his neck. The air gets oddly tight for a moment, making it hard to breathe. Silence hangs as each demon thinks about his question, making his cheeks flush brighter with anger as the seconds tick by.

"Why can't I find your digital trail?" Zavida finally breaks the quiet with the one thing bothering him. "I've broken into… ridiculous amounts of systems, used magic, and even passed through the royal servers. You're like a ghost."

The injured kid makes a pitiful growling sound—though it's getting better—and thumps his fists on the blankets. "I. Don't. Know. I'm not bad with tech, but definitely not a hacker or this place would *not* have been my only choice for college. As far as I know, all my records are in the normal law enforcement and human services department file storage like any other… kid."

His pause was odd, and that gave Jasper the impetus he wanted. "Why did you pause before saying 'kid?' And why would it be in law enforcement files?"

I have a feeling this answer is very important.

"Because… because I'm having trouble admitting the whole 'demon' thing and…" He sighs and rakes his hand over his messy, dirty hair. "I'd be in both because of the other word I prefer not to have associated with me—victim."

That startles all of us, though Kit's favorite three grimace. They must know things the rest of us do not—or at least, pieces of Kit's story we haven't heard. Cracking my neck, I move to the end of the bed, sitting on it gingerly. My weight makes the mattress dip and I lose my balance, making Kit laugh softly. My eyes shoot up to his when the sound makes my insides warm. Maybe Jasper's right about one thing.

"Tell us what you are able," I say as he looks at me fearfully. "I will make sure your boundaries get respected."

I mean that, oddly enough.

"I've had four foster families since the end of middle school." Kit licks his lips, and the kinkajou squeezes him, which seems to help. "I had more before that—some good, some bad. Legend says I got dropped at some hospital as a toddler; who knows, though? Anyway, 'victim' applies to either end of the timeline, but more so to the years I mentioned."

"I'm going to *hate* this," Xerxes whispers before taking a seat on Anton's lap.

Neither of them have had an easy time with their families, especially because of their sexuality and gender. But they know if we're having a shitty parent contest, Jasper and Oriel win hands down, followed by me and Zav. We've borne both physical and emotional torment much worse than their bigoted asshole birthers—which is saying something.

"I sure as fuck did," the kid mumbles as his eyes fall to his hands. He's fidgeting with the blanket now, and I feel the anxiety ramping up around him. "Bad choices were made in that first year of high school and I was… attacked. It was bad enough to force the very uninterested fosters to shuttle me to therapy four times a week, which led to me getting the boot to a new home by summer. Each placement after that was its own challenge until I landed in Brett and Allison Jameson's house before the beginning of my senior year."

Jasper's eyes widen as he connects the dots, and I shake my head. The fucking idiot didn't realize all Kit's weird behavior was tied to trauma, likely as deep as his own. Obviously, I figured it out and adjusted; I'm not as stupid as he intimated, and he knows that. I beat his ass for using *my* father's method of emotional torture on me, especially in public, so we're even.

But I didn't tell him what I extrapolated and now he looks like a fool—punishment complete.

"Attacked how?" Anton asks. We all breathe a sigh of relief, because no one wanted to be the one to request elaboration. The prideful peacock can rarely keep himself from saying shit like that, though. He's caring, but he also believes his needs trump civility.

Kit glares, then slumps, and my heart hammers in my chest. X is right; none of us will like this. My hand has a mind of its own, lifting to rest on his calf as I wait. I half-expect him to kick it off, but he doesn't. He just keeps picking at the blanket while we sit in silence. "In the way you're thinking, obviously. I was in therapy for physical issues for a few months, and I've been working through the PTSD and my high-functioning anxiety ever since. That's why I…"

"It's why you had the panic attack," Salem murmurs. "And also why this dick knew how to help."

That brings on another round of quiet, but while we're all digesting his truth, the little rat comes skittering down Kit's leg to look me in the eye. It's weirdly intelligent, and I agree with the assertion that it's a familiar. Holding one finger up, I squint as I wait for it to do something. A soft chitter echoes in the room, and before I know it, I have a goddamn rodent on my head.

"What the—"

The smile that comes over our new member's face is so bright I have to swallow hard to keep my thoughts in my head. "Dottie gives her blessing. Maybe I don't need seven."

Seven? What the fuck is he talking about?

Zavida shuffles over, surprising me as he damn near dances on his toes before he looks at Kit. "I'm really sorry. I was doing what I thought—well, that's not important, but if you're telling us the truth… maybe someone else hid your background."

"Fucking duh," Kit grumbles. "That's what I've been saying, but Prince Prickface wouldn't listen."

A snort falls out of my mouth before I can stop it and they all stare.

"Traitors, all of you," Jasper growls softly. "He might have a good sob story, but only he can verify it thanks to the missing files."

"Uh, nope." Our attention switches from our angry prince to the kid on the bed again, and he shrugs. "I've got a copy of every single piece of paper in my file from every incident. Part of my therapy revolved around being able to admit all the things that damaged me. I made the shrink request my entire foster care record and all the case file materials through FOIA. I'll give them to Zav if I have to."

My brow arches. I don't know what that is, but it sounds important. However, his statement is very specific. "Only to Zav?"

His voice is raspy as he ducks his head again. "There are some… pictures I'd rather people not see."

Oriel shoots to his feet, glaring at Jasper. "You'll do no such thing. You've admitted to something painful that *no one* would make up. Salem and I witnessed your attacks more than once. You don't owe him or any of us that kind of intrusion."

"Yeah, I agree," Salem says slowly. "I wouldn't want some dicks I just met to have shit like that. It's a bullshit ask, and I'm with O."

X nods, then Anton joins him. "Us, either, I'm afraid."

If I agree with them, it's beyond the point of argument, but Jasper is going to freak out.

"I know you're going to be pissy, J, but…" I sigh and scratch my chin. "I can't get behind making him, either. No one who's been violated like that should have to do it again to prove themselves."

Zavida dances from foot to foot again, looking unhappy, but determined. "I don't want them, Kit. It's not a fair request."

"For fuck's sake, don't you see that he's using your—"

Everything stops as a loud siren echoes through the dorm room like a klaxon, and I jump to my feet.

"Fuck, that's the gathering circle alarm." I get my shit together quickly, devising a plan before anyone else can even register the noise. "Salem, fetch Kit's uniform immediately. Oriel, find the hidden weapons and distribute. Zav, hack into the alert system for info."

Kit just gapes at me. "What the hell, Slash?"

"He's my *general*, you dipshit," Jasper smirks. "I only called him dumb to piss him off. You should try playing chess with this giant fuckface."

"Or Go," X mutters.

"Poker," Anton grimaces.

"Warhammer," Zavida says with a pout. "It's all ridiculous, and he sucks."

Grinning with all my rows of teeth, I shrug. "It's who I am. I can't help that you're all handicapped by three-dimensional thinking."

"Someone better tell me what the gathering circle alarm is. I can whip Slash's ass in games later."

"You wish, little demon." I take his animal off my head, passing it to him as I stretch my arms out. "But I'll humor you with a few rounds. For now, this alarm means we have to gather in the summoning circle in the stadium. Since there are no events or lectures today, I do not know why, and I don't like it."

Jasper nods, sharing a look with me. "Agreed. I'm going to get my things. Someone help him not look like our weakest link, please?"

He strides out with a flourish and Kit mumbles some *vulgar* curses he must have picked up during his classes.

I suppose even in Hell; you adapt or you die.

kat/kit

As curious as I am about Slash's gaming prowess, the tone in his voice when he gave the orders told me this alarm thing was serious. It hurt, but I scooted myself to the edge of the bed until Salem returned with my stuff. Luckily, I keep nothing incriminating about my real identity where someone snooping would stumble across it. Otherwise, I might have had a heart attack when the shark shifter sent him to find my shit.

I look at Anton, X, and Salem pointedly as they lounge on the chairs. "Um, can you…" I wave my fingers at the door and they nod, though the panda shifter frowns. "I'll call out if I need help, promise."

My quiet addition seems to pacify my roomie, and he follows the others out the door, closing it behind them. I'm not wearing the same clothes I got buried in, and when I stop to sniff the shirt, I realize it's a loaner from Salem. That explains why it's huge, but not how much Dank really knows. My binder is still on, dirty as it is, and I won't be able to change it before I head to this fucking emergency. I probably stink, and I have to do something about it before I put my clothes on.

Wincing, I scoot forward until my feet touch the floor and ease myself up to a standing position. Fuck, that hurts. Having a ceiling fall on you is a 'zero out of ten—do not recommend' experience for goddamn certain. Dottie makes soft clicking sounds I think means she's worried as I pad across the floor in bare feet until I get to the dresser. I need something to make sure I don't smell like two days of bed bound nastiness, even if dudes frequently don't care about smell.

Demons wear deodorant, right? Fuck, I hope so.

There's a spray can of something in the weird demon symbol language, and I squint at it. Maybe if I glare hard enough— Suddenly, the symbols re-arrange into letters and I'm looking at a can labeled 'Old Scratch Flaming Spicy Scent' that *has* to be some sort of demon smell good shit. My hand shakes for a second, but I gather myself and pull the cap off. Spraying it under my arms, up my back and between my boobs, I pray it helps. I don't know what in Pandora's box just happened, but I also don't have time to figure it out. One of those impatient fuckers will knock on the door soon and I'm not even closed to dressed.

"Dottie, shit is getting weird up in this house," I mutter to my pet as I grit my teeth and make my way back to the bed. She blinks at me, then nods, her gigantic eyes full of understanding. I wish she could talk because I'd feel like I had someone besides the ocean of testosterone to communicate with, but alas, that's just not how it works. At least, I think it's not.

Who the fuck knows what's going to happen next in Hell?

As carefully as I can, I pull on the uniform pants, my socks, shoes, and then my button-down shirt. My body is aching by the time I get to the tie, and I groan as my arms feel like limp noodles. I can't fucking do this shit, and I'm going to look as bad as Jasper thinks when we go to this bullshit.

"Kit? Do you need some help?"

Salem's soft question makes my chest flutter, and I put my hand on it. No time for weird feelings. I have to finish this crap and get moving. "Um, maybe with my tie? My arms are—"

Before I can finish my sentence, the big dude is in the room, kneeling in front of me with a lopsided grin. "No problem, man. You're still recovering. Glad to help."

He's really close—like super duper scary close again. I lick my lips nervously as he fiddles with the accessory until it's close to my normal messy knot, grinning up at me proudly when he finishes. We keep looking at one another quietly until I clear my throat, hoping the flush on my cheeks isn't as bright as it feels. "Thanks. I'm trying, but um… I hurt a lot."

"Oh, shit. Kit Kat, we could give you more painkillers. Dr. D left some and if you—"

I shake my head emphatically. "No fucking chance I'm going to this thing high as a kite, Salem. Maybe when I go to bed, but not now. I can suffer through as long as you guys just… keep an eye? I'm stubborn and I might… not have a great gauge of my ability to fool the masses."

His grin is damn near brilliant as he nods. "Assignment accepted. Keep Kit Kat upright and looking pissed during the meeting. Got it."

Of course, I'm asking the guy who falls asleep at the drop of a hat, which might not be my most intelligent idea.

"Make sure Oriel and X know, too?"

"Done," Salem says as he holds his hand out. "Come along, roomie. Dottie, you, too. We need to get out there so Oriel can give you back the knives the doc took off you."

My face gets redder and I mumble, "Trauma."

Salem frowns at me. "Being armed is *not* considered weird here, little man. You don't have to explain. But Dr. D couldn't leave you strapped while he examined you. What if you woke up and stabbed him? It'd take hours to regenerate."

Regenerate? What the bloody fuck is Dank?

Instead of asking him, I nod and take his hand. Dottie scrambles up my arm to perch on my shoulder, and we head into the main room. I blink when I see Oriel handing out various small weaponry and the rest of them dutifully stowing the gear under their uniforms. X places a wicked-looking dagger in their thigh sheath and I make a note to tell them how fucking badass *that* set-up is. I feel like I'm in the middle of a scene from Vampire Diaries or Buffy—and I'm definitely fucking Xander. I hate that asshole, so I cough softly to get the crow demon's attention.

O's dark face brightens a bit, and he strides over to hand me the knives I had hidden under my binder, and at the small of my back. "Kit Kat, these are pretty cool. Let me help with the other one so you don't have to bend, okay?"

I wait for panic to grip me at the suggestion he touches me, but surprisingly, my stomach doesn't do a backflip. "Okay. Thanks."

That's all I've got for now—I'll deal with the rest later.

He drops to his knees, lifting the cuff of my baggy pants to put the small ankle sheath on me. I swallow hard as I watch a hot guy kneeling in front of me *for the second time in an hour*, hoping I don't make an idiot of myself. His hands are gentle as he adjusts it so it doesn't slide down, then pats the cuff into place. My skin feels like it's on fire, especially the weird patches. The temperature change tells me those spots are in more places than the ones on my arms the guys showed me and I have to shove my hands in my pockets to hide the shaking.

"There we go," he murmurs as he stands and brushes the knees of his pants off. "All good here. Where are Jas and Slash?"

"In the hall waiting," Zavida says as he peeks in the door. His red hair is sticking up all over and I think he's been running his hands through it in frustration. He looks worried, and since he's one of the three closest people to the prince, that means the dickhead is as well.

Just fucking great; we're all going to die.

"Your aura just got super weird, Kit Kat," X says. "You okay?"

I shrug, holding onto Salem's hand as much as I can until we're in public view. "I don't like surprises. They've never been a source of good things for me. It makes me anxious."

"Don't worry," Anton says confidently. "I know you can't help it, but you're part of us now. We're bound to help you, no matter what. Just put your chin up and give everyone the glare you give Jasper. You'll be fine."

Salem snorts as he squeezes my palm. "If you give them that look, it'll wither their balls off. Good idea, Annie."

Ducking my head, I grin a bit, then nod. "Alright, let's go face the music before they come in to blame me for making us late."

If I can keep my resting bitch face on, I'll be okay—that's what they said, right?

THE TRIP TO THE STADIUM WAS FULL OF QUIET BROODING—MOSTLY FROM Prince Cocknozzle—but I noticed that none of the caliphates or unmatched students looked any less worried. Even the demons in the upper classes look as if this isn't a normal occurrence, and I can't help wondering if my presence triggered this. But then, Jasper's guys being here could be the reason just as easily. They've made it very clear they're up to shit with his dad and don't get along with Lucian.

If their bullshit is putting me in the thick of things, I'm going to strangle someone.

"Stay stoic. Do *not* let any emotion show when they tell us what the fuck this is about," Slash says under his breath. We're all walking close enough to hear, so he continues. "You can look amused or haughty, but *not* concerned or afraid. Whatever it is, we need everyone to believe it's meaningless to our group."

As we approach the stadium, I let go of Salem's hand and Dottie hugs me tightly. She knows I was using the connection to settle myself, it seems, and I'm grateful for the added support. Every inch of my body is aching from the induction or itching with my anxiety. I'm grinding my back teeth hard to keep the bored expression plastered on my face as instructed, but this is the most demons I've seen since I arrived. The lunchroom isn't even this crowded, so I assume the older demons must take meals elsewhere.

Jasper and Slash lead us to a weird open space that swirls with magic, and I stop short. The Prince rolls his eyes dramatically, then walks into the void without a word. He disappears and I look at the others wide-eyed.

"What the fuck is that?" I hiss in a low tone.

Oriel looks chagrined as Slash chuckles and does the same thing Jasper did, completely dissipating from the spot. "We forgot. This is… think of it as a portal elevator combo. It's how we get to the royal boxes. Only those in the bloodlines or tied to them can access it. You just walk in and… yoink."

Oh, I'm going to murder these idiots when this is over.

"Fine," I grit out as Zavida takes his turn. "But if I re-appear missing limbs or fucking pants, I'm punching every one of you in the balls twice."

All the remaining members of my caliphate wince and I smile triumphantly. Obviously, that got my message across. Swallowing hard, Anton nods, then walks into the void, followed soon after by Xerxes.

"After you, Kit Kat," Oriel says. "We'll come after, so you feel safer."

"Oh, gee, will you?" I sniff in irritation, ambling toward the weird transport with my girl clinging to me. This is ridiculous and I'm probably being set up, but what choice do I have? I can't stand here and make a scene with thousands of demons wandering about.

Once more into the breach, I suppose.

Dottie and I step into the whirlpool of magic and my body feels like it's being ripped into pieces, then reassembled just as quickly. When my eyes open, I'm facing a fancy ass open air box full of students I don't know and insanely opulent decorations. I look up when a glint catches my eye and I realize the awning thing over us is made of a precious metal mesh dotted with jewels in an intricate pattern. Everything here is over-the-top rich demon shit, and I don't get to take it all in before Salem and Oriel appear behind me. The latter takes my elbow surreptitiously, guiding me towards the highest section in the booth where the others are sitting.

"Who are these people?" I ask him quietly.

"Other royal caliphates and dudes within all the families' structures. Not anywhere near our level, but they get access just the same. Jasper hates it, too."

For that reason alone, I kind of want to mingle with the other hybrids, but I know that's a bad idea. I'm not full strength for human Kit, much less for what I need to represent to rich demonic classmates. "Got it."

Once we join the rest of the guys, I settle into my seat in relief. This makes it much easier on me, and I'm glad we're in the fancy place, so we're at least comfortable. It's not my usual style to enjoy this kind of excess, but *fuck*, my body aches. I need the support.

"Slash told you all what to do. Don't disappoint me," Jasper growls as we stare at the big screen projecting the stage full of faculty on the stadium floor. "I've had enough of that for today."

I don't blame him for being pissed—the entire staff is down there and he's up here with us.

Something bad is coming.

I *don't like it one fucking bit.*

This random call for the entire university to gather in the stadium on a Sunday evening is not only unprecedented, but it has that scheming son of a bitch Lucian's name written all over it in blood. There's no way he missed the power surge Friday, unless he slipped out of the pits to the surface again. My source in his office told me he's been doing so frequently since last term, and the idea of him slinking around the human realm is no less disturbing than him knowing my caliphate destroyed the damn temple.

My hands grip the arms of the plush chairs in our section of the royal box, but I can't stop my tail from twitching below. Everyone forced back our animals before we left the rooms, but there's still an aura of power surrounding the members of my group that can't be hidden. The little shit who still might be a spy is cowering down by O and Salem, and I have to bite my tongue to keep from saying anything.

I'll never admit it out loud, but Slash was right; my reactions have been more harsh than warranted. Kit hasn't displayed a damn hint of being duplicitous other than the background being wiped, and Zav seems satisfied with his explanations now. I'm not, but that's because I know plenty of good liars with smooth words who'd risk discovery to seem innocent. He didn't want to give up those files, although he definitely has them, and we played into his hands when the guys respected his privacy.

But why did he gamble with something so obviously dangerous to whatever he's hiding?

"I don't like this."

Turning to my second-in-command, I arch a brow. "Oh, *now* you want my input?"

Slash rolls his eyes to the awning above us as if asking for help, then grunts. "Look, Jas. You knew you were being a dick. People tried to reason with you, and you ignored it. What the fuck was I supposed to do? I would never let you go full-on Tarron without stepping in."

Huffing as I flick my gaze to the scrawny guy, then back to my friend, I press my lips together. I don't get why they're all so taken by him. He's little, weak, and knows nothing of our world. Kit isn't even fucking model hot like X or Anton, nor dark and brooding like Oriel. He's not even cute like Zavvie.

What's the draw?

"Fine," I sigh, giving up on figuring out what the hell is happening to my only actual family for the moment. There are bigger things to focus on, and I can't let my frustration with my newest inductee cloud my vision. "I don't like it, either. My source tells me that the slimy fuckwit has been slipping through the void to the human realm and I don't know why. It makes my tail twitch."

A loud crackle comes from the enchanted speakers on either side of the screen and we both sit up taller. The answers are coming, whether we like them or not, and I don't want to miss a thing. "Record this," I growl at Zav on my other side.

He nods, pointing his phone at the screen and getting ready without a second thought. "On it."

"Good evening, faithful servants of Hell!"

I knew it. Fucking Lucian Darkstar.

"The faculty and staff of Discordia University hope you've had an informative first week of classes at your home for the next four years. Normally, we would allow you all more time to get settled before making any large-scale announcements, especially ones that will affect the entire campus."

"However, we were honored to be chosen for a pilot program being implemented across the universities in our dark lands next year. Discordia University is the premier educational facility for demons and their hybrids already, but the boon bestowed upon our students was so great that we are implementing the beginning stages next week."

"Fuck," Slash mutters and I nod. "We were right; this is terrible."

"No shit."

"Tomorrow morning, you will head to class as usual, but unfortunately, all extracurricular activities will be postponed for the year so we can use the time for our new program."

A roar of outrage fills the stadium, even in our booth. Not only did that asshat take away the fun activities demons like X love, but also the professional ones Zav and Salem take part in. Worst of all, I know this includes dueling—a fact that will *cripple* any player who has hopes of going pro after college.

Anton whistles softly. "That's rough. It will not win them any favors. In fact, it might cause a—"

The stands erupt in loud shouting, and within seconds, there is a blast of magic in the air. Anton was going to predict a riot; he wasn't wrong. Demons in various classes are already fighting one another as loud crashes echo around the space. I squint at our booth, daring anyone in here to even consider fucking up my private space. I'll end them without batting an eyelash.

"Enough!" The voice booms through the stadium loudly enough to make all our ears ring and the fights stop as demons clutch their heads. "You will sit down and listen or you will be sent to the pits for a month!"

"Is that bad? It sounds bad," Kit whispers to Oriel.

What a naïve little shit—it's the pits of hell, of course it's bad.

"You don't want to know."

I roll my eyes at O's sugarcoating and focus on the screen, looking at Lucian and the other staff. The professors, including the one I work for, look nervous as fuck. Not one appears to be happy about this situation, and that does not bode well for any demon at Discordia. This change is not something they're part of—no, they're props.

"By his most royal decree and the agreement of the seven families, with the approval of Discordia University, this year will mark the first Caliphate Games in two millennia! Congratulations on being selected for this most prestigious honor, demons of Discordia. You will all make us proud—or you won't make it at all."

Oh, shit.

"Caliphate Games? What's that?" our new member asks curiously. Salem and Oriel shrug, then they all look up at me.

I'm sure I'm as white as a fucking soul spirit, but I clear my throat to answer. Only Slash and I know how absolutely fucking horrifying this announcement is—the last time the games were a yearly occurrence was before my father and his cohorts made a play for the throne. They used four years of team efforts to weed out the competition and train so they could wage war on the throne after graduation. It almost decimated the houses within the current royal lines.

Not to mention it's eerily similar to my plan to unseat my dickhead birther.

"The Caliphate Games were a yearly tradition at all the universities in Hell before... the war," I say, hoping my voice is as strong as I'm trying to project. "They were played through the entire year amongst all levels of demons and groups in the school to weed out the weak. At the end of the year, every school had more than a quarter of their campus gone. Then they'd recruit new first years and start again."

Kit's eyes widen, and I almost feel his panic rising.

"Anyone who survived all four years of it became royalty after they instigated the coup that put my father on the throne."

The rest of my guys suddenly understand that I'm saying *their* older relatives are the survivors of games at various schools. Obviously, the court now is packed to the brim with former competitors, but that's not why I'm concerned. The King and The General orchestrated their treason while their caliphate played in the games all those years ago.

Why the fuck would they start this shit up again?

"Jasper..."

My gaze flicks from Slash to Zavida, then down to the others. I don't have promising information for them; this caught me off guard despite all the spies I have in every corner of the campus. It's an intel failure and I'll handle that, but for now, I can't reassure them. I know they want it, but it's just not possible.

The dark-haired thorn in my side heaves a sigh before he speaks. "So this shit is atomic bomb level bad, huh? You didn't know it was coming, which is probably pissing you the fuck off. But maybe the question we really need answered is why? Why this, right now, and whose idea was it?"

Slash grins. "On the nose, little demon."

"For fuck's sake..." I growl in irritation, but rein myself in when I remember what my best friend said. "*Yes,* that's the key question we have to ferret out. They've angered every student in this damn place, and most of them won't understand how dangerous this announcement is. Notice the other royals in this place have cleared out while we were talking."

A quick glance confirms I'm telling the truth, and for once, the human doesn't shoot back at me with a poisonous barb. "They're scared."

"They should be," Slash rumbles. "Jasper wasn't lying when he said the schools lost much of their student body every year. Demons are hard to kill for other supes and humans, but less so for other demons. These trials—because they *are* trials, not games—are designed to kill and maim those who shouldn't be here."

"You think your father had something to do with this," Kit says as he fidgets with a spinning ring on his thumb. "That's why you're grimacing so much."

"Bingo was his name-o, Kit Kat," Salem sing-songs. "Tarron and the other advisors—that would be our parents and some other staff fucks—would have to approve something this dramatic. More so at Discordia than any other school because so many demons from their houses go here."

I watch the kid take in that response, biting his lower lip as he thinks. Once he's ready, his eyes meet mine and the intensity in his gaze shocks the shit out of me. "It's not me they're aiming for, then; it's you."

Damn, he's smarter than I thought.

"Possibly," I say casually, shrugging as if it doesn't matter that my father might try to get me killed. "They might also try to take out as many caliphates as possible to solidify their reign for longer."

"That would be a shit idea if we got invaded," Slash grumbles. "Our enemies aren't just down here, and we all know it. The damn Society wants us to join them for that reason. If some rogue supes want to take on most species, they have to take on them as well. Your father won't play nice, so if vampires or some shit made a play, we'd only have ourselves. Thinning the ranks would make for a small goddamn army."

Nodding in agreement, I tap my fingertips on my chair. "Unless that's *exactly* what Lucian and whoever he's aligned with wants. It wouldn't be beyond his wheelhouse to have people working on the surface to form an alliance with other rebel groups. If they help him take Hell, he could grant them anything from trade rights to alliances in wars against others."

"Wait. Wait." We turn to look at Kit, who is frowning darkly. "Are you saying that pompous ass who brought me to you is trying to take over Hell with secret forces after these games take the powerful out?"

Xerxes leans forward, looking at me seriously. "Should we just… let them take your dad out? Two birds, one stone."

"That won't work. Lucian and whoever is helping him plot will be far worse than Tarron and the families." I look at Zavida, noting the fear on his face for the first time. His parents suck a lot and he's not worried about them being murdered as much as the alternative. "Jasper, we can't let his scheme succeed. You know the only demons and supes up there who would be interested in Hell wouldn't stop with this realm."

He's right; no one wants Hell for the sauna, they want it for the army of demons and hybrids with ancient powers.

Kat/Kit

I f I thought Jasper was a grouchy dickhole before, now he's literally giving off steam as his dragon tries to take control. We're trudging back to Canto IV at the head of the throng of demons escaping the stadium. No one is talking, but Salem and Oriel refused to let me walk without holding onto their arms. Slash growled when I protested and I sighed, giving up the illusion of choice until we're out of public view.

I'm not sure why they're so damn worried if the Games don't start until tomorrow.

"Stop looking at people," Anton orders as he catches me studying some other demons who are moving in groups.

My nose wrinkles in confusion. "What?"

X spins on their heel, walking backwards as they grin at me. "Demons aren't like humans or the other supernatural, Kit Kat. We don't play by strict rules like your kind, so it doesn't fucking matter if the Games officially start tomorrow."

"They'll take me out today for looking at them?" I gape as Dottie squeezes my neck. It shouldn't really surprise me to find that out, but I'm having a hard time processing at the moment. "And no one would get in trouble?"

"Is he really this dumb? He *can't* be this dumb," Jasper mutters, and I narrow my eyes.

I am so over his shit.

Speeding up, I drop the guys' hands and stomp up to the prickly asshole and punch him in the kidney. I hiss when my hand hits something that feels like a goddamn brick well, shaking it as he stops and whirls around.

"What. Is. Your. Problem?"

Sucking in a deep breath, I push all the fury and outrage I've felt at being the outsider looking into my voice. "You, Jasper Eversore. *You* are my fucking problem. I have been patient, and I have been the bigger person—"

"Not likely, shrimp."

The others form a circle around the two of us as we stare each other down. No one tries to stop what's happening, so I glare at the haughty prince. "I am *not* a shrimp. I'm normal sized, you giant spiked fuckwit."

Jasper stalks closer, going toe-to-toe with me as I drop my bag on the ground. "Small enough to roast, then snack on, but not an entire meal. Thus, shrimp."

What the fuck is wrong with him? I'm five foot nine!

"You need a pair of glasses, you royal asswipe." I lean in, my eyes dark with anger that's been pent-up far too long. "And maybe some intense therapy because this shit is classic fucking trauma dumping. I've been very clear about my boundaries and you... you just trample on them like I'm not worthy."

He arches a brow, looking at me with equal rage in his yellow eyes. His demon is out to play, and I can't even find it in me to care. "Look, shrimp. I've said it time after time. You *don't* matter. There is *nothing* you could do that would convince me you are worthy of my brothers, much less me. You should go home."

"Jasper Elias Motherfucking Eversore!" Slash roars as he rears back. "What the *actual* fuck, man?"

Dottie is clinging to me hard as I back up, looking at him with so much emotion threatening to burst out of me that it scares me. I don't pick up my bag; I don't look at anyone but him. Slowly, I walk backward out of the circle until I'm free, then I take off at a run towards the dorm. I haven't run like this anywhere but a track and... once, in the past, but I don't have an option.

I have to get away from them.

My throat is tight as I huff and puff, my arms pumping as I ignore the sounds behind me to dart into the throng of people near Canto IV. Ducking my head, I dodge and weave in between people as quickly as I can. I don't want any of the caliphate to find me. The only way to deal with what's coming inside of me is to find a nice, quiet, dark spot where I can hide while my body and mind disassemble.

By the time I get to the door of the dorm, I'm sure I lost them. I know going to my room won't end well, so I walk swiftly through the common area and past the small gaming area to the set of stairs that lead down to the subterranean study rooms. Guaranteed, the guys don't have a clue these are down on the bottom floor; their rooms are far too large and comfortable for them to seek places beside their rooms to relax. I can hole up in one of these until I get through this attack.

After I'm back in control of my faculties, I can make better decisions about the future.

"Just hold on a little longer, Kit," I mutter to myself as I scramble down the stairs as quickly as I can. My hand is trembling when I find the knob to the first empty room, turning it before throwing myself inside. My back rests against the hardwood as I pant from both the run and the panic running through me like a freight train.

I sink to my knees, burying my face in my hands as the sobs shudder through me. The stress and pressure from the past few weeks of college uncertainty, the Jamesons, coming here, and everything else crash into me. I topple to the ground, curling into a ball as hot tears run over my cheeks. Crying isn't really my thing, but my therapist kept saying it would help. Since I don't have one here, I might as well try whatever I scoffed at in the past.

What the fuck else am I going to do?

Going back to Brett and Allison isn't an option—not just because Dank burned the bridge to ashes, but because I know too much. The world up there wouldn't be the same and I didn't even like my life up there. I wouldn't be able to transfer from the secret demon school, so I'd have to take whatever job I could until I got better work. With little to no experience and no home, my prospects top side are looking shitty as fuck.

But I can't stay, can I? Jasper is determined to drive me over the edge and I'm hanging by my fingertips as it is. Even telling him my story didn't fix his goddamn bullshit, so I know he doesn't have a shred of humanity in him. He'll keep coming until I do something I swore I wouldn't ever do again.

I respect myself too much for that, even if he doesn't.

Shuffling toward the middle of the room, I splay out on my back in the darkness, then look up at the ceiling, letting the tremors and tears work their magic. If I don't fight the symptoms, maybe I won't fall so deeply into the hole and not be able to get out. My eyes close as I whisper the mantras to myself: *five things I can smell, four things I can hear, three things I can touch, two things I can see, one thing I can taste…* I switch it up, forcing my brain to focus on the answers to those questions rather than the ache in my chest.

I'm not upset that Jasper refuses to see me; there will always be people who don't accept you. That is a fact of life, and worrying about everyone liking you is a fool's errand. But his words triggered a response I've worked so hard to keep at bay for years. I'm frustrated I couldn't control it, angry that he saw my emotions, and feeling helpless about how to proceed. My options are severely limited now—especially after that stupid ceremony—and the trust I attempted to give to the others is shriveling inside of me like a dead flower.

For someone with my issues, allowing *anyone* inside of my heart and mind is damn near impossible. I don't blame Oriel or X or any of them for his behavior—no, Jasper owns his shit. But my fucked up psyche went into 'red alert' mode the moment the slap of betrayal hit me. I don't know if I can or want to fix that problem. The walls are back up, fortified stronger, and I'm safe inside my little tower if I leave this be.

Is having friends… or whatever… worth taking that risk again? They can't stop him.

Digging my fingernails into my palms, I sigh in relief at the bite of pain when they break the skin. Sometimes, I need that sensation to get my head on straight during an episode. My therapist said it's self-destructive, and he's right, but I don't give a shit. When you're headed into the darkness, you'll use whatever tools you have at hand to stop the descent.

"God, Kit, you sound like a fucking idiot," I murmur to myself. "Normal people don't have to lie in the dark scratching themselves to ribbons so they can prevent a goddamn meltdown. No wonder everyone thinks you're a freak."

"You're not a freak."

My heart rate skyrockets as I gasp, scrambling to a sitting position so I can scoot as far away from it as possible. Fear floods my system—I'm alone, in the dark, after they announced a 'to the death' competition in Hell.

How stupid am I?

"No," the smirking voice drawls as I hear footsteps come closer and see glowing green eyes floating in the pitch black. "You're a little bitch boy who strayed way too far from his keepers."

A chorus of *Beavis & Butthead*-esque laughter echoes in the room at those words and I lick my lips. There's at least four of them, and I can't make out a damn thing. I picked the absolute *worst* room in the building to have my breakdown. Dottie is silent next to me and I'm sure she's trying to figure out how to help me. I don't want her to—she could get killed by some stomping dickwaffle with combat boots on.

"Leave me alone," I growl into my cupped palms. I'm hoping if I create enough bounce to the sound, they won't know what part of the study area

I'm hiding in. My hand grazes a piece of furniture as I move and I realize I've found a desk. I make myself as small as I can, tucking underneath it as they continue to snort and snicker.

"I don't think so, bitch boy. If you want to suck a major demon's dick so badly, you'd have to stand in line for the Prince. But for me? I'm right here."

Time stops as I see the sliver of light from the door they entered fade out as it clicks shut. I've been in this situation before—not exactly the same, obviously, but close enough for my PTSD to make my vision blur and wretched sounds fill my ears. I swallow hard, biting my lip until it bleeds to keep my wits about me. They haven't found me yet and I don't feel my girl.

Maybe she got out before they shut the door?

Jesus, Kat, this isn't *Lassie*. Your kinkajou will not bring the fucking cavalry to save you. Just like before, figure out how to save yourself. I suck on the bloodied lip as I force my brain to slow down so I can assess my options. I have a knife at my ankle and one in the small of my back. There's another one between the boobs I don't want these motherfuckers to realize I have. I feel it will only make this worse for them to discover my secret.

Men like this are fucking trash, and it rarely matters to them who they're hurting as long as they can inflict pain.

My hand slips down to my ankle, and I pull loose the smallest blade. I don't want anyone to realize I have backups if they get a hold of me, so we'll take this one stab at a time. Gripping the hilt of the tosser, I wait in complete silence as my body quakes with fear. A hand grabs my foot and I scream as the dickwad drags me out from under the desk toward the middle of the room. I lean forward, slashing blindly toward it, and I'm rewarded with a shout, a sharp pain, and freedom.

Scrabbling again, I move away from the idiot I stabbed, fear bubbling up in my gut as I try to find another hiding place. Before I'm successful, I run flat into a pair of legs and I'm lifted off the ground, making me drop the damn blade with a clatter.

"He's not armed now. Pin him down."

Fuck. No.

I flail as much as possible, hoping my attacker will drop me while I try to get the much bigger K-bar at the small of my back. It's the one I sleep with under my pillow since the incident and I'm very comfortable with its grip. I grab it, but the force of being slammed to hard concrete knocks the wind out of me. Someone steps on my wrist until I let go of my favorite weapon, but I don't cry out. They will *never* get a sound out of me; it's the fucking first rule of 'foster care fight club.'

No one gets your screams.

A fist crashes into my jaw, followed by kicks hitting my ribs, and I clamp my mouth shut hard. Every blow feels like they're using goddamn Thor hammers, but I don't let even a whimper escape.

"Boy, this little bitch likes it rough. No wonder Eversore and his freaks wanted him all to themselves."

My beating continues, and I let myself float away, rising above the battering of my body by whoever these abusive shitstains are. If all they do is beat me, I can take that. I've survived so much worse than this. I have to stay in the happy place and it will all be okay.

The sound of a belt opening stops my heart and my breath in my chest. I know that sound; I know it like a dog knows the sound of a whistle from far away. Tears gather in the corner of my eyes as clothes rustle above me— more than one set. I grit my teeth, unable to get to the last blade between my breasts because hands are pinning my limbs. Spots dance in front of my eyes as the true descent into the black pit begins…my mind *knows* I'm about to be re-traumatized and it's protecting me.

"Get the *fuck* away from him!"

The room lights up and I blink in confusion as I'm blinded. I slam them closed again, squeezing hard to mitigate the stars in my vision. A roar like none I've ever heard in my life fills the entire space, vibrating over my skin as the hands holding me down disappear. Loud, crunching sounds and screams echo off the walls, and all I can do is roll to my side. Tucking myself into a tiny ball, trembling fingers grasp the razor blade from my binder, gripping it hard in case the intruder comes for me next. More cracks and the sound of breaking bones signal the final stages of the surrounding battle, but I don't open my eyes when all the noise fades to my soft pants and a low rumbling snarl.

Suddenly, the temperature in the room ratchets up, and the smell of burning flesh is in my nostrils. I gag, coughing with my head aimed at the ground so I don't choke on vomit if it comes up.

"Ah, fuck, don't fucking puke," the voice says.

It sounds like it's at the top of a well and I shudder slightly. I have to come back from the place I'm in to interact with actual people. The galloping of my heart doesn't want to, but I've always known I can't stay in the safe place forever. That way, madness lies.

"I'm… not… trying… to." My voice is raspy, little more than a croak because of the heat in the air. When I pry my lids open, I almost pass out from shock.

Kneeling beside me in the most awkward position possible is a half-shifted Prince Eversore, the dick who sent me running here in a panic, and the room behind him is full of flames.

Did I die? I must have, right?

"Can I help you up?"

The question has me reeling—since when does this fuckhead ask anyone permission? But I nod slowly because I doubt I'll be able to stand on my own in this state. I'm fucked up—mentally and physically—and the room is goddamn *en fuego*, so we need to get the hell out. "Y-yes."

Jasper takes my hand gently, then my elbow, supporting me as I do my damnedest to make sure he doesn't hear a single sound of complaint. I'm not giving *him* my screams, either. He sure as fuck hasn't earned them. Once I'm upright, he offers his arm for me to lean on without saying one nasty word.

I definitely died.

Unfortunately, the first steps I take are a bust, and he heaves a deep, irritated sigh. "I'll have to carry you. Those corpses are going to catch the rest of this place on fire soon. You, shrimp, are flammable, even if I am not."

"Okay."

That's all I got because he hauls me into his arms, stomping out of the room like a scaly firefighter. He doesn't look back and I consider asking him who the hell those guys were. Worrying my bloody lip with my teeth, I decide knowing feels like it might be worse than not, so I'll have to save that truth for later.

"Stop that." His grunt makes me focus again, and I look up at him with a dazed expression. "You're making it worse."

I shrug, but that hurts like a motherfucker. "It helps me."

"Well, don't. You're going to Dr. D's. The rest of the idiots will meet us there."

A soft chitter sounds and my eyes widen as Dottie scampers along behind the dragon demon with a big grin.

Well, I'll be damned—I actually got saved by a fucking kinkajou.

What are the odds?

Want more? Go here for a bonus story.

Preorder Book Two in the Discordia series now!

Read along with the Vella of Season Two.

Reviews, Print, and Merchandise

If you have enjoyed this story, please review it.
It helps other readers find my work,
which helps me as an indie author.

Thank you!

Reviews are appreciated on the following platforms

TikTok
Instagram
Facebook
Bookbub
StoryGraph
Threads

To purchase print copies or merchandise, go to The Worlds of Cassandra Featherstone

GET A SECRET BONUS SCENE!

For another secret bonus scene that follows *Veiled Flame, click the link below, sign up for my newsletter, and get your freebie.*

Get your bonus scene here!

Sneak Peek: Bloodthirsty

QUEEN BEE

They dim the lights in the club, and the spots click on as the curtain slides open.

It's a full house tonight in the little burlesque club off the Rue Pierre Montaine.

Chez Arc En Ciel is not well known compared to the *Moulin Rouge* or *Le Lido*, but the wealthy from both sides of the Seine gather here for shows four nights a week. If you pass the various layers of security checks to even be permitted to book a reservation, you also have to be able to afford the two thousand Euro per guest cover charge. If you don't eat or drink anything, that's all it will cost; however, that would get you blacklisted.

Intro music pumps through the speakers and I stand on my mark in the opening position. My cane is resting on the wooden boards of the stage by my front foot as I pretend to lean on it. Roars of applause echo through the room as our troupe of dancers catch the lights, sequins sparkling like diamonds when the stage lights rise. We're dressed in pinstriped black pant suits and fedoras to match the big band style opening to the song. As soon as the horn-filled intro finishes, the dance begins.

I follow the routine with precision, snapping and popping my hips to the beat as we spread out across the stage. You wouldn't know by the fake smile on my face that I'm scanning the crowd. Two fan kicks later, I've rotated past the proscenium, and I think I've found my mark. Twirling, I stop in the place I need to be for the bridge, singing along as if my life depends on it. It might, to be honest, because I need to sell my cover tonight, so no one notices me.

The Guillotine moves in the shadows, but tonight, she's in the spotlight.

My ass shakes as I dance my way through the song, swinging the prop cane I'd replaced with one of my design. You wouldn't know by looking at it, but it's not the painted balsa the other dancers have for a very specific reason. I need it to complete the mission that forced me to spend two months in Paris working my way into this job at *Chez Arc En Ciel*. If I can't strike tonight, the surveillance, counterintelligence, and time spent building this cover are wasted because my mark is leaving for Asia tomorrow.

Tonight, the Cobra dies for his sins.

The break of the song slows the music and the dancers pour into the crowd to wiggle around the rich assholes. It's choreographed, but it's also to advertise each girl for private dances in the lounges upstairs. We're not strippers— not that there's a damned thing wrong with a woman using her body to support herself—but we do bare more skin in the closed rooms. The *laissez-faire* attitude of the owners means as long as we kick them thirty percent of the fees for those dances, they don't care what any of the girls do in the rooms. I'd find it sleazy, but the girls who work here are highly skilled performers who choose to make thousands of dollars a night rather than peanuts in some ballet troupe or chorus line.

By the time I've flirted my way to the VIP tables, the Cobra is staring intently at all of us. Spotlights pin each one of us on the floor at the bass hits, and I swivel my hips as my free hand slides down to the secret spot on my jacket. In unison, we tear the jackets off to reveal rhinestone studded bras with straps crisscrossing our waists like shibari ropes. A lift of the fedora and pop of my hip, along with the beat, draws the fierce-looking brawler's eyes directly to me. I pout prettily and stalk towards his table with the swagger of a tiny dicked asshole that owns a monster truck.

His thin lips pull back over the famed curving fangs he had implanted. Dark, glittering eyes follow every move I make as I approach, and I pretend to whip my hair from side to side as I check for his guards. They're here somewhere, but I need them to be far away so I can beat my escape before they notice. When I get within inches, I tap his leg with my cane and spin around to shake my ass in his face. The grunt of approval makes me want to heave, but I turn, holding onto the prop with both hands. My feet click on the floor in a soft shoe step as I make 'fuck me' eyes at the dirty bastard. He leans back, his pants tented as he gestures towards his lap.

Fucking gross.

I don't care about his weapons trade or what happens when people get the shit he moves. I have no clue why I have to take him out. The reason they have sentenced him to death isn't part of my contract, and I'm nothing if not a dispassionate observer of the darkest parts of human desires. Twelve years at *l'Academie* ensured I care very little about anything that isn't directly related to my ability to complete my jobs.

Sighing, I dance closer and drop onto his rather unimpressive erection and wiggle. There's plenty of cloth between us to prevent him from doing anything I'd make a scene over, so I focus on the task at hand. I slip the cane behind his head, resting the wood against his neck as I tug him forward. The move reads as playfully bringing his face to my breasts, but at the last second, I click the release built into the custom weapon. One end slides open to reveal the razor sharp garotte and before he can say a word, I yank it through.

Faint gurgling is the only noise besides the end of the song, and I carefully slide the sides of the cane together. Climbing off the nasty fucker, I put my hands on his cheeks so I can pretend to flirt with him while I arrange the head so it looks as if he's leaning back in the booth. It needs to look realistic to allow me to return to the stage with the others. When I have it settled, I back away from the booth, blowing fake kisses as I walk backwards through the crowd. I almost collide with a dark-haired guy with his collar pulled high as I head for the stage, and I roll my eyes. Whatever celeb that is trying to keep their face away from the paps is doing a shitty job of it.

The entire troupe takes a few bows and shuffles off of stage left to the wings. I exhale a sigh of relief when the next group enters on the opposite side. I haven't heard shouting yet, so I don't think the Cobra's men realize he's down. Now I take this emetic pill, have a vomiting episode, and I'll get sent home.

That's when Arabella Montaigne, the burlesque dancer, will cease to exist, and Remy Arsine Benoit will re-emerge.

I smile to myself as I chew on the tablet that will have me retching my guts out in a few moments. This is a more complex extermination than I usually prefer, and I can't leave my normal calling card behind. The Cobra's head had to remain in the booth rather than get delivered to his home in a basket.

Such a shame, that. I quite enjoy the reactions my little gifts engender when they're discovered.

Walking into the dressing room, I carefully strip my costume off, putting all the pieces in my bag. Every item in the locker room that belongs to gets placed in the duffel carefully as I wait for the effects to hit me. It won't do to leave loose ends, even if my prints have never touched a single surface in this place. My gut roils and I turn, facing one of the other dancers as the vomit finally comes. Gracelia screams like she's being skinned when I hurl on her and it's everything I can do *not* to smirk through the chunks.

"C'est la merde!" she shouts, running for the showers as if she's on fire.

It takes less than a minute for the owner to send me home for the night. I walk out the back door of the building with everything just as the sirens scream.

Perfect timing, as always.

I jump into the first cab I can hail, directing him to the *Hôtel de Crillon*. Their suites are the ritziest in Paris, and it's my go-to hideout when I'm here. I used to only stay in the Bernstein Suite, but some rich fuckwad purchased it six months ago. If I could track them down and beat the hell out of them, I would, but I booked my schedule until late 2025. Assassins with my skill set and accuracy are getting harder to find. They forced the old guard into retirement because they refuse to adapt to the digital age. Too many cameras, crime labs, and hackers running about to do everything Cold War style.

The future of murder for hire is millennial, people. We're old enough to be stable, but young enough to be agile with new technology. Plus, most of them are broke AF from crooked ass student loans.

It's not an issue I have, but I've been in the business since I hit double digits. You don't survive *l'Academie des Invisibles* if you haven't killed someone before the end of primary school. It's unheard of.

I was eight the first time I used the weapon that would become my signature.

Shivering, I tap on the window of the cab and bitch the driver out. He's taking a longer route than necessary to raise my fare, and I'll have his guts for garters if he doesn't knock it the fuck off. A string of curses in French erupt from him when I voice the accusation, and I slam my palm on the window with enough force to crack the plexiglass barrier. He almost drives into another car, but when he regains control, he makes the requested adjustments to our route.

We arrived at the front entrance after a few more arguments and a traffic jam around the *Champs*. I throw the euros at him in disgust, memorizing the medallion number for later. He's not worth my time, but I have quite a few contacts who might be interested in blackmailing a cabbie in town. Getaway cars are cliche in the crime world now. Most ne'er-do-wells like myself find greater comfort in anonymous taxis or ride-share accounts hacked through the deep web accessed on burner phones. If your ride doesn't know you're a villain, there's no one to flip if law enforcement comes looking.

I never look the same for any job—ever.

I will not use Arabella Montaigne as a cover in the future, and once I move to the location of my next job, I'll ensure that she meets with a terrible fate. It's a lot more work to slowly kill off my alters once I've used them, but it's also why I've never even come close to being caught. The dancer with long wavy red hair, freckles, and big green eyes will never grace the streets of Paris again after I hop a plane. She will, however, get a minor story in the paper and an obituary when I decide how she tragically dies.

The Guillotine will rise from her ashes and be reborn.

Sneak Peek: Come Out & Prey

Just A Girl

Delores

Sighing, I look around my bedroom at the posters and decorations covering my walls. My obsession with pop music, musical theater, and high school rom-coms sickens my parents. They would prefer me to be into heavy metal and horror movies like the other kids my age.

Being the only child in a family as prominent as mine is difficult when you don't fit the mold. My parents—like their parents and all my friends' parents

—are apex predators. Preds rule our world, and the division between us and prey is so severe that we regulate them to a completely different echelon of society. Prey shifters are weak and beneath our lofty abilities. The ruling class of elite predator families stretches back generations, and they've evolved into a bunch of assholes who only care about succession and greed.

My animal has not manifested yet, but it will soon enough. Luckily for me, none of my friends have manifested their inner animals, either. I'm part of the in-crowd at school, and my boyfriend, Todd, is the most popular guy in my class. While he and I aren't officially engaged yet, we've talked about it enough that I know it's only a matter of time before he puts a ring on my finger. I should be on top of the world, but I can't help but feel like my life just doesn't fit me the way it's supposed to.

Every teenager wishes their life was different, but I dream of becoming an entirely different person. Not inside, mind, because I'm pretty comfortable with who I am. I don't want to be part of this legacy, this society, or even this family. They are all focused on competing to be the richest, the deadliest, or the most powerful, and I want no part of it.

I walked over to my closet and pulled out the outfit that I had chosen for my tour of Apex Academy. My mother hired her personal designers to create a custom school uniform for today and expects me to present the 'appropriate' image of the sole heir to a Council seat.

I hate having to pretend to be like them because I'm nothing like them.

Regardless, I pull on the short, pink pleated skirt, three quarter length sleeve blouse, knee socks, and Mary Janes that comprise the uniform for my exclusive private high school. Since I'm using a 'college visit' day to tour the Academy, I'm expected to represent Shifter Secondary as well.

Shifter Secondary is the most exclusive high school for unmanifested shifter teens on the East Coast. Unfortunately for me, it was not my parents' first choice for my education. They hoped I'd follow in their footsteps by choosing to force my animal to emerge early. If I had done that, I could have attended *Apex Academy Lower School.*

I didn't have the stomach to use my body in that manner at fourteen.

Their heirs followed my lead, which made my mother and father furious and their hoity-toity council colleagues angry. My closest friends, the Heathers, also refused to force their animals to emerge, as did Todd and his friends. That was the first time the adults in our circle decided I was a bad influence. After that, I had to toe the line at every turn, ensuring that I followed all the strict rules and regulations that govern the heirs to council seats.

Everywhere I went, I had to dress in a manner befitting the next Drew to sit at the table. They forced me to take dance lessons, piano lessons, diction lessons, and other more humiliating tutorials to prepare for the day that I became a true predator. In our society, teenagers have no say in how we prepare for our animals to emerge.

Your parents make all the decisions, choose your friends, choose your mates, and decide every detail of your life down to what you eat every single day. At least, that's how it is in my family, because my mother is from the old world.

She came over from Slovenia when she was incredibly young and met my father on the society fundraiser circuit. Her idea of preparing her daughter for the future involves lessons in makeup, clothing, jewelry, and on how to keep your mate satisfied. Lucille is completely unconcerned about whether I end up happy, only that I attend to my council seat and my husband's *needs*.

Once I get dressed, I grab my vintage Vuitton bag and peek at the mirror for a last check before I head downstairs. I tuck my perfectly highlighted blonde tresses behind my ears, and the smokey eye and winged liner are on point with this year's fashion trends. I apply a quick swipe of cherry red lip gloss and open my mouth, inspecting my teeth to make sure they are pearly white. Even though once I develop threatening incisors or sharp fangs, something will inevitably cover them in blood, my parents want my smile to look like a toothpaste commercial.

It's all such utter bullshit.

I take a deep breath and turn on my heel, heading for the door. I can already hear my parents yelling in a Scotch and vodka induced rage in the drawing room. It's only eleven thirty in the morning, for Hera's sake.

Lucille and Bruno don't fuck around with cocktail hour. They are nicely sauced by ten a.m. every day, without exception. I can't remember a time when my parents didn't get drunk off their asses at an event or party, much less in our 'home'. They liquor up and fight until they part for the day, and then start again once they arrive home from their daily commitments.

I brace for the barrage of criticism my mother will subject me to when I cross the threshold. Closing my eyes, I whisper words of encouragement to myself via lyrics to some of my favorite songs, desperately trying to hype myself up before she can tear me down.

"Delores! I hear you breathing at the top of the stairs, darling. Come down this instant and let your father and I inspect your presentation."

My mother's purr *sounds* friendly, but believe me, it's not. I roll my eyes as I make my way down the stairs, knowing my mother won't hesitate to send one of the staff if I don't acquiesce to her command. Most of their staff would gleefully jizz themselves with being chosen to drag me downstairs for inspection.

At this time of day, the only servant in the drawing room will be Matilda—my ex-nanny turned personal assistant—and that request would test her loyalties. As the only person in my household who has my back, I don't want to put her in that position, so I answer. "Yes, Lucille. I'm on my way."

I'm not allowed to refer to her as 'mother' because it makes her feel old. 'Lucille' is always what I've called the woman who supposedly gave birth to me. I'd be tempted to disbelieve we shared any DNA at all if it weren't for our similar bone structure. She's about as nurturing as a rattlesnake, and if it weren't for Matilda, I might have died as a child. If the kitchen staff whispers are accurate, I have to accept that my mother neglected to feed me much of the time.

"You coddle her far too much, Lucille," my father growls. "As the heir to our family seat, Delores will come without being instructed to do so. We will not tolerate her insolence after her animal emerges. She will behave as I command or suffer the consequences."

The last of Bruno's rant echoes off the marble walls of the foyer as I step onto the hideously expensive, endangered teak floor. Schooling my features into the mask of indifference I wear whenever I have to deal with them, I enter their den of drunken fights with my spine steeled for an emotional assault.

"I apologize for my tardiness, Father. I only wished to perfect the image I will present during my tour of Apex Academy. I realize it is imperative I impress the Headmistress and her staff."

The humanoid features of his face shift seamlessly, and the hungry crocodile inside of him gives me a toothy smirk. "You will impress them, daughter, or so help me… I'll send you to Bloodstone Isle."

My stomach drops like a stone as I barely suppress a shiver.

Bloodstone Isle is a reformatory school. It's surrounded by spells and enchantments to prevent students from escaping—a feat that has only happened once in its one thousand years of existence. The most feared cat group in the shifter world—the Khan ambush—runs the school, and they're rumored to consume errant students when the Council allows it.

It's the threat both rich and poor shifter parents used to keep their children in line. Wealthy parents like mine use it as a method of controlling any heirs that refuse to conform to the rigid structure of our society. Predators don't value the lives of those who are weak, and they label heirs who refuse to take their rightful place at the top of the food chain weak. Everyone knows Bloodstone is full of criminals, miscreants, and psychos, and even they don't seem to survive.

Bloodstone is a death sentence—pure and simple.

"Y-yes, Father. I understand," I croak out. As if the pressure of touring my new school isn't enough, now I worry the Dean will relay something to my parents that gets me shipped off to Death Island.

"Bruno, darling, if you scare her, she'll frown. That causes wrinkles. Delores, chin up and smile for us."

Swallowing the lump in my throat, I flash my mother my brightest smile. Her blood-red lips curve, and her leopard fangs burst free as she all but purrs. "I will not have you sullying the family name, Delores. It's bad enough that your education gave you ideas about your value beyond breeding stock. You will take the seat on the Council when it is time, but the husband we select will control the business—as nature intended. Do you hear me?"

My eyes narrow briefly, and for what is possibly the millionth time this week alone, I nod at my mother to appease her temper. "Yes, Lucille."

"Excellent!" The leopard fades as she claps her hands. "Matilda!"

The tiny woman steps up, her eyes wide behind her glasses. She's a pred, but the smaller size of hawk shifters puts her in the servant class. I believe she genuinely lives in fear of one or both of my parents deciding to eat her. "Yes, madam?"

"Fetch Bruiser. He will accompany Delores to the academy for her tour. Tell him to take the Escalade—it won't do for her to arrive in a tiny car—it will draw attention to her extra weight. We must make an impression."

Matilda nods, and I feel the fear radiating from her, and I don't blame her. Bruiser is one of my parents' bodyguards and our frequent chauffeur. He's a Komodo dragon shifter and the house staff are terrified of him. It's hard not to be, given that he prefers to play with his food, then eat it after it's dead. The kitchen crew believes he 'handled' the gardener that looked too long at my mother when I was ten. He disappeared without a trace.

Once Matilda scurries away, I watch my parents drink and bicker about their plans for the day. Bruno is going golfing with a congressman, and Lucille is going to the spa. We all know that both outings will include stops at the homes of their current pieces of ass for a quickie, but no one talks about it. The appearance of the loving couple has to be maintained, although neither of them has slept in the same room since I was a baby.

They don't give a damn about fidelity; I learned that at an early age. Children often discover things they shouldn't because of adults discount their ability to understand the conversations happening around them.

I stopped keeping track of who they're boning long ago, because I'd need an assistant to keep the affairs straight.

While my parents' marriage is a sham, I remind myself that my boyfriend, Todd, isn't like them. Yes, his parents only own half the live entertainment industry, but my father allows me to see Todd. The other parents will force the Heathers to accept an arranged betrothal, and I'm grateful I'm lucky enough to have found the perfect match on my own as my high school sweetheart.

"Delores, Bruiser is ready to escort you to Apex. He's pulling the car around now," the hawk shifter says softly.

Snapping out of my reverie, I smile at the trembling woman. Bruiser must have scared the living hell out of her. For no other reason than it amused him, I'm sure. He's as much a brute as his name implies, and I don't look forward to riding alone to the academy with him.

Something about that shifter gives me the creeps…

Sneak Peek: Children of the Moon

PROLOGUE

Twenty-one years ago…

A powerful wave of apprehension hits me as we approach Claridon's house. Pausing at the edge of the forest, I wait until we can see what awaits us. The silence is deafening as we take in the wreckage of what was once the home of our dear friends.

They splintered the heavy cabin door in pieces littered around their yard like an explosion sent the shards flying. When the wind shifts, the foul stench of death and rot slams into us, making my wife gag. Lights are flickering ominously in the shattered windows and another scent—burnt food—catches the breeze as we approach.

"Cast protection before we reach the porch," I murmur.

"Ego invoco deus ab mihi. Protego mihi ab hostili et malum.[1]*"*

I nod solemnly, repeating her words to invoke our Goddess' watchful eyes on me as well. The scene in front of the house does not inspire confidence about what we will find inside.

The air is thick as we step onto the porch and another smell wafts towards us—blood. Its metallic tang invades our senses almost to the point of tasting copper on my tongue. Climbing over the debris, I look at the once cozy living area. Shredded cushions, torn drapes, stuffing, and other destroyed furnishings lie scattered around the room. When I bend to examine the destruction, I find coarse animal hairs embedded in the remnants. I pick some up to sense the aura of the creature it came from, but all I feel is death.

The bloody hoof prints puzzle me—I do not recognize them as belonging to any creature I'm familiar with. Whatever came to this house was not a normal shifter, nor was it a common magic user. The level of malice and lack of emotion concerns me. Its aura is like that of a necromancer or one of their creations.

I follow a set of heavy prints to the hallway leading to the dining area and kitchen. Swallowing hard, I prepare myself for the carnage I know will appear. The rotten food and decomposition scents are so bad I have to raise my shirt to cover my nose before I vomit.

It is certain our friends are dead; no one can lose the amount of blood that coats the surfaces and walls while staying alive.

"What made those claw marks? I've never seen such deep furrows," my wife whispers.

I shake my head, holding a finger to my lips to keep her quiet. I've never seen that type of mark, either, but we don't know if there's anyone still here. We must stay silent while we explore. The food on the stovetop is burned and has flies on it—that's the rotting smell. Wood is barely burning in the oven, just a few embers remaining, but it tells me our friends were caught unaware.

It means the malevolent being that attacked the wolves did it within the past few hours.

My heart stops when I remember their baby girl. Feray had to be here when it happened; it's the New Moon and both of her parents stay home during the start of the new lunar cycle.

"Freya, forgive me. I almost forgot the baby," I hiss at my wife.

Her eyes widen and her hand flies to her mouth. I see the tears forming as she thinks about what the condition of this place means for a defenseless infant. Together, we leave the kitchen, intent on heading back through the outer room to the stairs.

Just beyond the landing, we stumble over the body of Claridon. His corpse is mutilated, but I recognize those battered hands anywhere. He clearly put up a hell of a fight to keep the intruder from making it past him. Despite that, it ripped his chest open and his intestines are hanging out. Blood spatter decorates the once lovingly decorated walls, painting them vermillion and signaling his desperation to protect his family.

Swallowing again as I look at Imogen, I tilt my head at the trail of bloody hoof prints that lead to the nursery. We were here when they found out they were expecting, when they assembled the room, and even after Feray was born. Now the beauty of that memory has been sullied by the scene before us.

We have to be strong…

Once we're both ready, we follow the prints to the door of the baby wolf's room. The sight that greets us is horrific: it splayed Lyra out as if nailed to a cross and impaled her head on a post of the baby's crib. Blood is dripping down the whitewashed wood, making its way to the pink carpet. Dead eyes stare sightlessly at us as we hold our breath and enter. The injuries to our friend are a testament to how hard she fought to protect her child, though in the end, she also failed.

I don't want to see what this monster did to the baby we considered a sister to our child. Forcing myself to approach, I stare at the empty crib in astonishment. There's no sign of Feray, nor that it harmed her in this room. I whip my head around to look at my wife in shock.

Was this a kidnapping? Why would they kill everyone so brutally instead of simply sneaking in to snatch the baby?

My eyes dart around the room until I reach the closet. I stalk over, throwing the door wide. There's a pile of dirty linens and blankets in the bottom, which is unlike Lyra. She always kept everything tidy, so much so that we all teased her about it. Tossing the clothes over my shoulder, I dig down until I reach the floor. I call for light and my magic brightens the dark space enough for me to see a tiny seam at the baseboard.

Claridon was always paranoid, and I never understood why. We both lived simple lives in a small town of magic users and shifters, well outside the dangers of the big city. He was a master craftsman and Lyra ran a bakery; there was nothing to worry about. Humans were far away from our little town and the stench of corruption from the gangs and Councils doesn't exist in Silver Falls.

But I recognize a bolt hole when I see one, so I search frantically until I find the lever that will spring the door open. It takes several tries to successfully open the door—Claridon was top-notch at his trade—but when it swings out, I gasp.

There, wrapped in her father's shirt and Lyra's clothing, is Feray. She has the warding amulet Imogen made for her on her chest, and I realize that even while scared for their lives, Lyra and Claridon ensured the beast wouldn't find their child. Between the magic of our amulet and their scent swaddling her, the baby is hungry and tired, but safe.

I lift the tiny infant out of the hole gently, my eyes filling with tears. Her baby scent makes my heart hurt for my fallen friends and I clutch her to me tightly. It's our responsibility to take care of her now; I know that. Imogen nods when I look at her with a sad expression, then walks over to the dresser, opening a drawer. When she hands me the baby sling, I know she feels the same.

Once I secure Feray to my body, we make our way back to the stairs and head out of the house. It will need to be burned to keep that creature or anyone else from following the scent trail to our home. We don't want anyone to know Feray is alive; she will be safe with us as long as we continue to have her wear the amulet that suppresses her wolf.

Raising her with our daughter, in a new town, is the only way to keep her alive.

I didn't wake up this morning knowing I'd have to abandon my entire life and our home, but I know as surely as the sun will rise tomorrow what we must do to protect this baby. Looking down at her curiously, I ponder the situation again. A magical beast used as an assassin seems like overkill if their target was the infant. Slaughtering her family was also unnecessary—that thing could have slipped into her room and killed her before anyone knew it was there.

Lifting the magic on her amulet for a moment, I wait until Feray opens her eyes. That's when I realize why my friends put it on her. My wife walks up beside me and runs a finger over her cheek. Her red hair looks very much like mine and as long as we keep the magic refreshed for the spell, she will look as though she is our natural daughter.

"We must pack up and move immediately," Imogen says as we walk out. "The capital city is vast, and no one knows us there. That will allow us to raise her as our own—a sister to Fiadh."

"Yes," I murmur. "I will send a message to the local council to inform them we are moving. The death of our friends and their daughter are too much for us to bear here. You simply need to keep her secret in our home until we leave."

She nods. "What about the monster who did this? Who would send it to kill a baby, and why?"

"Someone who scared Claridon enough to make a secret bolt hole in the nursery and forced Lyra to ask us for that amulet. I don't know what they were up to, but obviously, it was much bigger than our tiny town."

Imogen frowns. "We made three amulets, love. Why weren't Lyra and Claridon wearing theirs?"

"I don't know, Gen. Whatever the reason was, they took theirs off and someone powerful hunted down their daughter. Nothing is what it seems here, but we must protect Feray. We will keep her wolf suppressed for as long as possible—up to her Ascension if we can. She'll grow up and if she's destined for something bigger, she'll be able to assume that mantle when she's ready."

Taking this baby on and keeping her secret violates our coven laws; we both know it. Hiding her means we will always be on the run—we need completely new identities when we flee to the capital. It's a lifetime commitment, but the look on my wife's face tells me she's certain this is the right thing to do.

I know without a doubt that being was pure evil, and it came with one purpose: *assassination.*

Tomorrow, we begin our lives on the lam with two babies—there is no other option .

Get it now: **https://books2read.com/newmoonrisingCOM1**

---

1. I call on the gods. I protect myself from enemies and evil

About Cassandra Featherstone

Cassandra Featherstone has channeled her lifelong passion for writing into a flourishing career, a journey that started when she first grasped a pencil as a gifted child with ADHD.

Her debut novel, born during the solitude of COVID lockdown in March 2020, draws on a tapestry of personal encounters and insights that resonate deeply with her readers.

An international bestseller, Cassandra has topped Amazon charts in categories such as LGBT Anthologies, LGBTQ+ Mystery, and Bisexual Romance, among others. Her works navigate the complexities of bullying, PTSD, body dysmorphia, mental health struggles, personal reinvention, and the empowerment of claiming one's own space. Importantly, Cassandra offers a thoughtful and respectful portrayal of LGBTQIA+ relationships, subtly reflecting her own connection with the community through her narratives.

Her literary repertoire spans sci-fi fantasy, urban fantasy, paranormal, and comedic genres in academy whychoose settings, with a strong commitment to portraying consensual, safe, and accurately depicted BDSM and kink lifestyles. Her books are an invitation to explore transformative stories that are both inclusive and engaging.

Often affectionately called 'The Muppet' for her wacky theater kid personality, she resides in the Midwest with her tech-savvy husband, their creatively inclined college student, a literary-minded dog, and four scheming cats.

READ MORE AT CASSANDRA'S WEBSITE OR HER FACEBOOK PAGE. SIGN UP FOR EXCLUSIVE CONTENT AND UPDATES HERE.

Join her Master List for promo and ARC opportunities by scanning the QR below:

ALSO BY CASSANDRA FEATHERSTONE

THE MISFIT PROTECTION PROGRAM SERIES

Road to the Hollow

Return to the Hollow

Home to the Hollow

Rejected in the Hollow

Revealed in the Hollow

Healing in the Hollow

Revenge in the Hollow

AUDIO OF THE MISFIT PROTECTION PROGRAM SERIES

Road to the Hollow

APEX ACADEMY CAPERS

Come Out and Prey

Let Us Prey

In Prey We Trust

Oh Holy Spite (3.5 novella)

Eat. Prey. Love.

Prey It By Ear

AUDIO OF THE APEX ACADEMY CAPERS SERIES

Come Out & Prey

Let Us Prey

In Prey We Trust

TRANSLATIONS OF THE APEX ACADEMY CAPERS SERIES

Come Out & Prey (German)

Let Us Prey (German)

In Prey Trust (German)

DISCORDIA UNIVERSITY

Veiled Flame (Book One)

Quiet Burn (Book Two)

SECRETS OF STATE U

Blood on the Ice (Book One)

Suspicions on the Stage (Book Two)

FAETAL ATTRACTION

Hell on Wheels (Book One)

Book Two Title TBA

VILLAINS & VIXENS

Bloodthirsty (Book One)

Ruthless (Book Two)

Wicked (Book Three)

AUDIO OF THE VILLAINS & VIXENS SERIES

Bloodthirsty

Ruthless

TRIANGLES & TRIBULATIONS

Hoist the Flag (PQ)

Yo-Ho Holes (Book One)

CHILDREN OF THE MOON-
WITH SERENITY RAYNE

New Moon Rising (Book One)

Waxing Crescent (Book Two)

Waxing Gibbous (Book Three)

Full Moon (Book Four)

Waning Gibbous (Book Five)

Waning Crescent (Book Six)

RISE OF THE RESISTANCE

Ream Exclusive Prequels

Hooked on a Feline (Book One)

Peacock Me Like A Hurricane

Book 3 TBA Title

REAM SERIALS

Secrets of State U

Discordia University

Denizens of the Dark

Faetal Attraction

Agents of the Ouroboros

Rise of the Resistance

F.E.A.R. Academy

ANTHOLOGIES

Unwritten

Shifters Unleashed

Jingle My Balls

Love is in the Air

Silent Night

Snowed In

All Hallows Eve

Discordia University
Student Dormitories
Library
of the
Ancients
The
The Wastelands
Staff Housing

Canto V
Region: Hell
Arena of Lost Souls
agic Enclave
Knowledge Enclave
Administration
& Health Annex